The Northern Roseaarde Series

Book 3

EXISTENTIAL PEST

R.E. Holding

CLIFF CAVE BOOKS, LLC

EXISTENTIAL PEST
Book 3 of the Northern Roseaarde Series

For information contact:
https://www.cliffcavebooks.com

Edited by Sara Kelly
Cover art by Mighty Pejes Studio
Interior design and propaganda pages by R.E. Holding
Cover format by R.E. Holding
Map design using Inkarnate by R.E. Holding
Previous Title: Reaper's Legacy

ISBN (paperback): 978-1-963125-35-1
First Edition (under new title): January 2026
10 9 8 7 6 5 4 3 2 1

Contents

The Story So Far 12

PART 1

Ten Years 19
Eastern Visitor 25
A New Life 27
Golden Passage 36
Finding Color 43
New City, New Rules 49
Their Plans, Then Hers 54
Hole 61
Triple E and C 67
Her Plan Now 72
Only Hope Remained 77
Quiet At Last 82
A Bag of Surprises 90
Eulogy 96
One Last Night 99
Enemy 104
Sea Bound 111

PART 2

Surprise Catch 116

Temptations 122
Fired 131
Orange Cat 133
Journey 138
Passenger 140
Homecoming 145
Escape From Secas 149
Reunion 155
Jack and Verena 160
Bunker Stuff 162
Mister Shadow 167
Practice and Focus 175
Reflections 182
Return 184
Shattered 196
Death's Wake 203
A Most Unfortunate Row 208
Ten Years 212
Lor's Resolve 222

PART 3

The Plan 227
On the Move 230
Going In 242
The True Realm 248
Nothing Is Real 255
Death Cycles 259
It Is Done 265
Ten Years 270
Epilogue 276

Other books by R.E. Holding

HORROR:
Metaxysm
Hillbilly Vamp
Subcutaneous (coming 2026)

FANTASY:
Nefarious Gift (book 1)
Despicable Boon (book 2)
Existential Pest (book 3)

COLLECTIONS:
The Artist's Soap Making Workbook
The Northern Roseaarde Omnibus (2026)
Infinity Hall: An Anthology of Sorts (coming 2026)

SIGN UP FOR THE NEWSLETTER for upcoming releases and freebies by visiting HTTPS://WWW.REHOLDINGAUTHOR.COM, OR BY SCANNING THE QRC below:

STAY UP TO DATE WITH extras at the Cliff Cave Books website by visiting HTTPS://WWW.CLIFFCAVEBOOKS.COM OR SCAN BELOW:

INDEX

Read as a reference to the main text - reading ahead may contain spoilers.

Anglia: a race of people marked by their paper-white skin and hair. Eyes are typically light-colored and can even manifest as pink or red.

Arts: a non-Guild sub-faction career path that includes crafters of all kinds, entertainers, guides, storytellers, and musicians.

Ascendia: the Engineering capital of Roseaarde. It lies in a cluster with the other seven cities on the western bank of the North continent.

Audioxine: an illicit street drug, claimed to be crafted by the Yeunish and circulated to the youth.

Audun: the capitol city of Roseaarde. Officials control the activities of the northern continent and the southern morass.

Beast Tamer: an enhanced version of a Shepherd, only present in the Yeunish.

Black eneris (obsenis forturum): life essence that comes from a failed pull. It can be used as ink or if corrupted, can become toxic.

Blood fish: Carnivorous fish that generally live in deeper parts of the sea.

Blue eneris (lapis piscus): the life essence that is pulled from aquatic creatures.

Breach: the festering rot at a root of Great Tree sealed shut by Maron Valoa'brenga.

Cap 1 and Cap 2: periods of time marking the beginning and end of each year.

Celerity: the Reader capital of Roseaarde. It lies in a cluster with the other seven cities on the western bank of the North continent.

Chitter Birds: Small, quick and dark colored birds that can swarm. They are known for being early risers and waking citizens in the desert with their calls.

Chromatis hominum: a special kind of essence pulled from a Weggevens skin walker midway between human and animal.

Cirv'e: the beast of the breach and tormentor.

Corl: small fishing town south of Kanckette on the coast where the border blends with the southern continent. The town is widely ignored by Audun, and its residents live off the land rather than ration blocks.

Danashi: a race of people marked by their dark skin and hair. They can have any color eyes, including hazel and dark brown.

Desert Maelstrom: the annual energy storm that occurs in the middle of the span that begins around day 140 (middle of period X) and ends around day 180 (beginning of Split 2).

Deygo Lilac: Multicolored flowers that bloom just before the maelstrom. Pleasant scent.

Draught: also known as a "pot," these are solutions crafted by Formulators.

E-disk: a communication device popular with the citizens of Roseaarde. Its functions vary from making calls to sending QuickChats, watching holofilms, and performing daily tasks, such as depositing plats.

Elementalist: a new type of Weggevens that manifests as the controlling of elements. Ayala is a fire-based elementalist and Quint is an ice-based elementalist. The power is strong and capable of rapidly draining the host if used for a prolonged period.

Eletonk: a species of large land mammal typically residing in the desert.

Eneris: the essence of life pulled from recently deceased (or living) organisms.

Engineer: a Guild member who can sense the potential of materials to craft technology.

Flash ink: a type of tech text meant to disappear once the intended reader takes in the message.

Formulator: a Guild member who can sense the potential of eneris and other formulations to craft draughts.

Foscan: a race of people marked by their grayish-tan skin, black hair, and white eyes. Foscans were accused of rebelling against Audun hundreds of years ago and have been forced to serve as slaves for various households and businesses.

Giltberries: A special gold-colored berry that's been extinct for ages.

Gold eneris (auris hominum): a special essence that comes from a Reaper who pulls their own. Extremely rare and widely not practiced.

Great Tree: an ancient tree that used to grow at the northeast tip of the North continent. It has since burned to ash.

Green eneris (verdigris plantum): the life essence that is pulled from plant material.

G-scan: a tech device that uses a touch of blood along with a fingerprint to determine genetic markers, as well as any hidden Guild talent. Eloria was subject to a G-scan when receiving her diagnosis, and Lor was given a G-scan when confirming his Yeunish identity (not explicitly stated in the text).

Guild (see Engineer, Formulator, Reader, Reaper, Shepherd): a special title given to individuals who attend the Heart Island program and leave with a special ability.

Guild Central: the Eastern branch of the Seven Cities, commonly abbreviated GC. Working at GC means living in the apartment halls, with all expenses paid. Working hours are, however, long.

Haerow: a small coastal area known to draw individuals seeking private, and oftentiems salacious vacations.

Hanso Fruit: A type of island fruit with a sweet smell and bitter flavor. The residents of Heart Island are fond of the aroma, and it is ever present at the resort.

Holoconfetti: a special virtual confetti used in celebrations to reduce litter.

Holofilm: a type of entertainment loved by everyone, starring non-Guild members of the Art faction of storytelling.

Holopic: an image viewable in 270 degrees.

Howie Rod: a popular construction piece meant for sturdy buildings. Made of metal.

Igni: an extinct race of people who were former guardians of the Great Tree.

Ivory Saltpeter: a white eneris-based formulation invented by Jack that acts as a mild poison and potential explosive, depending on use. Dill shoots Hammer with Ivory Saltpeter to weaken his strongman ability.

Jaune Spirit: a yellow phial invented by Jack that gives the user an intense burst of energy. Dill used the phial in the cavern tussle.

Jumper: a type of on and off-roading vehicle with large spherical tires that can rotate in all directions. Popular choice as a taxi vehicle.

Kanckette (a.k.a "tent city"): the only city in the desert zone known as the Span.

Kanckette is the last train stop, as the Desert Maelstrom always destroyed any further travel east. A band of people live under the tracks in a series of tents, usually collecting any discarded items from the station above to use.

Lapis Evening: a Yeunish sleep aid draught invented by Jack. Used by the team to keep Hare sedated.

Last Grudge: an offensive phial invented by Jack and using Fowler's chromatis, tossing the formulation creates a multi-colored windstorm intense enough to cut like razors. Anything caught in its path is obliterated. Crow was a victim of the draught.

Law: a non-Guild sub-faction career path that includes roundsmen, judges, officials, and barristers.

Leaper: a small amphibious creature inhabiting the Southern Morass. Not edible.

Medicine: a non-Guild sub-faction career path that includes medics, observers, apothecarians, and advisers. Mesaman: a race of people marked by their tanned and ruddy complexions. The most diverse race, their hair can range from light to dark, with eyes typically light and no darker than hazel.

Milaris: the Formulator capital of Roseaarde. It lies in a cluster with the other seven cities on the western bank of the North continent.

Mount Gehenna: the towering mountain on the northeastern tip of the North continent. It is known for its black sands and constant guard.

Nazagora: Dark alien creatures that inhabit the morass. Predatory, but edible with body parts that grow back. Amphibious.

Newslite: an old-fashioned news delivery format requiring a subscription.

Non-Guild (see Arts, Law, Medicine): any profession that doesn't fall into the Seven Cities' definition of prestige.

Noxeine (a.k.a. "Klik"): a recreational substance mostly used by teens for a numbing high. Hare claimed his childhood crush, Tilly, traded sexual favors for the drug.

Oatcress: a ration block consisting of oats and protein.

Obsidia: the Reaper capital of Roseaarde. It lies in a cluster with the other seven cities on the western bank of the North continent.

Orange eneris (naranis corpum): the life essence that is pulled from a specific species of fruit.

Pandemonia: the Weggevens capital of Roseaarde. It lies in a cluster with the other seven cities on the western bank of the North continent.

Patch: crafted from ancient tech and a silver alternative, the patch is a device surgically attached to a Weggevens to prevent the drain. Invented by Verena and using Jack's alternative silver, the patch is proprietary and not shared with the Seven Cities.

Pau'tan virus: a type of infection that became a pandemic in Lor's early years, and took many lives. The cities now have a cure.

Peakwood: a mid-sized city just outside the peninsula of the Seven Cities. Lor's hometown.

Phial: a specialized glass vessel used to collect eneris for Reapers or to store draughts for Formulators.

Phillo bloom: a pink bloom in tropical areas with a light perfumy aroma that goes well with the scent of hanso. Flowers are not edible.

Plat: the system of cash, with the symbol of pL.

Pohay'an: a small tourist location north of the Seven Cities and nestled in the mountains. Location of the famous ivory forests and hot springs, and home to Val when not serving in the program.

Puck: a species of fish.

Purple eneris (purpuris porum): the life essence that is pulled from any purple-colored plant.

QuickChat: a message sent to another user via e-disk.

Reader: a Guild member who has the ability to read minds. Skilled members can even push ideas and thoughts. Gaining the ability naturally isn't as common as a Shepherd spending plat to earn special training.

Reaper: a Guild member with the ability to pull life force (eneris) from any recently deceased (or living) thing. Other abilities granted to a Reaper have been shrouded in mystery.

Reaper's gold: the gold eneris within a Reaper, extractable only by self, or by tough metal gloves employed by the cities made with enhanced tech.

Red eneris (roujis emporum): the life essence that is pulled from land creatures.

Red Mash: an offensive phial invented by Jack that absorbs through the skin and erodes in a series of large blisters. Used to attack Hammer in the cavern.

Roseaarde: the world.

Runner: a type of Weggevens ability that grants super speed to the user.

Sarga Fruit: a type of yellow fruit that is sometimes sent in rations. They're juicy, fitting in the palm of the hand, and are a favorite of Lor's.

Saxeroot: a root vegetable, blue in color, that's been thought to be extinct for centuries.

Second sun: a purple-colored sun that rises at the 24th hour and lasts a standard hour.

Seven Cities (see Ascendia, Audun, Celerity, Milaris, Obsidia, Pandemonia, and Wild Crag): the cluster of cities on the western bank of the Northern continent that serve as governmental rule for Roseaarde, consisting of representatives for each Guild house.

Shepherd: a Guild member with the ability to communicate with animals.

Silver eneris (argenis hominum): a special type of essence that comes from humans.

Skin walker, or skin changer: a type of Weggevens ability that grants the ability to transform into an animal to the user.

Southern Morass: a second continent loosely attached to the North by stretches of sand banks. The morass is a bog-like zone where the cities banish the Yeunish to die.

Span: the entire middle section of the Northern continent, covered in desert and mostly uninhabitable except for the city of Kanckette. Several encampments litter the sand underneath the trains, and the vast poverty of the zone has bred brigands.

Split 1 and Split 2: the periods of time in the middle sections of the year.

Storyteller: a non-Guild profession in Entertainment. Someone who acts in holofilms.

Strongman: a type of Weggevens ability that grants inhuman strength to the user.

Trega's Sky: a city on the West coast, just north of Peakwood, where most holofilms are made. A very affluent city.

Two-mind: a type of Weggevens ability that involves the attachment of another "mind" to the user. Known to possess secrets of the dead. Highly deadly affliction.

Valoan (see void brothers): a cult group of members who forsake bonding with the Maker in favor of worshipping the breach.

Vegemeal: a ration block consisting of a variety of vegetable and fruit matter compressed together.

Verdigris Biosore: a deadly phial that can degrade the flesh rapidly. Its intensity depends on the strength or weakness of its victim. Pigeon was killed with a needle of biosore, and Hare was threatened with it.

Verdigris Mend: a potent and almost instant healing draught invented by Jack, that uses a small drop of Reaper's gold to formulate. Used to mend Verena after her attack, Gale after his attack, Hare after getting punched, and Lor after being shot by Crow.

V-Note: a touch sensitive tablet that is widely used as a job-related recording system. Lor uses a V-Note to capture his visions when reaping, and medics use V-notes to record patient data.

Void brothers (see Valoan): a cult group of members who forsake bonding with the Maker in favor of worshipping the breach.

Volatile: a new type of Weggevens with random and serious outcomes. Each one has a unique second personality that can come out in violent ways, often resulting in the death of the host.

Waterbird: a species of bird that congregates around larger bodies of water.

Weggevens (see runner, strongman, skin walker/changer, two-mind, volatile, elementalist): a Guild member with an unpredictable outcome. Whatever the outcome, the ability is volatile and has consequences for the user.

White eneris (witis volatus): the life essence that is pulled from air creatures.

Witis Rejuvenate: an important drug invented by Jack to help treat a Weggevens suffering from life drain.

Wild Crag: the Shepherd capital of Roseaarde. It lies in a cluster with the other seven cities on the western bank of the North continent.

X: the period of time in the middle of the year, marking the beginning of the Desert Maelstrom.

Yeuni / Yeunish: a race of people born by the Anglia and Foscan. Their kind is hunted and banished to the southern morass for reasons lost to history.

Climate and standard annum

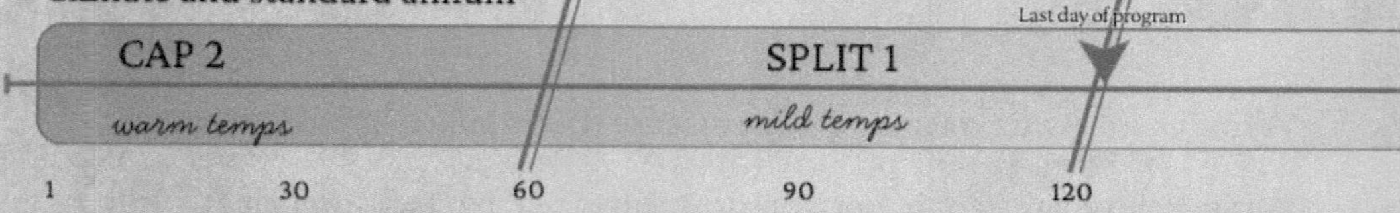

Daily sun rise & sun set

ONE DAY, 30 HOURS:
1st sun rise: 08:00
2nd sun rise: 24:00
Evening: 26:00-07:30

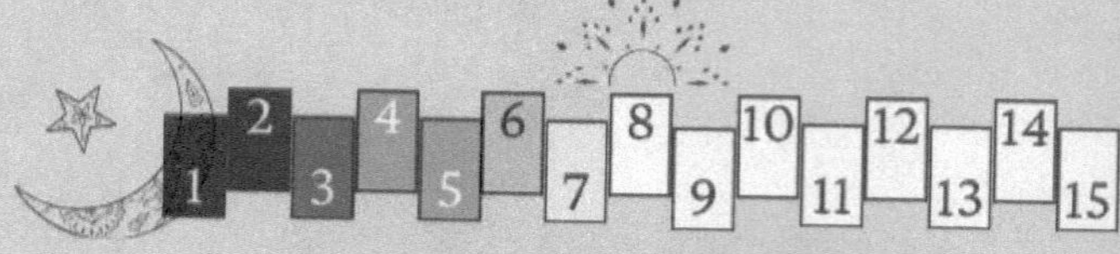

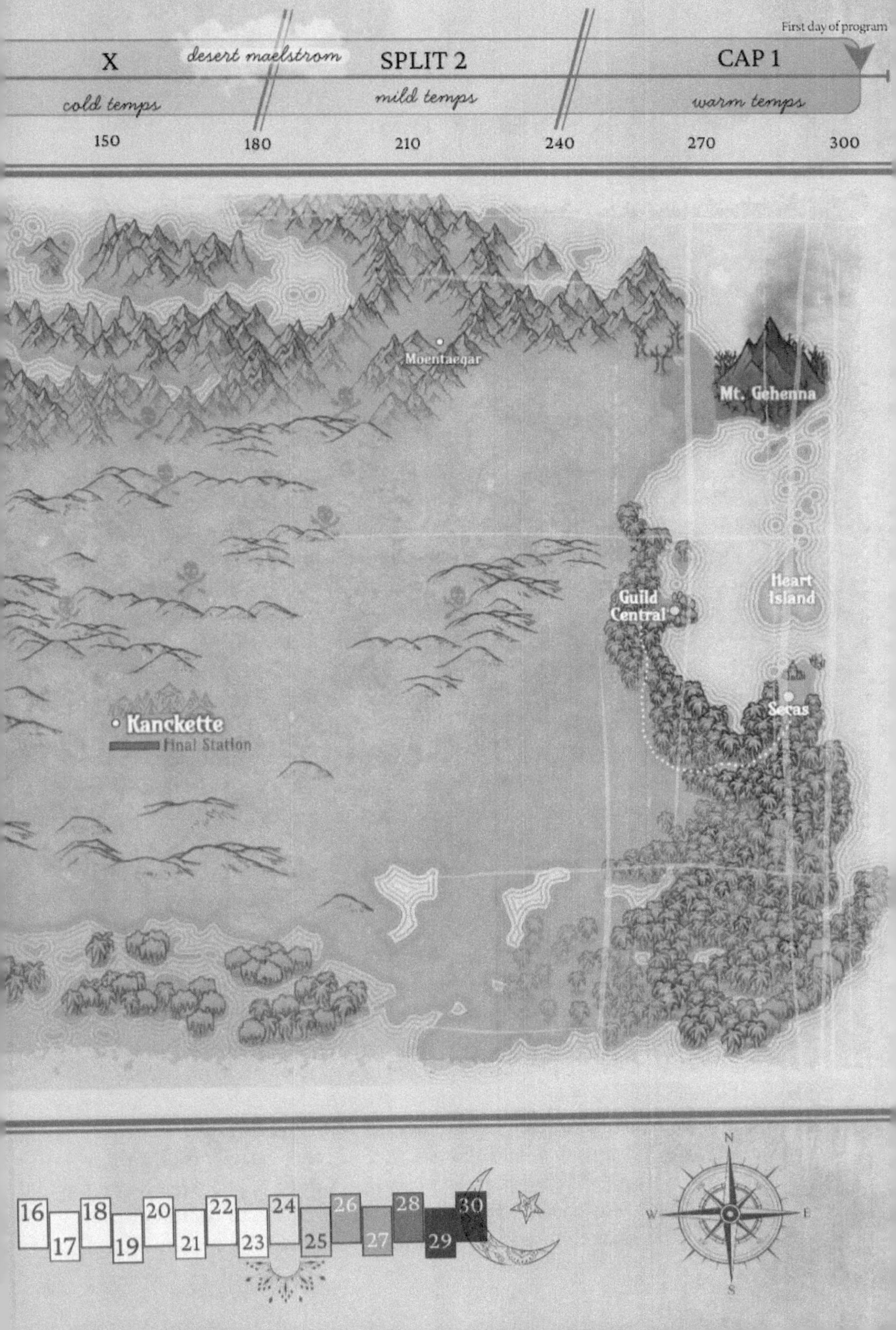
First day of program
X
desert maelstrom
SPLIT 2
CAP 1
cold temps
mild temps
warm temps
150
180
210
240
270
300
Moentaeqar
Mt. Gehenna
Guild Central
Heart Island
Secas
Kanckette
Final Station
16 17 18 19 20 21 22 23 24 25 26 27 28 29 30
N
W
E
S

The Story So Far

Book 1: Nefarious Gift

Loren (Lor) Turtingas lives with his stepfather, Gale, in the mid-sized city of Peakwood which lies on the west coast of the Northern Continent near the Seven Cities. Living an isolated and lonely life, Lor has been studying the non-Guild *faction* of Law, specifically the role of the roundsman. Gale tries hard to convince Lor to enter the Guild program on the far east coast at Heart Island, but due to a bit of a misunderstanding and a dash of disrespect, Gale gave up being nice and forced Lor to go despite the cost.

On his first day in the program, Lor meets Paerli (Par) Harea, a beautiful Danashi stranger that takes an instant liking to him without any effort. However, once Lor meets Damaetra, his attention shifts to the demure Anglia, who teaches him about faith and how it might be connected to the colors he has always seen whenever he closes his eyes. Shortly thereafter, new friendships are forged between the handsome Mesaman, Nico Dicus, and the goofy fun-loving Danashi, Dill Storgut.

After a harrowing death in the first week of the program, the friend circle begins to question their safety and make the choice to remove the implant imposed on them on the second day.

As time carries on, each member discovers their ability: Damaetra and Nico as Formulators, Dill as an Engineer, and Paerli as the coveted Reaper—a class capable of pulling life essence, known as eneris, from the living and recently deceased. The odd man out is Lor, who doesn't discover his ability until the final week of the program when he has a violent seizure that turns him into a Reaper like Par.

Without much time to learn how to use his ability, and cryptic advice on avoiding "yaslecha" by the island Foscan, Val, he leans heavily on his prior connection to a strange Weggevens skin changer named Fowler that he met on the train on his way to the program. The group moves to Guild Central, where Fowler serves as their sponsor. While the job placement seems like a dream, they discover quickly that work is demanding, and they hardly have time to spend with each other, except for Lor and Par, who happen to be in the same apartment hall.

During a rough day at work, Par comes to meet Lor at his apartment that night, dropping a huge surprise on him by telling him that she has always been a Reaper and was specifically looking for him. She divulges a plan for them to become immortal together, but his fierce loyalty to Damaetra infuriates her to the point of assault.

The next morning, there is a box from Par on his floor that contains a phial of her gold eneris along with a note meant for him to drink it and bind himself to her. Stashing it away, he goes to work without her and meets up with his Foscan mentor, Krik'tha, for duties that day. While on the job, Lor asks Krik'tha how a Reaper can pull their own eneris, and it immediately sours Krik'tha. He refuses to talk with Lor for the rest of his shift.

When returning to the court, he runs into Nico, Dill, and Fowler, but no Damaetra. After putting the pieces together, Lor realizes Par kidnapped her and he has no choice but to find a way to gather his own gold and to drink Par's. That night, Lor reconnects with Krik'tha, who teaches him how to perform the "Ritual of Self" that withdraws his gold. After nearly bleeding out, he succeeds in pulling the gold and makes plans to meet with everyone to confront Par.

Once he drinks Par's gold, she finds him, instructing him to meet her team further at the edge of the desert. It is here Lor sees that Par's "team" has captured Damaetra, and that one of their members happens to be Nico's estranged twin brother. More secrets are revealed when Par drinks Lor's gold and discovers he's Yeunish—a disreputable race of people with a city-driven bounty on their heads.

Lor and his friends are ill-prepared for the encounter when Fowler transforms to get help but is immediately shot down by Par's team member, Crow. When Dill tries to go to him, Nico's twin, Hare, restrains him and ultimately blinds Dill while cutting off Nico's legs. As Lor tries to fight back, he's hit with another of Crow's projectiles and left to die in the desert until he is rescued by Gale, a revealed Weggevens runner.

Lor awakes in a modest farmer's home, where he discovers that Par's team mate, Jack (a.k.a. Cricket), has defected from her because he also hides his Yeunish heritage. Jack has powerful formulations that can heal Lor, but are unable to help Fowler, who exists in a fatally deformed transition state. Fowler begs Lor to put him out of his misery and pull his eneris, which ends up being an ultra-rare substance called chromatis.

The team returns to Guild Central, preparing for their next move to rescue Damaetra. Jack leaves Nico with some recipes to try, including a mysterious "last grudge," which contains Fowler's chromatis. Dill creates Engineering eyes for himself, and hyper fast modules for Nico's preserved natural legs. During this time, Lor also discovers the danger of pulling eneris when angry.

Once prepared, they venture out to Mount Gehenna, or the burnt husk of what was once Great Tree, where Par holds Damaetra. They reconvene with Jack, and the guards allow them through the gates by the instructions of a woman on Par's team, Livia—a Reader with the ability of the push. Lor is led to the entrance of Gehenna by remembering a dream he had, and after they crawl inside, they see how much life has grown inside.

Par's team finds them, and Par leads Lor down the umbilicus while the rest standoff in the main cavern. Down in the deep corner of the umbilicus, the half-living ancient, Maron Valoa'brenga has been trapped for over a millennium, sealing the breach with his own body. They use a reverse reap to pull him from the breach, and afterwards, Lor attacks Par. He escapes the umbilicus with Damaetra and Livia.

Lor meets up with the crew in the main cavern just before they unleash last grudge on Crow. An enraged Par comes after them, and they escape when she is stopped by Maron, who tosses her necklace to Lor. He now carries it with him, not knowing what it's for. They capture Hare and impulsively bring him back with them to Guild Central, with no idea what to do with him next.

As the maelstrom dies down, children play in the desert, smelling a rotten odor. Just as the smell hits them, one of the children, Zane, seizes uncontrollably until bursting into flames.

BOOK 2: DESPICABLE BOON

AFTER LOREN RETURNS FROM MOUNT Gehenna with everyone, they're now faced with handling Nico's rogue twin, Hare. They attempt to bribe him with witis rejuvenate in order for him to reveal what he was doing with Paerli. Damaetra struggles with her own identity after having been held hostage by Paerli and her "team" for three days. She reluctantly stays with Nico, as her need to not feel alone supercedes the fact that his apartment is also home to Hare and Jack, both former members of Paerli's team.

The group reconvenes, deciding on a plan to take care of their new situation while the maelstrom rages: Lor debates returning to Peakwood with Gale, as long as Damaetra goes with. Jack wants to return to his place in the desert of Kanckette. For now, they continue their work until they can take action, and Lor learns more about what it means to reap humans, while Nico discovers what life was like for his twin, Hare (Niki) while in banishment.

Despite being outfitted with new tech restraints, Hare (Niki) is able to escape and disable Nico, fleeing to the Kanckette tents. Lor, distraught at the news, seeks a way to converse with Horace, the suspected Weggevens two-mind, to find out more about what happened after opening the breach and whether Hare is a threat to him. He travels to Heart Island with Gale and Damaetra, learning more about the void brothers, and having an interesting conversation with Horace that reveals Gale's old school friend, Greg, is the second mind he carries.

While caught up in revelations and the nostalgia of Heart Island, Lor proposes to Damaetra with a piece of ancient tech he finds in the sand that is perfectly ring-shaped for her. She agrees, and they return to Guild Central, agreeing with everyone that they would move to the cities and find work. They learn about the tragedy of the boy, Zane, in the desert, and realize they've opened a floodgate of Guild abilities that overtakes ordinary citizens in new and profound ways.

In Act 2, the young Ayala wanders from her tent in Kanckette, reeling from the death of her friend Zane, and the oddity that now simmers in her hands: the gift of fire. She encounters a band of criminals who intend to take her, but she sets him on fire with her ability while the tent residents come to her rescue. Her mother, Verena, is a skilled Engineer, using her specialty in electrics to help take the brigand down. The life drain begins its work on Ayala, and she falls asleep with Verena left to stress about what to do.

Jack returns to the desert to a warm welcome from the resident children, as well as Verena, whom he has an unspoken love for. He is able to stop Ayala's life drain with his witis rejuvenate before accidentally blurting out how he feels about Verena. Turns out, she feels the same, and they share a kiss along with a budding relationship. Ayala accepts Jack as her new dad, and he also discovers Hare has returned to the tents.

Meanwhile, Loren and his friends arrive to Gale's home in Peakwood, while Damaetra returns to her home with Thea and Aedras to figure out what's going on with her sisters. Once at Gale's house, Lor discovers in the most embarrassing way possible that Gale is married to his real mother, Dag the Small, or Els'daegal. Gale fills him in on his real father, and the relationship he fostered with Dag.

Jack and Hare forge an uneasy alliance, as their supplies of silver have dwindled following their fallout with Paerli. A new challenge arises when residents begin succumbing to the breach's effects. Jack and Hare realize that a steady supply of silver is critical to the survival of Kanckette.

Lor and his friends are able to find work in the cities, living out their daily lives while Lor attempts to nurture a relationship with his mother. He learns she is a Reaper also, but doesn't use her ability. They discover the strange vibrations between them when their hands touch. Nico begins a budding romance with Eva, while Dill reconnects with Emilia, one of their former classmates.

After settling in, Lor and Damaetra get married, with their wedding crashed by three different people: Hare, Maron, and a shadowy figure only Hare notices. Lor and Damaetra discuss the danger of having children due to his Yeunish heritage, and she disregards his concerns to chance. Following their fresh marriage, both Damaetra's sisters (Eloria and Caella) get hit with Guild abilities; Eloria a Reader, and Caella a Weggevens skin changer. Eloria receives a diagnosis of her ability from a medic, whom she pushes to prevent registration by the cities. Through Eloria's accidental Reading, she overhears Damaetra's concerns for her new pregnancy.

In order to help Eloria, Caella temporarily moves in with Nico to receive witis rejuvenate and to allow Eloria some peace while she manages her new ability. It's through living here that she meets Hare, who's been stalking Nico. He gives her a new patch Verena invented, using an alternative to silver created by Jack, that works better than witis rejuvenate, and they begin a soft relationship.

During Damaetra's pregnancy, Loren has an encounter for the first time with cirv'e while he meditates on his colors. He's rescued by his mother, who he can feel inside the dream through the vibrations.

Not long after, roundsmen come to Kanckette, looking for Jack and arresting him for being Yeunish. They suffer a few strikes from the children of the tents, but ultimately Jack is taken for banishment. At the same time, Damaetra is giving birth to the twins, delivered by Gale at home. Once they are born, the roundsmen arrive, murdering Dag and nearly murdering Gale before Lor shows up, the target they'd been looking for. Lor realizes that the roundsman that has been tracking them and seeking justice is Hammer, the strongman from Paerli's team they failed to vanquish during their encounter in the cavern. He outfits him in a special pair of gold-draining gloves and hauls him away.

While going through the banishment process, Lor recognizes Jack, and also discovers the mechanism of his immortality through repetetive, unsuccessful brandings to the forehead. They're loaded into a boat to make their final voyage to the southern morass.

After the fallout of Lor's capture, Damaetra is inconsolable, and Gale nearly takes his life. Nico prevents Gale's attempt, then returns home to learn about the relationship between Caella and Hare, creating a thin reconciliation with his brother. Afterwards, everyone looks after each other, each offering their own prayer for Loren as he struggles to survive the drop off.

Chased by alien monsters, Lor is separated from Jack and another Yeunish man named Brit, sticking close to the young Zary. Just as they're about to get eaten by the large alien creatures stalking them, Jack runs in to save them and bring them to a long-term southern resident, Karl, who's been looking for them. Brit doesn't make it.

With Karl, they camp out and eat a regenerative limb from one of the creatures, known as the Nazagora, then arise the following morning to continue to the community. Here, they're thrown into an initiation ritual where they fight each other to maintain strength in a place that can eat them alive. Jack quickly taps out, but Loren gets angry enough that he can't stop beating the ground until the gold-sapping gloves snap off. He earns the title "Gold Fist" from the others by his chaotic display of anger and grief.

Karl has a talk with Lor afterwards, telling him as a Yeunish Reaper, he has the ability not only to take life, but to heal it, and orders him to heal Zary's brand. After a few failed attempts and a lot of emotion, Lor finally learns to feed good memories into the host to pull out the injury, thereby healing Zary's forehead. Jack foregoes the healing, choosing to live out his life with the brand.

Back in Peakwood, Gale has gathered everyone into his home, including Hare (Niki), to discuss their plans for the future and how they need to take action to make Roseaarde a better place.

In the epilogue, Loren has been living out his days in the morass, becoming a formidable fighter alongside Jack and Zary. In the cities, a report comes in for Renae, the leader (princeps) of Audun from a Reader. Renae is angered by the note, reaping the life from the messenger, and swears to stop allowing new captured Yeunish prisoners to live to become a part of Karl's plans, who happens to be Renae's nephew.

PART 1

Chapter 1

Ten Years

Loren

Day 5

To my beautiful bride,

How did we find ourselves here? My greatest fear since the moment I met you, was the day I would never see you again. Here we are, distances apart... I'm in a strange land with even stranger creatures, and I fear I'll never make it home to you. It was mere luck (and desperate pleas to the Maker!) that I made it through day one. I'm not sure if my immortality would let me lose my head.

On my second morning, after being rescued by the scouting squad (I call them that, they don't call themselves that), they forced me to fight. It was weird at the time, but I understand now why they do these things. The land is treacherous, full of the beasts known as "the Nazagora." Not only must we adapt and get stronger, but if we don't, we'll die. Well, they would die.

Resources are very scarce here. We have a meager plot of land that I'm going to have to learn how to tend with the others. I'm surprised at how well things actually grow here. There is a lot of water and mud, though, so maybe that's why.

So, the Nazagora... I mentioned earlier that I wasn't sure I could lose my head and live. Well, one almost took my head on the first day. But the weirdest thing happened, you'd never guess. We were able to eat one of its limbs, and they grow back! We've been getting our protein from them for now, but we really need to find something else for protein. It was super off-putting at first, but honestly, their meat tastes like fresh fish. I think you'd like it, especially since you loved that plate of stone head roughy you had at that restaurant, right before you got pregnant... what was that place called? The Sunny Side, I think. I don't want to forget any moment I had with you.

Anyway, I have this journal from Karl. He said he's had it for a long time and never used it, so he gave it to me. Like I said, resources are scarce here, so once I fill the pages of this up, that's it. I wish you could read it.

Love, Loren

DAY 8

Dearest wife,

I miss you so much. It kills me to think of you and the babies. I don't even know their names. I hope you picked some beautiful ones—ones that have special meaning.

Every time I pick up this pen, I strive to write positively on this paper. If I dwell on what happened the day you gave birth, it would ruin my day. I can't let my day be ruined if I plan to someday at least try to come back to you. My trainings are intense, but the more I do them, the more I hope to survive in this place, to protect the others. And I can't let sadness ruin that.

However, I will let myself have this one grace: Gale and my mom are dead. I saw them die. I can't change any of that. I had a moment the other day that was a bit of a struggle, but Jack helped me past it by offering to hold a small memorial for them. It was me, Jack, and a young girl named Zary who had the memorial, and it was nice. For now, I will move on. Oh yeah, Jack is here with me.

Love, your Loren

DAY 15

My Violet Lady,

I think about you a lot. Writing that reminded me of the day you asked me to be yours. I guess nothing has changed! Man, that feels like ages ago, but I remember our time together so vividly. I remember lying in our bed, just taking in the scent of your hair as you slept next to me, belly pushing into my side. One of our babies kicked me in the ribs, and it made me laugh. I couldn't believe how well you slept through all that jumping in your belly! You are just amazing, that's all there is to it.

But hey, I forgot to tell you that I can heal! Karl told me that it's because I'm Yeunish... normally Reapers can't do that. Once I figured out how to do it, it's been such a blessing here. So many people need patching every day. Plus, my healing works by remembering all the good things about life, and usually that means I get to see you again in my head (and my mom, Gale, Eva, Dill, and Nico).

I'm finding that a lot of the Yeunish here that have abilities have them a little bit more amplified. I mean, we knew Jack as the best Formulator we'd ever known, and now I can heal, but there are a few Beast Tamers here also. We call them Beast Tamers and not Shepherds, because they control more than just birds and crawling things. They can control these Nazagora out here—a creature so bizarre, I had never even heard of them before! And they're really big and crazy vicious.

Love, Loren

Day 45

Precious wife,

I regret not writing for a while. Things can get busy here... as much as I hate to admit it, there were things about living in the North that the cities made much easier. Here, just getting food takes a lot of work. And really, that's pretty much all we do. We fight, we grow, we feed, we (sometimes) sleep, we fight, grow, feed... The days seem to blend together.

We've stopped sending scouts back to the North. Remember when we saw one getting arrested on the train going to Pohay'an? Well, that was Fil. He's back here with us, and they apparently hurt him pretty bad, so Karl said no more scouts. Plus, it was extremely hard to get them up there—lots of bargaining with unscrupulous people on the coasts for transportation, and the results were not worth it. Karl used literal birds with messages on them to communicate with those coastal criminals. And we're not talking trained birds, just random ones around here! So once they were out of range for our Beast Tamers, they often got lost or came right back.

I'm sorry, that's probably boring to you.

We have interesting seasons here. It's very wet most of the time, but we have our little clearing that we've settled in and farm on. The rain is like the maelstrom, except we have about a standard month of nothing but rain. The Nazagora are attracted to this rain, so they get really close to our settlement. This was my first season experiencing that, and I'll admit, I got a little worried at how near they were.

Karl says they've never gotten in; they just stand at the border and watch us through the trees. Then before you know it, the season is done and they leave. Gives me the creeps, though.

Love, your salty flower

DAY 104

My dearest wife,

I know you'll never see these, but I can't help but feel guilty at how long it's been since I wrote. Like I mentioned before, the work here is hard and takes a long time. After the duties are done for the day, I usually just want to eat and go to bed. I've been using Lapis Evening a lot to knock myself out. We have plenty of blue and white to use around here, so Jack can still make it for me. Sometimes I wonder if it's doing more harm than good... I haven't had a dream in a long time.

Love always, Loren

STANDARD YEAR 2, DAY 426

Sweet wife, love of my life,

I've been here nearly two standard years now, and nothing has changed. We get new exiles about once every standard month, but we've lost a few as well. Mainly from age but also to melancholy. I hate to document that here, so I won't record these things, only know that it happens. We're pretty good at avoiding the Nazagora, as they're really only active at second sun, so I haven't seen any losses because of them. At least, not since my first day.

Anyway, I'm the only healer here, so I have a lot of work to do when we fight, when we forage and hunt... it can be a little taxing, only because sometimes I don't want to share my memories with anyone. They're mine. But I know it's the right thing to do, and recalling them to heal someone else is a vivid enough vision that I feel like I can reach out and touch you.

Interestingly enough, I don't even know what I look like anymore. I can sometimes catch a glint of my reflection in the murky water, or in the flat side of Karl's switch, but really, I'm not trying too hard to look. But you? I could never forget your white gold hair, the way your cheeks flushed, or your eyes that seemed to change between blue and violet in the light.

Love, your Loren

Standard year 3, day 732

My lovely bride,

I can tell I've gotten bigger. I punch harder, and I'm really hungry all the time. There's this interesting plant we've been growing here that I've never heard of. Karl says it's long extinct in the North, so that makes sense. Anyway, it's called saxeroot, and it's the best thing for filling us up with just one or two. And they thrive in this place—we almost have too much! They're great for, well... not starving, but they're the best substitute for protein blocks. Plus, saxeroot tastes better. And they're blue!

I worry about you and the children. I try to imagine their faces as they would be now, but I can't. I only saw them so briefly, which breeds in me my own flavor of melancholy. Don't worry, I'm not going to do anything impulsive. Karl and I have been trying to come up with a plan to get home. Unfortunately, the cities want us gone so badly, the only thing we could possibly do is declare war against the capital. There's no way we could win, just us... no matter how strong we get.

Especially if our numbers stay pretty much the same. There are forty-six of us, hardly enough to take on the thousands of roundsman in every corner of the North.

Love forever, Loren

Standard year 5, day 1384

Dearest Damaetra,

I lost this journal for a while and thought it was gone forever. It's weird to go back and read these entries... it's like I can peek into my state of mind all that time ago and see a different person.

We had a scary moment last year, and most likely if I knew where the journal was, I wouldn't have written it in anyway. Jack came down with the Pau'tan virus... you know, the one that took Gale's first wife, Surai? Well, we don't have the cure here in the South, and I've learned there might be some limits to my healing ability. Either that or I just haven't mastered the skill to kill off a virus. There were moments when the fever got so strong that the times I stepped in to help, I couldn't even hold on to him. Crazy enough, he made it through, but it was a trying time that tested us all. We've all grown so close that I don't know what I would have done if he died.

I'm afraid to admit that this is my life now. Even in the rare moments when Karl and I try to come up with ways of getting back North, my heart knows there's nothing we can do. I miss you so much... I hope the children are safe and happy.

Love, your husband

Standard year 7, day 2,055

I'm sorry, love.

I'm sorry I haven't come back to you. I'm sorry I'm not there to help raise our children with you. Worst of all, I'm sorry I'm missing everything in their lives—in your life. I miss Eva, Nico, and Dill. I wonder how everyone is doing.

My hands are rough and chapped. My skin has burned and peeled from the sun. My dreamless sleep has stolen all the color from my world.

I must carry on, no matter how hard it gets. And by hard, I mean to say that I live in a home that doesn't belong to me. A stranger more than a guest, but forever held here.

Have you changed like I have? Have lines formed around your mouth from smiling? Or frowning? Did you grow your hair back out or leave it short? No matter what, you are beautiful. I pray you've found companionship in friends and family.

Forever yours, Loren

Standard year 8, day 2232

My darling,

This will probably be my last entry. There isn't much paper in this journal, and I'm running out. This is my life now, and I'm going to have to come to terms with the fact I will never see your face again. I will never meet my children, and I will be forgotten by my sister and my friends.

I've had terrible thoughts... terrible ideas about the cities' treatment of our daughter. Please keep her hidden and safe. I don't ever want to see her here.

Chapter 2

Eastern Visitor

Through those annoying wavy lines of heat, the dark figure got closer and clearer. It was her stranger. He had a name of course, but she didn't tell anyone about him. She wanted his stories all to herself.

The shadow got even closer, a twig of a man through the wriggling heat squiggles coming off the sand. A quick glance over her shoulder, and she saw the tent flaps secure. It was still early, and Mom napped inside. Another scan to see she was alone, then she jogged the rest of the way to meet him.

"Mister Shadow," she whispered.

The stringy man knelt before her and hummed. "What did I say about calling me that, young one?" his deep voice admonished her sweetly.

Her dark hair flapped over her pale face in the harsh wind, and she used a finger to slide it behind her ear. "It *sounds* cool," she said.

"You are quite the strange child," he said. "Come, sit with me."

He led her to the stone ridge, not too far from camp, and not too deep where the bad people were, and they sat in the bit of shade the rocks made. The stone ridge was her most favorite spot, where she spent her days with Mister Shadow. He was kind, fed her stories, and best of all, he was just like her. No one was like her except him. Maybe she could someday be a shadow person to another *young one.*

Mister Shadow straightened his legs out in the sand and leaned back on the smoothest boulder. His pants were ripped in places and stuck to his knobby knees. He needed new clothes. She thought about helping him out, but no one at camp was as tall and skinny as him.

"Tell me again about the East," she said, cupping her hands at her chest, giving him the most pleading eyes she could make. It made him laugh, and she liked it when he laughed. He usually seemed sad.

"Ah, the East," he said, gazing into the horizon where the black mountain stood. It seemed so small from here, but she knew from Mister Shadow that it was actually really big. She squinted at it, trying to picture all the glowy plants inside like Mom told her about.

"The East was a fascinating marvel of the time," he said, "but you know much about the East already, don't you, child?"

She scooped up the yellow sand, letting the grains drizzle from her fist. "I like your stories."

Mister Shadow chuckled. "Of that I have no doubt. But yet this time, I have a question I must ask of you."

She perked up, peering into his perfect face, cut in two by the boulder's shade. "Me? What would I know?"

"I must know if you have spoken to him yet. Have you practiced what I taught you?"

More sand trickled from her fist until she slapped the rest down and stared at her own hand, half buried in the grains. "I practice and I practice, but I'm useless, Mister Shadow."

"You are not useless. You are still very...*young*. This might take some time."

She blew out a breath from her lower lip, letting the black chunk of hair push out from her face, then started to hum an old song she heard Mom singing once. Mister Shadow let her hum for a bit while she fanned her hand through the yellow grit, watching it wave over her fingers.

Then she remembered something and sat upright. "You know, I did practice a lot yesterday, and after I went to sleep, I think I saw him. It was really fast, but I dreamed about him."

"Oh?"

"Yeah! He didn't know I was there, and I couldn't say anything to him, but I know it was him. It had to be."

"And how do you know for sure?"

"Easy, Nate *looks* just like him... except younger and weaker. Not Daddy, though... he's a real tough *fighter*!"

Chapter 3

A New Life

Loren

Maybe this was the Maker's way... Lor flexed his bicep as his knuckles connected with Ivon's ribs. The tall Yeuni stumbled back with a cough and a short bark of a laugh, bolting forward to return the favor.

The crowd erupted after Lor braced his core, only to get faked out with a right hook to the mouth. A quick duck, then an upper cut to the chin rang Ivon's head, and he backed off once again to the raucous cheers of "*Gold Fist! Gold Fist! Gold Fist!*"

The earthen flavor of Immortal Green coated Lor's tongue, as it did every time he took a biting hit. He spit out a mouthful of clotted blood and grinned. Through the crowd's chants, Ivon tapped out early.

Boooooo!

They jeered at Ivon's early defeat, crying out "*Gold Fist*" again and again.

"You've become quite a force, Gold Fist," Ivon said in a muffled lisp. His jaw lilted to the side, a swollen split already forming. He bent over, breathing heavily. A dribble of blood dangled from his chin where a front tooth passed through his lip.

"You and I, we're equals. Call me Lor, remember?" He held his palm over Ivon's chin, closing his eyes to remember his mother and her smoky laugh when he mispronounced her language. One time she had sassed Gale in a way that reminded him of himself, and he smiled. All the fond memories of her concentrated at Ivon's jaw, snapping it back into place.

Ivon stood upright with a deep belly groan. "Thank you, Gold—I mean, Lor." He palpated at his ribs with a meager grin. "It stings, but I am well."

"Good," Lor said, patting Ivon's arm, "go get some rest. Let it finish its work in you."

Whatever "it" was. There was nothing fancy about his healing. No lights, no fanfare... nothing to suggest anything at all. It was better that way.

The crowd, along with Ivon, dispersed for the afternoon. They weaved through rows of huts made of mud and thatch, some climbing their rope ladders into crude elevated tree homes. Others with field duty returned to rows of saxeroot, begrudgingly tending to the crops with bare hands or wooden handmade tools.

While watching everyone go, a light breeze teased at Lor's neck, and he turned toward it. The dark mouth of the entrance to camp gaped in the distance: the overgrown entry point where he stepped through all those years ago to discover his new life in the South. Ten long years... he'd stopped marking the days in his journal. Could it have really been that long?

He could almost hear the residual memory of his squalling son and see the curious gazes of his daughter. When he nearly lost his head to the Nazagora, his children were so close. Now, barely there. He didn't even know their names. Would he know them if they stood right in front of him? Or worse yet...were they still alive?

He thought too deeply of them, trying to scratch out the true memory of them and not the echo he'd repeated so often in that place. So deep, in fact, that the abrupt *ahem* that came from over his shoulder nearly caused him to piss himself. He spun back around, away from the brambled exit.

Jack stood there, hard-lined and arms crossed. "Karl needs to see you." The old Formulator flexed his jaw, as his biceps bulged from the scrappy white shirt he found years ago. Its threads had thinned, showing more than Lor cared to see underneath.

"Can't you just tell me what he wants, since you're his favorite?" Lor teased.

The unhealed brand on Jack's forehead puckered from a Y-shape into a fat V-shape. "I could, but I'm not going to. He wants to talk to you personally is my guess."

Lor groaned, running his hands down the wrinkles of his wrap, catching a finger on a small hole in the fabric. "Alright, fine. I'll find you later."

Jack nodded and left. Karl's hut was closest to that tree-lined exit hole. It was bigger, more cozy, and built as a gift to him years before Lor showed up. They used to use it to regroup and create strategies for getting back North... sessions that became fewer as the years went on.

It was probably for the best anyway. After all, what would they do if they made it back North? Hide in the mountains? Live by the sea? There was no way they'd integrate back into Audun society. The moment a roundsman caught a whiff of Yeunish funk, they'd either be back facing the Nazagora all over again or some other worse fate.

Only a few long strides from Karl's hut, and he caught the eye of Hahn, a newer beast tamer to the group. He was passing the opposite direction and curled a dry lip at Lor as if he was the one with the right to be disgusted. Lor knew the type of guy Hahn was. He was, generally speaking, an asshole. As they crossed paths, Hahn rammed his shoulder into Lor's, nearly knocking him back and sending a jolt of pain down his arm.

"Watch where you're going, *Gold Dick*," he said with a sneer.

Lor rolled his eyes. "Very clever, did you come up with that all by yourself?" He rubbed his arm, tasting a hint of that familiar syrupy grass that must have come for his bruised shoulder.

Hahn spun toward him, squeezing himself crudely. "Yeah, I did. You like it? I thought of it when I saw your hot wife in the hot springs. If only you'd shown me her tits."

Lor felt his features fall, and he stared up at the jerk with a deadened glare. The dead man was certainly pleased with himself as he walked backward, tongue unfurled and fists knocking together twice. He turned back around to continue on his way, his laugh an echo toward the falls.

Lor cursed under his breath. If there was another way to heal without sharing his precious memories with scum like Hahn, he would have done that. If he'd known Hahn was a creep to begin with, he'd have let the guy heal on his own.

Or die.

He regretted the day Karl's collection team brought a weak and cowardly Hahn into the fold, showing him the ropes and being told to train him to be a fighter.

All of that regret and rage boiled as he watched him continue to saunter away, still laughing to himself. A dark ring fizzled at the edge of Lor's vision, filling his sight until all he saw was Hahn's bobbing head, laughing. Why not remove it from his shoulders?

Before Lor could even consider centering himself like Zary tried to guide him, he marched toward Hahn, and fast. He didn't see it coming when Lor gave him a good clout to the back of his head. The knock choked the laugh from Hahn's throat, and then he dropped to the ground, rolling over with a pair of wide black eyes in a mix of fear and pleasure.

Each fist swung at cheekbones in resonant thuds as Hahn manically laughed, spitting out a tooth at one point. In one hard hock, he spit a fan of blood at Lor's face, a stinking hot and foul mess over his nose and mouth, forcing him to quit punching and recoil.

Hahn moved fast, throwing Lor from his vantage point to lying on his back. Thick fingers found his throat.

"Show me your tender little daughter next," he growled as he squeezed, giving Lor's head a small shake.

Lor tried to gasp, feeling the pressure rise into his sinuses, then into his eyes as he scrabbled to pry those rigid fingers from his neck. He could reap him… right here, right now. It had been years since he reaped a human. The warmth of Hahn's grip against his neck pulsed with life as Lor gasped for his own, and he bucked under the man, feet sliding over the grass in desperation to gain leverage.

The taste of green flooded his senses with each shake and squeeze. Hahn grimaced above him, face shadowed by his long black hair and a bloody vein of drool that hung from his lower lip.

Do it, Loren. Reap him.

The dark voice whispered in his ear.

Pull him dry.

Lor squeezed Hahn's wrists to try to pry them from his neck. Hahn's red grimace contorted over him into something primal, and he had to do something. It was only a small zap, but Lor dipped inside that vicious mind for only a brief moment.

Scared little bully… eternally jealous. An only child, he was raised in secret by one of the many death camps in the desert. His heart grew hard and cruel there, and he'd seen his share of death. He'd seen his own mentor burst into a volcano of red pulp when they tried to snatch that young fire elemental.

Air at last! Lor gasped, taking in wafts of cool air in greedy rushes when Hahn rolled away and into the grass. Hahn blinked rapidly, darting his eyes this way and that. Once he got a feel for his surroundings, he found his hands, shrunken into dry hooks. The fingers were curled inward, braided together in a useless fleshy cane. With his lips puckered into a little "o," he held his new hands to his face as he worked the tendons white. They rolled about, leaving the fingers to fend for themselves. Then he screamed.

Lor made a dry heaving cough through those screams. His palms were smeared blue-black with silver as more of it slithered down his forearms. The screaming drew everyone's attention, even Jack and Karl, as he poked his head from the big hut door.

Between the screaming and murmurs, Lor thought he heard Jack ask him if he was all right, grabbing his arm and helping him to his feet. The others swarmed Hahn sitting in the grass, who wailed in pulses while gaping at his hands.

A cold shadow crept up behind Lor and clasped his shoulder. "Come see me when you're done here." It was Karl. He barely acknowledged Hahn, but his face had soured when he looked over the scene.

Lor hated using the waterfall for dirty jobs, but he had to give his face a good scrub to rid himself of the dried bloody spit. Afterwards, he tapped on Karl's driftwood door with a knuckle. Broken planks at the top gave him a view of the inside either way, where Karl stood over his wood scrap table. The surface was littered with old food and bits of dry plant life that had made its way into the hut through uncovered windows. He popped his head up and motioned through the gap in the planks for Lor to come inside.

"We needed him, you know," Karl mumbled as he picked up a curling brown leaf from the table, turning it back and forth before tossing it to the floor.

A slit of light cut through an upper window, lying across a rugged tome sitting among the leaves between them. Dust motes spun and lit up in the beam, twirling in eddies at the disturbed air.

"He tried to *kill* me," Lor protested.

"You can't die."

"All the same..."

Karl grunted, shaking his head. "I'm sorry that happened."

"Why are *you* apologizing? Last I saw, it wasn't your face hovering over me, trying to choke me out..."

He put up a hand. "I was worried his old habits might show themselves. I knew who he was before, so for that, I'm sorry. He will be supervised at all times from now on."

Lor rubbed his neck. The shot of history Lor acquired from his short reap told him all he needed to know about Hahn's *old habits*.

"Jack said you needed to see me?" he asked.

Before answering, Karl shifted the tome toward him, sending up more dust whorls that had no business looking as magical as they did. "We need to make our move, and soon."

With a low tut, Lor shifted his weight. They'd been through this before. "Make our move? Have you changed your mind?"

"We don't have much time."

"What does that mean? How soon are you saying, and how are we supposed to do this?"

There was a circular device Karl made that he hung on the wall to keep track of the days. When he glanced at it, he made a sharp nod. "After the North's maelstrom."

"You're talking *this* year?"

"That's right."

"And did you have some secret plan to do this, or...?"

"That's why we needed Hahn."

"Well, his hands are stumps now, what's your second plan?" There was nothing Lor could imagine that Hahn could possibly do better than they had in the past ten years. The thought upset Lor.

"Our intel on drop-offs has been tainted." Karl didn't answer the question as he picked up a different stray leaf to fidget with it. "That alone has us losing more recruits these days."

Lor chewed a lip. After meeting Horace, he never thought information from a spirit could actually be bad. Yano, the Yeunish two-mind, was immune to the never-ending life drain and had quite the head full of knowledge, even if his spirit was a bit lazy.

She doesn't like crossing the water, Yano had told him once.

"So, is Yano's spirit just being lazy or what?"

Karl closed his eyes and sighed. "I don't think so, but she's either given up on living in Yano's head, or there's someone in the cities that is so good at faking their own intentions."

"Send me out on a collection, I'll find out what's—"

"No. I can't risk our only healer."

"In case you forgot, I can't die. If you don't want me out that way, what did you want to see me for?"

Silence encroached the space between them. After a moment, Karl tapped a finger on the old tome. "Have you ever seen one of these before?"

Lor tilted his head to get a better look. When he did, he realized that "old" wasn't a severe enough word for the book Karl had. The pages were yellowed and thin, with a few sheets poking out from the binding with wavy edges.

The tome itself was hand-bound in dark leather, worn and swollen in areas from water damage, where the delicate golden emboss work had lifted and flaked off. Strange symbols ran the perimeter of the front cover, which seemed too familiar to Lor.

This tome wasn't just old—it was remarkably *ancient*.

"Can't say I have. When you say 'one of these,' do you mean to say there are more of them?"

Karl ran his finger along the swollen bubble on the cover, tracing it up the length of a gold border. "No. I believe this is the only one left."

The hairs stood up on Lor's neck. A lost tome like that held who knew what. There was no title that Lor could read, other than the rambling symbols up the side. Hand-bound, no mechanical markings... it held the character of a project someone sometime in the distant past took great care to create. If this was the last one, what made Karl think Lor would ever have seen one?

"What is it?" Lor asked.

Without answering again, Karl opened the book, flipping to a page near the end. As he read the passage, it wasn't immediately clear that he spoke another language. Lor tried to decipher the arrangement of vowels slurring along with an occasional throaty click. To say it was lovely was an understatement. It was like a song. He wasn't acquainted with many languages outside of Northern Common, but it certainly didn't sound like the little Foscan he knew.

Once Karl finished, he left the page open, staring at it. The typography on the pages resembled the same symbols on the cover... strange combinations of hashings, circles, and lines. Where had Lor seen those before?

"So, what exactly was that?" he asked.

After clearing his throat, Karl touched the block of symbols in the center, where Lor assumed the passage came from. "It's Eastern Common. I might be the last person on Roseaarde who knows it. Well, me and my bastard of an uncle."

It was the first time Karl had mentioned family. The entire block of time he'd spent in the hellish mire, and Karl had never mentioned family. Lor raised an eyebrow. Two stunning revelations were in Karl's answer: first the uncle, second... Eastern Common. The East did not exist. It was a made-up fable for children. Wasn't it?

"*Eastern* Common? The East doesn't exist... does it?"

Karl tittered at that. "It doesn't anymore. But when this book was stitched together, it did."

"I hope you can enlighten me more about that sometime," Lor said, arms crossed, "but before you tell me about your uncle, would you please translate that passage you read?"

More silence. Although this time, Karl seemed to be thinking of how to form the answer. "I'm not sure how to explain it, but I believe it's referencing a reckoning that's meant to happen in the North, involving the tree."

"You mean, Gehenna? Great Tree?"

"The very same."

"So, what makes you think this didn't already happen in the past?"

He stared at the block of symbols again, pointing at a specific one. "Because this one references the tree as it is in its current state. Withered but not gone."

All of that life inside the mountain...

"Karl, what *is* this book?" Lor asked. "And tell me plainly."

A smile tugged at the weathered corners of Karl's mouth. It wasn't a grin that conveyed any sort of happiness. Rather, it was wistful with a touch of melancholy. "This is the sacred text of the Maker. It survived not only the war, but even the destruction of the tree."

The ancient war. The war responsible for leaving detritus all over every beach on the eastern coast, tugging at his shoes, stubbing his toes. The tech that he put around his wife's finger. The pieces that confounded most of society, that Dill was able to manipulate for Nico. The symbols from the book... they were the same Eastern Common engraved over every edge of that ancient tech. The old memory flashed in his mind as an orange ember. As soon as it came, it was gone, but now he felt closer to history—a hidden history the North completely forgot. Or purposely erased.

Lor stuttered, "Whu... Why?" Wrong question. "I mean, what happened to the other copies?"

Karl tittered. "Banned, buried, shot into the sky... I don't know what happened to them. I just know the world forgot their Maker in order to forge their own way, resulting in a war that broke open the thin film between us and the otherworld."

"*Other*world?" Lor's mouth had gone dry.

The golden dust motes continued to swirl over the pages, giving the sacred text a certain magic. Karl lightly tapped the page. More dust bloomed at the tip of his finger. "The other dimension that was the playground of Cirv'e. Now Roseaarde is its playground... and my uncle its puppet."

"This... is a lot," Lor said, blowing out a sharp breath. Curse his shitty memory. Horace had told him some of this, and he should have remembered. Why was it so easy to forget? Throwing up his hands, Lor blurted the next encroaching thought. "How did something like this survive for over a thousand years? It's animal skins and *paper*!"

"Animal skins, yes... paper, not so much," Karl said, tapping the page again. More gold ballooned out. "You'd be surprised at how innovative your ancestors were."

"My ancestors? Do you mean... the Igni?"

"The very same."

Lor slumped down on a partially rotted stump by the table, most likely meant to be a visitor stool. The wood splintered under his weight.

"So, this idea of the passage you read... Do you think this is like a prophecy or something? I've seen enough holofilms to know that prophecies are usually self-fulfilling and kinda ruinous."

Karl raised a thick brown eyebrow and smirked. "Ruinous? Big word for you. I'm impressed."

"I need to write all of this down. Have you told anyone else here about it?"

Karl made that same solemn smile as he closed the book. "Not yet, but soon. I promise."

Lor observed the book while it sat in its golden magic dust. Did Karl see it too? He snapped out of his reverie and faced Karl. "Alright, who is your uncle?"

Karl smirked. "I think you know by now."

Chewing a lip, Lor closed his eyes, hoping for some colorful revelation beneath them, but it was only black. As much as he didn't want to admit it,

Karl was right. He had an idea of who his uncle might be, and he didn't like it.

"So how *did* the princeps get mixed up with Cirv'e? And why are you here if you're family?"

"Simple, I'm a sympathizer. There are no exceptions for family. As for how he fell under Cirve's spell? That's a longer story. He needs salvation."

CHAPTER 4

Golden Passage

CIMMA

A STRONGER, HOTTER BREEZE MEANT MAELSTROM soon. Yellow eyes scanned the dunes as their dust gave up offerings to the sky in twists.

"Cimma, come," a voice called from the tent, "your mom wants you."

Cimma glanced over her shoulder to see the hem of Verena's skirt get swallowed back inside. When she turned to face north again, a heavy yellow haze had already closed a curtain over her view of the mountain. The storm was too close for Mister Shadow to visit and probably already began where he stayed. Too bad... she still had a lot of training questions.

The tent flap billowed in the breeze, and the men would have to tack it down before second sun to resist the side winds. Cimma ducked inside and worked on setting the trap. Mom sat on the sofa, right on the edge with her head in her hands, like she did when talking to the Maker.

Cimma knew not to make too much noise during quiet time, but Mom lifted her eyes when the low buzz of electricity traveled through the perimeter wire.

Her voice was groggy, half speaking and sighing at once. "Where's your brother?"

"He's with Quint and Mister Freely. Why?"

"Is Ayala with him?"

These questions were their own type of tiresome for Cimma—she was not Nate's keeper. "Isn't she *usually* looking out for him?"

Mom took pains to roll over her right hip to stand. When she got close, she always had a habit of fussing with something on Cimma. Clothes, shoes, the dirt on her face... this time, Mom brushed a stray black hair from Cimma's yellow-smudged cheek. She had to look up at her to do it, as Cimma's legs were already long and lanky, and she could see the top of Mom's head.

Mom smiled, even if her eyes were pink and puffy. It looked like she had been crying again. Every year she seemed more tired. Cimma frowned.

"What's the matter?" Mom asked, still fussing with Cimma's hair.

"Nothing, Momma," she lied. She didn't like seeing her that way, but it didn't do any good to talk about it. There was a journal Mom wrote in, and she knew there were stories in there. Probably stories about why she still cried.

"You got your sass from your dad, you know that?"

If Cimma only gave up a grin, Mom wouldn't know how much hearing about Daddy hurt. "Do you need me to find Nate for you?"

"No, he's fine with the Freelys for now. I just wanted you inside. Did you set the trap?"

"Yes, Momma," she said, foot dangling down the bunker to make her way down for the long season.

Each season spent underground was more bearable than the last as more passages were dug out and the machine almost ready. It was still boring, but at least it was less irritating than sitting in the dim light listening to hums and snores.

A few standard years ago, Papa helped Uncle Nico and Uncle Dill dig out their own spaces, which made it so much more roomy for them. Verena still called theirs the hub, because they had the water tank and one of the few ladders that came down here. Uncle Dill called it a hive, like the little bugs that made that sticky sweet stuff in connected holes where they store their young. Everyone was connected.

Last year, they even dug out a deeper passage dedicated to the bucket. The bucket always made her feel sick when it was in the room with them. It was warm and smelly. Either way, it was Nate's turn to take *care* of it.

Even if the underground was getting more bearable, she still dreaded it. By maelstrom end, she was ready to feel the sun on her face and breathe in fresh air that didn't smell like Nate's legendary poops.

When she glanced around the bunker, she noticed Betta had already set up a game of Gehenna's Pass, ready for battle. Games with Betta were fun because a lot of times, she let Cimma win. Only, Gehenna's Pass was at least a three-player game... she hoped Quint would play.

If she passed through Uncle Niklaus's bunker, then west, Quint lived *there*. When she got older, and if she ever wanted a boyfriend, it would be Quint. He had nice, cold skin that he could hug her with when she got too warm. Plus, she heard about the time when he was just a kid, and he almost took out a roundsman.

Her other friend, Treece, didn't like to play games, but she was really good at making up scary stories and talking them out with all the different voices... Treece could be kinda scary herself.

Best of all was Ayala. She was her best friend, and talked to Cimma like a real person, not just a child.

She poked her head through the fabric flap between theirs and Papa's bunker. It was empty. "Hey, Momma!" she shouted up the ladder, "where'd Papa go?"

"He went to Secas this morning for some things. He'll be back soon," Mom called back in that same groggy voice, but it was getting stronger.

Verena came in from Uncle Nico's side, with a thick blanket rolled up under her arms. "Hey, hon," she said while flattening the blanket out over her bedroll, which she'd already opened up and inflated.

"Are you not going to play?" Cimma asked, nodding at the Gehenna's Pass setup.

"Nah, not tonight, sweetie. I'm going to read for a little bit. But you all have fun."

As she finished speaking, Nate's white-capped head poked into the bunker from Uncle Niklaus's connecting passage. He glanced around with the fabric piece still draped over half his head.

"There you are. Mom's looking for you."

His whole body stumbled inside by a nudge from a giggling Ayala. He rubbed his arm with a scowl. He was always so serious. And sensitive.

"Ready for the seasonal underground party?" Ayala said, pumping her hands above her head with a wide grin. She was everything Cimma adored. Everything she wished she could be: beautiful, capable, older...

"Did someone say party?" Papa slid down the ladder, tossing a fabric bag to Cimma. She caught it by the neck, and it twirled heavily in her hand. Inside were several of her beloved yellow-skinned sarga fruits.

"I almost shocked myself on the trap overshooting my run," he said, heaving a series of long breaths as he picked at his Weggevens patch. The skin around it had gotten red and wet.

"At your age, we can't have you doing that." Mom followed Papa down the ladder. She always took her time down the rungs, but she made it, giving Papa a long hug. When she pulled away, she noticed the blistered redness around his patch too. "You should talk to Nico about that."

Papa shrugged with a smile, then went to the back and set his bag of supplies on the workbench. It brushed against the long ripper blade hanging from the wall. It was sharp and scary but necessary. Cimma didn't like it.

"Speaking of Nico, you should ask him to come play Gehenna's Pass tonight," Ayala called from the game setup. "He said he wanted to learn."

There was no problem with that. The more players, the better the game, and Cimma only hoped there was enough room for Quint. Nate protested, only wanting to watch.

Wind howled outside, and more voices spoke inside the hive of bunkers. Everyone had begun to settle in for the season, and all bunker curtains were pulled back for first night's community.

Nate sat on the floor, watching as Betta returned to tend to the game setup. Cimma sat next to him, resting her head on his shoulder. She always liked the way her brother smelled. It was like flowers and reminded her of Mom.

He put his arm around her. "Mom said you were outside alone all morning," he said.

Cimma clicked her tongue. "I'm here now, bubbie."

"I don't like it when you're out there for so long by yourself."

"Why do you worry? I know what I'm doing."

"As your *older* brother, I need you to not be gone all the mornings unless I'm with you." He nudged her with a smile.

"Two standard minutes is hardly older," she said through her grin as she nudged him back.

"Old *enough*. What if a bad person comes for you to turn you in?"

Cimma sighed. "Then I'll punch them really, really hard in between the legs like Verena said to do."

"What if it's a *girl* bad person?"

"Then I'll punch her in the..." She looked up to see where the adults were. They were talking among themselves about the upcoming game night. Then, she cupped the side of her mouth and whispered, "I'll punch her in the *boob*."

Nate giggled with her. She herself hadn't grown that way yet, but since she was getting taller already, she was starting to look grown. Mom said it's because she's Yeunish, like Daddy. In all the dreams she had, though, she didn't look anything like Daddy. There were times she felt maybe it wasn't him in her dreams after all, but something in her belly told her it had to be.

Nate's worry for her wasn't his fault—she was wanted for some reason like Daddy was. Mom wouldn't tell her why the people in the capitol wanted her, but Mom was too tired to force her to stay in the tent and too loving to not let her just be a child. Sometimes Verena acted like a second mom, keeping an eye out for her. Probably because her husband was wanted and taken too. She didn't like to talk about it, though.

As everyone started to gather for the games, Mom and Papa decided the machine needed work and went through the second hatch at the far wall to get into the cockpit.

The room got a little too crowded for Cimma's taste, but she liked to look at Quint, even if his eyes were always on Ayala.

The games ended before Mom and Papa came back from the cockpit. There must have been a lot of work to do down there, and Nate would be excited to see all the improvements. She didn't care much for the machine.

The bunker grew nice and quiet as everyone went back to their rooms and the family began falling asleep. With nothing but the dark underground and pitiful tech lights to go by, it was hard to tell when first sun was up. The few of them that still had their modded e-disks could tell them the time, and right then, it was supposed to be bedtime. But Cimma couldn't rest.

For this season spent underground, Cimma was determined to practice more of Mister Shadow's lessons. No goofing around, as much as she wanted to, because there was much to do.

The dim orange tech light flickered in the corner where Nate snored on his bedroll. That wouldn't do at all. Cimma nudged his shoulder to roll him over, and he obeyed without even waking up. The hocking drone became low, heavy breathing, and that would have to be fine. All other shadows were silent in sleep.

The practice worked best when she sat upright, so she crossed her legs and straightened her back, preparing to close her eyes. There was nothing in her stomach to distract her, and no other noise to confuse her, other than Nate's low breathing. She blew out the last of her own cautious breath and closed her eyes.

A deep violet hue swirled in slow puffs as Nate's breathing continued to drone in the background. Violet was Nate's color. It was lovely, but she was looking for something else in the dark... something vaguely gold-like. It was usually shaped like a door or something. It was too pretty to be a real door, though. At least, prettier than anything she had in the desert.

Mister Shadow taught her to focus on anything she could remember to bring it into focus. Problem was, she couldn't remember a thing. Mom told her that Dad was taken the day she was born, so she relied on old holopics from her and Papa. Stories from Uncle Nico and Uncle Dill helped fill in the gaps, and the rest she tried to imagine, hoping that her imagination was enough to conjure that door.

Nate's tech light was too bright, coming through her closed lids. So she tossed her little deflated pillow at it, snuffing out its glow for now.

With the orange halo no longer creeping into her side vision, she settled in to focus again. Old holopics, stories, and raw imagination, all under the swirling violet of Nate's breathing.

And there it was—beyond the violet curls, deep in the dark, the glint of something golden shimmered in the distance. She willed herself to move toward it, but she felt stuck in place. Mister Shadow told her to imagine floating through the dark, but it was hard to float when she was being weighed down by the violet current.

The snoring got louder, with the colored torrent coming in blasts. She loved her brother, but Maker help her, she hated him in that moment.

Ignore it.

Mister Shadow's voice echoed in her mind. He'd told her this many times when she struggled with extra noise. She brushed away the violet swirls and passed through them. They had an interesting smell too... like spring deygo lilac.

The golden passage got closer and closer as she put the snoring behind her. Yet, the lingering aroma of the spring flowers clung to her senses. It didn't bother her—she liked deygo lilac.

The door was solid, decorated in curls of gold that were faded and chipped in places. This time, she needed to use Mister Shadow's technique to open it.

An unwilling door is not so easily opened... he had told her before. She didn't think the door was unwilling, though. It was stuck somehow and needed help to open.

In her mind, she stuck out a knuckle, attempting to rap on the door to see if she could feel it, or if it would make a sound. Neither happened, as her knuckle slipped through air and the door loomed before her, shut tight.

Hmmm...

She had to open it soon, because having her eyes closed like this was making her sleepy. The low snoring drone in the background didn't help things at all.

Hellooooo...

She called into the void in her head. Mister Shadow said head voices could be heard too, but only by the Maker... and the *worm*. When Papa had told her about the worm, it kept her away from the mind place for a while. No worm was going to wriggle in her brain; that was a fact. She harumphed at herself.

No sign of the worm yet... maybe the Maker could open the jammed door.

Please help me open the door?

She stuck out another metaphysical knuckle, but the door absorbed the tap, sending ripples outward. It was hypnotic, making her more sleepy. The darkness was getting darker.

I can't do this by myself...

Her plea tapped into some strength that lifted a load off her mind, and it made her light enough to float a little from the ground. A sound, like the spring of a lock, clicked, releasing the stuck door. It creaked open just a crack. A beam of sky light came through, and Cimma swam toward it.

As exciting as this was, the swim toward the door tired her even more... but she made it far enough to peek through the crack.

He was there, sitting by a waterfall all alone with his head down. Did he talk to the Maker too?

Look up, look up, look up!

Her mental strength waned as she stared into the scene, wishing to be there with him. With Daddy. He glanced up and stared right at her staring at him with shining gray eyes.

Did he know me?

The blackness took over, and she finally succumbed to sleep.

Chapter 5

Finding Color

Loren

No matter how relaxed, centered, or mindful Lor became, or how many hollow prayers Zary directed him to say, his colors remained smoky and fizzled. No pattern and no message lay within that darkness. It was a quiet cavern under his lids, and a part of him ached because of it. It didn't help that his head buzzed with anger at Hahn, and every thought centered around the filthy thoughts that scum had about Damaetra.

It was pointless. He slapped his eyes open.

"Anything?" Zary asked, sitting next to him cross-legged with her own eyes closed.

"Nothing," he said.

No longer the sixteen-year-old jilted girl, Zary sat before him, a mature, young woman of faith. A smile crept across her face as she opened her golden eyes. "Your mind is a mess," she said.

Perhaps she was right. Lor found himself too often rubbing his face the way Gale used to. Middle-age frustrations hit him in his thirties, and his stepdad's bad habits became his.

He groaned. "I don't know what to do."

"Maybe you should stop taking Jack's Lapis Evening," her answer came quickly.

"If I don't take Lapis Evening, I see the worm."

"If you learn how to *focus*, you can resist the worm."

Lor rubbed his face again. The first time he healed someone instead of sucking out their eneris, he thought it would bring him closer to the Maker, like he was when he didn't even realize it. Years of healing and "centering" had gotten him nowhere. The colors hadn't gotten worse, but they weren't the same shape and vibrancy as when Damaetra touched him. He wondered if she had moved on from him. The thought burned his gut, but no young widow of banishment with two children should suffer to be alone...

"You're scattered again," Zary said, poking a finger on Lor's forehead. "This is part of your problem."

"It's hard not to be."

"I get it... I do. But the further you drift from focusing on your goal, the worse your mental state becomes. Here, let's try again."

The weight of her request made his shoulders slump, but he closed his eyes anyway, trying to see anything but the smoke and the black. What even was his goal? The words she spoke in an attempt to get him into a calm state droned in the background as he tried to remember what it was like to see his colors when he was younger.

The first time he saw them, he passed them off as nothing but an active imagination. They swirled in vibrant shades, altering to customize to the color of his current company, or whoever was talking at the moment. Some shades were nothing like he'd seen in nature. He lamented the past thinking about them now. Things seemed so simple back then... back when he wanted to go to Peakwood for Law to be a roundsman. Such a stupid kid back then.

It wasn't until the program when those colors crystallized into traversable portals. When he thought about it, the portals didn't even show up until his first day on that beach with Damaetra. Destiny, perhaps?

Destiny. What a concept. Of all possible outcomes for him in adulthood, his "destiny" pulled him into the realm of the worm, making him shun all portals by taking Jack's drug. Even if he knew Cirv'e wasn't the only one he could meet inside.

"Just focus, Lor," Zary said. The shock of her voice snapped him out of his own mental meanderings. A small poof of blue smoke came and went under his lids when she spoke. Not near the intensity of what he used to see. Hell, he wasn't even sure he remembered it properly.

"Let me ask you something, Zary," he said, still keeping his eyes closed. There was no color for his own voice, just the same black void.

"Hmmm?" she answered with meditative calm.

"Do you, or have you ever seen... colors? Like when you close your eyes? When people speak, or when you focus?"

"Colors? Can't say I have. But I'm a fisherman's daughter... not really the creative type."

Lor tittered, opening his eyes to the blinding light of midday first sun. He squinted in reflex, shading his eyes with a rigid salute. "I'm not creative either. I just used to see colors and now I don't."

There was no purpose in telling her any of this. He never talked about his colors outside of his wife—not to his best friends, his sister, or even Gale. He wished he had when Gale was still alive. The colors used to mean nothing to him. Now, he knew they were something, but he didn't know what. Gale was smart and probably would have figured it out. Telling Zary wasn't going to change anything.

A moment passed while he thought about it when Zary opened her eyes and looked up at him. "Interesting. Tell me more about your colors."

How to begin… He could tell Zary about them, she could think he was crazy, then move on. Maybe he could tell Jack about them too. Or Karl.

So, he told her everything he knew… from the random color swirls that came when someone spoke, to the fractal lens that formed portals he first spoke to, then went through. Sparing her the more embarrassing details of his encounter with the worm's portal, he told her about that too.

"No wonder you've been drugging yourself. These colors made portals you could go into?" she asked. When she swallowed, the sun rippled over a pale scar running across her neck.

"Yeah…" He hesitated. "But it was probably just me making stuff up out of the weirdest corners of my mind."

"No." She sat up and frowned at him. "No, that's not it at all. You *traveled*."

"Well, in my mind I did."

"No, you don't understand… you've told me about your encounter with Maron and his wife. You saw the past when you peeled him from the breach."

"How do you know it was the past I saw? You're not some ancient immortal too, are you?"

She chuckled. "No, not immortal. If I were, I wouldn't have this, now, would I?" She drew a finger across that thin scar with a forlorn smile. "Know what I think? I think you accidentally went into the worm's *lair*. Then it tormented you, as evil likes to do. I mean, when you heal, you project things from your life. It's all got to mean something."

"Like what?"

She twitched a shrug. "Don't know. Let me meditate on it a bit. Maybe I'll find something."

He wore his face pink with a sigh, feeling the nice rub against his sinuses. "What would your insight look like?"

"It's hard to explain… it's different than your colors. It's more of a feeling."

"I'll sit with you," he said.

"Good. Maybe you can work on your focusing too." She smiled, closing her eyes again and turning her face away to leave him with his own thoughts.

Zary had his trust, and he was glad he told her. During their banishment, she had made great strides with her relationship to the Maker, which made her a spiritual help of sorts. But she had no visions, no colors, nothing tangible to see or touch, which to Lor was more powerful. It was all inside, hidden in her gut. Supernatural, even.

Her advice to quit taking Lapis Evening was probably the right thing to do, but he was afraid.

Years of hardened fighting, and whenever he thought of quitting, he was reminded of that stinking hole, that creeping cold settling into his chest before thinking and feeling the vilest things he didn't even know existed inside himself. The force that managed to pull him out was his mother's connection. And she was dead.

When he closed his eyes to see nothing but the blackness of his eyelids, the notion of quitting Lapis Evening started to make more sense. The idea that he might skip his dose that evening thrilled and terrified. Knowing that his mind had become so far from the Maker, he felt a strong possibility that his first lucid night would open his mind to dark forces.

Whatever the worm could show him was a gamble—would it be rage? Lust? Violence? All of it? Either way, the real question would be whether he could resist it.

Concentrate.

Zary hummed to herself in a joyful low tune, barely audible. He'd seen her color before—a deep blue that showed itself in smoky outlines years ago. Despite her hums, the color couldn't pierce the nothingness. He sighed.

"Just try think-talking," she whispered.

Damaetra told him the same thing during the program, and that was the first time he saw the white-gold portal. Only his imagination could tell him what possibilities were inside it. If only he had the foresight to enter *that* one instead of the black one.

Concentrate.

The blockage couldn't have been yaslecha. He rarely pulled anything in this place, and he felt... fine. Surely yaslecha didn't come through healing. On second thought, he gave away so much of his personal memories, maybe it did.

Never did he imagine he would lose the ability to see his colors. They were so vibrant... so very present. Even stronger still when he learned to channel them through only the smallest urging from Damaetra.

He frowned. How many people had he fed his memory of *her* to? That vile Hahn had pieces of her in his mind. But so did others that were not so vile. He tried to savor a memory only for himself.

A random moment popped in his head. It was from the program years ago, when he sat with her on the pink beach that smelled like salt and fruit. A gentle lapping of the water along the shore played in the background. As she sat with him, she placed her hand over his like she had hundreds of times before. The feel of her warm palm lingered for a moment, as if she were there with him. When he turned his hand to grip hers, all he managed to hold on to was air and sweat.

"Remember to focus, Lor," Zary reminded him.

The sound of her voice blew a puff of blue smoke through his vision like a dusty fart. It was something, and in his excitement, his eyes popped open.

The daylight burned. Zary sat in the same position next to him, eyes still closed with the slight smile baked onto her face. *Glad* she's *having fun...*

"Question for you," Lor interrupted. Zary grunted, not a single crease around her calm lids.

"What do you think of Karl? I mean, what do you think he's about?"

Zary opened her eyes and glanced toward the big hut near the entrance where Karl stayed. "I can't say I know how to answer your question. Can you elaborate?"

He chuckled to himself at her question. She had become so eloquent over time that it was hard to remember her ever speaking in her jangled fishing town slang like she did when they arrived together. No longer the naive child in love with a jerk willing to sell her out, she had grown into a competent young woman.

"The thing is"—he paused to consider his phrasing—"I've always thought Karl was just so different than any of us. Not just that he's a Mesaman sympathizer or anything. He seems like he *knows* things. Do you know what I mean?"

She droned a low hum while pressing her lips together. "Well... he *has* been here a long time... I guess I can understand why you'd think so."

"It's not about how long he's been here, though. He has this book in his hut. It looks ancient, and he claims it's written in *Eastern* Common. It sounds crazy, I know, but he could read it too—"

"Wait, he has a book written in Eastern Common?" Zary's eyebrows were nearly at her hairline.

"That's what he says, but—"

"Can you show it to me?"

Lor glanced at Karl's hut. "I don't think I have the power to do that, but maybe if you ask him...?"

"I think I will." Zary stood and turned to him. "I'll be back. Keep focusing."

With that, she marched toward Karl's hut. He worried he shouldn't have said anything. But Zary was going to do what Zary wanted, so he resigned himself to whatever retaliation Karl had in mind.

Alone again, he searched the area for anyone that might bother him. Particularly Hahn. The good thing was the guy left him alone for the most part after he pulled a little of his silver. Maybe the silver he pulled was the evil bit. It was a thought. He closed his eyes.

Again, blackness.

Maker, just show me something. Anything... from you, not the other thing.

Silence and blackness.

He tried to picture all the times he saw colors, portals, smoke, static... anything to spark them up again.

What he ended up seeing instead was something different. A point of light warbled in the upper view.

Interesting...

It hovered and buzzed in place—a solitary point of yellow light. As he thought about reaching out to it, the point drew a line down the entire length of his head cave, splitting open in the smallest of cracks.

It didn't feel like the worm. So he watched the slit of light and hoped that whatever watched him back was on his team.

It was a girl. Young and Yeunish, staring right back at him. It wasn't possible, was it? Before he could get a really good look at her, the golden crack fizzled out, and he was back in the dark.

Chapter 6

New City, New Rules

Caella

Atop the tallest apartment building, Cae watched the city below. People hurried back and forth, not taking too much time to converse with each other. The slightest dissent would clap them in chains, or possibly banishment. As a cat, she spent many days off observing the decline of the citizens from the roof.

One particular man she saw regularly had a new set of eyes on him for a while. She'd been watching him for standard months as he stood at the corner, trying to catch the attention of people passing by.

The cards he passed out usually ended up in the nearby bin, but she caught one once blowing through the alley.

Come learn the truth about the great lie. Ask me how.

It was decorated in a beautiful image of nature, and she had a feeling it was his attempt at persuading citizens to defect against the cities. Very bold and not smart to do alone. About two standard weeks ago, her sharp eyes caught another watcher.

The poor man had no idea. It had to be either an undercover roundsman or a city sympathizer that watched him. They wore all black, positioning themselves between the buildings across the road. Today was different. The other watcher made their move.

As the corner preacher held out a card to a sharp-dressed woman passing his corner, the other watcher stepped out into the light, strolling directly toward him. This time, the watcher wasn't alone. They were flanked by two thick roundsmen.

Before Cae could consider what was happening, the two roundsmen jogged toward the man, and one of them slapped a cuff on the man's outstretched hand.

"Hey, what are you doing?" His voice was barely audible against the winds blowing on Cae's roof, so she hopped down the escape stairs to close the gap between her and the commotion.

"I didn't do anything to you!" he shouted in the struggle.

Cae caught the tail end of them pulling the chain, dragging him from his spot.

No one stopped to help or even watch. Most heads were down, with the occasional curiosity peeking up to catch the roundsman's next move.

He wriggled in his confinement, kicking a leg out as he stumbled backward toward the cruiser.

When he lost his balance, he went full-on squirming to try righting himself again. He shouted over the din of foot traffic, "Don't succumb to the lie! Your soul is precious! You are worthy!"

The roundsman clocked him across the cheek as he sputtered out the rest of his sentence. It caught him off guard, and his legs buckled. The roundsman reached up and brought his stick down on the man's head again.

"You are worth everything!" He sputtered blood from his mouth.

Cae shrank back, but she couldn't look away. The violence wasn't uncommon in the cities, but she never got used to it. And it was getting more common. She wanted to get back to the desert... to get away and fight back. They would have to take it all back.

The crack of a projectile rang out, and she jumped. There was only smoke and a thin trail of blood. All of it came from a red hole in the man's head.

And no one helped.

They dragged him through the street to throw him into the back of their cruiser. A single protest for a medic cab was silenced by the roundsman pointing the weapon at whoever dissented.

Cae had watched that man for months—meek at first, and with a few friends. Every week, one less friend joined him, but rather than despair, he got bolder. Whether his message of warning landed with anyone, she couldn't say, but she was sure he had an impact on at least one person. That one person was enough; she had to hope.

An uneasy emptiness pulled her heart at his loss. She wished she had talked to him. If only she had the nerve to have that conversation, to tell him to hide. Then, maybe he'd still be alive.

She bowed her head in a brief moment of silence for the man, then turned to get the hell out of there.

Along the way, she heard whispers of women's gossip. Some were shocked, some were glad. Those who were glad were far from redemption. She avoided the feet of those women, who would gladly step on her cat form for sport.

She climbed the next escape stairs to the top of some finance building and made her way back to her apartment.

A few blocks later, the open balcony window welcomed her home.

"Please tell me you're going to take a shower." Eloria half turned from her spot on the sofa and pointed at the greasy smears all over Cae's white fur.

Cae dove under a blanket, and her filthy face emerged with a frown.

"So, I'm going to have to wash the blanket too, I take it?"

Cae huffed, "I'll get it, sheesh." She stood, taking care to cover herself with the blanket.

"Hey, you alright?"

"Saw another execution today. Right in the middle of the street."

Eloria pressed her lips together and glanced down at the floor. "Another one?"

"I just want to forget about all of it," Cae called over her shoulder as she moved farther down the hall toward the bathroom.

The tub swirled gray water down the drain. As Cae pondered the last year or so of spying on the residents of the area, one thing was certain... Life in the Seven Cities had gotten dangerous. Even work had become divided... more support for the princeps and Cirv'e had increased there, and she wouldn't even dare open her mouth. Before, if she was caught speaking against Cirv'e, it could have cost her job. Now, after what she witnessed on the street, it might cost her life. As much as she loved Arts, she knew it was going to end. And probably soon.

She poked at her Weggevens patch that sat right above her heart where she had moved it after meeting Niklaus. It wouldn't be hard to live life as a cat... get away from everything. After all, cats can kill worms.

That wouldn't be fair to Niklaus. He wanted a wife, not a pet. Just thinking about him made her sad. She should have been in the desert with him. At least they'd be happier. But they needed funding, and her anonymity was their advantage. So, she worked. Nothing like sticking it to the man while taking city plats and funding the rebellion.

She sighed, rinsing foam from her hair. When she was satisfied the alley funk had been sufficiently purged down the drain, she stepped from the shower. The small silver band sat inside a black bowl on the sink. Her ring from Niklaus. It glittered where she left it, and she slid it over her middle finger with another sigh.

Back in the living area, Eloria sat on the couch, reading a rather boring-looking manual.

"Work stuff?" Cae asked, nodding at the manual.

Eloria looked at the cover as if she didn't know what she was reading, then grunted. "I'm behind on a few new laws." She smacked the manual shut and tossed it on the table. "It's getting harder and harder to control these guys."

"Maybe you should quit. I was just thinking even I might quit."

Eloria rolled her head back and forth, letting her neck pop a few times. "I've thought about it. But what would the desert do without the Triple-E Bank?"

"And C. Don't forget about my measly contribution."

Eloria tittered. "Every little bit counts. Besides, it's Eva and Emilia raking it in with Engineering plats. Sometimes I wish I *had* registered as a Reader."

Cae plopped down on the couch. "I still think you should quit. I really don't like how close you work with that Hammer guy."

"I've heard it all from Mom and Aedras. I'll think about it."

"We can both quit and go live in the desert with everyone."

"Cae, I know it's hard to be away from your husband, but we have to think about what our funding does for their cause. *Our* cause."

She wasn't wrong about that. If they both stopped working, that would cripple them a bit. Mom and Aedras pulled some plat in, but they still had a good chunk of debt to take care of on the side.

Too much time had passed since she saw Niklaus that she let her emotions get the best of her.

Biting a lip, Cae picked up Eloria's discarded manual and flipped through it. The newer section was easy to find, right in the front.

> Law No. 1084.56, Section 3, Index 2: At no time must a citizen suffer insult as it concerns the affairs of the new deity. The offending party must offer no less than a day's wage, pre-tax, as penalty dictated by small court.
>
> Law No. 1084.57, Section 3, Index 2: Consider it unlawful to manufacture insult against a citizen regarding Law 1084.56. The individual responsible for false reporting shall offer no less than a day's wage, post-tax, as penalty dictated by small court.

"Wow, this *is* boring." Cae shut the manual, tossing it in the same way Eloria had. "Why can't they use normal Northern Common to word these things?"

"Tell me something I don't know," Eloria said, rubbing her temples. "The bad thing is these new laws pop up faster than I can remember them. It's going to get harder to do my job *and* push Hammer without looking obvious."

"I say quit."

"You don't understand, it's not just about the plat. I have to keep that guy in check, because if he tells the princeps about Dame, or even Nico and Dill..." She sucked in a breath. "Maker forbid the children."

"Honestly, does he even remember them at this point?"

"I don't know... all I hear in his noisy head is all the nasty stuff he wants to do to all the women around him. And *me*." Eloria shuddered.

"Ew... for real?"

The slight nod her sister gave wasn't reassuring. In fact, it made her wish the guy would just die already.

"I wish he'd just die already," she said.

"I knew you'd say that," Eloria said with a smirk. "Maybe the princeps will get annoyed enough with him that he'll pull him. Hey, don't look at me like that."

"I don't want *you* to get pulled." Cae picked up the manual and handed it to Eloria. "I'll let you study."

As she made her way to the kitchen, Cae's thoughts drifted to all the ways Hammer could disappear. She could lure him to the desert and let them unleash Last Grudge on him. The sand would bury his blood, and none would be the wiser.

"That's great and all, but you realize I'd have some explaining to do at court if my partner disappeared," Eloria said, peeking up from her manual, eyes dark.

Cae twisted her lip into a grin. "Hey, stop reading my mind," she said.

Chapter 7

Their Plans, Then Hers

Cimma

"See this one here? It controls the throttle. Cimma, come take a look," Momma said while sitting with Nate at the machine's controls.

Truth was, Cimma didn't care much for machinery. Nate loved to learn all about the knobs, dials, and buttons to mess around with, but for her, there were more important things to worry about. Like finding Daddy. Ayala missed her daddy too. Why was no one looking for all the daddies?

"Ugh, fine," Cimma responded, sliding from her perch at the back of the cockpit.

When she got to the two of them sitting there, pale skin glowing in the blue overhead light, it made them both look like ghosts. Surrounded by the darkness of the cockpit, it was the only light there. The small mirror near the control panel caught her reflection, and in it, her eyes were green. If only she could walk around like that.

The section of panel Mom focused on had a series of levers and knobs of varying colors. Red, white, black, yellow... it was hard to know what was what. This was why Cimma didn't like machines.

"What's a throttle?" she asked. Nate tittered and rolled his eyes. He was never mean about it when he looked at her like that. He just knew it wasn't her thing.

"It controls the speed of the engine, silly," he said while motioning for her to come to his side of the panel.

As usual, Cimma dragged heavy feet to the place she didn't want to be but felt obligated to go. Nate stood up so quick the chair swiveled before he snatched it back and asked her to sit. She did, falling as hard into the seat as her footsteps across the floor. It must have been the air in there... sterile and full of some mild electricity.

Nate pushed her toward the controls, leaning his chin on her shoulder like he did when showing her anything. Pointing at a green button, he looked over at Mom before explaining what he thought he knew. "See, here's the power," he said before moving his finger to a white lever, "that's the electrical feed"—he moved his finger to the yellow lever—"and *that's* the throttle."

Cimma sighed after Mom praised his machine smarts. She was a daydreamer, living in other worlds and learning from a man she called Mister Shadow. There would never be a moment where she shone, or a moment where her mind would be useful to the team. And she was cursed, just like Daddy. She cast her eyes down to the dim glow of the panel's various buttons and whirling machinations that only attuned minds like Verena, Uncle Dill, Aunt Eva, and Aunt Emilia could build.

She sighed again.

"What has you down, sweetheart?" Mom asked, patting Cimma's knee.

Cimma tried not to let a tear come from her eye. With a short sniff and casual brush of the cheek to check for any rogue wetness, she mumbled over the panel, "I'm just not good enough to learn this stuff. I won't be useful when we do this."

Mom clicked her tongue and turned Cimma's chair toward her as Nate sidestepped to keep his chin attached to his twin. "Don't talk about my beautiful, brilliant daughter like that."

Nothing witty came to Cimma's mind to respond, but she wasn't sure she wanted to argue. Mom would always tell her kind things, because of course she would.

"Am I like Daddy?" she blurted.

It wasn't a question meant to make Mom sad, but her eyes showed it even if her smile didn't. "Oh, honey, you're a lot like him. In so many ways."

Cimma thought about that for a moment. In all the practicing she did for Mister Shadow, it didn't occur to her that neither Mom, Nate, Papa... nor anyone really knew what she knew. It was a piece of knowledge that she could use to help maybe, instead of machine smarts... she had something else.

"Do you actually think Daddy is dead?"

Nate abandoned Cimma's shoulder, and Mom looked up at him with the pitying kind of face she did too often. "Cim, we've talked about this," she said.

The cold cockpit got colder. They would never believe her. "You said he was banished. That doesn't mean dead."

"Please, you're upsetting your brother."

"But you should *know* that he's still alive." The blue light reflecting over Mom's eyes gave them an animal glow in the dark. Cimma shouldn't have said it. She wasn't prepared for the questions they'd ask.

How would she know? Who told her? Then she'd have to tell them about

Mister Shadow... and she didn't want to tell them about Mister Shadow. Or maybe she should.

"Who told you this?" Mom asked.

She wasn't ready to tell them about Mister Shadow. "I just knowit," she mumbled her words together and tossed her head to the side—anything to keep from looking into those glowing eyes.

"Cim..." She patted Cimma's leg. "The South is where they sent him to die. No one makes it out of there alive."

"But, Daddy, he—"

"Cimma, stop. You've already made your brother upset, and I won't hear any more of this."

Mom stood sharply, locking her knees to tower over Cimma sitting there. As she watched her, her eyes went distant, and she fidgeted with the ring on her finger. The ivory one with the same markings as bits of the machine down here that she said Daddy found for her in the sand.

"Actually, I'm a little tired. I'm going to go rest for a while," Mom said as she drifted toward the exit. The billowing pants she wore reflected the blue light as she ascended the ladder back into the bunker.

"Way to go, Cim," Nate said, wiping his palm across a cheek as his lip trembled under it.

"Hey, I'm going to prove to all of you Daddy is alive, just wait."

"Stop it already!" His whine came out more agitated than sad.

She sighed, looking at her brother's quivering face. There was no use talking about it; she would just have to find a way to prove it. She jabbed a finger at a section of the control panel not yet connected to any electricity. "What's *that*, anyway?" The levers and buttons were lifeless.

Nate sniffed. "Uncle Dill still needs to hook up that part of the machine. I think Aunt Eva and Aunt Emilia are still putting it together."

"What does it do?"

"Don't know yet," Nate said as he moved toward the shadowed section of the control panel. He ran a finger down the side and struck one of the buttons like a desert snake. It clacked in response, a hollow thud of plastic disconnected from a power source. "I bet it'll be cool, though."

Up in the bunker, the air was a little warmer, though still cool. Cimma wasn't sure if she preferred the coolness of the underground or the heat of the desert sun. Both were pretty great. The curtain to Papa's room was open a crack, and she could hear Mom inside talking with him. So much for resting.

"It's already too far gone at this point, I'm sorry." Mom's voice was hushed, as if she knew Cimma could be crouched at the opening and listening.

"There has to be a way to reverse this... I've failed before, but I can't... I won't fail you or the children," he responded in the same hushed tone.

"I've made peace with it. I really have."

"Well, I haven't. And Nico probably has some formula he could create for you."

"We've tried Verdigris Mend. It doesn't work on this."

Papa coughed, and it sounded wet. "I wish you had told me sooner. Why didn't you tell me sooner?"

Cimma leaned her ear closer to the crack in the door. The long silence made her heart pump. What was Momma hiding?

"I love you, Gale... you know I do. I've missed Loren for so long, it has quite literally eaten away at my bones. And I'm just so tired of fighting..."

Papa paused. In barely a whisper, he murmured something she couldn't hear.

As Cimma leaned in closer, a whump and groan came from the bedroll behind her. "You shouldn't be *listening*, Cim," Nate said just loud enough to rouse Mom's attention.

Heart racing, Cimma bolted from the door toward the water tank and snatched the nearest book as if she'd been calmly sitting there the whole time reading. Mom came through the door, eyeballing the upside-down parts catalogue in Cimma's sweaty hands. Her smile was soft and sad.

"Why don't you two find Quint and Ayala while I rest for a little while?" she said, strolling toward her bedroll. She spun it out, and it lay flat on the sandy ground as the foam inside inflated. Before fully filled, Mom fell into it, curling into a ball to face the opposite wall.

Papa was still sitting at his small table, chin over fist and searching through articles on his modified e-disk. His black med kit, worn and limp, sagged on the table next to his elbow.

"Hey, Papa," Cimma said quietly as she shuffled inside. He perked up and smiled at her.

"Hey, little miss sneaky. What have you been up to?"

The table he sat at had only one other chair, but she skipped to it with a grin and sat across from him. "Mom was showing Nate the machine again."

"Is that right?" he said, shutting down his e-disk. He paused and studied her, widening his grin and taking off those thick-rimmed glasses to peer at her with that look he always gave her when he knew she was up to no good. "And what else have you been doing?"

Cimma tried to will herself from going pink, but her cheeks got hot, and she knew she was caught. "Nothiiiing," she drew the word out, knowing she wasn't good at lying.

"You *sure* you weren't listening at the pass-through?"

Cimma knew she turned red. Hopefully Papa didn't notice in the dim light.

Papa laughed. He was about to say something else, then reached toward his arm and patted the skin around his Weggevens patch. There were red scratch marks from his nails, and one of the corners looked swollen and angry. He caught her watching him pick at it, then softened his face in a defeated smile. "My body doesn't like Verena's patch," he said.

Cimma frowned. "You know health stuff, don't you? Can't you fix that?"

He chuckled again, more muted and humorless. "Perhaps someday," he said, pulling out a phial of green goop from his bag. Using a thumb, he popped the cork from it and dribbled a small drop of the syrupy liquid onto the swollen part. "For now, I need to just keep doing this. But I will run out eventually." He shrugged and put the cork back on. "There's no more gold to make more."

The concept of eneris was still something Cimma struggled with. Gold was in that liquid. She only knew that because Uncle Nico told her. Gold was the type she knew came from Daddy... but *only* Daddy. Why only Reapers? Her thoughts drifted to Mister Shadow. Maybe he could help.

When she saw Papa looking at her the way he did when her thoughts wandered, she straightened her shoulders. "What were you reading about?" she asked, nodding at his quiet e-disk.

"Oh, nothing. Just trying to keep up with current affairs." Papa curled his fingers over the disk.

"Is Momma sick?" she asked, folding her hands in front of her.

Papa's throat bobbed up and down. It looked like he was choking on the words he tried not to say. He tittered a bit, and she wondered if he wrestled with whether he should lie to his granddaughter or not. Cimma made a quick prayer that he wouldn't.

"She's a little ill, yes," Papa said, choosing truth. He had to know she heard part of their conversation.

"Does she have the virus or something?"

"No, nothing like that... but let her tell you herself, alright?"

"I guess." Cimma frowned as her disappointment furrowed her features, but Papa wouldn't give in. He only smiled at her before standing from the table.

He flicked the side of his e-disk, and it wobbled as it spun in place. "Let's go find Uncle Nico," he said, waving her to come with him.

Sound asleep on her bedroll, Momma snored a little. Next to her, Nate napped too.

Cimma's gaze lingered on the lump of her mom. She remembered getting sick with Nate a few times—usually during colder days, and that one time Betta sneezed on her. That sickness made her tired too, just like Mom... but she got better after a few days with Verena's cactus dew petal broth. And Mom's special orange formula she called feverdrip. Couldn't Mom just try the feverdrip too? It was weird that Papa wouldn't tell her about Mom's sickness.

Nate and Mom didn't hear them shuffle past as they crept by, and it made Cimma proud to feel as nimble as a cat.

The passage for Uncle Nico's bunker was on the wall next to the food bench, which slowly starved for lack of food storage as the storm carried on. Papa pushed the cloth to the side, and Mom and Nate still didn't move.

Inside, the room was dim, lit only by a warm yellow tech light overhead. Uncle Nico sat at his small table, hunched over a phial of a crystal-colored formulation, dabbing a small drop of it on his tongue. He jotted his notes down, going for another taste.

Verena sat opposite him at the table, with a magnifier draped over one eye and a slender tool picking at a thin piece of ancient tech. Neither of them saw Cimma and Papa stroll inside.

Papa cleared his throat.

Both of them bolted upright, twisting to look at them—Verena with her eye all big in the magnifier and Uncle Nico with a partial drop of the formula shimmering on his lower lip.

"Oh, hey!" Uncle Nico said, wiping away the glossy drop. "I think I'm close to coming up with a substitute for Verdigris Mend. It won't be quite as good, but at least we wouldn't need gold."

"We were just talking about that," Papa said as he motioned between himself and Cimma.

A shadow stirred in the corner. Uncle Niklaus had been sleeping there. "You all are loud," he mumbled with a great yawn. Curls the color of bone stuck out in all directions, and he ran his fingers through them.

"Hey, you wanted to be in here." Uncle Nico put the cap on his blue phial.

"My bunker is lonely."

Papa pointed at no one. "Oh, I meant to tell you," he said, "your wives are planning on coming back a few weeks after the storm ends. I just got a message from Emilia about it."

"Why not right after?" Uncle Niklaus pouted.

"Because Eva is finishing up her parts for the new attachment for the machine. Emilia's aerosolizer won't work without it, and they need the resources she can get from Ascendia, that's why."

The new attachment must have been what Nate was showing Cimma earlier. She made a note to ask Papa what an air-o-so-lies-ur was.

As the adults talked about adult things, Cimma found her mind wandering again. She normally liked to listen to the adults talk, but she'd been bothered a lot lately about the visions of her dad.

Mister Shadow told her to focus and find him, and she did, so they needed to just go get him. It was what Mister Shadow wanted too, she could tell. But he wanted to wait. Why wait when they needed him now?

There was a way to do it, though... she learned about it from Uncle Nico. He seemed sad to tell her about it, but learning was good, and she liked to learn. But to get Daddy back, she'd have to use herself to get it done. She knew it would be worth it.

Chapter 8

Hole

Loren

Two standard hours before second sun, and another tip from Yano's spirit told Karl of two outcasts being dropped off that day. The usual crew gathered at the tree arch leading from camp, with Jack strapping on Karl's pack-sack while they held their torches. Lor watched from the falls with Zary in meditation at his heels in the grass.

The stocky shadow pointed at him as it sauntered back to his cabin. It was Karl. Nothing got past him—he knew Lor wanted to go. In Karl's stead, he had been sending Jack, who truthfully had become a force of his own. The hut door slapped shut, swallowing Karl inside...

Now was his chance.

He was quick, slinking away from Zary and slipping behind the huts before ducking into the tree line. With no torch or pack-sack of his own, he had to be quick to find the others.

A dead branch snapped across his throat, sending the dry, dead stick soaring into the muck. First sun was still high overhead, so he had time. In a half jog, he wove between reeds and debris before reaching the long trail to the drop-off. Five figures moved together on the trail. No doubt it was Rik and Jack at the lead, with the three other beast tamers, Davy, Oren, and that prick, Hahn. Though, why they kept him by their side as a beast tamer was a mystery, since his hands were destroyed.

He chuckled to himself.

A quick jog to catch up, and he found himself passing through the camp site where he had his first taste of Nazagora. It had been a while since he'd been back to this place, and it had changed. It was more overgrown with piles of deadened debris and still lifeless. The stumps he remembered sitting on while having his first meal in the bog had rotted halfway into the ground, splintered and mossy.

The fire pit foamed black and wet, no longer suitable for any great fire, but maybe enough to roast a bit of meat. There was nothing better than that first taste of the weird flesh. The Nazagora flavor was amazing—simple char, no spices—and much more satisfying than the protein, oatcress, and vegemeal bricks from the cities. It was even better than the stuff they'd been growing and foraging.

He'd never forget that first taste.

There was a pinch at his neck from a biting fly, and he slapped it away before glancing up to find the scouting group had spotted him following. They stood together, watching him and waiting. Jack crossed his arms and shook his head.

Lor jogged to the group and hid his embarrassment with a smile.

"Why did you follow us?" Jack asked.

"I had to see for myself what Karl was talking about." Lor stepped forward, leading the rest to follow.

The cold sigh behind him followed too. "Don't get yourself killed," Jack said.

Lor chuckled. "As if I could die."

Hahn sneered, holding up a hooked hand as if to send him a rude gesture. Lor didn't understand Hahn's new ways of being an ass, so he ignored it.

The newest tamer, Davy, broke the silence between them. "I've seen your fights," he said, stepping in sync next to Lor. "I hope I can fight like that someday."

Lor tittered. "Don't worry, you'll eventually have to. Everyone fights."

"Yeah, but did you see me get crushed by Zary? And she's just a girl!"

"A woman, you mean. And a tough one at that, with strong faith. Don't underestimate anyone in this place." Lor took a look at Davy. He was young and fresh, choosing a close-cropped haircut, having nicked his temple with whatever implement he used to cut it. With eyes wide and a grin spread across the smooth skin of an unchallenged life... he was a little too excited to be an exile. Some Yeunish were born to expect banishment.

"Yeah, I like her a lot," Davy said with the same silly smile.

His casual innocence was infectious. Lor knew what he meant, and he was sure Zary had little interest. Knowing what he knew about her first and last relationship, she was more focused on forgetting anything outside of her devotion to the Maker. "Well, get up to speed with her. Otherwise, she won't think twice about you."

"Ooh, harsh! But point taken. Would you teach me?"

"I can teach you some stuff, but my fights aren't the most fair. You know I heal, right?"

“Yeah, duh, I knew that.” Davy smirked and shook his head.

Rik halted in front of them and held up a fist. Everyone shut up immediately as he crouched behind a set of hairy bushes. It took a second or two for Lor’s ears to get accustomed to the sudden silence. It was an eerie silence. As they attuned to the lack of noise, a stray gee fly buzzed past his ear. Even through the thickness of the air, he smelled the funk of bog sweat and blood.

“Hear that?” Rik whispered.

Amid the thrumming drone of silence, the faintest wet sounds made their way through, just beyond the next patch of dripping trees.

They crept through the mud in silence toward the next tree bank. Each man took a tree to hide behind while craning their necks toward the drop-off spot.

“Damn,” Jack whispered under his breath.

It was then Lor caught what Jack saw. The hulking black mass of a lone Nazagora hunched over its meal in the mud. Now it was clear where the smell of blood came from.

“Where’s the other one?” Rik hissed, scanning the bog.

“I don’t see anyone else,” Lor said.

Jack peered around the tree at the Nazagora, oblivious of their presence. “Intel said there were two.”

Rik sighed. “Well, come on, let’s take care of this one.”

They marched toward the creature and its corpse meal, sending it quivering onto its haunches. Its guttural clicks and alien whimpers almost made Lor feel sorry for it. After all, it was just trying to survive too, right? A creature that size wouldn’t be able to survive on bog water and a handful of jumpers alone.

“Back, Nazagora!” Rik shooed the creature away, and it slinked backwards before scurrying off into the mist with its melancholy whine.

The corpse was a woman, and Lor’s gut squeezed into a knot. Too old to be his daughter... too young to die. The Nazagora made short work of her insides, but her face was intact, looking off to the side, as if waiting for a friend to come for her up the horizon. Only she was half-buried in the swamp, surrounded by water-logged reeds and grasses.

Jack’s fingers were clamped around her jaw, moving her face back and forth. He clicked his tongue. “I should have known,” he said. “Someone put a round in her.”

A deep black wound opened up her forehead. It was unlike anything Lor had seen. At the look of it, she didn’t suffer... and for that he was glad. That Nazagora happened to stumble upon her after she had died at the hands of the mysterious boatman.

There were no other signs of a second body. Whoever she came here with was out there somewhere. Either that or their intel was bad.

"What do we do with her?" Davy asked. Deep wrinkles cupped his mouth as he frowned.

Rik scanned the area again, and Lor followed his gaze, hoping to spot the other outcast somewhere on the horizon. "We have to leave her," he said, avoiding looking at the woman. Lor did the same. It was uncomfortable to see her in that state.

"Can you get silver from her?"

Lor recoiled. "What use do we have for silver out here in this place? Besides, I haven't done that in..."

"Days," Hahn said with a sneer. He hooked the wrinkled end of one of his useless hands into his nose to dig around.

Damn, that guy was disgusting. But he wasn't wrong. Lor had forgotten all about his accidental pull. Reaping was something he'd never forget how to do.

"I'm not pulling her," he said.

Oren stepped forward and bent down next to her in solemn prayer over her body. Rik and Davy did the same, and Lor wondered if he should too. But he feared that whatever he prayed for would have the opposite effect against his intentions. For a dead woman, what worse could he do to her? He stood and watched their quick moment of silence.

"We have about another standard hour or so to find the other outcast," Jack said, looking at the sun's position.

"Let's get looking then," Rik said.

Lor glanced for the last time at the woman in the mud. She had a name and a story... and now she was food for the beasts. It was hard not to think of her while they moved in silence through the rest of the tree patches.

That hole... black and wet right in the middle of her forehead... it went clean through. They were missing something important here. The woman was either killed because of her heritage or something else.

They combed each area as well as they could in their limited time for a missing person that may or may not exist. Based on their tainted timing information, there was a chance that the number of exiles was also wrong.

But the more they searched, the more it nagged him. If there was even the slightest chance his daughter could be on that boat, why wouldn't Karl let him join the collection party? Maybe it really *was* because he was the only healer.

At least, it had *better* be the only reason.

"Guys, look over there." Davy pointed toward a swath of trees in various states of life and decay. At the foot of one of them was a pair of limp feet cocked off in different directions and fitted with the signature tan-colored sack fabric. The fashion of the banished.

They jogged toward the spot, finding an elderly Mesaman lying at the roots.

"Is he alive?" Oren asked.

Lor knelt to the man's side, feeling his neck for a pulse. A low thump knocked back, and although subtle, his chest rose and fell.

"He's alive but passed out."

"Poor guy, he must have been running so long. And he's so old!" Davy said.

Jack pulled out a small bladder holding the yellowish concoction he called Jaune Spirit. Since the man was passed out, he took a sharpened hook fish quill to inject the decant into his arm. The yellow liquid worked fast, as the man opened his eyes with a frightened moan before bolting upright.

"Come, we don't have all night." Rik held out a hand and helped him up. As soon as he was on his feet, he wobbled in place, putting a hand to his gray head. Deep wrinkles fanned out from his eyes, and his tanned skin stood out from the pale Yeunish statues that surrounded him. Under a low brow, his green eyes were damp.

"Is this hell?" he croaked. His hand shook as he held it to his head, covered in dark spots and dry skin.

Jack shrugged. "Pretty much. But you're not dead yet. Let's get out of here."

After passing him fond memories of his time during the program, Lor healed the man's brand. He almost had a heart attack from the awe of it, then turned to cursing the cities for keeping the Guilds to themselves.

The man's name was Darius Fatheree, and he lived through many generations, speaking in strange revelations about the length of time the current princeps had been around.

Renae was middle-aged when I was just a teen! he had said. The proclamation elicited a few side-eyes among the group, each look speaking untold worries of the possibility of early onset senility or just an honest case of mistaken identity. As far as Lor knew, the princeps had a record of his life on public display. He *had* to, if he were to become princeps.

The proclamation was even curiouser still considering their new exile's appearance...

Hovering at the ripe standard age of seventy-six, Darius was a Yeunish sympathizer, sent to the bog with the woman he hid in his basement. He couldn't recall what the cloaked boatman looked like but remembered the dark hole of the tech shooter pointed at his friend. Her body hit the ground before he could blink.

"You were very lucky," Jack murmured as he lifted a branch for everyone to duck under.

"I wouldn't call it luck, son," Darius said. He walked with a bit of a limp—not one from immediate banishment pains but one that had set in his bones years before.

"What would you call it then?" Jack asked.

"Is there a such a word that works here? I mean, one that would describe mentally jarring someone enough that they might just want to give up and die?"

"Yeah, it's called cruelty. I'm sorry."

"Ain't your fault, boy. But I'm just an old codger with neither wit nor will—and not long for Roseaarde soon, I gather."

"What does that mean?" Davy asked, while hopping over a small mound of waterlogged earth.

"It means he's going to die soon, dumbass," Hahn interrupted. He poked his hooked hand back up to his nose, trying to scratch or pick it.

"Aren't you charming," Darius said. His eyes followed the twisted cane of flesh corkscrew around in Hahn's crusty nose. "But yes, that's what I meant."

"Well, welcome to the rest of your life," Jack said, as he pushed away the final canopy of weeping branches to reveal the open camp. The sight of the rushing waterfall, the handcrafted homes, and the bustle of people made Lor wistful for his first time in that place.

Of course, Karl stood several paces inside with his arms crossed and a frown. Zeroing in on Lor, he shook his head and motioned for him to follow.

"I'm in trouble," Lor said through a grimace.

Chapter 9

Triple E and C

Eva

Tick, tick, tick... The mechanical clock beat above Eva's head as she spun the microdriver on a converter joint. The part was small, and the magnifier she swiped from her lab in Ascendia worked wonders for the finer details.

The constant ticking of the clock brought a kind of serenity to her mind as she worked, each spin rotating to the beat. That was why she made it. She often got lost in those mechanical beats, so when she finally looked at its face, she was already running late. The others would be waiting for her at the Iron Eletonk Cafe, with Cae probably feral with hunger by the time she got there.

One last turn of the microdriver and she set her work down to swing her dark green jacket over her shoulders. It had been raining for days and didn't do any favors for her mood.

The last few meetings with her girlfriends didn't go very far. It was always plat this, plat that, transfer, don't transfer... It was tiresome waiting for the day they'd take back the tree. Every day that passed without action, the cities grew more restless with their increasingly oppressive mandates pouring from Audun. If Eva were to be completely honest, things were so far gone that she didn't even believe getting rid of the worm would set everything straight again. At least not right away.

The ID lock at her front door bolted it shut, and she raised her jacket hood. The old cream-colored cruiser she bought in better times sat in the circle drive. She sighed, jogging toward it as raindrops plipped over her hood. With all the plat they funneled to the desert project, she couldn't afford to replace the cruiser. It was reliable, though, and she hoped she could squeeze a few more years out of it.

Once inside the cruiser cabin, she started the silent ignition to turn over the power bank. The last playlist she had on in there crescendoed. She listened for a few moments, hands limp on the wheel. The music reminded her of Nico. The low drone of the lead singer for My Haerow Honey belted out the tune they listened to when he kissed her for the first time.

That smile he wore... so cock-sure and charming. They had dated for a while at that point, but he was a gentleman. Still a gentleman. That first feel of his face so close to hers and all the newness of their relationship was stored in the notes of that song. It brought the slightest sting to her eye when hearing it. Seeing the local band live was one of their first dates.

She blew out a long stream of air and took off for the cafe, praying that Cae's stomach would forgive her for being fashionably late.

It had been too long since she'd been able to visit Nico in Kanckette. If the heavy rains meant anything, it was at least a sign of the maelstrom coming to an end soon. Once the desert was calm, she'd take some time off and off-road this cruiser into the dust, not stopping until the green fringe of his tent opening was right in front of her windshield.

Besides, she also had some duties to the machine. There were new components to add to the aux panel.

A cramp dug into her side, and she belched, feeling the tired nausea that wracked her for the past standard month. Nothing sounded appetizing for lunch. If anything, she'd stick to cold water and maybe some stale toast.

Just as she thought about it, the orange holo sign for the Iron Eletonk Cafe buzzed ahead. Swiping over her e-disk, she was only twelve standard minutes late. One last moment listening to My Haerow Honey, and she passed her e-disk over the meter to pay before shutting it down and marching into the eatery.

She saw Eloria first, still in uniform, waving at her. Emilia and Cae flanked her sides, leaving the one spot open for Eva. It had her back facing the open, and she hated that.

No one spoke. All e-disks were off, and they motioned to each other in a signing code they made up years ago.

You're a little late, Cae signed harshly to her.

I know, sorry, Eva signed back.

It's alright. Eloria motioned. *Let's order now so we can discuss.*

Cae raised her hand at one of the Foscan servants. She was a tiny thing, dressed in all white with her black hair cut short, unlike a typical Foscan. When she greeted them, her smile faded a touch as each of them zoomed in on the digi-menu to whatever they wanted without a word.

Eva touched her lower lip, as a way to tell the Foscan they were mute. The servant's smile returned, and she trotted away with their orders. In public, there was no telling who listened. With e-disks off, being recorded was lower risk but not foolproof.

Toast? Really? Cae signed to Eva.

Eva pulled her lips to the side and made a face while rubbing her stomach. A part of her felt bad for not indulging in real food found only in the cities anymore. Surely Nico was eating scraps and rations with the rest of them. They were blessed... for now.

The big guy is still looking for our men. Eloria motioned. *He needs a push almost every day.*

That's bad, Eva signed.

It's under control at the moment. The man is exhausting and has a foul mind.

The Foscan delivered their dishes. The brown stack of crispy bread was boring next to the simmering glazed meats, fresh fruits, and variety of steamed greens on everyone else's plates. Cae didn't wait to dig into her blood fish steak.

And the princeps? Emilia signed as she tossed a small red fruit into her mouth.

More devout than ever. Completely worships the worm. Eloria motioned back.

Cae tapped the table with two fingers before signing the news of her own eavesdropping in the alleys. *I see more and more arrests all the time. Don't know how much longer we can go unnoticed by them... They're getting very violent.*

Eva nodded, crinkling her face inward, lost in thought. She took a small pull from her toast and washed it down with a sip of water. The mineral flavor of the cold drink turned her stomach. She tapped her two fingers toward Emilia. *Do you have the aerosolizer parts yet?*

Almost, Emilia responded. *How about the pulse shot?*

Eva held two fingers together in a pinch.

We should be close to taking it all back. Emilia grinned.

We should plan to go to the tents after the maelstrom, Eloria signed. *Maybe for a little longer. I've been saving my vacation time.*

The mention of returning to the tents and seeing Nico again made Eva's heart race. Everything inside her wanted to be near him, yet she was afraid to face him, and she had no idea why. Another bite of the over-browned toast and she wanted to retch.

Are you alright? Emilia signed to her.

Eva shook her head with another sip of the dusty water. A quick sign that she'd be right back, and she left the women to ponder her abrupt departure.

The bathroom had a cold smell, sharp and medicinal from a scented formulation they pumped in there, but someone had recently fouled up a stall. She leaned over the sink and looked up at a mirror tainted by some murky spray, as if someone spit straight on it.

Behind the spitty film, her skin was sallow. Her once vibrant red hair had dulled, hanging limp over her shoulders. As she stared at herself, a cold sweat broke over her brow as the bitter flux pulsed at her throat. She ran to a stall and threw up nothing but watered down bile with pieces of soggy brown toast. The sight of it gagged her two more times before she slumped to the dirty floor, waiting for the cold chill to disperse from her forehead.

The bathroom door creaked open, and she heard her name whispered though the crack.

"I'm in here," she mumbled from the floor.

"Oh no, why are you on the floor?" It was Emilia. She knelt down next to her, putting a warm hand on her back.

Eva shivered at Emilia's touch and moved a shaking hand to the paper roll. She dabbed a wad of paper over her mouth and tossed it in the toilet. She sighed and pressed a toe to the rusty floor flusher. *I'm alright,* she signed.

Emilia said nothing, crouched next to her wearing pressed lavender pants and glossy black shoes. Her white blouse practically shone against the dingy stall door with her signature pearls clasped around her throat. It was a sight to see such a polished woman in a place like that, but Emilia was classy inside and out. Her gaze moved between Eva and the toilet, and the look in her eye told Eva that she was severely misjudging the scene.

"Are you... pregnant?" Emilia whispered.

Eva tittered. "No, not pregnant."

Her friend sank her shoulders and stuck out her lower lip. "Bummer. I was about to get so excited."

Eva glanced around and went back to signing. *We can't raise a baby with the way things are going right now. Maybe after, when we get everything taken care of.*

Well, we better work quickly, then... We aren't getting any younger, Emilia signed. The smooth pink smile that spread across her face was probably meant to placate Eva, but she wasn't hopeful; she was terrified.

I'm afraid, Eva admitted. *This world... this world is so messed up. I think Faelice has been watching me at Ascendia.*

Emilia frowned. *Faelice? Is she that Anglian admin?*

Eva nodded.

She's an old moldy hanso tart... Why do you think she's been watching you?

Eva chuckled at the insult, trying not to hack out vomit breath. *It was right after we came back from the desert the last time.* She clenched her jaw shut, craning her neck to make sure they were still alone.

She caught me scanning out some schematics I wanted to reverse engineer for the machine. I should have been more careful... but ever since then, she's been following me around. She thinks she's being sneaky about it, but I'm not stupid. If she says something, I could be thrown in gaol.

Emilia hummed. *I can listen around, see if I hear anything. Maybe spread a rumor or two about her being passed around the city and catching something that made her crazy. Two can play these dirty games.*

Eva laughed. *Dill is a bad influence on you.*

I learn from the best. Emilia winked and helped Eva to her feet.

Back at the table, the twins bickered in muted gestures. Eva caught the tail end of Eloria signing *not right now*, before stuffing her hands in her lap and facing away from Cae.

What's going on? Eva signed.

As Cae lifted her hands to respond, Eloria turned with a glare. Even if she did hesitate for just a moment, it didn't stop her from going on a wild signing tirade.

My dim sister overheard the big dummy having a conversation with the princeps about a potential mole in their force. I told her she needs to quit immediately, but she won't do it, because he needs a push daily. We can deal with that guy, don't you think? I think we can. Niklaus knows more about his weaknesses... We can totally take him. She needs to quit now. Tell her she needs to quit!

Her hands flew in such wild motions that it drew the attention of a nearby table. Attention that Eva could do without, knowing she potentially had eyes on her at work. Now with this news, her stomach flopped.

Nausea waved over her again, but she swallowed the bitter tang and tapped the table in front of Eloria.

Maybe Cae is right. Maybe you should quit. She signed to an exaggerated eye roll from her old friend.

Not you too... Eloria sighed.

It sounds like it's getting dangerous, Elo. If your partner is suspicious of a mole, it's only a matter of time before he suspects that it's you. We can't have you protecting us all the time all by yourself!

Eloria clucked, picking at the remnants of her plate. *I'll think about it,* she signed.

Chapter 10

Her Plan Now

Cimma

Remnants of the maelstrom belched little versions of their twisters into the air. The fresh tang of electricity in the atmosphere was a welcome fragrance to the month-long underground smells of sweat and poop.

A crimson phial peeked through Cimma's clutched fingers, moving with the sway of her arms. The night sky held little light as she moved through the desert, cloaked and sort of armed.

Unknown dangers lurked in the shadows, and the phial of Red Mash would probably be just enough to let Cimma escape anyone who would pursue her. Last Grudge would have been the better choice, but she once told Uncle Nico that it scared her a little after it ripped through a band of death camp brigands.

Brigands. That's what Mom called them. Cimma didn't know what that word meant, but she knew it meant the bad people in the outer areas in the desert. Either way, Last Grudge sacrificed some *brigands* that scary day last year, spraying their life into the sand. It made orange stains in the yellow sand, and Cimma knew it was because orange was made with yellow and red. That orange splotch stuck around until the maelstrom took it away.

She knew they were bad people, and Papa said they deserved it, but maybe they just needed help becoming good people. That's why she chose the red phial. As far as she knew, it wouldn't kill anyone, just hurt them a little. As long as she was careful to stay under the tracks above, the lights and the train would help keep the bad people away.

Subtle noises of the desert pulled her attention, and she listened specifically for any footsteps. Nothing but insects of the night chirping in a beat-less song. Without the bustle of home, the night noises were eerie. Wind rustled a cluster of nearby shrubs, and it sounded like someone hiding in it. She squeezed her phial a little tighter.

Whenever she got to where she was going, she would have to figure out what to do with the phial if she never used it. A weapon like that would surely turn heads, and she didn't want to make too much of a scene. Worse yet, she wanted to get *caught,* not killed.

An old station lay just outside the boundary of Kanckette. It didn't show up on Papa's e-disk map, but she remembered seeing it one time in the distance. Papa told her about it when she asked, but he didn't think it was used anymore. She hoped someone was there; otherwise, it would be a very long walk to the mountain station. Probably days... and she only had one phial.

There were bad things beyond the safety of their tents. That was what Ayala told her the day she herself wandered off and killed a man. They were the same age when she did that, and Cimma worried about killing anyone. No fire came from her hands that she knew of, though. Raising her phial hand, she examined her fingertips. Nope.

Several standard hours passed, but she didn't know how many. The stars had shifted, and there was a peek of light on the horizon. The moment Mom fell asleep was the moment she wrote her note and slipped from the tent, so she knew she had walked through the whole night. She felt bad worrying her, Nate, and Papa, but the gift she would bring to them was just... the best.

A distant arc of light flickered ahead—small and dim, lining the top of an entry archway. Light meant power, and power meant people, so she threw her shoulders back and continued her walk, red phial at the ready in her fist.

The light took forever to feel any closer as she walked, but eventually it did. She made it to the mystery station. Her shoulders were sore from holding them back, and the phial pressed fancy dents into her skin.

Other than the tech lights on the archway, the station itself was dark and quiet, a passing breeze the only whistle moving through it. A thin layer of sand blew across the stone walkway as a lone scrap of paper twirled around near the deserted entrance.

She snatched the paper, turning it this way and that to piece together whatever propaganda had faded from the surface. Fortunately, Uncle Dill taught her letters, so she knew them well... It was a poster for the worm. Of course, the poster didn't say "worm" on it exactly, but she knew what Cirv'e was. Mister Shadow taught her all about Cirv'e.

And Mister Shadow would *know*.

When she looked up from the paper, she glimpsed a handful of train gates that had to have been nice looking a long time ago. Now, peeling colors and broken tech lights that probably once made the station a happier place were crusted in muted shades of age. She didn't like it here... It was a station of ghosts.

A bin at the entrance had a ration wrapper poking out of the auto lid, like a green tongue sticking out at her. She took the worm propaganda, crumpled it into a tight ball, and tossed it at the can. The lid responded in a rusty whir, gulping it down with the rest of the ration wrapper.

"Who's there?" a deep voice called from the end of the station.

Cimma's heart leaped. It was time. She lowered the cloth from her mouth and lifted her green-colored goggles, hovering her hand over the bin to drop in the phial of Red Mash. It hit the wads of paper at the bottom with a crinkly thunk.

"Identify yourself," a shadowed figure called again, making their way toward her. A second shadow trailed the first, and she was suddenly afraid.

She regretted throwing out the Red Mash so soon. What could she possibly say?

"C-can I get a ticket here?" she called back, her voice high and shaky.

Both shadows slowed their hurried steps, taking a more casual stride. A jangling noise came with each step, and based on what Papa told her of roundsmen, she guessed the shadows were them... with their beaty sticks.

Don't be afraid.

She took in deep breaths to calm the cold chill crawling down to her fingers and toes.

The first roundsman came near, and he was dark and stocky. Kinda like Uncle Dill, but big.

"Holy shit, Marko... it's a Yeuni." He turned to the trailing shadow.

She stood her ground, flexing her hands at her sides to get rid of the shivers. If she kept her face tough, they'd know she was tough. She prayed that her willingness to go with them would keep them from beating her with those sticks. She'd heard stories from Ayala. *Don't talk back and don't fight back, no matter what.*

The one called Marko got closer to her, rubbing the bags under his eyes before popping them wide to get a better look. Her "tough" face quivered as they continued to eyeball her without saying anything.

"Dude, she's just a *kid.*" Marko crinkled his bushy red brows to the center of his forehead. He glanced from her to his partner several times, waiting for the first roundsman to say something.

"Bounty went up. It's a hundred thousand plat now. Can't pass up a gift that just walked into our station." The bigger partner arched his shoulders back, the way a chitter bird would puff its feathers up against an enemy.

Second guesses are for weaklings... don't be weak like your brother.

It wasn't her voice in her head, but she listened to it. She matched the chitter bird's puffing feathers and straightened her shoulders with chin held high.

The skinny one, Marko, wouldn't look at her, watching his large partner instead. "Sammy, she's just a kid. If we send her back where she came from quietly—"

"No. Kel's sick, and I need the plat. Come, little one, come!"

Cimma obeyed.

"You're a sick ass," Marko said. He still refused to look at her—gazing into the sky, at the station gates... anywhere but at her.

Even though she wanted to get caught, the man, Marko, seemed like a decent person. Ayala had nothing good to say about roundsmen, but maybe she didn't meet the right ones. Maybe she never met Marko with his skinny arms and red hair like flames.

"It's alright, Mister Marko, sir," she said to him. He jerked his head toward her. He had nice green eyes. "I'm here on purpose."

The big one, Sammy, chuckled a little, then frowned. "You *want* to get bountied?"

That wasn't a familiar word to her, but she guessed it meant getting turned in. She put on the tough face again and nodded. Both men glanced at each other before skinny Marko knelt in front of her. The desert sun had painted tan freckles over his pale nose. They were neat in all their random, splotchy weirdness, and she wished she had some too. "Why would you want to be caught?" he asked.

"I-I..." She paused. "Please, just turn me in... make me *bountied*... and get your money. But don't hit me, please."

Another glance between the men. Sammy shrugged and held out his thick hand, which she took. It was rough and hard, like someone who used tools a lot. It reminded her of Uncle Dill's, bumpy and callused with dry patches that scratched her palm. Knowing that her hand in his was her ticket to the South, she tried to picture holding Daddy's hand. He was tough, too, and probably had hard hands like these. Then she smiled.

Skinny, freckly Marko wouldn't come, shaking his head with a deep frown as they made their way to Sammy's cruiser.

He didn't talk much at all to her, only asking her name and why she wanted to go south. Her first name was fair enough, but her reason was an answer she wouldn't give up. No one had to know Daddy was there.

"They'll brand your pretty head," Sammy said. If she knew what that meant, maybe she'd feel some way about it. Instead, she didn't answer him, looking forward as the vehicle pulled up to a mushy shore. The smell was different. It was salty, with a familiar kind of aroma. Like the one she smelled after the brigands died.

She turned to him before he rose from his seat, and he looked back at her. He had a lot of hair above his lip, and it curled outward like little handles. Silver strands threaded through it, and Cimma guessed he must be really old... like thirty or something. But his face was kind, and she thought about what he said.

"Do you really think I'm pretty?" she asked.

He sighed, his whole face melting. "Are you sure you want to be here?"

The question was confusing. For one, they were already there. Second, she told him before she was going to the South, why would he second-guess? Like a weakling? Plus, he didn't answer her question.

"Yeah, I asked to be here, didn't I? But do you really think I'm pretty?"

Sammy tittered, making the hairs right under his nose jitter. "You're a kid, so don't look at me like that. The Yeunish are a pretty race, I can't deny it."

They sat in the cruiser for at least a standard minute. Big Sammy had a nice smell, like sweet things and hard wax. He held the cruiser's lever for a while as he stared out the fogging windshield. "You could die, you know?" He whispered it, and she sensed his hesitation.

Mom thought Daddy was dead. She knew he was still alive. Maybe they heard stories... scary stories to keep them afraid to disobey. Maybe the whole thing was like nothing at all.

Before she could ask any other questions, Sammy slid from his seat and led her out into the swamp from the other side.

Chapter 11

Only Hope Remained

Damaetra / Gale

Mom and Nate,

You didn't believe me when I said Daddy was still alive, so I'm gonna prove it to you. I'm going to the South to get him back for good. Then everything will be better.

Cim

The little piece of jagged parchment floated to the sandy floor without a sound. How did a mother gather seasons of pain and swallow it down to remain the rock for the rest of her family? A warbled cry pulsed from Damaetra's throat as the too-familiar salt sting swelled at her eyes. Her chest rose and fell in short bursts.

First sun had only just picked itself up from the horizon, and her daughter was long gone. Her stubborn, naive, and vulnerable daughter was gone. Soon her sensitive son would wake up and find out. The news would crush his heart—he was so fond of his twin sister. It was double the pain for her.

How could she even think of doing something like this to the family? Her lungs beat in her chest, trying to pull in air that wouldn't come.

"Is everything alright?" A sleep-drunk voice slid up from the bunker. Gale slipped into the main tent where Damaetra still stood, slack-jawed and panting.

He tilted his head at her, then found the parchment on the floor. "What's that?" he asked.

She couldn't even look at him. It was all her fault. A corner of the paper lifted in the breeze when she looked down at it. An imperfection woven in the paper press drew her attention, not the black letters scrawled in a child's mediocre handwriting. Her face flushed as the air wouldn't come into her body.

"Damaetra?" Gale asked. She scooped up the note and thrust it toward her father-in-law. He could read it for himself. She had to have read it wrong.

The paper slid from her fingertips, and after a short pause, Gale mumbled, "I don't understand. Where's Cimma?"

The damned air wouldn't come into her lungs. The early yellow of dawn sliced through the thin seam in the tent opening, cutting into the room. Cimma knew her way around the tent. She knew how to disarm and rearm Verena's trap.

The story of Ayala nearly getting snatched by the group of death camp criminals was a tale reiterated time and again to Cimma when learning how to disarm it.

You remember what Ayala told you about wandering alone at night? Her own words echoed in her mind. Cimma was the same age as Ayala then. What if she was brutalized by them? The whimper returned to her throat as she tried to unlock her vocal cords and attempt to breathe.

"Dame, *where* is Cimone'a?" Gale hopped toward the entrance. For a fifty-eight-year-old man, he made short work of that trap, twirling knobs and flipping switches.

Once the low hum of electricity waned, he whipped open the tent flaps, shouting into the open air for his granddaughter.

"Cimma!" His shout was ordinary. A passive call for sundown. "Cimma!" That call had a hint of panic. "Cimone'a Turtingas!" The tail end of his shout screeched through the wind.

"Mom? Papa?" Nate crawled up from the bunker, still rubbing sleep from his eyes. Seeing him there, his innocent little head poking up from the underground hatch, Damaetra's heart broke. He waited, blue-violet eyes just like hers wide and watching.

"Honey," she warbled out the word, tempering her gasps to stay strong for him. Gale's distant calls down the tent line stole Nate's interest as he craned his neck toward the entrance. "Did your sister say anything to you last night?"

"No, why?" He yawned, still trying to look from the tent, brows crinkled together. "Why, Mom? Why do you ask? Why are you breathing like that?"

The casual tone he brought with him morphed into the terrified urgency of finding a venomous sidewinder in the sand. Gale cried out again, his voice joined by the Freelys and a few other residents.

"We're, ah... having trouble finding her."

Breathe, breathe, breathe!

"What?" His eyes bulged when he gaped at her.

Such a sensitive boy, water already rimming his lids. Her body felt heavy, her head light, and she flopped onto the sofa, head in her hands. Each new trial ate at her bones and sucked at the marrow.

From the moment she was born, Damaetra knew Cimma was headstrong like her father. Even more so like her grandmother, Els'daegal. She struggled to find words for her prayer as she begged the Maker for her daughter's life. There was a limit to how much stress her body could take.

"Cimone'a!" Gale cried through his worn throat. His chest heaved as he tried to stifle his panic.

She was gone... she was gone.

Mister Freely combed the other side of the nearest dunes with Quint and Ayala, sending birds as far as they would listen to him, but it was pointless. Ayala's tears told Gale everything he needed to know.

That round face tottering about the bunkers, her mischievous giggles, how she pestered her brother... all the memories of his granddaughter rushed into his mind in unquenchable regrets. She was stubborn always, asking questions she shouldn't have the foresight to ask, and constantly listening to the world around her. All the same, she cared deeply about family, even through the stubborn veneer. She was so like his Els'daegal.

He almost missed out on all of it when he pulled that shooter from the mantle. Thank the Maker for Nico. But now Cimone'a was gone.

It made him sick to think of what could have happened to her. The brigands seemed to increase in number year after year, influenced by evil notions. If he ever found a camp that was responsible for hurting her...

He wanted to run. He could run to the cities and be back in time for dinner. Trouble was, he knew she couldn't possibly be there, and he didn't want to risk being there either. He ran his finger over the swollen corner of his patch and called for Niklaus.

The sand plumed up next to him as the scrappy twin obliged.

"Go to Secas and try to find her there. I'll run West," he said. Niklaus nodded, activated his patch again, and left in a cloud of yellow dust.

The closest area west of them was the small train station that was barely used and nearly defunct. He'd check there anyway.

Careful not to show his ability to the strangers he might meet, he stopped short of the station and strolled casually through the gate. It was littered with rolling ration wrappers, a crumbled Yeunish wanted poster, and a swirling layer of yellow sand. The single trash bin sat near the archway, corroded at the bottom with a layer of redness, still wet and familiar. Gale bent down to examine it.

"Stop there, sir." A roundsman approached from down the station.

Gale complied and stood upright.

"Had a nasty incident with that can, sir. Didn't want you to poke around at it," the roundsman said as he got closer.

"What is it?" Gale asked.

The man shrugged. He had a shock of red hair and freckles splattered over his pale skin. "Some wild formulation, we think. Burned our maintenance guy pretty bad."

"Why don't you get rid of the trash can?"

"It's still under investigation. We need to keep it where it was when the formulation was found. Anyway, what can I help with here? Train's not running today."

Hesitant to pull out a holopic of Cimma on his modified e-disk, Gale stopped short of his pocket. He rubbed his hands over his pants as if he meant to do that. "I was wondering if you've seen a young girl here recently. Dark hair, pale skin, about this tall." Gale flattened his hand almost up to his nose.

The roundsman put up a finger and turned to look over his shoulder. Gale took a look too, but they were alone. "You mean a young *Yeunish* girl?" the roundsman whispered.

"A-ah..." Gale swallowed and swiped at his brow. He took a few standard seconds to weigh his odds of admitting he was a harborer. It was Cimma, though, and he had to know... If it came down to it, he could completely outrun this chump. "Yes, yes... Have you seen her?" Gale whispered back.

The red-headed law man eyed him. "You know harboring is a crime too, right?"

Gale's heart sped up as he readied his sprint foot. "Have you seen her?" he asked again.

The man's face softened, and he took in a deep breath, jetting it back out through pursed lips. "There was a girl here at first sunrise."

"You saw her? Where is she now? Is she here?" The station was empty, but Gale couldn't help but crane his neck around and scan the area.

"I'm sorry to tell you, but my partner cashed in on her."

Gale's whole chest deflated. So that was it. She was really, truly gone. Darkness bloomed in his core as he thought about the rumors he'd heard from Eloria of unlawful executions happening at the drop-off. She was going to die, if she hadn't already.

"I didn't want him to, though," the roundsman continued, "to turn her in, you know. Are you sure it's the girl you're looking for? I mean, maybe it was a different one or something."

Gale closed his eyes and bobbed his head. "Thanks for your help," he said, turning around.

"Stay safe out there," the roundsman called as Gale waved his acknowledgment and stepped back through the archway into the sand.

The news would wreck Dame. She was already hurting so much, he couldn't possibly tell her this. He didn't want to lie to her, but he also didn't want to see her spiral. As long as there was hope Cimma was still out here somewhere, Dame could hold on to that hope. And if Cimma did return, they could celebrate. Nico could have something figured out to cure Dame, and things could start going back to normal. It was easy to picture it in his head.

The irritated edge of his patch wept through his sleeve. He activated it anyway and turned around to see the roundsman was gone.

By the time he'd returned to the last tent in the row, the wet spot on his sleeve had gone red.

"Damnit," he hissed to himself as he peeled the fabric away.

Residents continued to call out for Cimma, but Gale went to the back of the tent and wept. As he silently shook with his face in his hand, a can of water plunked into the sand next to him from above.

With hand shielding his eyes, he looked up without finding the person who dropped it. So he picked the can up, studied it, and cracked it open for a sip. It was still cool. Not cold but refreshing enough. It was enough to pull the heat back from his collar and straighten himself.

He blew out a tight breath, wondering about the strangeness of people but thankful for the drop. It was enough to cool his grief and present himself back to the family as the rock they saw him as. He needed to be that rock for them. They needed someone to lead.

Chapter 12

Quiet At Last

Eloria

There was a feeling, the kind Eloria would get when she knew she had a bad dream but only remembered the darkness of it. It was that kind of morning, a bad omen. She rolled out of bed, massaging the sides of her weak knee. A chord strummed in her neck where she slept funny.

Getting older really sucked.

Joining the force at her age was frowned on, but she did it anyway and began enjoying the benefits of suffering for it.

Pushing Hammer had its fun moments at least, and she could smile about that. The small grin pulled at her sore gums from where she took a hit from that crazed Weg volatile earlier in the week. It still hurt... That woman was fierce.

The crisp air in her bedroom still had a lingering aroma of washing soap from the night before, and she savored it. Not too overpowering, it smelled like sweet fruit and the dampness of rain, making her feel feminine again. Wrangling lawbreakers during the day took its tithe of her grace.

Putting weight on her feet activated the deep ache in her heels as she limped toward the bathroom. The swelling had gone down at her cheekbone, leaving a nice purplish half-moon under her left eye. She poked it, feeling the squishy sore spot.

Her white hair touched her eyelashes, and she needed a trim again. If she'd known it was mandatory to keep it clipped above her ears as a roundsman, she might have reconsidered. For some reason, her own twin pulled off the hairstyle better than she did... She missed her long hair.

Eloria sighed, gripping the sides of the hand basin and observing the bruises on her pale arms and legs. Forever destined to be single with this rough mug. There was a time she was always beautiful—hardly needing to convince anyone of that, with or without a push.

The one time she considered—truly considered—spending the rest of her life with someone was in her role in Arts when she fell in love with the talented glass crafter, Benni Vetreu. The scent of his skin was a warm ambered wood and his eyes the color of blue night. He wore his brown hair longer, tucked in a frizzy tail, and the thick stubble that traversed his face rubbed her chin when they kissed. All of those things, those wistful memories, latched to her core.

But she left her low impact job in Arts to be beaten up regularly in Law, and Benni chose someone else. It didn't take a Reader to understand what happened, and it was crushing.

As she examined her aging imperfections, poking at a puffy spot here, dragging a wrinkle there, a low mumbling rose from the other room. Cae was awake, visiting with Mom and Aedras. They always visited on the first day of weekend start. She closed her eyes to focus on Cae's voice and isolated it in her mind.

"I don't like this at all," Cae said. Her footfalls drummed to a pace.

"It's probably nothing," Mom said.

Each voice struggled to pass through the walls, but Eloria heard well enough. It had been a while since she needed Dill's dampening halo, which sat on her nightstand. The poor gadget would probably never get used again, since tuning out the noise had become second nature.

Listening to criminals to get the upper hand was one thing, but listening to her family between walls made her reconsider, so she turned it off. She splashed warm water from the basin on her face, and she relished it before making her way into the family fray, still in her night clothes. No matter how quietly she stepped through the hall, there was no sneaking around Cae. Her sister's animal ears heard her before she turned the corner. She jogged across the room to meet Eloria, in her hand a bouncing memo written in flash ink.

"This came for you," she said, holding out the note. The transparent memo reflected the glowing words Eloria knew would vanish the moment she read them.

"What is it?" Eloria pinched the edge, plucking it from Cae's hand.

"I couldn't tell you... It's from the city. You know... THE city."

A rush ran down Eloria's neck. If it was from Audun, she had a duty to comply with whatever it said, lest she get tossed in gaol with the dregs she helped put away. She straightened out the note and cleared her throat, preparing to read it in front of everyone for posterity:

> Miss Eloria Praes,
>
> You have been summoned to the court of Princeps Renae for an accounting of current activities in your district. Please make haste to the inner court during your allotted time of one standard hour prior to second sun on the eve of this day.
>
> Thank you for your service.

As she read the words out, they vanished, leaving her with a clear nondescript swatch with the standard navy and gold seal of Audun glowing in the lower corner. So much for the weekend.

"Is that pretty routine for your type of work?" Mom asked. She sat on a stool at the kitchen, facing Eloria with her ankles crossed, always demure.

"No, not really," Eloria said, giving Cae a look.

"So what happens if you don't go?"

"Gaol," Eloria said with a small cough.

The pristine white stone path leading toward the capitol spire was meant to evoke calm and cleanliness. In Eloria, it was like a cold sentencing. Her hand shook as she swiped her badge at the opulent entry.

All afternoon, she had checked and double-checked that her report was thorough and without any mistakes. Then she triple-checked that the file was in her e-disk to present to the princeps.

The front desk administrator gave her the penthouse key and waved her through after check-in with an unnerved smile. No one was safe from scrutiny. It made Eloria sweat a little more.

She entered the lift and slid the antiquated metal key into the slot for floor twenty-five, then cranked it to the side. Only the penthouse required a key, and her name was attached to it from check-in. To prevent any other reason to have her tossed in gaol, she jammed it into her pocket before stepping onto the white marbled tile of Princeps Renae's suite.

This was only her second time here. The first, when she was hired. She brushed her sweaty palms down the wrinkles in her uniform and patted her pocket for the e-disk.

A mechanical timepiece in the hall told her she was a little early, but she jerked her head forward when the harried cries of a protest came from the end of the hall. A terrified Shepherd wailed in fatalistic sentiments for his life.

He begged the Maker for mercy inside his mind as the dull thumps of knuckle on bone beat in a slow tempo through the hall. Her throat stuck together when she tried to swallow a dry lump.

The pleading came from where the princeps maintained his office... past a custom lounge, entertainment center, bathroom, and even a sanctuary. The hall was an endless serpent, and her stride became less certain with each louder thump and howl.

This man must have been their mole suspect. She should have been relieved, but instead she felt pity for him, saying a quick prayer for his life to be spared.

Their voices sharpened when she got closer.

"I swear it, please!" the Shepherd wailed, his consonants wet with what she could only assume was blood.

She hovered her hand over the door handle, listening for more, when a final whap and sputter caused Renae to demand the Shepherd removed from the office. Heavy footsteps approached the door, and she drew back just as it flung open with a badly beaten and barely conscious younger man being dragged out by two Foscan servants. She sucked in a breath.

"Ah, Ms. Praes. Please, come in." Renae nodded her inside as he spun a red knuckle into a silky white cloth.

He stood next to a long black table she remembered from the day she was hired, signing paperwork and dreading her new reality. That day he wore the same dark suit he wore then, navy maybe, with a sharp silver-gray tie. The matching silver cuff links reflected the overhead light as he turned his hand in the cloth.

He took a few steps backwards, watching her with his salt and pepper mustache twitching up in a grin. His matching hair perfectly swiped across his brow, with sides trimmed neat against his temples.

Reaching out a hand, he motioned toward a spot on the table in front of a tall-backed chair, carved with intricate animals, that had been tucked at the head position. The chair's wood had a blackened stain to match the table, decorated with deep gold colored padding, and all of it stood stark against the sterile whiteness of the room.

It was a beautiful throne, but he didn't sit in it.

Eloria stepped inside. The casual mannerisms he presented relaxed her the slightest bit. That was, until she spotted a Foscan on her hands and knees wiping up drips of the Shepherd's blood from the floor. That made her relax a little less.

"Apologies for the Shepherd," he called from across the room. "We have a bit of a situation that needs handling. If you would hurry, please, I have more than enough districts to cover today." Renae flipped open a smoking case, withdrawing a hand-wrapped black cane, and clamped it between his teeth.

Eloria's clunky steps dragged across the tile in that long, cold room. The chill cut through her uniform. Aside from the handful of Foscans in the room, they were alone. It was strange.

Renae outstretched his hand, and she stared at it while fumbling in her pocket. She heard rumor of his strong reaping ability, and she was careful not to touch his skin, even if it did look ordinary. The e-disk left her fingers just above his hand.

He noticed her hesitance and tittered, swiping through to find her report. As he did, overhead tech lights bounced off the black stone ring he wore. Red stars glimmered within a magical beauty that enraptured her. It was an uncomfortable sort of feeling.

"Here it is," he said, taking a puff of his smoking cane, letting the orange smoke make lazy trails from his nostrils.

A few more sharp swipes from his forefinger, and he projected the report from the disk between them. Only, the series of charts and gradings she expected to find hovering there were instead three rows of ten numbers that looked familiar to her. Some were blue, some were green. She tilted her head to study them, trying to understand where she had seen them before.

As the numbers hovered there, another image came into view, fading in with dramatic effect. Renae watched with concentrated intensity. More orange smoke curled around his gentleman's mustache before he stubbed the cane out into the glass dish on the table.

Then it hit her, and the heat pulsed from her collar. The 270-degree holo print of her own thumb hovered over the numbers, glowing in brilliant shades of green and blue. The memory hit her hard, complete with the thumping music she remembered from the attractive medic.

"You're good, Ms. Praes, I'll give you that." Renae's voice yanked her from the old memory, and she glanced up at his smirking face. Her lips parted, but no words passed through the terror that tightened her throat.

"This report is from, what, ten standard years ago? I'm not surprised very often, but this was certainly... surprising." He snapped his fingers toward a pair of Foscans standing stiff-legged nearby. In one synchronous movement, both of them scattered toward a door at the back of the room—most likely a servant's living closet.

"How long have you been pushing your partner?"

"M-my partner? Pushing Milo?" Eloria couldn't look at him. "I'm not sure what you mean by pushing."

Irritation blew from his mouth in a hot sigh. "I'm not an idiot, Ms. Praes. In all the years Milo has been at his duties, it wasn't until *you* became his partner that his odd obsessions became less tiresome."

"Sir?" she asked, but she knew.

You should quit. Cae's voice poked her frontal lobe.

"His weird ob-*sesh*-uns. You know what I'm referring to because you've been erasing them from his mind. There's no sense in playing coy, Eloria. I don't care about his need for revenge on you and your friends. I *care* that I've had a Reader with quite dangerous skills operating right under my nose, doing who knows what to myself and my court."

"I haven't—"

"Maybe you haven't... It doesn't matter. You are unregistered, operating as a roundsman, with the potential to do so. By the looks of this report"—he poked a finger into the projected thumbprint, which rippled at his touch—"you also pushed the poor medic treating you that day."

The sting in her lower lip ached where she bit down a little too hard. There was nothing to say... He knew she was a Reader. Worse yet, she *did* actually push that medic. It's not like she knew what she was doing... Surely he had to know that?

"So, Ms. Praes. If you were me, what would you do in this situation?"

"I-I, uh..." She paused. Maybe if she took a small peek into his mind, if only to get the answer to his question right. There'd be no harm in just a peek...

She opened her mind to an assault.

The sounds penetrating her head were all at once inhuman. A deep drone vibrated her eardrums, a sound almost out of reach of human hearing, with tortured wails jabbing needles in her ears. Scratching and screeching, they forced her to double over with a half-suppressed cough.

Renae clicked his tongue with a malicious hum. "That's *cheating*, Ms. Praes." He strolled toward her, the scent of another smoking cane reaching her nose.

The sounds... unbearable... sharp, screaming pains... She couldn't turn it off. What she wouldn't give for Dill's dampener that she had tucked away, unused for years.

The white marble floor seemed so much brighter than her eyes could handle, until that eerie black stone, with glittering red stars set in gold on his fourth finger, entered her field of view. He lifted her chin, forcing her to look at him. "What did you find in there, hm?" He blew a puff of the orange smoke in her face, and her eyes watered. It was a sweet smell, almost sickening. She swallowed the bile in her throat.

"Here, let me help you." Renae watched her watching him as he made a fist, twisting it next to his heart. Whatever that movement was made the noises stop, and she couldn't have felt any lighter.

She stood upright once again, throwing her shoulders back and rotating her neck.

"Better now?" he asked, taking another drag.

Her meek smile placated him. If she played nice, maybe he'd let her go. He could fire her, or she could quit—she could still find a way to push Hammer. Leverage... there had to be something she could use.

"Milo is unregistered too," she barked with a flush creeping up her neck.

The confession was enough for him to raise an eyebrow. "Is that right?"

"He's a Weggevens strongman. Goes by the name *Hammer*."

Renae studied her. Lips pulled to the side around the stub of his smoking cane as he pinched the end and drew in a drag. Once the smoke dribbled from his nose, he flicked the butt onto the floor, where it continued to burn between them. A growing black ring smoldered around it, smudging the glossy white tile.

"Tell me, Ms. Praes..." he said. His shoulders were square, arms crossed, suit uncannily pressed smooth. "Why is it that no matter what I do for you people, you *insist* on stabbing me in the back?"

Her holo print still hovered over the e-disk on the table next to them. She glanced toward it.

"I...I didn't—"

"But you *did*, didn't you? You and that *oaf* of a man!"

"I could help you," she said quickly over his rant. Unlike most leaders, it caught his attention, and he studied her again, relaxing his face. She cleared her throat. "I could find any threats to you—help you sniff them out."

He chuckled and dropped his arms to his sides. "You're good, Ms. Praes. I think you know that."

There was nothing for her to say, so she watched him mindlessly tap her e-disk, letting it wobble furiously. Her only hope was that he'd agree to it and let her go... and possibly rid her of Hammer for good.

He closed the small gap between them with a gentle smile and an outstretched hand. The same hand with the stone. It made her desperate to leave—to put this day behind her and run to the desert. But he smiled, and it was charming.

A little disarming.

He reached out, touching her hand, and her heart pounded.

"That's a great idea, Ms. Praes," he said. The cloying smell of sweet smoke lingered around him, and the smoking butt still simmered on the floor. She let out a long breath and relaxed.

It was a new opportunity for her to get behind the scenes. She wasn't sure how she could help the others if she was on Renae's team, but she'd figure it out. She always figured out a way.

Gain Renae's appeal, and she could neutralize his connection to the dark influence of his zealotry for the worm. His warm fingers still clutched her hand, and she prayed he wouldn't come on to her. She couldn't even think of going back into his screeching mind to find out.

He tsk'ed at her and smiled again. "The only thing is, Ms. Praes... and believe me, I'm not one to be flippant about matters such as these..." He paused, his gentle gaze lingering deep into her eyes—more like a mentor than a lover. That relieved her, knowing she wouldn't have to do double duty to repel his advances.

Then he squeezed her hand. "The thing is... I just really *hate* Readers."

She didn't know if she could scream. Her lips parted as a belch came out in a spatter of silver. And she shook... oh, how she shook. She could only stare dumbly at her arm as the veins swelled and contracted. Jagged icicles pulled through them from deep inside her core, ripping and freezing every piece of her as silver shot from her rigored fingertips onto the floor. A ribbon of her essence slapped over the smoking butt, snuffing it out.

The thing about pain was that no matter how fleeting, it took its time. She felt anything inside of her that was made of flesh ripping apart. All the while, the man responsible smiled at her, holding her hand, as if serving her a warm cup of her favorite tea.

Vile. Evil. All faces of the lord of death... the one called Cirv'e.

And such a waste! Everything that made up her being, gave her life, made her *feel*... well, it squirted in crude shimmering slate to the floor, to be wiped up by an abused Foscan and thrown into the bin.

Her arm broke... then the other.

The plea of her twin was a distant echo in her deafened ears.

You should quit. Tell her to quit. You should quit.

Her knees buckled. Watching her own feet curl up over her shins like a shriveled night vine gave her a mild chuckle, but only of disbelief. Goodbye to Mom and Aedras... goodbye to Dame... goodbye to her dear twin, Caella. Oh, how guilty she felt for hating her so much during her most vulnerable moment—her Weggevens transformation. It ate at her one last time.

While her death wasn't one she pictured in this way, she was glad. She would die for her family—for their cause. It was only a matter of time, one of them would die—and it was her, because of course it was.

Maker take me.

The princeps... the puppet, Renae the Fool, grinned at her. It was the stained ivory mouth of imperfect teeth that became the final image she would ever again see in life.

Chapter 13

A Bag of Surprises

Loren

At the news of the next drop-off, Lor visited Karl for his blessing.

In the dusty cabin, Lor marched to the table where Karl stood, reading the ancient text.

"Let me go with them. We'll ambush the boatman and collect before it can kill anyone."

Karl glanced up at him, closing the book. "It?" he asked.

Lor shrugged. "I don't know what it is. Do you?"

Karl eyed him pensively. A twitch pulled at his eyelid as he stared for a standard minute too long. "I don't like it," he said finally, holding the last syllable under his tongue with that same searching stare, "but not only are you an adult, you won't listen to me anyway."

"Hey, that's not true..." Lor's voice trailed off when Karl gave him *the look*. "Alright, I'm stubborn, what can I say?"

Karl tittered and waved him off. The grin sank into Lor's face, but he wasn't about to let Karl think he had that effect on him. No matter how passive, it was nice that he agreed to the plan.

"I'm taking this," Lor said as he swiped Karl's switch from the table.

Karl sighed. "Try not to do anything extreme to the boatman, though," he said, rubbing the stubble across his chin. "If you kill... '*it*,' the cities could retaliate, and it would be devastating to us."

"So when's the next drop-off?" Lor asked.

The funk in the air was thick and cast green mist in low clouds. It was enough to have to hold back involuntary gags as they passed through particularly heavy patches of it. The only other thing that made it worse was how warm they were... baking in the midday sun.

"Blech!" Hahn retched, spitting fat and juicy into the water with a plunk. "Watch the gee flies. They're all over." As he said it, his eyes rolled toward Lor before he crossed them and wrinkled his face. Lor was desperate to punch it again, waving his hand back and forth to shoo away the little black bugs. It was all he could do to keep them from sprinting up his nose.

Intel had the drop-off happening two standard hours before second sun, so five hours should have been plenty of time to beat the boat.

Based on Darius's account of his arrival, the group should have enough time to make a plan before anyone else died. Nazagora should still be at rest, and maybe the secret of the cloaked figure could be revealed. It was a mystery long overdue.

He made a promise to Karl that he wouldn't kill it, but he didn't say anything about not uncloaking it... He chuckled to himself thinking about a skinny dork in their undies standing there without their coverings.

Then again, it was probably just another brainwashed city drone with his or her own problems. Maybe he'd use Karl's switch to stab it a little...for Darius's friend.

For now, they walked. Davy passed the time by lobbing question after question at Lor between dodging watery holes and skipping toward dry banks. Sometimes his questions were about fighting, with a sprinkling here and there about Zary. It was nice to feel like someone worthy of looking up to. At least, that's how Davy made him feel. After what her last boyfriend did to her, he was pretty sure Zary wasn't interested in anyone—something Davy had a hard time accepting. *But I'm Yeunish too*, he'd whine. He'd learn eventually.

The drop-off spot opened up in front of them, the water calm and undisturbed by boat trails. This was where they would wait... out in the open. No one thought this through very well.

"So, how are we going to ambush him if there's nowhere to hide?" Lor said, scanning the area.

"Oooh, we can hide in the trees just over here." Davy pointed at the nearest cluster of weeping branches.

"It's too far away," Jack said, folding his arms. He hummed as he glanced back and forth between the drop-off and the trees. "If they have a projectile weapon, we wouldn't get the jump in time."

Silent brainstorming among the group turned to harried pacing through the mud as they split up, searching the horizon. Ankle-deep in the mud, Lor stood there. The image of Jack slipping into a sink hole as soon as they disembarked all those years ago gave him an idea. Then the wind whistled through dead reeds, filling his ears with a melancholy droning.

The reeds were hard and hollow, sticking out of the mud in clusters. They swayed in the breeze, lightly knocking each other and whistling. He glanced back and forth between the reeds and the deeper edge of the water.

"I have an idea," he said, his voice cutting through the silence. The dry reed snapped easily when he snatched it from the cluster. It was just wide enough as he stuck the end in his mouth.

Hahn folded his arms and sneered. "Dummy, we're not hidin' in the dirty-ass water."

It was getting harder to restrain himself around that impossible ass. Lor opened his mouth before Jack strolled forward and snapped off a reed for himself.

"That's exactly what we're going to do," he said, winking down the rod to examine it. He pointed the reed at Hahn, holding the hollow end over one eye to peer at him. "This will work."

Two crisp snaps rang out behind him, and now Davy and Oren had their own reeds. Maker, he hoped his plan didn't get these guys killed. Except Hahn. He could die. Lor tittered at the two younger men examining their new breathing tubes, pressing them to their mouths and tilting their heads.

"Once we see even a hint of the boat's shadow on the horizon, that's when we'll hide," Jack said, pointing north through the boat's course. "It's a clearer day today, so it shouldn't be hard."

Lor dipped a toe in the water. The hardened scales on his heels from years with no shoes repelled the wetness. "We can slip into the water once we see them and hold on to the mud wall for leverage. Once the boat is close enough, we'll ambush."

A sneering belly laugh from Hahn crowded out the sound of him kicking a reed in half for himself. Everyone glanced at him as he hooked the floating stick out of the water in his stiff hand. "And then what, Gold Dick? Are you going to magically fly from your shit hole to jump the cloak?"

All the bones in Hahn's face begged to be broken. Lor sucked in a breath and snapped back, "Next time you need a heal, I just might pretend I forgot how to do it and watch you squirm."

"You *have* to heal me, prick. Code says so."

Lor looked around with brows raised. "I don't see Karl here. Why, you just might have a little accident."

"You threatening me, boy?" Hahn's nostrils flared as he approached Lor.

"I'm so scared of your little dried meat hands," Lor said between his teeth.

"Stop it, both of you," Jack hissed. "Hahn, shut your stupid mouth and follow the plan. If you get hurt, I would hope our healer would step up to help." Jack glanced over at Lor with a tired look.

"Get your reeds, guys," Oren said, pointing off in the distance.

A blurred shadow manifested on the horizon.

"Quick, get in," Jack said with a shove to Hahn. All four of them slid into the dark waters, reed in mouth.

Warm, greenish water enveloped the top of Lor's ash-blond head, giving it a ghostly translucency as it waved at the sides of his temples. Eyes open, the sky glistened overhead with occasional detritus floating by. He prayed the bugs found typically in Haerow stayed in Haerow and didn't find his eye jelly to be tasty.

No flavor of Immortal Green coated his mouth, so the water must have been harmless enough. Gross, but harmless. Everyone else made black shadows in the water, barely visible through the disturbed silt. He clung to the wall, fingers and toes buried in the slime, and waited. Listened.

Slow breaths whooshed through the reed.

Hoo-haaah...

An air bubble escaped his left nostril, tickling the skin as it rolled up and out.

Hoo-haa...

A shifting scurry from below made him worry about pinches to his feet from an ornery pincer crab.

Hoo-haaaah...

There it was—the faint buzzing drone reached his waterlogged ears.

Hoo-haah...

It was the smallboat.

Hoo-haaaah...

Oh crap, there was a motor on that thing.

Hoo-haah! Hoo-haah! Hoo-haah!

He shimmied farther down the mud wall, away from the drop-off point, and repositioned his reed.

Between shifting and righting himself, the muffled scream of his name pierced the water from the air. It couldn't have just been his imagination; it was Jack.

With a deft stab of his toes into the mud, he jumped out of the water, seeing the boat just as he expected, but surrounded by a red cloud. No time to think about it. Someone was already hurt... or dead.

The cloaked boatman had its back turned when Lor snuck inside and squeezed an arm around its neck, pressing Karl's Engineering switch against its throat. A gurgling laugh pulsed the switch up and down. Lor realized it was stretching its arm forward, pointing a silvered shooter at Jack and Oren, who dragged the new exile through the grass.

They were oblivious to their bodies in the blast radius, tending only to the stranger. But Lor flicked his switch hand and sliced clean through its wrist, dropping the shooter into the water, fingers still clawed around it.

The boatman screeched when the blackest blood pulsed from the stump. It drew Jack's attention as Davy jumped into the boat to help.

"Who are you?" Davy shouted. Bits of moss and algae clung to his neck and cheeks.

The boatman let out a low laugh once again. "I am no one," it said.

Lor pressed the switch harder against its throat. "You work for *them,* so stop screwing around. Who are you?"

"I sssaid I am nothing and no one at all," it repeated. Its voice, familiar and inhuman... it unnerved Lor. The silvered eyes in his sleep, the ones that watched him at night before his date with Lapis Evening... the slithering urge of vice and terror.

"I will cut your throat," Lor shouted, tightening his grip around the handle.

Another mocking laugh carried with it many pitches and tones. Too much familiarity in this thing, and he wanted it gone. Dead or gone—either way, away from him.

"You think you can kill me? Loren Benedict Turtingasss?"

It knew his name. It could have learned it from the day he was taken there, but ten years was a long time to remember one name.

It gurgled another chuckle, bobbing the switch up and down at its neck. "You cannot hurt *me,* foolsss of the Maker. I am eternal."

The switch straightened under Lor's grip. Karl's warnings be damned; this thing had to die. With a quick flick, he sawed the edge hard to his right. He expected more black blood to jet from the slice, but his arm fell to his side while stumbling forward a step and losing his payload. The boatman crumpled into thousands of meaty worms, wriggling from the cloak into the water.

"What the—" Davy's mouth dropped open as their tails disappeared into the deep.

Worms. It was a bag of worms. A sentient mass of writhing flesh that steered them to their banishment. A bag of wriggling pink strips shot Darius's friend dead. That almost shot Jack and Oren. He swore he cut off a whole, five-fingered hand. Craning his neck to where it plopped in the water, he hoped to see it there and confirm his sanity.

"What in all of Roseaarde's watery hell was that?" Davy said with heavy breaths.

In the wake of the wormy escape, Hahn's limp body bobbed in the water, a trail of red blooming at the neck where a mess of meat and bones remained. The boat's engine sucked his head inside of it. Davy breathed in and out in loud shudders at the sight of it. Lor felt next to nothing. In fact, the small bit of anything he felt was a relief, bordering on joy. What if reaping just once, he'd fallen farther into yaslecha and he became an inhuman monster? There was no healing that, even if he wanted to.

"Guys..." Davy said in a quiet calm. Lor was sure Davy was still too green to have seen death in one of their own. "Hahn is dead."

"Oh... oh *nooo*..." Lor said, drawing out the last word and watching more scarlet ribbons curl from the jagged stump. "That really *sucks*."

"Don't be stupid, Lor," Jack said. "You hated him, and now you got your wish. Now help me with the new recruit."

Water splashed around Lor's ankles when he plunked down from the boat. The recruit lay on the ground—small, not like the usual Yeunish—more like a child. A cord around their neck fixed the bag over their head, and Jack worked the knot with fumbling fingers.

"Since when did they start putting bags over their heads? Here, watch it," Lor said as he bent down to angle the switch under the rope to cut upwards.

Three sawing slices from the ultra-sharp edge and the rope broke free. Whoever the tiny Yeuni was under the sack didn't open their mouth. Not to cry out, not to whimper, sing, hum, belch... nothing.

Jack glanced at Lor to shrug before sliding the sack away. Once freed from the bag, long black Yeunish hair slapped onto the wet grass, and Lor fell to his knees.

"No..." he whispered. "No, no, no, no, God, NO!" He pulled at his hair, staring at the new recruit staring back at him. Young, yellow eyes.

Each day, he drowned his thoughts in waves of Lapis Evening to forget the worm. A part of him wasn't even sure he remembered the faces of his best friends. No amount of Lapis Evening, dreamless sleep, and passage of time stole the distinct bone structure, delicate lines, and round cheeks of his wife from memory. This recruit resembled her mother.

With her innocent face of youth—so much older, but still so young—with the raw red Y emblazoned on her yet unblemished skin, she parted her mouth to utter a foolish child's words: "I came to get you, Daddy."

Chapter 14

Eulogy

Caella

Her holopic was small, her audience minuscule. There wasn't much sympathy for the woman who attempted to assassinate the princeps. Cae knew better... she felt it in her organs. No, literally, she felt the moment that evil man pulled Eloria. He may as well have pulled Cae too with her writhing on the bathroom floor soaked in sweat and shivering cold. When it was over, darkness spread in her gut.

The cold and the dark followed her to the memorial service. Not even the warmth of her parents standing behind her could pull her from that pit. She shivered at the podium in front of a handful of fake supporters, then cleared her throat with a glance at the glossy dark wood casket. It was small... square. The perfect size for a human reduced to compressed skin and bones.

Cae rested her hands on the podium. Each moment of grief wore the wood into smooth impressions where her predecessors once stood. All eyes were on her. Aedras put his arm around her. "When we were in first levels," she said, "Eloria had all the answers. She was the smart and serious one, telling me I needed to settle down and focus. As adults, that never really changed."

The stupid slip of notes she had in front of her blurred. She wasn't going to cry at this thing, but even saying her sister's name was a bitter bite on her tongue.

"She left Arts for a more noble pursuit," Cae continued. *It wasn't really more noble, it was necessary.* She bit her lip. "And in the end, she died serving us."

She brushed her hand across her cheek, glancing up at the small audience. Eloria didn't serve these *freaks*, but she served the ones she loved... the family. But it was best to keep her language neutral in this meager audience of pretenders.

She could smell Aedras's faint cologne. It was the smell of serious events, joyful events, any event that was out of the ordinary. He wore it to Dame's wedding and to Eloria's badging ceremony. And now, to her funeral. That smell would forever burn in her memory as the fragrance of death. Even with his arm still wrapped around her, she couldn't feel his warmth.

Cae straightened her paper, blinking away the rogue tears that made it hard to see. "I remember one time, when we were still pretty young, we got a pair of matching sleepwear on our birthday..."

She told the story in a trance. It was one of her favorite stories, and she knew it backwards and forwards. The audience seemed to like it too, but it wasn't something that truly captured who Eloria really was. Who she really was to Cae... and how terrible Cae felt for not doing better as her twin.

But it was enough for them—catharsis for strangers to snatch their moment of closure to move on and go home, forgetting Eloria forever. By the time she was done telling her story, her cheeks were wet.

Whoever thought that serving food at a memorial was a good idea needed to feel the ripe stick of a pin in the eye. All these fake people, munching on appetizers, talking like they knew her. They didn't know her like Cae did. No one did—not even Aedras or Mom.

She swirled the glass in her hand, three fingers of warm fruited zinka... the kind that Niklaus liked. Mom did not approve, but Cae was an adult and could get drunk if she wanted to. The last mouthful went down her throat, and she tapped the bar for another.

"Are you sure about that, hon?" Mom put a hand on her shoulder as her glass steamed with more fruity spirits.

"Never been more sure in my life," she drawled. The bored sarcasm came from her in a fluid stream—a habit she picked up from her ornery husband.

Mom could sigh and bemoan her choice all she wanted; it wouldn't change a thing. But she didn't do any of those things. She wrapped her arms around her daughter and kissed her cheek. "I love you so much," she said with the faintest warble.

As soon as the embrace began, it ended, and Mom wandered away from the bar. That was how Cae remembered it.

Everyone was fake. All she wanted to do was leave. Too long had she put up with sneaking around, hiding her faith, her identity... Tomorrow would change all of that.

The next morning held an extra edge. Whether it was the hangover or just straight ang-grief, it messed with her head.

If the cities thought Caella Dicus née Praes was going to tie up her loose ends before abandoning them, they were dead wrong. Screw the cities. Screw the cities and screw the princeps. All of them could die and she wouldn't care. In fact, they should all die.

Conforming, pathetic, weak citizens, too yellow to take it all back. She'd seen enough. She'd had enough. Even Mom and Aedras couldn't muster enough will to avenge their daughter.

Anger won't bring her back, Mom lamented while Cae took the steps she needed to get far from that place. All she felt was anger. A primal, animalistic anger. A blood-red peripheral to her vision that she couldn't shake. Maybe it was the cat in her, but either way... screw Cirv'e.

As soon as she knew how to rip its head off, she had to get as far from its sphere of influence that she could. She had to go see Dame and Niklaus at least one last time before she ended it all.

Feed it... give in to the anger.

That inner voice coated her brain like a parasite. It had gotten louder lately, and after Eloria's death, it was screaming. The calm her sister always imparted to her had vanished—all that was left was rage.

Getting back to the desert by train would be hard... with her name plastered all over tickets, boarding placards, and whatever else the stupid cities used to monitor everyone, leaving her job and everyone behind would be impossible without tracking. No, a jumper cab and raw plats. All the way to the tents—it was the only way.

The Danashi driver didn't ask questions, and she found respite in that. She was in no mood to answer them. Armed with nothing but the clothes on her back and a rather small pouch only large enough for a handful of physical plat tickets, she was ready to disappear.

The ride through the cities was long and bumpy. They winded through side streets and off-road terrains until finally sliding into the open desert where the jumper tires glided through the grains. Other jumper cabs darted around on chaotic open land, but the Danashi knew their vehicles, and they drove them well. None were too eager to head in the direction of the tents, nor were they bold enough to travel north though the undulating dunes full of hidden death camps.

Cae's driver made a straight path along the base of the train rail, because everyone knew that near the end would be the cluster of impoverished desert folk.

Chapter 15

One Last Night

Niklaus

Niklaus was already outside, scanning the open desert dunes, reshaped by the storm and framing Mount Gehenna. It was windy that day, not something many people cared for. But he adapted to it and grew to prefer it. His vision had acclimated to manage the haze of particles and other obstacles from years of running, so he took it upon himself to keep watch on any encroaching death camp activities—especially during windy days.

Bonus if there was any sign of Cimma.

He'd grown to adore his cheeky niece, and he took her disappearance rather hard. Maybe she would find Loren after all.

A low hum rumbled in the distance. It wasn't terribly odd to see a jumper cab making its way down the track line. Though, it wasn't normal either. A yellow bloom of dust jettisoned from the tail end of the jumper cruising fast down the lane, leaving everything behind it in a blind cloud to him.

It was moving too fast, and straight at him. He readied himself in case the thing planned on plowing into his tent. He lowered his goggles as the spray of sand got closer.

It came to an abrupt halt a tent away, and a blurry white shape stumbled from the guest seat as the dust settled around it. He recognized that blurry white shape—the specific way she jerked her arm when righting herself and her signature swagger gave her away no matter how much yellow dust the jumper sprayed in its wake to get the hell out of there.

Though she didn't walk... she ran to him.

When he opened his arms, Cae crashed into them, burying her face into his chest.

"Why are you here?" he asked, stroking her hair. "I mean, I'm glad you're here, but I thought you had to wait, like, another standard week or so?"

She wouldn't answer. In one swift move, she smashed her mouth against his as if letting go would cause him to float away. It was kind of nice at first, but then he felt his lower teeth pressing too hard into the tender meat of his lip. Not just pressing hard, he tasted a little blood.

He broke away and stared at her. "Ow, Kitts," he said, running a finger down his gumline and pulling back a red tip. "I've missed you too, but what the hell—"

"Eloria is *dead*," she blurted. Her cheeks had a dark flush against her paper white skin. Several tears rolled down them, but the thirst of desert air claimed the water halfway.

"What?" He blew the question out like a plume of smoke.

"Eloria is dead," she repeated, "and I want to die!" Her last words choked out of her, sputtering and wet, before clutching him once more. The sharp heat of her breath pulsed into his shirt as she screamed into his torso.

There was no way this was real. He looked around for signs of strangeness—anything that would tell him he was dreaming. But the pain in his lip was real, the smell of his wife, and her hot cries into his shirt.

"H-how? No... What?" Ever the eloquent speaker, Niklaus sucked his teeth.

"I told her, Nick, I told her to quit. I told her to leave, and she *died!*"

So he held her, rested his chin on her head, and stared off into the hazy horizon. Cursed cities. A boiling crock of evil. He never liked them. He couldn't remember the last time he actually cried, but he felt his nose getting hot and his eyes warming.

"What... exactly *happened*?" he asked in nearly a whisper. Although, he wasn't sure he wanted to know.

But she told him. He learned about the suspicions they had, her summons in flash ink, and the shit form letter they received with a meager sum of plat to placate the family. Five thousand plat... that's all Eloria was worth to the cities. It wasn't even enough to bury her.

"Did you know that dickhead turned her into a shriveled ball? I didn't even know a body could do that. Aedras had to spend extra to have a special casket built for her." At that point, she'd returned to speaking into his chest, muffling her words. "He sucked out her whole life! All her silver, gone! Garbage! Where is she now? Where IS s-she?"

Her sobs pulsed into his chest.

"She's in the Promised Land, baby," he whispered, trying to soothe her feral grief.

It was the thing people told each other to make them feel better about death. No truth in the words was strong enough to take away the hurt. They actually felt hollow to himself as he said them. They didn't take away Cae's tears either.

"Is she, though? Her silver was trashed!"

Niklaus bit his lip. They had no idea what eneris was. What silver was. For a moment, he considered that Eloria was just gone. When people died, it was tradition to pull their silver. But now, he really wondered why.

A long afternoon of silent sobbing passed with Niklaus pacing and trying to come to grips with their new situation.

Dame didn't take the news well either, spending the rest of the day in the lower levels, curled up in the cockpit. No matter how much Gale tried to comfort her, she wallowed and wailed down there, crying out for her mom and dad.

Nate was near catatonic, and he mumbled to himself a lot. What he said was barely audible, but Niklaus sometimes heard him pretend as if he were talking to an invisible friend.

You're called Mister Shadow? he once said between tears. In truth, Niklaus worried for Nate's mind. For a child like that, family trauma clung on for as long as he'd let it. Niklaus knew this too well.

Nico was a small comfort to the boy, taking each free moment to tend to him. Hopefully it was some help, as Niklaus spent all of his time worrying over his own frantic wife.

She said strange things, muttered and cursed. Under a curled upper lip, she seethed and bit at the skin of her lower lip, making it bleed. He tried to guide her to sit or lie down, but she felt cold and prickly. It was as if her every pore readied for a fight.

She wavered between wanting to murder Renae to wanting to die, and these feverish convictions had his nerves on end, worried that she would do something stupid. As she raged throughout the day, Niklaus swore he saw her become a more feral version of herself—something he had no idea how to help with. She was quick to remind him, rather frequently, how helpless he was with her situation. While it angered him, she wasn't wrong.

Back to pacing, listening to her foam, and catching snippets of conversation between Nate and his imaginary friend "Mister Shadow."

Tonight would be better. They could rest, pray, recharge... it was a nice thought. It would be even nicer if Caella could. It was the middle of the day, but he was anxious for the night.

In the darkness of the bunker, Niklaus slept the moment his head touched down, and his subconscious drove straight into a twisted dream. In it, he sat at a long table with mostly faceless people, but his wife was there, next to him. Her hand was on his thigh, squeezing it with a strange grin on her face. There was food—lots of food in front of them, and the growling hunger in his stomach ached for it.

The rumblings of every stranger's gut gurgled as they gorged on the buffet, unable to sate their appetites. Niklaus only looked at the food, raw and dripping, masticating in slobbering, greedy mouths. Cae's squeeze on his thigh tightened as she partook in the feast, tearing at the meat on the table.

It was hard to say how many people sat at the meal, but it wasn't long before the food found its way into the fires in their bellies, leaving them wanting more. So they fed on each other, biting and tearing. A sharp pinch closed down on his arm, and it was Cae, teeth sinking into his flesh. She looked up at him with those light blue eyes he loved, warped into a darkness of hunger and misery. Revolted at his blood spattering up on her cheeks when she tore at his arm, he watched helpless as his tendons snapped into her mouth.

Stress, sadness, or fear could have been the thing that woke him in the middle of that night, but it was none of those things. The light pressure of pale thighs gripped his waist, bringing him out of the macabre dinner party.

In the darkness, the single orange tech light split Caella's features in half. One soft orange side and one completely masked in shadow. Her bright blue eye had dulled in that meager light, its only reflection a crazed glimmer.

"Kitts, what are you doing?" he asked. Rubbing an eye, he felt her on top of him, running her hand up his belly.

She only wore her sleeveless undershirt. It was loose and falling from her right shoulder.

"Caella?"

She still didn't answer, drumming light fingers over his chest.

"Hey, let's lie down, alright?" he whispered, trying hard not to let his baser functions override reason. The pinch lingered on his arm where she ate at him, and the orange glow did nothing for her beauty. The odd lighting pulled back her skin, showing the bones of her face and a mealy grin that reflected the one in his dream. He gently grabbed her legs, the burn chafing his arm as he tried easing her off. She squeezed.

"I haven't had you in so long," she said in a breathy groan. The sharpest parts of her face illuminated before him. Once again, and with much resistance, he tried to ease off the strength in her legs.

Desperate to keep quiet and not wake the others just beyond the thin curtain between their bunkers, he made a pathetic attempt to clear his dry throat. "Babe, we've been through a lot... let's just rest. Here, lie next to me, and we'll go to sleep," he whispered.

"I'm your wife, don't you *want* me?" Her voice morphed into something not of Roseaarde—a two-sided inflection that raised the hairs on his arms. It came with that same flesh-eating grin. Her eyes were so sad.

"Yes, I want you," he hissed, "but not right now, alright?"

She sat upright, ceasing her tempting undulations. "And why not?"

"Sh!" He listened for signs of the others waking. "Dammit, Cae, because you're not yourself! We just lost Eloria, and you need to take some time to grieve. *I* need some time to grieve... not act... *deranged*."

"So, you think making love to me is *deranged*?"

"You know that's not what I said."

"Fine, whatever, Nick." She rolled off him and wandered away from their bedroll into the darker part of the room. Her bright figure was swallowed into the dark corner.

"Please come back to bed," he pleaded with her, patting the fluffed mat.

"Not right now. It would be deranged." Each word pulsed from the blackness, carrying that same dual-toned pitch.

He refused to respond to the taunt. This was going to be such an up-and-down ride to get her through the grief. Hell, it would be hard for him... Eloria was just as much his sister too. He rolled to his back with a sigh, pressing the back of his fingers to his eyes.

A cruel reminder nagged his thoughts back to that moment in the desert years ago when he took Nico's legs. His *own* twin... Maybe he didn't truly understand her. The raw embarrassment he felt for doing that hit him in a hot wave. He hurt someone who cared about him to show off for someone who couldn't care less about him. Cae did nothing but love her sister, and she lost her completely. It didn't seem fair.

A part of him debated just doing it and letting her get it out of her system, even if he thought she might bite it off...

Nah, better to help her pull through this in other ways. "Kitts?" he whispered.

She wouldn't answer.

Chapter 16

Enemy

Loren

"What were you thinking? Who told you to get yourself caught? You were almost killed!" Lor paced frantically, pointing a finger at his daughter for each reprimand that she took with grace and a gentle stare back and forth as he moved.

She kept quiet, letting him yell at her. For all he knew, she was just as in shock to see him as he was her. He struggled to process the maelstrom of emotion: if he'd ever see any part of his family again, what they looked like, how she was nearly destroyed by a sack of worms disguised as their boatman...

Her face—she was Damaetra in Yeunish form. She was relaxed, demure, and hiding a form of mature wisdom brought on by diligent observation.

"What do you have to say for yourself?" He stopped to cross his arms.

As she continued to remain quiet, considering her words carefully, Jack cleared his throat. "Hey, Lor, we probably need to get back."

"Yes, I'm *aware*, thank you, Jack," he said harsher than he intended. Jack raised his hands and shrugged at Davy.

A distant wail echoed through the marsh. Its alien gurgles and clicks sounded close. "Great, now we have to worry about the Nazagora," Lor said through his teeth.

"Don't worry, I can handle them." Davy clasped his hands together like an eager child, cracking his fingers at the middle knuckle.

Lor nodded at Davy, then turned back to his daughter. In the aftermath of intensity following her arrival, he forgot to ask one of the most important questions since finding her. "What is your name?" he asked.

Finally, she grinned at him for the first time. When she opened her mouth, the sweetest, tiny voice he'd ever heard came from her. "Cimone'a. Mom calls me Cimma. She said it means *the Maker answers*."

A stuttering sob broke from his lips as he sank a knuckle into the bridge of his nose. The pressure held back some of the tears but not all of them. "And your brother?"

"Nate. I mean, Nathanael. It means the same, I think."

The Nazagora's cry rang out again, and they all looked off toward the sound. It replaced his heartfelt reunion with urgency for her safety, and he reached out for her hand.

"We have to get back to camp. I'll heal you when we get there," he said.

Another alien cry harped in the distance, and they picked up their pace to a jog.

But Davy hesitated.

"What are you doing?" Jack hissed at him. "We have to get moving!"

Planted firmly on the spot, he held up a finger. "Hold on, guys," he said, tilting an ear to the sky. He continued to hold the finger up as he listened to the Nazagora's call. "It sounds different this time. I think we should find it."

"Are you crazy?" Lor squeezed Cimma's hand a little harder. "This is my *daughter*—we have to get back!"

"No, seriously, I think we need to find it. I have a feeling..." Davy was already moving through the patch of forest back into the open swamp, with Oren close behind.

Jack wore his frustration in the deep crease of his brow but followed after them. Lor gave Cimma a gentle tug, loading her onto his back, and they, too, were on the move.

As they wandered the bog in silence, with Davy occasionally tipping his ear to listen to the woeful dirge that became louder, Lor found the sun's position in the sky. It was too early for a Nazagora to be out and about. If it was too early, maybe that meant Davy felt something unique in its cries.

Passing through patch after patch, each cry became closer and closer until the shadow of a rounded black body lay within a cluster of weeping trees the next bank over.

"There it is," Davy whispered.

They watched the creature lay there, unmoving but groaning in its strange bleating. "What is it doing?" Jack asked no one.

"It looks hurt," Cimma offered, squeezing Lor's shoulders.

Without permission, Davy tiptoed toward the next group of trees where the hulking shadow moaned. It was a sad tone, really. It was possible that the thing was hurt and crying out in pain—or for one of its mates to help it.

"What are you going to do?" Jack whispered at him, still following close behind.

Davy didn't answer, keeping to his mission forward.

Jack looked around anxiously. "What if this is a trap?" he said.

"The Nazagora don't set traps," Oren said with a chuckle as they stepped through the edge of the tree line.

In between one tall weeping tree and another toppled over, the creature lay on the ground, pinned under the broken trunk.

Lor had never seen one like this before. The closest he'd been to a Nazagora in the past was when one tried to bite his head off at the drop-off, and when they used to get close to camp during heavy rains. Even then, he didn't pay too close attention to details when all he saw was an open maw full of pointed teeth.

The successive squeezes he got from Cimma were wordless expressions of fear and curiosity.

"Look at it." Davy pointed at the felled trunk pinching the black flesh of three tentacles. The limbs bent at an upward angle as the tips wriggled sluggishly. The Nazagora gurgled.

"I'm sure it'll be fine," Jack murmured. He took a step back, anxious for the horizon.

Lor considered the creature and its situation. If the Nazagora had any kind of intelligence, he could help it... maybe make their colony less hostile toward their community. Cimma squeezed again, as if reading his mind. He leaned back to her to whisper, "Doesn't it scare you?"

In return, she whispered back, "It can't do anything to us while it's under that log."

Lor shrugged and carried forward with her hanging on his back, while Davy and Oren jogged toward the beast.

"This is so dumb," Jack muttered.

"Are you scared?" Lor asked Jack, not unkind.

"Aren't you?"

Up ahead, Davy rested his hand on the tip of the creature's tentacle, and it shifted at his touch. Oren fussed with the waterlogged trunk, trying to lift it and failing. He stopped to soothe the creature.

"A little help?" Oren motioned to Jack.

The two of them lifted the log, freeing the broken tentacles. The Nazagora didn't move, mewling at them.

"Do you think you can heal it?" Davy asked, holding one of the tentacles as the Nazagora lay pliant.

Lor didn't have an answer for that. He'd never healed anything other than a human before, let alone some previously unheard-of creature from the South. A strange black bubble of a creature at that.

"Don't their limbs grow back?" Lor asked.

"Not this one, see? The log hit it too far up. This here is the regrowth nerve stem." Davy traced a finger around a circular bundle of yellow cords in the core of the tentacle. "It's cut clean in half."

The idea of a nerve stem cut in half sent electricity down Lor's neck. The Nazagora had to be in a lot of pain.

"I've never healed so much as a bird before, let alone a *creature*."

"Hey, Teddy isn't just a creature," Davy whined.

"You named it?"

"Maybe."

"I like Teddy," Cimma chirped.

"Guys, figure it out, we're running out of time," Jack cut in, folding his arms.

Lor sighed. "I can *try*," he said. Bending down, he let Cimma slide from his back next to Oren, then approached "Teddy," squinting and pursing his lips. It was the same look Jack said he imagined it was like when Lor stared into a dirty toilet. He made that expression the first time he was ordered to heal Hahn after he picked a non-ring row with another member. Basically, he didn't want to do it.

He flexed his fingers, scanning for a place to hold on to, but there were only slick surfaces constantly undulating. If he even found somewhere to grab, then what? Did the Nazagora think like humans? Would a human memory do anything for it? He folded his fingers together, cracking his knuckles with a flourish, and wandered closer to the beast.

It lay on what Lor assumed was its back. He couldn't tell if it was male or female, but one thing he noticed was a flap of flesh that resembled a built-in pocket on its belly. It was thin, and he almost missed it, but it was definitely there. Stories of other animals that carried their young in a belly pouch were told in first levels, but he'd never come across any. First levels also didn't have the Nazagora in their texts.

This pouch could probably fit at least five humans.

Lor shuffled toward the broken cluster of tentacles, observing the one in Davy's hand. The tree had done a number on it, breaking it open and exposing the pink meat inside. There was no blood, just weeping clear fluid that looked sticky. It dribbled from pores in the pinkish meat, swirling in globs on the surface of the puddle nearby. If he reaped the thing, would the eneris come out red or blue? Maybe black? Or something else entirely?

He'd never felt a Nazagora before. When his fingertips brushed the slick surface, the creature twitched with a sad groan. Which memory to feed this thing? Something it might recognize, like the Yeunish here. He could send it a good memory of the camp, and maybe it would endear them to itself.

Maybe...

Lor shook his head. If there was a way to fortify a relationship with a potentially intelligent beast of prey...

Time to test the theory.

While trying not to let his fingers slip on the slimy skin, Lor wrapped them around the tentacle. The Nazagora squirmed a little, but Davy soothed it with whatever magic he had in his beast-taming fingertips. Hard scales lined the underside, and they flared out a bit, digging into the underside of Lor's hand. They were sharp like fingernails, threatening to cut into his own flesh.

He closed his eyes. The first set of memories came in broken waves. First came the moment he earned the nickname Gold Fist. Second was building shacks together with Jack. It was the first time in a long time he'd seen Jack smile. The rush of the waterfall behind Zary as they spoke of the Maker, and Karl showing him the sacred text.

It was the image of the sacred text that he felt the most power move from him. The Nazagora knew the text somehow, and the wriggling arm snapped into place, sealing the wound with the faint dribble of slime at the seam.

Once Lor had finished healing "Teddy," the creature made the strangest jovial noise. It was a low purr, like some of the cats he'd come across in the past.

"Alright, he's fixed, let's get out of here," Jack said, urging them on.

Davy waved at the huge black bubble lying in the grass. "Bye, Teddy," he said as its tentacles undulated with new life.

Lor swore he heard a low whimper. With each footfall toward camp, a quiet shuffling followed them. Teddy was at their heels, low to the ground.

"I told you this was a bad idea," Jack said, pointing at Davy and Oren.

"It probably loves you now," Cimma chimed in from her vantage point on Lor's back, squeezing his shoulders again.

They took a few more steps, and Teddy followed. Lor sighed. "We can't bring a Nazagora to camp with us," he said.

"You think?" Jack shot back. "Tell it to go back to its home."

"Um, I don't think it works like that..." Oren started to say.

"Here, I'll try." Davy stepped between them, making a series of motions with his hands, then resting them on his chest before pushing them out in front of him.

The hand movements didn't do what he thought they'd do... The creature only moaned again, getting close enough to Davy for a small nudge. It stayed low to the ground, shaking back and forth like a house pet.

"What's it doing?" Jack asked.

Oren put a finger on his lip. "Well, he's in a position of submission..."

"He?"

"Yeah, this one is male. You can tell by the—"

"Sh! Not around my daughter," Lor said, trying to reach his hands up to

Cimma's ears.

Oren laughed and pointed at the small ridge running across the body over the eyes. "I was going to say, you can tell by this small ridge here. It's what they use to sing out into the wild for their next hot date."

Cimma giggled, and Lor huffed. "Really, Oren?"

"Sorry! I'm not used to talking around kids anymore."

"We still can't bring him with us," Jack said, folding his arms.

"I don't know what you want me to do," Davy said, biting a lip. He reached out and patted the top of Teddy's bubble, and he gurgled.

"Just let him come," Oren said. "It doesn't look like he's going to hurt anyone."

Jack groaned and threw his head back. "I hope you know what you're doing. Karl's going to be pissed."

They made their way to camp, yet Teddy wouldn't come through the entrance, even with Davy beckoning him forward. Teddy just looked at him through little black eyes and took off, back into the swamp.

"Well, there you go. He left," Davy said to Jack.

In a strange way, Lor was sad to see Teddy leave. It was a unique bond that felt somewhat comforting in that last standard hour of travel. Even Cimma talked to him as he followed, and she seemed smitten with the thing. She called out to him as he left, then whined when he didn't listen.

It wasn't until the next day that any comfort he felt at that connection wavered. Because the next day, Teddy returned to their camp with friends.

Nick,

I'm leaving. I'm going to live out the rest of my life as a cat. I'll go to Secas and disappear into the cat colonies. Maybe I'll come back someday, but don't come looking for me. For what it's worth, you were great.

Kitts

Chapter 17

Sea Bound

Loren

"Oh... Good... *God*," Karl uttered as the row of Nazagora stood outside their borders, tentacles undulating. "What did you do? What did you *do*?" he hissed at Lor.

"Don't look at me!" Lor jabbed a thumb at his chest.

"Davy! Oren! Rik!" Karl called out.

Each beast tamer came from their corners of the camp, Davy stopping dead in his tracks with his eyes on the Nazagora.

"Fix this," Karl said to the three of them.

"I—" Davy stammered.

"First you let Hahn die, and now we have the beasts at our gate. Fix this!"

The looming darkness continued its slow rippling beyond the border, and all Lor could think of was his daughter, sleeping ignorantly in his tree hut. Silent, watching, they didn't instigate anything, as if they were simply waiting.

The three beast tamers exchanged looks—Davy swallowing with a grimace, Rik shaking his head, and Oren with fingers steepled under his nose.

"I told you Karl would be pissed," Jack scoffed.

Lor tilted his head toward Davy. "Is Teddy with them?" he asked.

Karl barked incredulous laughter. "Teddy? You *named* the damn thing?"

"Sh, don't upset them," Davy said as he pressed a finger to his lips.

"Then go soothe them, or whatever you need to do to make them leave us," Karl said.

"I... don't think they're here to hurt us. At least right now."

"Well, that's a great comfort."

"I mean, maybe Oren and Rik can speak up, but I think they're here to help us? Maybe to pay us back for helping Teddy?"

The memory of the old tome Lor fed into the wounded creature had a profound impact on the healing. Karl didn't have it on him, but they could grab it.

He turned to Karl. "Is the sacred text in your hut?"

"Yeah, why?"

"I think we should get it."

"No way am I risking destroying the only copy on all of Roseaarde."

Lor huffed, stomping toward the hut, with Karl fast on his heels.

"Lor, I'm not risking it." He tried grabbing Lor's arm, but he dragged him along.

"It won't be destroyed, I promise."

"You can't make promises on behalf of a herd of creatures." Karl's protests continued until Lor kicked open Karl's door and swiped the tome.

"There's something about this they're drawn to," Lor said, holding the tome up. Karl couldn't reach the book as Lor held it above his head. It was one of the few times his height gave him an advantage.

"Come on, Lor, please don't—"

"It'll be fine, trust me. But I'm going to need you to help me."

Throwing his arms up in defeat, Karl blew out a sharp breath. "If I must."

They took their time walking back to the rest of the group, now growing with terrified yet curious exiles. Zary had made her way to the circle.

Her face lit up at the book in Lor's hand, and she clasped her hands together. "You got the sacred text!"

"Stay where you are, Zary," Lor said, pointing at her. She raised her hands in compliance, backing up.

When they got closer to the tree line separating them from the monsters, Lor flipped through the pages of the text. The beast tamers stood nearby, waiting for their instructions.

Nodding at Karl, Lor continued flipping through the pages. "Where in this text does it refer to these creatures?"

Karl stammered, focusing his gaze between the tome and the tree line. "Maybe closer to the beginning?"

"Is that a question?"

"Very funny. Let me see, please," Karl said, holding out a hand.

One of the creatures slapped an appendage down, taking out a sapling and startling Karl to nearly dropping the tome. He sucked in a sharp breath and shook his head. "Be on the ready," he said, nodding to the beast tamers.

A string of the foreign language Lor had heard before came out of Karl's mouth in a lovely verse. The others gaped at the sound, mostly in wonder at it. Yet, nothing happened.

"What was that passage? Can you talk a little louder?" Lor asked.

"It was the passage of creation, and no."

"They can't hear you."

Karl gave him *the look* from under bushy brows. With a hearty eye roll, he read the passage again, louder, and nothing happened.

"Alright, try something different." Lor poked at the tome, and Karl brushed his hand away.

A little further in the text, Karl recited another passage, to receive the same reaction, which was none. The line of Nazagora waited, oddly patient for a pack of predators.

"Wait." Lor put his hand out to touch the tome again, and Karl brushed it away... again. "What was the passage you read to me that day you told me about this text? Something about the tree in its current state."

"That has nothing to do with the Nazagora," Karl said with a sigh.

"Even still, it's what you showed me that day, and it's what I showed... *Teddy*... when I healed him."

"I'm sorry, did you just say you healed a Nazagora?"

"Yes."

"You healed it..."

"Yes!"

The creature line bobbed up and down, their swelling bodies pulsing at the exchange. Each beast tamer tensed up, waiting for any signal they might attack.

"Just read them that passage," Lor whispered. He never felt so sure of his intuition in that moment. Even through the exasperated glare from Karl.

Karl flipped to the passage and recited it. Something about his voice changed—or it seemed like it changed. As the words burst from his lips, they carried a command with them, and a leader's confidence. The bobbing creatures quickened their pace as he spoke, causing sweat to run down the temples of their tamers. One of the Nazagora rolled over, back and forth, snapping dead twigs and smashing rotted logs.

"What the—" Rik mumbled as he stood at a squat, holding his hands at the ready.

"Read it again," Lor urged.

The scene intensified, and Karl licked his dried lower lip. With a sharp bark to clear his throat, he read the passage aloud again.

More commanding and more confident, even Lor joined in. He heard it enough to speak it along with Karl, as they repeated the simple three-line passage several times to the dancing row of black monsters. The rolling Nazagora extended its travel to the space behind the whole line. Back and forth.

"Guys, this is freaking me out!" Davy hissed.

The largest of the Nazagora slapped tentacles to the ground and wailed. It had to have been a male with that hard ridge behind the eyes, vibrating out a type of song. When he did, the row completely stopped their strange dance, lying down in what Oren called the "position of submission." Everyone in the crowd gasped.

"You killed them all!" one of the spectators crowed.

Then a low murmur spread. *"What do we do with all that food? Is that all of them? Maybe we're safer now!"*

"They're not dead," Oren whispered to Lor and Karl.

The murmurs continued until Karl turned to them. "Quiet!" he said. Lor was impressed at Karl's commanding presence. It was enough for the entire community gathered there to snap their mouths shut. "So what are they doing?"

"Can't you see?" Oren asked. "They're submitting to us."

"Just by reading a passage from the tome?"

"Apparently. I mean, I've had a feeling for a while now, but I think the Nazagora are connected to each other."

"That seems obvious now," Lor said with a smirk.

"It makes sense," Davy chimed in, "you showed Teddy that passage, now they all know it."

"But why are they attracted to the tome?" Karl asked.

"No clue," Lor said. He watched the row of stone-still Nazagora lying prone at the border.

Lor tucked his fingernail between his teeth and watched the absolute stillness in the creatures. They were land creatures, yet aquatic, desiring the rain. Many times they'd come close to camp during the season of rain, gulping it down with their alien sounds while terrifying the camp.

Teddy taught him a lot about the Nazagora. They were connected and familial, as if they could reach into each other's minds and share knowledge... emotions. They had their own leader—and their leader was now submissive to the community. They all had pouches, regardless of gender. Large pouches fit for at least five... and they could swim. Lor glanced at the tree hut Cimma slept in, then back at the Nazagora, still prone on the ground.

A single pouch, fit for five. Swimmers.

Lor swung his hand back to his side and turned to Karl. "Hear me out. I have an idea."

PART 2

CHAPTER 18

Surprise Catch

BLACK SKY STREAKED IN COBALT lit up with stars over the tide. The weathered hand of a small fisherman, rife with old calluses, grasped a beach-side fishing line, jiggling the pole as eager as a starving vagrant. It was a good season for pearl-scale roughies, and the line held the type of bait strong enough to entice them to beach themselves.

They'd feed for months on a catch like that. At least, that's what he remembered the last time he tried this trick. Or was it the lace fin carp? Either way, pearl-scales sounded tasty.

Evening crawler vines began their unfurling process, opening their luminescent purple flowers. It was risky to start fishing before this happened, since their light prevented visiting boats from crashing into the shore, but his meat stores were low, and he was hungry.

It was quiet, though. No boat sounds or anything of the sort. The night only gave up sounds of foam sliding across sand and the hollow thunk of wooden chimes clunking together in the light breeze.

The dead quiet also meant no fish—no tails thrashing or wild flapping in the water close by. The fisherman sighed, looking out at the glistening horizon, a gentle rippling under the stars. He hummed to himself, a low dirge written by his wife the day their young daughter was ripped from the family.

She was sent out there, somewhere, beyond the horizon where the moon hovered. Many nights he mourned himself to sleep knowing she was probably dead. He thought about her then, and how she so often begged to fish with him at night—not for the activity but to watch the crawler vines. It did no good to dwell on it. She wasn't coming back.

After waiting a standard hour with no hint of movement in the water, he pulled the line, ready to head back. Baela waited for him at home.

A rushing sound sucked at the surrounding air. Perhaps it was finally a fish! He scrambled to reset the line, praying he wouldn't miss the giant pearly or lace fin.

The water roiled and zig-zagged into a churning up ahead, breaking the star's reflections into several dark voids. No pearly was that big. He stepped back, dropping his gear, and watched the sea surge.

A dark bubble rose from the surface, bobbing up and down as it made its way to shore. As the bubble slid toward the shallows, he took several steps back, looking up and down the shore, turning a foot, ready to run.

Meaty tendrils slapped into the sand, hauling a monstrous body onto the beach. Gurgling clicks came from its alien throat when it lifted its face—or what might have passed as a face—to gaze in the direction of the frozen fisherman.

"That's no pearly," he whispered to himself, ready to release everything he held in his bladder. He took his first step to run home, catching his toe in the soft sand and sending him sprawling and kicking himself backwards.

The slick black creature crawled up to him in wet thumps: a towering beast, rimmed with tentacles and a dark mouth full of teeth. The fisherman closed his eyes, waiting for his inevitable end, when a muffled voice came from nearby, as if spoken through a pillow.

"I think we're on shore now," it said.

It was another man's voice, deeper notes reverberating from within the flesh of the beast standing in front of him. As the voice spoke, another creature crawled to shore with their own voices inside. And then another. The fisherman let go of his bladder.

Tears streaked his face, blurring the dark shadow before him, tall on its limbs—tall as a middle-aged tree—before lowering so close to the ground, it looked like it would take a nap right there on the beach.

The fisherman cleared the wetness from his eyes, in time to see a man sliding from a fleshy flap on the beast's back. The new stranger rolled off the creature and thumped into the sand. A dusting of grains collected over his entire left side, and he was followed by a woman. She landed on top of the man, and they both grunted. Both rolled apart for the next person to be birthed from the monster, landing between them.

Oh, that creature, such a strange thing! Terrifying, yet docile as a pup, lying still with closed eyes and a gaping mouth spread into a satisfied grin.

"Damn, it was stuffy in there," one of the strangers crowed, oblivious to the fisherman watching them.

The other sets of beasts unloaded their cargo as well, with their monstrous heads resting on the beach wearing those same dreadful smiles. How many people came from these things? Twenty? Maybe thirty?

The strangers helped each other, fussed with the rags they wore as clothing, re-tying long, black hair if needed, yellow eyes glinting in the moonlight. The Yeunish...

This was a dream, limbo, or something in between. Audioxine poisoning perhaps.

But it was her. It was the face of his daughter—older, more mature. A slender scar cut across her throat, pale under the night's glow when she turned to see him there, sitting back in the sand, slick with urine.

"Father?" she said.

He swallowed, staring up at her as she made her way to him. "Zare-bear?" he croaked.

She offered him her hand, and he hesitated a moment before grasping it. It was solid, tangible... and held him, pulling his weak body from the sand to stand with her. Her golden eyes held on to his white ones as they stared for an indeterminate amount of time.

"Dad," she said, lip quivering and hand tight around his.

He pulled her in and held her. She had grown even taller, and his small Foscan frame barely reached her shoulder. It was her. It was her.

"Your mother will die when she sees you."

The Nazagora were content floating in the water nearby. If they could sleep, Lor assumed that they did just that. Rik and Oren volunteered to corral them back to the morass to get the next round of Yeunish in the morning. Until then, he had to come up with a plan, because at the moment, he had none. According to Cimma, he knew his family was in the desert, but he had no way to get there other than his feet.

Zary's father, Tur'laethe, whom the town called Url (or Turse the Burdened on a rare occasion the city came calling), had lit a fire for them on the beach. The poor guy had quite the surprise when they showed up, and Lor felt bad for that. His modest home was barely big enough for his family, but his hospitality went beyond that of a typical Foscan, setting them up in a quiet cove nearby. Karl insisted they catch their own meals, but Url wouldn't let them do it alone.

An ember popped in front of Lor. He was too tired to be startled by it, gazing into the fire with red-rimmed eyes and convinced he'd fall asleep sitting upright. His meal of blackened fish and creeper tubers sat mostly eaten in front of him, with the remaining bits and crumbs getting colder by the minute. The small hump of his daughter curled up beside him, already passed out and silent.

As his eyes fluttered in a fight to stay awake, the fire popped again. This time, the outline of Gehenna traced itself in the orange flames. He blinked a few times, knowing it had been a while since he slept without the calm of Lapis Evening, and before he could protest in fear of what he'd see, his body collapsed to the side in the cool bed of sand and he had a vision.

Great Tree blazed in the distance, throwing giant living embers from its branches. They floated to the ground like fiery dancers twirling mercilessly in their own patterns of war. Once the embers touched down, the land turned black, spreading out to the sea and all around.

But then it moved in reverse. The land renewed and the embers floated upward, reconnecting to the tree and extinguishing the inferno. A majestic tree, the width of a city, and reaching to the heavens, stood firm in the ground as the branches swayed in the breeze.

Maron stood there, having a heated discussion with a Danashi woman at the trunk. It was Paerli, her face wet with tears and belly heavy with child, and she jabbed her finger at him in anger, then walked away. Her ghost stormed past as Maron descended into the tree.

Knowing Maron's fate, Lor turned to follow Par. Her trail led them to a modest home built into the side of the surrounding mountains. Once inside, the interior lit up with a pale light, spreading from strategic skylights positioned throughout. There were no tech lights, only the gift of nature.

Colorful twirls of green and blue ivy decorated the walls with white flowers glittering randomly throughout. A circle of cozy seats formed the living area, with hand-carved pictures and names in each one.

Several barefooted Foscan children of all ages filled the home, busying themselves with various chores. Once they saw Par, they greeted her warmly, and she responded in kind. One of the older children cradled a small child, about two standard, that Par reached for. She held the sleeping child close to her chest.

As she rocked slowly in place, a tear dripped from her chin.

Lor jerked awake. The fire had burned down to a dying radiant heat, and the cool breeze of night sea air sent chills over his exposed arm. Cimma still slept next to him, now with a thick and tattered blanket draped over her. Zary or Url must have stopped by and saw her exposed. The sooner he could get her back to the safety of home, the better.

A stick lay beside him, and he used it to poke the paltry fire, sending a cluster of embers into a frenzy like angry glowing gee flies. It woke Jack across the way, and he sat up, rubbing his face.

When he saw Lor, he nodded and yawned.

"Hey, Jack, I need to ask you something, and I need you to be honest with me. Please, just be honest," Lor said.

Jack raised his brow and nodded. "I'll answer as best I know how."

"You knew Par for a very long time, right?"

Jack tittered. "You know the answer to that already." He yawned again.

"What did you really know about her?"

"Not much really."

"Come on, Jack. I told you to be honest with me."

"Hey, I told you I'd answer the best I could, and there's nothing I can say that you don't already know. She was obsessed with the breach, you know that. She came to me when I was a dirt-faced orphan living in the tents."

The men looked at each other, letting the weakened embers float between them. Jack sighed at Lor's unrelenting stare. "Growing up," he continued, "she promised there'd be a day I could escape my life in poverty after I became an adult and followed her plan. I *lived* for the day we'd set off on that journey... but it wasn't until about thirty standard years passed before she felt another potential Reaper nearby to help her with that plan." He paused for a moment to narrow his eyes at Lor. "That's you, of course, don't need to tell you that.

"I was disappointed she wanted a team, but by that time, Hare was in the camps and was eager to please her. I think she felt sorry for him in that weird way only she knew how to feel. Either way, the team was formed, and that was it. When I was young, she never divulged any deep secrets. She only looked after me and told me how special the mountain was. I can only assume because now I know it to be the burnt-out shell of Great Tree and Maron's tomb."

Lor stared out at first sun's round, hairless head peeking up from the sea's horizon. "What about the surrounding mountains?" Lor asked. "I mean, the real ones, not Gehenna?"

Jack shrugged. "I don't know anything about those, only the city of Montaegar on the other side of them. But technically, that's something you should already know too from first levels."

Lor waved his hand in front of his face. The last images of the children living in the walls of the mountains stuck in his memory, and Par returning home to them. Surely evidence of their existence was still there... boarded up, closed up... something. He pondered it for a minute, lost in thought.

"Is that all you wanted to ask me?" Jack said with another yawn.

Lor realized his attention to Jack had glazed, and he turned to look back at him. "Did she say anything to you about the pendant she wore?"

Jack rolled his eyes and leaned on his knee, resting his chin on a fist, finding his own stick to poke at the fire. "I told you already... it was a bargaining tool against her, but you lost it."

"A bargaining tool for *what* exactly?"

"Hell, I don't know. She said it was passed down to her over hundreds of standard years and that it was special somehow. If you ask me, the stupid thing made her forget who she was."

All of those children in the mountain. They loved her, and she loved them. Nothing like the Par he knew... she hated the Foscans, using every opportunity to slander them. How his vision had her caring for a brood of them, he couldn't understand, but Jack had to be right about her forgetting herself.

"Why are you asking anyway? Isn't Par long gone?" Jack sat upright, cross-legged in the sand, and rotated his neck to popping. The sun rose steadily behind him.

Jack thought she somehow died in that mountain. He didn't know that she was never gone and returned to the rotting shell of her former home. She had to be there; it only made sense. "One last question, and I'll stop asking."

"Alright," Jack said with dubious side eye as he cracked his spine.

"You know she lived for over a thousand standard years. You know Maron was her husband. You said yourself just now that you thought she forgot who she was. I've seen visions in my sleep, and I've seen visions in the past. Is it possible... or is it *plausible*... that Par just might be one of the mothers of the Foscan race?"

Jack opened his mouth, letting out nothing but a gusty sigh. Then the fire finally died.

Chapter 19

Temptations

Nico

That darkness. No matter how bright the desert light, the darkness grew. Nico scanned the horizon, praying for the shadows of all his lost family members to appear. They were losing this war and losing fast.

It was up to him to make sure no one else fell, even if the weight of responsibility landed on his own shoulders for the sake of Cimma. It was a mistake to tell her about Yeunish bounties.

He tilted his head back and forth, allowing the pressure to pop in his neck. Physically, the pressure released, but mentally it remained—there was nothing he could think of that would change their circumstances, and all of it was his fault.

A strange fog persisted in his mind; it scrambled his formulation abilities, turned his fingers impotent when performing maintenance on his legs, and made him question his resolve. Where did it come from?

Each trip to the bunker where he needed the most concentration, the fog dug deeper. Every time he opened that Formulator chest, watching the phials of colors and formulas dangle there, he forgot himself. It had been too long since he'd created anything new. At this point, even Damaetra had surpassed his skill.

He wouldn't begrudge her for that, but he couldn't help but think about better times when he was comfortable in his own skin. When things were better.

He glanced behind his shoulder into the tent, where he caught a glimpse of Nate sitting at the table alone while scrawling out whatever he was thinking and mumbling to himself. Nico sighed. The poor kid had been through a lot.

All of this was because of Loren. Resentment wasn't the word he would use about the arrest of his best friend, but something malevolent tugged at his mind when he thought about the responsibilities he took on. Each year got harder and harder as he felt they weren't making progress fast enough. Every year he spent away from his wife buried that sense of lagging behind into his core, and he grew impatient.

While Dill and Emilia didn't care about putting off having children, Nico did. Eva was getting older, and he long gave up the idea they'd ever have some of their own while taking care of Nate and Cimma. And he lost Cimma a whole standard week ago with no hint of her anywhere. What kind of dad would he be if he so flippantly lost a child like that?

He clicked his tongue and shook his head at himself. Even worse, he was losing Damaetra to a sickness he couldn't cure. If he had the Yeunish touch, he'd know what to do... but even Jack was gone.

Verena and Ayala had long given up that they'd ever see Jack again, and maybe it was time he let go of his best friend too, along with any hope he might build a family of his own.

He glanced at the sky. It wouldn't be too much longer before second sun, and he needed to try one last idea for Damaetra's healing before it got dark. Nighttime was when the fog in his mind grew thickest, and he couldn't afford to lose more time, or another friend.

Turning back to Nate, he sighed again. "Come on, buddy," he said while closing the tent, "time to go downstairs."

Nate whined, drooping his shoulders and tossing his head back. "But I'm still trying to *learn*," he groaned.

Nico began the sequence of activating the trap. "Learn about what?"

"I'll talk to you about it tomorrow. Uncle Nico says it's time to go downstairs."

That was weird. "Bud, who are you talking to?"

Nate gathered his papers in a slop heap. "My friend, Mister Shadow."

Very, very weird. "Who is Mister Shadow?"

Nate shrugged and moved toward the ladder. "I think he lives in the mountains," he said before his head disappeared into the bunker.

Nico furrowed his brow, staring at the open hole leading into the lower level. *There goes the last healthy member of Lor's family.* Now he was losing Nate to psychosis. He remembered the promise he made to himself and the Turtingas family to protect them. They were each being picked off one by one.

Maker help them. Maker help him.

Light was thin in the bunker, but Nico had to work. Once he saw Nate to his room, he left for his.

The small table he had was cramped. His Formulator chest sat open on the floor as he pulled out the things he needed for the next experiment before his brain fog took over at nightfall. One by one, he set each previous test on the table.

The most recent formulation was a dud. It was great for dissolving scabs and making someone bleed, but that wasn't the right formula to replace Verdigris Mend, or for Dame. After his interaction with Nate, he felt compelled to create something to ease his nephew's broken mind.

Reaching across to grab a phial of yellow, his elbow caught the lip of a phial of orange, spilling it over the dry wood that soaked it up like a greedy, thirsty beast.

"Damn it," he hissed to himself, trying desperately to recapture any lost fluid. It was futile. The wood won, leaving an amorphous dark stain of rare eneris.

The little glass phial still had some drops along the neck he tried to tilt back inside, but his thick, callused fingers wouldn't let him. He leaned his head back in a groan.

"Formulas got you down?" Niklaus asked with a tease in his voice. He leaned against the open passage between their bunkers.

Nico responded with his favorite crude hand gesture, then mumbled a request for more orange eneris.

"Orange? You know how hard that is to get?"

"I know, I'm sorry," Nico said, capping off the last dregs of his spilled phial. "I'm just as frustrated as you."

"Doubtful," Niklaus said, sitting in the opposite chair at the table.

"If you go get some, maybe while you're in Secas you'll find Cae?"

Niklaus frowned. "Don't," he warned.

Nico raised his hands and shook his head. He was in no mood to dredge up his brother's melancholy. There was enough of that in his own head. Inadequate, unskilled, stupid... he ran over what he told Cimma about bounties and capture again and again, kicking himself for thinking it was harmless. Stupid, stupid.

Not only that, but his own ability betrayed him. Nothing worked anymore, and there was nothing he could make that would compare to a Yeunish formulation.

"What do you use orange for, anyway? Do you really need it?" Niklaus asked, pinching the neck of the mostly empty phial between two fingers.

Nico sighed. "Maybe I don't need it after all."

"Hey, I didn't mean anything by that..."

"Forget about it." Nico picked up his Formulator chest and set it on the table with a harder thud than he intended. Niklaus reared back a little.

If only he had been blessed with Yeunish intuition to come up with a new formula—an easier substitute. All he was able to conjure was a failed bleed tonic and something that would probably find its way onto an Audun anti-drug poster. Too long had he tried to troubleshoot something that should have been easy. At least, easy for a Yeuni. For Jack. He raked his fingers through his hair.

"I can get you the orange," Niklaus said, leaning back.

Nico only nodded, staring at his hands as he picked at his thumb's cuticle. Such worthless hands. A stupid tongue for the craft and a pitiable Formulator he was. He was due for a breakthrough. Just one win was all he needed—that, and Dame's forgiveness for driving off her daughter and making Nate crazy. And Eva. Maybe some new legs. And better skill. He could use a better relationship with Gale too.

"You look lost," Niklaus broke Nico's spell with his usual sarcastic drawl.

"What? No. I'm... just thinking."

"Don't hurt yourself."

"Very funny," Nico said with a sneer. The more he kicked himself, the worse he felt. The worse he felt, the more he felt justified in kicking himself.

The Formulator chest lay open next to him. Each phial dangled from their spot, waiting for him to befoul a formulation with them. The thought was frustrating, and the dreaded fog began its march through his brain. As he mentally berated himself some more, a false compartment in the bottom of the chest creaked open, revealing an alluring dark crack into a hidden space he'd nearly forgotten about. Inside that tiny treasure hole, red stars glittered.

The memory materialized, and his hand shook when he opened the compartment completely. The little black stone lay inside, atop a pool of its own gold chain, each red star practically glowing from within it.

When he slid it out of the compartment, it felt alive, a vibration in his hand, and the dainty chain lay in the creases of his hardened palm like a demure golden river. How interesting for him to find it now, after stashing it all those years ago when they were in a hurry to flee from the cities. Years of hibernation in a musty false compartment would turn any normal piece of jewelry into an oxidized crust, but not this one... The stone remained impeccably enchanting.

The same drawl of his brother droned under the hypnosis effect of the stone, and Nico couldn't hear it.

"Are you listening?" Niklaus asked, still a barely audible honk from across the table.

The black stone cast its darkness up the walls throughout the room, until the pathetic tech light disappeared and Nico's consciousness drifted into a dank, muddy space.

The soft, damp earth squelched between his toes. Toes! He hadn't had real toes in so long... where was he? Was he dreaming?

"Hello?" he called out into the void, but his voice cut short in his throat rather than echo. A pale light flickered on, deep in the distant darkness, and something answered his call.

"Hello to you," it said. It was neither man nor woman but an amalgam of both—eerily haunting yet oddly charming. Unlike the sound of his own cloth-stuffed voice, this one channeled directly into his mind.

"Where am I?" Nico asked, hearing nothing but vowels swimming over the deep cadence of his vocals.

"You are here," it said.

"How did I get here?"

"The void calls..." The dissonant voice sniggered, and Nico felt numb fingers curl over his arms, raising the hairs to a sting.

Every hair on his body stood up, including those on his legs—his real legs, which prickled the flesh into bumps. The feeling wrapped a haunted chill around his intestines, causing him to shiver: once violently, then persistently in subtle shakes.

There was fear, then there was terror, yet a wicked piece of him embraced them both with intense craving, and he didn't know why.

The distant light showed him nothing. It was dim, yet a painful shade of gray in his eyes. And still, he felt exposed to this entity, or entities, who spoke to him.

He was afraid to say anything further, and he didn't need to. The entity was already aware of him, reading his thoughts and reaching deep inside of him.

"You desire... intuition... intelligence... acceptance... you can have these things." The smooth offers commanded respect but held him like a lover.

A small squawk vibrated his throat, but he had no answer. He wanted these things. He was desperate for these things.

"I can give you what you desire," it whispered.

The soft brush of something cold and wet dragged over his calf, and he jolted forward a step.

"Would it be forgiveness?" it teased him, and another slick brush of the cold thing slid against his other calf. It made his legs go cold, sending more prickles up the flesh.

He closed his eyes to shut out the harsh gray light. Instead of the darkness of his lids, he was back in the desert, rescuing Cimma from brigands and bringing her home to her mother and brother. There was a great celebration, hosted by Gale, with piles of real food spread on a long table that fed the whole camp. When he opened his eyes again, the outline of happily feasting neighbors faded into the dark, leaving behind trails of skeletal remains rising from the sand in varying states of decay.

"Perhaps it would be intuition," the voice whispered as the last of the bones faded into the dark.

A pit of shame tugged at his stomach, knowing he wanted it. He wanted all of it. And he didn't have to close his eyes to see it. The newest formulation worked, and it was her salvation. Her pale hands slithered around his waist, and he melted in a sense of satisfaction and guilt, heart palpitating. Never had he considered a latent attraction to his old school friend... his best friend's wife... his dead best friend... but she was in front of him, vibrant and alive, full of his formulation and lips sweet in gratitude. Not just for her life, but for her son and daughter. They needed a father, and the mother a lover. He could be those things for them.

This was wrong.

"Power is what you need," the voice declared, "you only need asssk, and I would give it to you."

A small black stone, clasped in gold, slid down his bare chest, a frigid snap freezing his core. The stars inside were red like the lips of his wife, now at his knees and gazing up at him in wonder with his new pale paramour on his arm. The wife's hands found the back of his knees, a touch memory he'd long forgotten. As she knelt in front of him, he felt a clap at his shoulder from his father-in-law, the wide grin of consent spread across his face. The figure of his small and silly Danashi friend stood across from him, thumbs raised and teeth bared in an unconstrained smile.

Behind the praise, he felt their approval. Nico had money, status, and prestige as head Formulator in the great city Milaris. The Seven Cities awarded accolade after accolade to him that he wore within his flesh and radiated to all who gazed upon him. The ruler deferred to his instruction, and the fate of Roseaarde lay on his shoulders.

His wife remained at his feet, running gentle hands along the tender nerves at the back of his legs while the pale woman brushed her fingertips over his neck. He could provide for them, care for them, give them and everyone he loved everything they wanted. The black stone rocked back and forth against his skin, leaving cold trails that reached deep between his ribs.

"I can give you all of thisss," the dissonant voice said over Nico's failure to tame his erection. "The anssswer to all your quessstions... the knowledge of ssspirits... dominion and praissse. Real legsss made of flesssh."

The bellies of his wife and his lover were great with child. Both of them his, both of them healthy and ready to be born to him.

And he wanted it. He felt shame to want it.

Glancing to his pregnant wife, she smiled at him. She was lovely and loving, yet... different. What was her name again? His pale lover kissed his neck, belly pressing his side, and he struggled to say her name.

The man in front of him, still smiling, eyes missing, swaying back and forth with hands behind his back. Dark skinned and jovial, his name was short. But what was it?

His father-in-law had a name too, but it blew away in the wind. The man he craved approval from deep down, not knowing why, turned to look at Nico, grin hollowed by bits of bone blasted from his jaw... self-inflicted.

"It ssstarts with the formula," the voice said as an unnaturally thick book of formulations spun its pages in front of him. He tried to scan a page to memorize, but they moved too fast. "I know them all. Jussst follow me... and you can have it."

This was wrong but felt so good. Nico glanced down at the pendant around his neck. It had come to a standstill, searing hot ice into his chest. He wanted the formula. He wanted the knowledge of spirits. He wanted to make children, lots of them. He wanted all of it. He wanted his wife, he lusted after the wife of his dead best friend... He could have them both. He imagined the smell of them, their soft skin. One smelled of deygo lilac, the other of sweet violets. He cast his head back and groaned as all the hands touched him. It had been too long since he felt so alive.

"You alright, bro?" The familiar voice startled him, and he looked up to see himself looking back. The copy tilted its head, curls wild and wind-whipped. "I said, you alright?"

Eyes black, the copy wouldn't turn away from him. It advanced in stilted motions toward him, but he couldn't back away from it. The wife and future lover held him in place.

The pendant... Cirv'e.

Nico grasped at the stone. Its chill burned his palm. He yanked the thin gold chain until it snapped. The dissonant voice laughed in the dark, the deeper tones overwhelming the feminine.

The copy moved closer as Nico thrust the pendant deep into the void. Everyone but the mirror image vaporized with it. A slithering rush ran up the walls, pursuing his position as he stood there, stuck.

Once the copy was within arm's reach, he grabbed it by the wrist and sucked in a sharp breath before belting: "Niki, help!"

Warmth spread over his temples and down to his chest, where the ghost of the wicked pact once sat.

"You alright, bro?" Niklaus asked. He sat across from him with a pained and curious expression, almost as if he were about to laugh. He glanced down at his wrist, clutched and whitening under Nico's grip.

Par's pendant shook in his other hand, the gold chain threaded among his fingers. A cold sweat broke out on his brow as he came out of his stupor, and in reflex the pendant went soaring into a dark corner of the room.

"Whoa, what was that about?" Niklaus watched the corner where Nico chucked the pendant but turned back to his brother with eyes the usual crystalline-blue Nico was familiar with, not the black pools they were in his waking delusion. "Your face is paler than my ass. What happened?"

There weren't enough curses in Northern Common to accommodate Niklaus's question. Nico's lips popped open a couple times in an attempt to conjure something to relay back. He moved a hand to his chest, feeling the spot where his offer of a necklace once lay, and the remnant of coldness that fought for its existence. Nothing was there.

"I thought you were in a trance or something, then you yelled all kinda pathetic. It was like, '*meep meep meep*!'" Niklaus made baby bird noises, flapping tiny hand wings at his sides.

Nico didn't respond. Everything he was confronted with, whatever it was, reached into the furthest corners of his shame that he didn't know needed cleaning. Damaetra... he didn't think he could look at her right again.

"Dude, *say* something!" Niklaus slammed a palm against the wood, jostling the precious remaining phials sitting there.

"I-I..." Nico stuttered, the chill of the black room fixed in his lips and freezing them there. "I don't know. I don't know."

Niklaus sat back in his chair and bit his lip, continuing to watch Nico. He relaxed the frustration in his brow while he stared, until he let out a deep, quiet breath. "It was the worm, wasn't it?" he said.

The dissonant voice—the darkness and the promises—he'd almost forgotten his family and who he was. Nico threw his shoulders back. "Why do you say that?" he asked.

"What was on your mind just before? Were you feeling weak? Hopeless? Worthless?"

"Stop it, Niki. We've been through this already."

"No, I'm being serious. It feeds on your insecurities." He got quiet for a moment. "It feeds on vices, and it *lies* to you..."

Someone cleared their throat behind them. It was Gale. An intact version of him, to Nico's great relief.

"Emilia is coming to tent city to live. Eva's coming with her," Gale said.

"Right on," Niklaus said with a yawn. Then he sat upright. "Wait, so they're coming here to *live*? Like, forever?"

"That's right. They'll be here in about a few standard days, maybe a week. She didn't really give me details, but my guess is they're just being cautious. You know, after... everything."

"Damn, there goes all of our funding." Niki sat back again, craning his neck to look at the ceiling.

"We'll be alright," Nico added. He didn't know where the confidence came from, because he sure didn't feel all right.

"Guess it's back to stealing," Niklaus said with a shrug.

"Why are you acting like that?" Nico asked, brows creased.

"Acting like *what*?" Niklaus let his irritation show through his usual bored drawl.

"You're thinking of plats when your own sister-in-law is dead, and your niece *and* wife are missing."

"I said, *don't*, Nico." He clamped his teeth together and glared.

Nico turned back to see Gale gone and the flimsy partition fabric swaying in the breeze. He most likely didn't want to get involved. Not again. He turned back to Niklaus, who reflected his anger back at him.

Niklaus lifted his lip in a snarl. "Do you think I don't agonize about any of that?"

"Of all the things you could do, you could at the very least try to *look* for Caella!" Nico shot back.

Niklaus turned red. Every line in his face reminded Nico of the long week they held him hostage at Guild Central. "I swear, Nico," he grumbled, "I should have slit you off at the fucking waist."

"The *hell* you just say to me?" Nico stood on his black legs, joints squealing.

Niklaus stood too, neither one taller than the other, noses nearly touching. Nico clenched his fist, jerking it up. It made Niklaus flinch and touch the skin under his eye.

"Screw you, Nico," he muttered as he sauntered from the room.

"Go find your wife!"

"Yeah, sure, *bro*." His voice was already at top of the ladder, distanced enough from his brother.

A chill current flushed in the room, and he stood there, alone once again and left with his thoughts. Even in the shadows, the pendant he had pitched to the corner glittered in the dark. There was a foul magic in that stone... perhaps the very thing that made him rage at his own brother. Then there was guilt. He didn't have to prod Niklaus like that.

Shame crept through his chest, spreading through his torso in a crawling lace. It was pure embarrassment. Not only for his row with his twin, but for the way he felt about Dame in that nightmare, and especially his own wife. The distant sound of that unforgettable laugh echoed in his mind.

He had to get away from that pendant and get the warm sun on his face.

Chapter 20

Fired

That stupid woman. She just had to get into his head and tell the princeps his secret. At least she was dead. All snitches should die. Real justice was made with the hands of the offended, and he was so very offended. But now that she was dead, these hands had to serve justice in other ways.

The day was sunny, but Milo sat sourly on the park bench across from his former work building. Cracking a knuckle, he sneered at a pair of young children walking by with their father.

That stupid princeps should have died under his fists when he fired him. Why did he hold back? He was a *strongman*. Reaper or not, Renae wouldn't have stood a chance as his fists turned that smug face into a pile of mush.

Oh well. That business was over, and now it was time to rebuild his memories after that stupid Anglia partner of his stole them. He was free to terrorize whomever he pleased without the badge of Audun.

The first name he remembered was Loren Benedict Turtingas. And now that it was there, he couldn't forget that epic arrest. He grinned to himself at the sight of that bastard in gloves. But that guy was already banished and most likely dead. What he really needed was to find the rest of those shit birds that came with him that day to fight in Gehenna. What were their names?

He squeezed his shoulder, feeling the tight knot nagging him. The squeeze hurt in a good way, releasing a hot jolt of relief.

The wife... there was a wife. The widow Turtingas. He remembered using her implant signal to track where they lived, but he didn't have access to that system anymore. Where was that house he tracked her to? Pinewood? No, that wasn't right. Peakwood! It was Peakwood. He could go back there and finish what he started.

He could make a game of it. If there was a chance his old lover was still alive, he could work with her to wipe the lot of them out. But she was probably dead too.

The black e-disk was small in his meaty hand. He told it to show him Peakwood. The map fanned open in front of him, but there were too many streets. To filter it down, all he had to do was find the homes that had Foscan servants. Then he could find the homes in which their servants had died within the last ten standard years.

That narrowed it down to six homes dotted all around. Not many people had Foscans, and even fewer had ones that died. Those little parasites were resilient; he always thought so.

That narrowed it even further to two homes.

The Foscan he shot was a woman...right? Yes, because she was married to her owner. The thought made him want to retch. What a disgusting pair. At least the sick bastard of a husband was dead too. That sweet feeling of that man's flesh and bone caving in tickled his knuckle, and he had to adjust himself.

An older woman strolled by to see his hand shifting around where it shouldn't be, and she frowned.

"Want some?" he said as she scurried away.

He leaned back and smiled. Then it was back to focusing. Keep 'em coming.

The more he searched his mind, the more clear the memory was. There were holes, spotted by time... but at least it was there and not buried by that Anglian bitch.

He wished he'd been there when Renae squeezed her dry. Silver always tasted better when it was fresh.

Yeah, he drank silver before, so what? Everyone should try it. Everyone's silver had a different flavor, and he wondered about hers. Too bad it was wasted. She was pretty hot too.

He forgot what he was planning, pausing to glare at his former work building again. That whole place should crumble under his strength. He could start with the lazy administrator. Bash his brains into the counter...

Time to focus again. Once he found the wife, he'd find the friends. Then he could kill them all. Maybe bring a Reaper to pull them and he could sample their silver too. Then their souls would live on inside his veins, forever serving him and beating down anyone that stood in his way.

Yeah, that would work.

First, he'd have to retrace his steps to Peakwood.

Chapter 21

Orange Cat

Caella

The coastal town wasn't anything like Cae remembered. It used to be full of life and color... Now, well, it was drab and sad. People wandered the market with heads down under depressed rain clouds. Market vendors pitched their sales with little enthusiasm, and even the alley cats had given up on their humans.

The white cat weaved through the streets, collecting the grime of discarded beverages, spilled foods, vomit, and spit. The town was definitely *cleaner* the last time she visited.

Despite the dreary arrangement of the once bustling outdoor market, she felt it better reflected her current life. She didn't want the color. She didn't want the sunlight. She grasped her own storm cloud and carried it with her to the alley, under dry awnings.

For the past week, she'd wandered aimlessly, looking for scraps, and finding small, private moments to feel human again—alone, in the alleys. A woman was arrested in front of her for speaking against the worm. Knowing what she knew about her sister, these arrests most likely became executions. The thought brought up her despondence once again in a bubbling stomach ache.

Eloria wasn't the easiest to get along with at times, but Cae understood her. She was pretty sure she was the only one who did. It made sense, though—ever since they were old enough to have opinions, Cae always thought of Eloria as the other half to her whole.

Now that she was gone, she felt that part of her rip itself from inside her, and she was desperate to find a way to fill it again. At least to stop the bleeding. Niklaus was a good husband, but he wasn't her twin. He should know that... what it was like to feel torn from the person who shared his life, his face. She wanted to cry again, feeling the dark loneliness of her situation, then anger at his rebuffs toward her. Maybe it would get better if she found others, just maybe.

Time to find some friends.

There were at least eight cats that she saw in the alley behind the eneris emporium shop, sitting, bathing, curled up and sleeping... So she trotted up to the closest one—a slender striped tabby cat licking between her toes. As the tabby glanced up to see the bounce of white fur and pink-nosed greeting, she hissed and strutted down the alley toward a black tom to continue her grooming.

Whatever.

The white cat lay in the spot the tabby left, and the stones were still warm. It was here she curled up and finally rested after the long and hot morning.

So much to think about, too hurt to think about it. Cae's breaths came out heavy, and she was close to falling asleep. She didn't know anything about this cat colony and prayed they didn't try to kill her in her sleep. She was too tired to worry about it. As she closed her eyes, a set of bright orange-colored paws strolled in front of her. It was too late; she succumbed to sleep and just hoped the ginger cat came with good tidings.

In her dream, Eloria was with Cae in their home, and Niklaus visited. Nothing was out of the ordinary, and they played a few card games while watching their favorite holo series, *Blank Slate*. It was life going the way it should. Cae wondered if real cats dreamed of their families too, or if it was all chases and food. When she opened her eyes to the cold cobbled street of back alley Secas, she felt that sharp stab of regret in her belly. Nothing in her dream was real.

The odd ginger had never left, sitting nearby. When he noticed her eyes open, he made a purring click at her. In a strange way, she understood it. She got up, stretched, and followed him farther down the alley.

Second sun was rising, and the signature purple hue cast its first light across the market, tinting the shadows. It nearly created a beacon of purple glow on Cae's white fur as she moved from trash bin to trash bin behind the buildings. The scent of wet, stale dust hovered just over the cobblestones. As gross as the smell was, Cae much preferred it to the smell of hot garbage.

When they made their way behind a medic tent, the strange ginger leapt into one of the cans in the back. Cae twitched her nose, curious now as to why she followed him. When he jumped back out, he had a half-full blister pack of green and blue capsules.

The blister pack clattered to the stones, bouncing upside down to reveal a bold black drug name printed over the reflective foil: *Metamorfine*. The "a" and the "i" were punched out, and their wells collected drops from the awning above.

The ginger watched her for a moment before sitting in a proper pose on the stones. What did he want? He just sat there and... stared at her, in front of this pack of over-the-counter drug that sounded like it could be for...

The realization clicked when the strange cat ducked under a hank of brown cloth on the ground next to the can he pilfered from. A man's head emerged, and he tucked the covering around him. She tilted her head while watching the man bend down to grab the pills and dry-swallow two of them.

"Bigger dudes need bigger doses. So what's your deal, anyway?" He swatted a clump of fire-red hair from his face, already damp with the wet air. Lounging against the wall, his legs were spread a little too far.

Not even a week in Secas and she was discovered. There weren't any other coverings for her to convert and talk to him, so she sat there, keeping her gaze fixed on the stones of the alley, not the ones barely hidden by the brown cloth.

"I'm not stupid. I know you're a skin changer," he persisted, picking at a tooth and watching her.

Rather than gape at his indecency, she glanced up into his dull green eyes, then back down the alley where they came from.

"I'm the only one in that colony," he said. Unlike her sister, it seemed this stranger understood how to speak "cat."

The thought of Eloria brought Cae's mood back down, and she sauntered up to the back wall of the pharmacy, leaning against the cold stone.

"Here," the man said as he dug through the larger dumpster. He withdrew a large black plastic wrapping and tossed it at her. "It's been a while since I've talked to another skin changer."

The alley was clear once second sun took over, so she was safe from onlookers if she chose to change. The black bag wasn't her first choice, but she wasn't in her right mind enough to bring clothes, and no one was around anyway. She nuzzled down inside it, surprised that it didn't have a smell, considering the baked garbage in the alley. Careful to cover herself, she poked her head out and looked at him with her human eyes. Nothing seemed as vibrant anymore, and the dull, drab alley got even duller and drabber.

"There you are," the man said, "name's Quill. You?"

She cleared her throat, keeping her head down with an occasional side-glance down the alley. "Cae."

Quill sniggered and tipped his head at her chest. "I had you pegged the moment I saw you. What's that you got there?" He offered her the half-full blister pack of Metamorfine.

She crumpled her hands inward, taking fistfuls of the black plastic bag with them over her heart. Unless the guy was a complete pervert, the only thing she had there was the patch. She shook her head at the pills as politely as she could. "It's a Weggevens patch." With the answer, she considered her friends in the desert. Why had she run from them again?

"Alright... what's a Weggevens patch?" Quill chewed on something in his mouth. It could have been dry pill residue.

He watched her with innocent curiosity, but she wasn't sure how to answer his question. As far as she knew, Verena didn't freely give out her invention to Wegs outside the desert. Except her, of course.

"Can I see it?" he asked. Innocent or not, she wasn't about to flash her breasts to a man masquerading in the alley as a cat... even if she was doing the same thing.

"Um, no. I don't know you," she said, folding her fist a little tighter inward.

"Well, what is it then? Is it, like, something you can use instead of the pills? I think I've seen something like it before. Can I have one?"

"Hold on, you've seen one before?"

Quill chuckled and sat at the opposite wall. Second sun was almost completely overhead, illuminating everything with an eerie violet, casting shadows that hurt to look at. Cae wasn't in the habit of spending time outside during second sun and squinted.

He jabbed a freckled finger toward the open market. "There was a man over there a few weeks ago. He had it on his arm, though. I was right under him because he stopped near one of my sunnin' spots. I only happened to see it just under his floppy sleeve."

Perhaps it was Gale, or maybe Niklaus. They both still ran errands here. "What did they look like?" she asked.

He hummed and glanced upward. "Well, he was older..."

Must have been Gale.

"...he had these thick glasses perched over his nose as he looked at random stuff."

Definitely Gale...

"...and he had a lot of blond hair. Like a big bush of it."

Not... Gale.

She tilted her head, trying to conjure who could possibly have gotten their hands on Verena's tech.

"I've seen him before, though, don't know who he is. I've seen him here on weekends from time to time."

Quill's stare had gotten uncomfortable, and the fist she had clenched over the plastic was getting sweaty.

"Would you please not stare?" she said.

"Sorry, you're pretty and I'm lonely."

"I'm married."

"Oh?" Quill leaned back with a grin. "And where is your invisible husband?"

Cae couldn't tell this stranger she ran away on impulse, leaving everyone that loved her. Eloria would shake her head at her, tell her how disappointed she was. Cae frowned, and Quill picked up on it.

"I'm sorry, I didn't mean to upset you. I'm a little socially starved, if you know my meaning."

"It's fine, just... don't stare, please. If you want a lesson on proper social behavior, staring is weird."

He nodded with a grin, but his interest remained. It could have been innocent enough, but there was no telling by the look on his face. "So anyway," he continued, "maybe that guy'll come back and I can help you find him."

"Sure," she said. The prospect was intriguing even if she wasn't sure of this stranger yet. But just like her cat instincts, she was curious to know who else might have Verena's exclusive patch.

"So you wanna know the rules, or what?" he asked.

"The rules?" She raised her brow.

"Yeah, see, if you wanna roam around our colony, you gotta know what to do and what not to do."

The idea of following rules had no appeal. She came here to escape the stupidity of rules. Rules of the city had them all in chains. Maker knew what rules of the colony would do.

"We're the only skin changers here, though, aren't we?" she asked.

Quill pawed behind his ear for a scratch. "Yeah, but cats got rules. You don't follow them, you get bit. Scratched. You know, cat stuff."

Cae sighed. Before becoming a Weggevens, she knew nothing about cat culture. After becoming one, she ran alone in the alleys, spying on people on the weekends. There was no reason she couldn't just roam alone here.

"But don't be a perv," Quill cut into her thoughts. "Another skin changer used to roam around here a while back, playin' nice and lettin' women stroke him, if you get me."

"Disgusting," she said with a grimace.

"Yeah, that guy went straight to gaol. Well, anyway, if you want to roam with us..." Quill's explanation of the rules droned on. She was sure she didn't catch any of it as she pondered her stupid decision to leave her family.

Admittedly, she still wanted to find this mystery person that had Verena's patch. Something about the connection intrigued her, and she felt drawn to talk to him.

Once she found the man, she would make her way back home. Niklaus would forgive her, wouldn't he?

Chapter 22

Journey

Loren

Sunrise poked out from the horizon for the third morning Lor spent in the graces of Url's hospitality. It was time to make their way to the tents and get Cimma back home. To see his family again. As excited as he was to see them, he was nervous. The incredible change that must have happened with everyone within the last ten years... he shook his head at the thought.

Cimma's silhouette stood at the water's edge, letting the foamy water chase up her ankles and across the flat wet sand. The abundance of water had to have been something alien to her as a child of the desert. Had things gone differently, she would have been a child of the cold mountains.

"Do you like it here?" he asked her.

She turned to him with a smile, eyes wet, and nodded. "It's beautiful."

"We can come back," he said, holding out his hand to take hers.

"Mom is going to be so happy to see you," she said, squeezing his hand.

He smiled at her. "I hope so."

"It's finally fully charged, so you should be good," Url said, patting the scratched dust shield at the front of his sand skip.

"I... don't know how to drive," Lor said.

Url laughed, flipping a few switches at the front panel, then pumped a lever three times. "You learn fast when it's necessary."

"And the charge on this thing?"

Jack stepped forward, touching the handle. "My wife is an Engineer with a specialty in electricity. She'll have something when we get there," he said.

Url looked up at Lor with a smile.

"Are you going to be alright here with them?" Lor nodded at the hillside cave where the exiled Yeunish bundled inside. The black bubbles of the Nazagora bobbed in the water nearby, and Rik sat atop one of them.

"Well, life's full of surprises, but nothin' we can't make do with," Url said with a smile.

"I'm going to be a while probably. I appreciate you watching over them while we're gone."

"How long you suppose?"

Lor hummed. "I'm not really sure, but we need to do this soon, so I imagine I need a standard month or two."

Url's nod didn't instill any faith in Lor that he was thrilled with the idea, but he'd "make do." With how hospitable he'd been, Lor felt a little bad about that.

"Your kindness will be repaid a thousand times over, I just know it," Lor said, clapping a hand on Url's shoulder.

"I'm just beyond happy that you brought my girl back. I've already been paid."

Zary stood next to her father, a concentrated look on her face. "Be careful, Gold Fist," she said, drawing him in for a hug. "Remember to focus and practice."

Lor tittered and smiled. "By the time I come back, I'll be a pro." He withdrew from her embrace, holding her arms. "If you get bored and want to tutor someone in the art of focus, Davy is eager to learn."

She rolled her eyes, and the corner of her mouth turned up in a sheepish smile.

"Which one is Davy?" Url said, craning his neck toward the coast with his brows pulled forward. He cracked his knuckles one after the other.

Chapter 23

Passenger

Caella

Another hot day. Whatever moisture remained in the stones of Cae's alley had evaporated, leaving the baked stink of garbage. Quill didn't seem bothered by any of it, running his cat tongue up the length of his back leg. Of all things a cat could do, Cae refused to clean herself with her tongue. Disgusting.

Desperate for a dip in the water, she debated leaving the colony for a little while to wash the filth from her coat. So, she slipped away while Quill had his back turned.

The bay wasn't far, and the heat kept people indoors. It was nice to find the area mostly empty. The city of Secas was proud of their cleanliness, making sure the bay was a serviceable entry for recreational swimming. And it was impeccable. In the market, however, it was less so.

Alley dirt bloomed from her paw when she dipped it into the water. If she chose to dunk herself in, her cover would be blown. None of the market cats ventured into the water. A quick survey of the area, and she found herself alone. In and out.

She shook the extra water free, then sat for a moment in the sun, gazing off over the endless horizon, Gehenna a shadow in the distance. Her world was lonely now, a feeling that took hold once she found herself roaming the alley.

As she watched the water ripple in a trance, the silver nose of the Heart Island ferry appeared in the distance. It was so long ago that she watched this ferry usher her little sister back to the family from the program. The thought made her wistful for the past... the way things used to be.

It wasn't long before the ferry bobbed up to the dock, with a handful of people shuffling from their spots on board to descend the ramp. As they did, an older man with an airy mess of ash blond hair was among them, sporting a pair of glasses nested inside of it. He had to be the one Quill told her about. Nearly dry, she shook again and followed him.

The man walked everywhere. Being in her smaller form, Cae struggled for energy to continue following. He visited a diner, a clothing store, a fruit market... They were all the places she couldn't go as she was. After he emerged from Hanobi's Eneris Emporium, she was afraid she'd have to call it quits and rest in her alley.

Then he ducked between the emporium and the sweet meats shop into the alley. *Her* alley. It was great timing, and she hoped he'd stop there.

When she followed, she found him standing in the center of the clearing, back turned to her with paper sacks hanging from his fists. She hugged the alley entrance, strolling cautiously forward, then leaning against the wall. Then he turned to the side, skin dripping from his bones with age.

"I knew you'd come," he said to the wall. The loose skin dangled under his chin as he spoke.

Was he talking to her?

She took a few steps back when he fully turned around and locked eyes with her. "Why did you leave everyone?"

His words struck deep into her heart. The nagging guilt she carried seemed to transmit straight into this stranger's mind, and she felt naked for it.

The man reached into a bag, and she twitched, now wanting to run but too curious to leave. He pulled out a wrapped set of clothes.

"Please, let's have a conversation. Human to human," he said, offering the clothes.

As they were near the dead end of the back alley, she knew there was a private nook on the other side of the sweet meats building. She glanced toward it in her best cat-speak, and he tossed the clothes there, where she followed after them. It was probably the most private place she could go to transform but not the most ideal. It was tight, and she had hips.

Hips or not, she wriggled into the new clothes and found they fit just right. There was no time to get creeped out about that, so she stepped back into the alley to face the man that knew her pant size better than she did.

"That's better, isn't it?" he said while handing her a pair of slider shoes.

She gave him a brisk smile, taking the sliders and slipping her feet inside them before examining her hands. "Do you happen to have any hand cleaner?" she said, holding her dirty palms up.

When she glanced up, he had already pulled a small packet from his bag, printed with *Sweet Meats Eatery* in bold green letters. "Well, wouldn't you know?" He grinned at her, stretching out the packeted travel wipe from between two fingers.

Cae hesitated before reaching out for the wipe. "Thanks," she said, tearing it open and flapping out the disposable cloth inside. As she twirled the cloth around each finger, she sighed at the distinct hanso smell coming from it. She hated hanso.

The man waited with patient restraint, watching her go through the meticulous wipe of each finger, before adjusting the striped blouse that hugged her curves. Hands now clean and smelling of hanso, she ran them down the sharp fold wrinkles on the blouse.

"So tell me, Ms. Dicus, what brings you here?"

At the mention of her married name, she ran her thumb on the underside of her middle finger where she normally wore Niklaus's ring. It was back at the tents. Curiouser still, this stranger actually knew her married name.

"I'm sorry," she said, peering up at him, "am I supposed to know you?"

He chuckled, and it was charming... nothing off-putting about him at all, despite all the weirdness about him. "Sorry, miss, I lose myself sometimes. My name is Horace Wanner. I teach at the island."

They shook hands, and she withdrew quickly, wringing her hands together. "If you had a set of clothes fitting me exactly, you knew I'd be here. You know my name... Don't you know why I'm here?"

That charming laugh again. He shrugged, keeping a tight grip on his paper bags. "I do, yes. I want you to say it."

"I don't know you," she said with a raised brow.

"I told you who I am." He only smiled at her.

"Are you a Reader or something?" It was the first thing that came to mind, and she regretted saying it out loud. The only Reader in her life was Eloria.

"Oh, sweet woman. I'm much worse than that." The subtle laugh turned sour to her. The man being no longer charming, she was worried. She scanned the alley, frantically hoping for Quill somewhere to help her just in case. They were alone, as if the alley's schedule was cleared out just for them.

"Worse?" she whispered.

Horace ran his fingers through that mop of graying blonde hair. She found it funny that he looked uncomfortable, as if he was the actual uncomfortable one. After a quick pop of his lips, he pushed out a cryptic answer.

"I have, what I would call... a *passenger* of sorts. He tells me things. And I apologize, but for the sake of my well-being in this 'new' world, I can't say any more. But I am happy to say, my condition is under greater control thanks to this..." He lifted his sleeve briefly to show the lower edge of his patch, brushing the fabric back over it with great care.

Cae lifted her hand to her chest, feeling the edge of her patch. "Do you know Verena?"

"Not directly, no, but I do know her husband Jack rather well."

Cae never had the pleasure of meeting the legendary Yeunish formulator. Niklaus told her all about him, though she found his retelling of the man to be an up and down adventure of hate and admiration. That only made her more confused about him.

"So, please, Miss Caella, tell me why you came here." He lowered his arms and peered at her.

She didn't want to say. There was no reasonably explainable good reason. Not only did she wish for death, but if it wouldn't come for her, she was confused, hurt, embarrassed, and not in her right mind... hurt.

"I—I don't know," she said.

He tilted his head and frowned. "Please, for your own sake, you must confront your pain. Tell me why you came."

She wanted to die. "I lost my sister."

"And?"

Let the darkness swallow her. "My *twin* sister."

"And?" Horace nodded at her, and her frustration swelled. If this man knew things, why couldn't he just leave her alone?

"I'm hurt."

"Because...?"

"Because she's gone! I'm hurt because she's gone! She was sucked dry, and I felt every rip and tear—the agony of her death and only wanting it to be real for myself! The worst part? I don't even know if she made it to the Promised Land!"

Horace sighed and clicked his tongue. "You are a wellspring of pain, Ms. Dicus. Your loss is a blade to your belly, I know that."

Crying in front of a stranger wasn't an option, but the tears pushed hard against her eyes. "Yeah, it really freaking sucks," she said.

"And what of the little needles that prick your sides?"

"What's that supposed to mean?" His riddles had confused her on how to feel. Sad, or annoyed?

"You carry the one big hurt so heavily that you forget about those that are still here. Thea, Aedras, Damaetra, your niece and nephew..." He paused, watching her as she felt herself breaking. "...Niklaus."

"I'm ashamed," she mumbled. A tear broke free at last, screaming down her cheek thick and warm, coming to rest under her chin. She brushed it away.

"Yes," he said, placing a hand on her arm.

Her lip quivered as another tear fell.

"My niece is gone too," she mumbled, sniffing back the water in her nose.

"Not so," he said with a smile.

She furrowed her brow. "What makes you say that?"

In a frustrating pass on the answer, he waved it off and lowered his eyes. "There is a malevolent force that oppresses the North." He paused, and Cae narrowed her eyes at him. "That force... is rather strong inside your tent."

A numbing chill began in her bowels, shimmying upward to flush her face. "I'm sorry, what?"

"It seeks to tear your family apart."

"What force are you talking about? I'm so confused!"

"I'm sorry, Ms. Dicus, my passenger is the one who speaks in riddles. I believe in his boredom, he finds it funny to meander. Me? I find it a touch annoying."

Cae sighed, blowing a hank of hair from her eyes.

"He does want me to let you know that Loren needs to look for the stars."

"*Loren*?" She tried not to choke on her spit. "I'm sorry, but your... *passenger* is mistaken. Loren is dead."

Horace hummed. "Not so."

The hairs prickled on her neck, and she regretted leaving her family. "You're kinda blowing my mind right now."

He smiled at her again. It was a warm smile, a feeling she hadn't had in a while. "Would you do me a kindness and let your sister know that the city's order moves for the cause?"

"Another riddle? What do you mean?"

"Don't worry, she should know. At any rate, if it's of any help to you, Ms. Dicus, good things are coming your way. You just need to go back home to your family."

The clarity that came to her when leaving the tent made her wonder if there really was a malevolence that hovered in their space. She frowned. "My husband... I'm so embarrassed the way I left."

"He does miss you terribly, even if he won't let on. Now then, do take care, Ms. Dicus, and be safe. The cities are always watching."

Chapter 24

Homecoming

Eva

The early morning sun began to fill the living room with light, yet Eva had been up for hours, checking and double-checking that she tied up everything.

Dad's house... the one she grew up in... was going to become just a memory. Living alone for the last ten years, she found solace in her annual visits to the desert, but it didn't make leaving her home any easier. She lingered on the carved ivy fireplace, going back to much easier times when she was just a kid, Lor was just a Mesaman brat, and her mother was still there with Dag hanging around like she always did.

Now the house was empty—specters of scuffs in the floors from her childhood remained, with a fresh coat of bland paint covering the subtle grime from repetitive bumps against the walls. The grooves in the kitchen tile were long scrubbed clean of their gentle servant's blood, and the two blasts in the ceiling that Gale had patched years ago left the type of mismatch in colors that one would only find if really staring at it.

She stared at it. Her heart leaped at the idea of her father losing it in this room, and she said a quick prayer of thanks. But she didn't know how to feel, leaving it all behind.

Sighing, she chewed at her cheek. Her dark red hair was tied back into a sloppy knot, and dangling in her hand was one meager bag meant to carry everything to support herself. Her contribution to the machine was already loaded in the cruiser.

The sale of the house was complete, and she had to go.

The walls were empty of holo frames, the cabinets clear, and all the things in Lor's room sold off to strangers. All except the wool blanket she gave him all those years ago, with the silvered filigree. She clutched it in a folded wad at her chest.

It was hard to see random people carry off his things. But he had no use for them in death. Her lip quivered, and she shook it off, grabbing her e-disk and heading to the back.

Parking her cruiser in the rear seemed easier, letting her get in and pull away without the memory of her childhood home getting in the way of their goal. As she opened the back door, a splintering bang ricocheted at the front door.

She leaped out the back passage, pressing her back to the exterior wall, chest heaving. There was a small window in the back door next to her, warped with decorative turns in the glass. Still clear enough to see through, she peeked through one of the bubbles to see a beefy man standing in the front doorway, sniffing around like a feral dog.

Who the hell...?

Another figure stepped inside, creeping next to him. Once the eerie second person had their fill of the empty house, they tapped the big guy on the shoulder. "Looks empty to me," they said. Their voice seeped through the small crack where Eva hadn't fully closed the door.

The big man knelt down, feeling the floor. Then she realized who it was... the man who murdered Dag and almost murdered her dad. The man who sent her brother to his death. She'd seen him once with Eloria on patrol.

She took light steps to the cruiser, hoping not to draw any attention to herself. Sliding inside, she started it up, thankful she had gotten the upgraded model at the time, which had a silent ignition.

The playlist from Nico hummed softly in the cab, and she sped away, watching the house fade in her side mirror.

They were looking for them. They were looking to finish off the rest of the family; she knew it. With Eloria gone, no one had that man in check, and now he had a friend. Maker only knew what the friend's goal was.

She pushed the limit as fast as she could to pick up Emilia and get far away from Peakwood. The playlist rolled over, playing "My Haerow Honey" again. It made her more frantic to get to Nico in the desert.

Thank the Maker Emilia was reliably punctual. She waited in front of her apartment building, demure hands clasped around her lavender and ivory colored bag, pearls shimmering around her long neck.

Eva screeched to the curb, making Emilia jump. Once the door slid to the side, Eva beckoned her inside in frantic waves. Not understanding the fuss, Emilia obeyed and jumped in, cramming her bag on top of her lap.

Eva tore away from the curb, and Emilia jerked back with the force.

"What's wrong? Are you alright?" she asked, squeezing the bag.

"You tied up all your loose ends, right? Filed the final papers at Ascendia?

Sold off most of your stuff? Paid the rest of your lease?"

"Yes, of course I took care of all those things. What's going on?" Emilia panted frantically.

"I think the family is in trouble," Eva said while swerving to dodge a slow jumper cab.

"In trouble how?"

"Remember how my brother was banished and my dad almost died? And Dag...?"

"Yes, yes, I remember." Emilia's dark eyes widened.

Eva swerved again, eager to get out of the cities. She drove the accelerator lever forward a touch, knowing she was being erratic. Emilia squeezed her eyes shut and pressed her lips in a thin line.

"Sorry, we just have to get out of here."

"Don't let a roundsman catch us," Emilia said, prying her eyes open again.

"You're right, I'm sorry." Eva pulled the lever back, slowing down behind an old model cruiser on its last gear.

"Just breathe and tell me what happened."

"Right... right," Eva said with a sigh. "Well, the man responsible for all of those things I mentioned broke into the house as I was leaving. I think he was looking for someone."

"He broke in? Who could he be possibly looking for?" Emilia cocked her eyebrow. "I mean, Loren is gone, he thinks Gale is dead, and Nico and Dilly never lived there..."

"Oh Maker," Eva breathed out, "he's trying to track Dame."

Emilia sucked in a breath.

"He finds Dame, he finds them all." Eva swerved around the old cruiser.

"How much time do you think we have?"

Eva chewed a lip, studying the road. "Hard to say. Eloria was pushing him for so long, it might take a while. At least, I hope it takes a while. I need to warn them."

As she moved to crank the lever forward again, they came up on a set of station tracks with the safety barricades descending around them.

"Shit," Eva uttered, bringing the cruiser to a halt. Emilia put a hand to her chest, taking heavy breaths.

"I'm sorry, Emilia, please take some deep breaths. We're going to be fine. We'll be fine..." Her last word faded with the train whipping by in a loud honk. Despite telling her friend this, she needed to take her own advice.

She closed her eyes as they waited for the train to pass. The rhythmic bumping of the magnets eased her mind as her engineering brain focused on the off-kilter hum of it.

Someone should fix that...

The sound faded, and she opened her eyes to the safety rail reopening. She would take it easy driving through the cities for now. But the moment her wheels hit the sand, that lever would be pushed to the max.

Chapter 25

Escape From Secas

Horace was right. Cae bit at the skin around her nail and stared at the bright orange visitor center where she had to get a jumper back home. Plus, living like Quill wasn't anything like she expected. It was a lot dirtier for one, and scarier.

So, she said goodbye to him and told him she'd return to bring him a patch of his own, but only if she could. And Horace? She hoped he would be all right, and she prayed the cities didn't find out about his "passenger." When she got home, she'd have to ask anyone if they knew what that meant.

The visitor center hadn't opened yet, cutting back their hours by enough that first sun had already risen. Everyone was squeezing their wallets as the city demanded more tithes, even buildings owned by the cities.

She clicked her tongue and shook her head as she thought about it, feeling the fresh anger for Eloria all over again.

As she stood there, glaring at the closed building, a cool breeze brushed behind her. Every time she felt the wind like that, she imagined it was Niklaus running by. She hadn't been away too long, but the embarrassment was still a little raw, and her temples flushed at the thought. She barely remembered anything good about that night. If there was a malevolence like Horace said, she felt sick thinking that it had a grip on her. *Look for the stars...*

After a moment, the assistant passed through the door, performing her series of unlocks to allow the public entry. About time.

Cae strolled to the entrance and went inside. It stank like dust and mildew. The assistant was still arranging brochures in the display when she turned and saw her.

"Good colorful morning, ma'am. What can I do for you?" she asked. Cae could tell she didn't mean it.

"Uh, yes, um, I need to order a jumper cab."

"Certainly! May I see your identification?"

The small strap-bag she brought with her was only roomy enough for the essentials, including her ID. She handed it to the assistant. With a click of the tongue and a few taps into the system, she sighed.

"Oh, you're not a resident of Secas or Heart Island," she said, continuing to type away.

"Ah, no, I'm not," Cae replied, raising her eyebrow.

"I see, well, I just need to verify Guild affiliation. New policy, you see."

The woman pulled out a device that looked like a regular ID lock but more involved. Cae backed up, staring at the thing like a predator.

"What do you mean, Guild affiliation? I'm in the Arts."

"Yes, ma'am, I understand. After the attempt on the princeps's life, we have to check for any hidden Guild talents for non-residents."

Cae curled her fingers inward, putting her fist by her side. The assistant gave her an expectant look, jiggling the device to get her to put her hand in it.

Attempt on the princeps's life... yeah right. No doubt the lie about her sister spread like crazy. Bastard. Cae started to sweat. As the woman held out the device, her arm went a little slack, and she glanced behind her to the pair of roundsmen standing nearby. They stepped forward a foot, and Cae ran out the front door.

"Stop!" one of them shouted behind her, but she couldn't. She wouldn't.

The hot air squeezed her lungs, and all the colors of Secas flashed by her in a blur. It was still early, so not many people were out, but those that were gaped at her running by.

What was she going to do? Run back to the tents? She didn't think this one through very well. The market was nearby, so she ran for it.

The sound of their footsteps ground against the cobblestones behind her, but she dared not pause for even a standard second to see how close they were. She had to trust she made some distance.

The market opened up to her, and there were more people there than near the ferry. Good. She could hide somehow.

She cursed herself for leaving the tents, pondering over what malevolence convinced her to leave her family. Now, she was cooked. An older woman cried out when she ran past, nearly smacking into her.

"'Scuse me," she mumbled. That time, she turned her head slightly, enough to see the roundsmen were only just entering the market.

Good, but not gone.

Her thighs burned. All she wanted to do was transform and duck into a tight hiding spot.

If she changed, she'd lose her clothes.

Damn.

She couldn't run forever... she couldn't even run much longer. This was the end. It was gaol for her. How she wished she hadn't left Niklaus the way she had.

Good things coming my ass!

The open market gathered more crowds of morose people going about their daily drudgery, occasionally letting out a *woop!* as Cae weaved through them. The dodging slowed her down, and she could feel the roundsmen gaining on her.

When passing by a breakfast cafe, she impulsively popped a tray of full soup bowls up into the air when she slapped the bottom of it.

"Sorry!" she shouted to the waitress and patrons now covered in brown broth. The roundsman had only paused to shake off the salty liquid, continuing to chase after her. She'd just pissed off a bunch of strangers for nothing.

But she created some distance. Distance enough to pass through the small space between the last two shops in the market, leading to her alley. But not before accidentally shouldering the nearby patron, who shouted "*Hey!*" as she bolted by. Or did they shout... Cae? Too much wind in her ears to tell, but the only person that knew her in this place was Quill. The way that guy lounged around all day in cat form licking his balls, there was no way it was him.

There was nothing behind the shops to help her. She stopped for a moment to think. There was a wide opening in front of her she could run through quickly to get to the Chroma Night Inn. But it was long and risky.

She should have known, since this was the exact alley she met Horace in the day before and spent the last standard week frequenting. In a panic, she glanced around, trying to find ways to escape the roundsmen she knew were making their way to her location. She could transform and hide, but it made her small and vulnerable... and naked.

"Hey, you!" A third roundsman spotted her from the industrial opening, and she was glad she hadn't gone that way. But now she was trapped. She slumped her shoulders and closed her eyes, waiting for the slap of cold irons around the wrists.

The last thing she imagined was the disappointment of her husband's face when he read her letter, and her heart sank for it.

As she waited for the bulky roundsman to catch up to her, she swore she heard her name.

"Kitts!"

There was only one person in all of Roseaarde that called her that.

She opened her eyes and turned to see the shadow of her husband come out from between the eneris emporium and meat shop.

"Nick!" she called back.

It didn't take much for him to understand what it meant to see a member of Law jogging toward her, being a career criminal and all. Across his shoulders, he tugged at a decent-sized tote, which he pulled open and tilted her way.

As soon as the advancing roundsman saw Niklaus open his bag, he picked up speed, flicking open a set of chains, ready to make his arrest.

In a white blur, Cae shed her clothes and leaped into the bag before he bolted past the roundsman, through the Chroma Night alley, and toward home.

"Whoa, *whoa*!" Dill shouted at the burst of wind energy that blew his leaves of notes from the bunker workbench. "Niklaus, I *swear*!"

He began plucking the notes from the floor when Nico entered from his partition. "What was *that*?" he asked.

Dill opened his mouth to tattle, but he was interrupted by the muffled groans of Niklaus and Caella from their bunker. He grinned at Nico's increasing disgust. "Sounds like Niki's laying some pipe."

"Oh *God*!" Nico fled from Dill's bunker and up the ladder.

Dill hummed as he meticulously straightened his notes, slowly making sure each piece was in perfect order, and tapping them on his small workbench to the beats from next door.

"I'm glad I found you," Niklaus said with a sigh. One arm he tilted behind his head while the other held his wife against his bare chest.

She hummed, her arm across his stomach.

He ran his hand along her back, and tight bumps on her skin rose to meet his fingertips. She was warm, and her heart beat slowly against him. "Why did you run from me?" he whispered.

"I don't know," she whispered. "I was upset... Maybe a little embarrassed... And I wanted to die."

"Don't say that. Don't ever say that." He squeezed her closer, and she let him.

"Losing her was like... losing a part of myself, you know? And I was full of so much *rage*." Her finger traced the small raised freckle he had between two ribs.

"Yeah..." He gazed off into the darkness of the room, trying not to think about his childhood disconnect from his own twin. Guilt had never left him, even after the shallow reconciliation he had with Nico. It came to him in waves... depressing bouts that gave him cold sweats. This was one of those moments, raising bumps of his own over his arms.

He needed a distraction from his intrusive thoughts, knowing it would bring him closer to the suggestions of the worm. "Tell me about your time in Secas."

With a yawn, she smacked her mouth. "I'll tell you after a nap."

The thorn was there, festering in his side. Caella's grief reminded him of it, and he needed to excise it if he was ever going to rid himself of vulnerability. Draping on the best shirt and pair of shorts that he had, he left his napping wife in their room while he went into Nico's bunker.

His brother wasn't there, but the sounds of tools clinking and grinding came from the main tent. Niklaus climbed the ladder and poked his head through the hatch to see Nico's back to him, using a spanner on his knee joint. When he turned for the screwdriver, he caught sight of Niki watching him from the floor.

Nico tittered and grabbed the screwdriver. "Get it all out of your system?"

Niki didn't answer, observing the black metal posts that served as Nico's legs. They'd been fixed and patched again and again over the years, with additional modifications to repel grains from crushing between sensitive parts. A vertical slash in his shin rod had crusted over with a thin layer of red-brown rust.

With his back still turned, Nico continued to work on whatever new issue he had with his right leg.

"I'm sorry," Niki mumbled from the hatch.

"What?" Nico turned, still wearing the face of concentration as he continued spinning the screwdriver with some effort.

Niklaus rose from the hole and moved toward his brother while he kept spinning that screwdriver. As he got closer, Nico stood to face him and set the tool down.

The small smile he gave showed his frustration with the repair task. "Legs are getting rusty," he said. "We don't have the extra plat for Dill to make new ones—"

"I'm so sorry!" Niklaus fell into Nico, holding on to him, awkward, and not really knowing how to hug his own twin. He wrenched his hands on Nico's shirt, twisting it while sobbing into his shoulder.

As he held on, Nico stiffened, patting him on the back in a hesitant staccato. Then he felt the warmth of arms around him. "I'm sorry, I'm sorry," he repeated.

Nico held a little tighter when Niklaus thought he might collapse. "Please forgive me..." he moaned.

"What did you do this time?" Nico said with a chuckle. When Niklaus answered with a longer series of heavy sobs, Nico pulled back to look at him.

"It's been more than ten standard, Niki," he said.

"I know, it's just..." He paused, taking a step back, smearing his eye across his sleeve. "Something bothered me this whole time. A little here, a little there... and I realized, after Kitts lost her sister, that thing that always bugged me just under my skin was that I never asked you to forgive me. To *really* forgive me."

He drew back in again, clutching on to Nico and remembering the feeling of being trapped in a stunted thirteen-year-old mindset, desperate for approval from whatever kind of support figure he found in Paerli. All the times he stalked Nico, wished he could be him—the jealousy and anger—he felt guilty for it.

"You're my brother," Nico said, "how could I not forgive you when you grovel?" He chuckled a little, holding on to Niklaus. They stood there together for a time, while Niklaus took longer, calmer breaths.

"I'm glad you found her," Nico said.

Niki's intrusive hiccups simmered to throat bobs and a deep inhale before he broke away from the embrace and smiled.

"Aw, it's just so adorable!" Dill came up from the hatch and walked toward them, moving a glossy black sphere around in his hand.

"Shut up, Dill. What's that?" Nico pointed at the ball as Niklaus pressed his palms against his eyes to drag away the wetness.

"Oh, this? It's only the perfect fix for your right leg's ball joint." He held the piece out to Nico. As he was about to take it, Damaetra called to them from outside.

Chapter 26

Reunion

"Is this real? I'm not dreaming, right?" Damaetra asked as Nico and Dill joined her outside in the heat.

They glanced toward what she had been looking at, and a figure stood in the distance, a few paces from an old sand skip. The figure stared at them, hazy shadows behind drifting sand.

"Momma!" Cimma burst through the haze and clutched at her hand.

Stunned, Damaetra felt woozy. She wanted to cry, but her mouth remained parted, eyes roving over the scene with Cimma clinging to her. The pains of her illness shot electricity through her veins, and she stood there, holding her lost daughter with her still-open lips drying under the sun.

A small tug came at her hand from Cimma, and when she glanced at her, she grinned with pride. "I told you. I told you, and I told Papa and Nate."

Shifting her gaze forward again, she whispered to herself, "Is this real?"

The figure from the sand skip emerged… tall and muscular. A shade that she knew but didn't quite recognize. A more confident gait, not tripping over loose rocks or tech. She spun the ancient tech ring on her finger with her thumb—the one she remembered accepting in her youth from a man on his knees.

That same man, now collapsed at her feet and holding her ankles, called her name over and over again.

She fainted.

***

Her hair had gotten long again, the way he remembered. He took a coil of it around his hand as her head rested in his lap. Small lines etched on her forehead with age, yet she was still beautiful, smelling of violets.

"Is she alright?" Dill asked, kneeling down.

Old friend... darker, thinner. He'd ditched the engineered visor for tech eyes almost unrecognizable from the real thing if it weren't for the adjusting irises. The slashing scar that took them was nothing but a thin pale line.

"She's passed out," Lor said. He reached out and touched Dill's arm.

"Look at you, old man." Dill smirked, grabbing Lor's bicep. "Did you grow the one muscle that matters too?"

Same Dill. Lor couldn't help but laugh. Over by their tent, his daughter held on to Nico as he rocked her back and forth in his arms. He uttered "*I'm sorry*" over and over.

A woman emerged from the same tent, running toward the sand skip, calling out for Jack. On her heels was a young woman sobbing as she ran. Lor smiled as he watched them, knowing they belonged to Jack.

Turning back to Dill, Lor furrowed his brow. "Where's my son?" he asked.

"He's with his friends a few tents over, probably didn't even hear you coming."

Lor's smile trembled. "I have a lot to catch up on."

When Dill pressed his forehead against Lor's, the tears bit his eyes. "We'd given up on ever getting you back." Dill paused. "Which means we'd better get you inside before anyone snatches you away from us again."

"Good idea." Lor stood back up and scooped Damaetra up in his arms to carry her inside.

The tent his friends stayed in was thick and resilient, surrounded by traps. Lor never visited the tents at Kanckette, but seeing it now reminded him of the community he felt in the South.

The inside of the tent filled quickly with family. But he noticed, as he lay his wife down on a padded seater, a familiar face sitting at the table.

"H-hey," he said, giving Lor a meek half wave.

"Hey?" Lor glanced over at Nico, who came at him with arms open and tilted, ready to swallow him whole.

"I'm going to do my manliest attempt at not crying right now," Nico said, voice warbling and arms squeezing.

Lor squeezed his friend back, feeling how slender he'd become in the desert wasteland. "You've reconciled with your brother," he said.

Nico tittered and squeezed harder. "He's been invaluable to our efforts."

"Aw, that's the nicest thing you've said about me," his twin said from the table.

"Hey, that's not true," Nico said with a laugh, pulling away from Lor but keeping a hand on his shoulder. "I once told you what a great wife you caught in Caella."

"Wait, you married Cae?" Lor raised his eyebrows.

"That means you and *Niklaus* are in-laws," Dill said, strolling up to them and slapping Lor on the shoulder. Niklaus shrugged with a smirk.

"I'm going to need *that* story later," Lor said while chuckling.

The tent flap swung open, and an Anglia boy stood there, stiff and breathing jets from flared nostrils. The paper white skin of his mother flushed red, with wild, white-gold hair spun in suspended animation at his crown. Cimma stood behind him, wrapping her arms around his neck.

"Daddy, this is Nate," she said.

Nate's lower lip trembled, eyes locked on his father. Lor wanted to sweep him up and hold him, but when he stood, Nate took a small step back, tilting his head and absorbing the stranger before him that gave him the structure of his face.

"Are you really my dad?" Nate squeaked.

Lor got to his knees and held his arms out, waiting for his son to approach on his own. Cimma gave him a nudge.

"I am," Lor said as he closed his eyes.

When he expected blackness behind his lids, the clear scene that remained perplexed everything he knew. Clear enough to watch as his son hesitantly came to him among the swirling smoke of murmuring colors. So tempted was he to open his eyes, but watching his children wrapped in bright colors of tent conversation served him something magical.

Nate made it to him at last, falling into Lor's embrace and smelling like his mother. Purple gusts billowed from his son as he whimpered in his arms.

Nate pulled back, chin wrinkled as Lor remembered the day he was born right before he made his first cries. "You're tall. Am I going to be tall too?"

With a chuckle, Lor opened his eyes. All color vanished, leaving behind his son, plain-clothed and waiting, blue eyes damp. "Maker willing."

Lor drew him in for another embrace, feeling the cool shadow of another person standing behind him. All his senses had overwhelmed him, and he needed that little extra moment with his son before turning to see who else would greet him that day. But he didn't have to move—when a pair of arms surrounded him and his son, they were shrouded in a scent he never thought he'd get the chance to experience again. He fought the urge to pass out. Sheer shock punched him in the side, and all those years of grief felt like wasted stress and he hated the cities for it, for harboring The Hammer.

"I thought you were dead..." Lor's voice cracked through barely a whisper.

"I thought *you* were dead," Gale said back.

"Papa, my face is in your pit," Nate muffled.

They had a good laugh at Nate's expense, finally able to pull a smile from the boy. Through Gale's open smile, Lor noticed the few missing teeth that had been rudely knocked from his face and his city-based hatred boiled a little hotter. Otherwise, his stepdad showed no signs of that near-death experience.

Their mirth was cut short when Jack came through the opening with his wife and daughter by his sides.

"What happened to Damaetra?" Jack asked, pointing at her lounging on the sofa. When everyone turned to look, Jack's wife had already knelt at her side, fanning her with a weathered piece of paper.

Lor rubbed his face, standing with his arm around his son. "She fainted," he said.

Jack raised his eyebrow. "Well, is she alright?"

His wife stood and clucked at him. "She's fine, Jack. I'm going to get a cool towel for her forehead. I'm Verena, by the way," she said, trotting toward Lor with a hand out.

He shook it briefly, trying not to squeeze too hard, but the roughness of her hand surprised him. Dark circles swelled under her hazel eyes, still red and damp. "It's great to finally meet the woman who was able to break into this guy's hard shell." Lor chuckled with a thumb jabbing toward Jack.

She laughed at Jack's scowl, thin lines spreading from the corners of her eyes. Lor couldn't help but notice how different she was from Jack—full of expression, curvy with tanned skin, and long copper-brown hair. Their daughter was much the same, with less lines and a heartier laugh.

As Verena descended into a hatch in the ground, Nico leaned into Gale, whispering something Lor couldn't catch before coming back in for another tight hug.

"I can't tell you what it means to me to see you here with us again," Nico said, then tilted his head in a backwards nod at Damaetra. "Spend time with your wife, dad, and children... When you're done, it's my turn." He smiled, pushing his knuckles into Lor's shoulder for a light shove before following Verena through the floor hatch.

Besides Verena, Nico was the only one to leave the room, which was a little confusing in the moment, but Lor knew there would be time yet.

Gale cleared his throat. "We've been working on a plan to take back the tree," he said, nodding toward the hatch. "Nico's been feeling behind on his part, so he probably wants to work on a few things so he can focus on you."

Before Lor could say anything, Verena came back with a damp towel. "When Dame wakes up, she can show you our project," she said as she knelt down to start patting Damaetra's forehead.

Damaetra stirred, but her eyes remained closed.

Then, a different white-gold head poked up from the floor. "It's true... you *are* here!" Cae had filled out since he last saw her, keeping the short, boyish haircut he remembered from so long ago.

When she drew in for a hug, her eyes seemed tired, as if just waking up for the day. "I didn't believe it when he told me, but you really are alive!"

Lor sniggered and pulled back to look at her. "Who told you what?"

"It was a man in Secas, he told me that you were alive and that you need to look for the stars."

"Look for the stars? What in Gehenna does that mean?"

She shrugged. "I don't know. He said his passenger talks in riddles."

"Horace!" Lor blurted. "You talked to Horace..."

Gale frowned when Cae mentioned the "passenger," and Lor knew it was for his old friend, Greg, still chained to a living person. Gale opened his mouth to say something when a North-wide alert chirped from his e-disk.

When he swiped up to take a look, the rotating images of two criminals hovered there—Niklaus and Cae—wanted by Secas.

"Son of a..." Niklaus hissed. "Do I really look like that?"

Gale rubbed his face pink like he always had, blowing out a stream of air. "This is really bad," he said. "Our way of life is shrinking every day."

Chapter 27

Jack and Verena

It had only been a few days since Jack had arrived back in the North, and he almost forgot the South entirely. He followed Verena into the network of bunkers they'd carved out while he was gone, marveling at the change. A noise escaped him as they moved through their piece of the hive-like home, which happened to be the largest of the bunkers. According to Verena, it had been expanded for Damaetra and the children.

They even dug out small, private spaces for the buckets.

Verena led him to the far corner, tying a piece of red fabric on the hook at the entrance of their modest water closet. After passing through two short turns and a long piece of privacy cloth, they made it inside, where the squat bath basin hid. It was the same basin he remembered, already full of fresh water.

"We only have to reuse the water three times now before recycling," Verena said, while running her fingers through the clear and clean liquid. She gave him a playful wet flick over his neck. The droplets were cool on his warmed skin, and he smiled at her. The music of the rippling water triggered a quiet thirst in his throat, made louder by Verena undressing herself to climb inside of it.

"Not seven anymore?"

She smirked at him, draping her dress over a crude peg stabbed in the wall. As she strolled to the basin, he watched her move, forgetting his question. It had been too long. The water rose to her neck when she descended inside.

"Not anymore. It's been great working with Dill, Eva, and Emilia on the aquifer project. It's a smaller one, but enough to keep a somewhat steady supply of water for the tank."

Jack found the single stool in the room and moved it near her head to sit, holding an old mug they used for rinsing. The blue and yellow Audun logo had faded from the side over the years, leaving only the dull, mug-colored imprint behind. "You've been doing a lot here."

He filled the mug, letting the water pour from it over her sand-dusted hair. Yellow trails wiggled down her strands, revealing the coppery silk underneath.

"Everyone has been working so hard," Verena said with a sigh, lifting her hand from the water and watching it drip from her fingers. "My joints have been really achy lately."

Jack grunted, spotting a phial of washing soap resting on the floor in the corner.

"Oh, could you get that for me?" She nodded toward the phial.

He got up and in two steps snatched it from the corner, popping the top and dribbling out some soap into his palm. The scent of hanso fruit filled the room when Jack combed his soapy fingers over her scalp.

"Where did you get this soap? It's very strong." Jack wrinkled his nose.

Verena tittered and smiled. "Niki was running errands for us and picked that up thinking it was fancy." She paused with a frown. "I guess he can't really do that anymore."

The new wanted notice seemed to throw their routine into chaos, with no one eligible to run their errands the way they needed anymore. The plan she shared with Jack earlier gave him some hope they'd find a way to end whatever force was oppressing the North. If anything, they could at least heal the tree and live inside it, away from Audun politics.

Closing her eyes, she sighed. "I've missed you terribly... and Ayala was a wreck for the longest time."

He massaged her temples with the soap. "I won't ever let them rip us apart again."

Contentment spread across her face as she relished his resolve along with the tender hair care. After a time, she dunked her head to wash out the soap and emerged with water clinging to her eyelashes.

Jack tugged at his collar, leaving drips of foamy water along the fabric as he began to unbutton it. "Who gets the bathwater next?"

"Hm, probably Niki. Why?" she asked.

Jack smirked, pulling off his shirt and letting his pants fall to the floor. After years in exile, he'd gotten used to not wearing underwear. He stood before her in the low light. Where once sinewy tendons held on to slight bones, he'd become solid muscle. Verena gaped at his slender frame, cut with the labors of the South. Then she giggled as he crawled into the water with her.

Chapter 28

Bunker Stuff

In the darkness of the sub-bunker, the cockpit opened up to Damaetra and Loren. Once she woke up again, the news hit that she was volunteered to explain the project. But she was happy to have some time alone with Loren. No better time than now to get him caught up on their work in the desert, seeing as how her sister and brother-in-law were now criminals to the cities, and their window to take action was closing. Loren hopped down into the cockpit behind her, remarking at how nice and cool it felt.

"This is the driver's seat," she said, running her hand across the back of the motley chair, pieced together with random bits of fabric Niklaus had found here and there in Secas.

"And these controls... they're meant to activate with this." She held her hands together at her chest, using one hand to slowly rotate the ancient tech ring around her finger on the other hand. "Dill's work. It's ingenious really. But don't tell him I said that," she said with a smirk.

He stepped closer to her, and she could smell his familiar aroma that she missed so much. His ash blond hair had gotten shaggy, cut in jagged edges with some primitive tool. She'd give him a haircut. A fresh nick at his neck told her he had recently shaved. He never wore a beard before, and she wondered what he'd look like with one.

His fingers brushed at her hip, and it tickled a little. She giggled at his touch, staring into his gray eyes. Turning toward the panel, she pointed at the slot where the ring went.

"Sliding it in here will power it on, like an ID lock, or a key. Then these levers here will be how we drive it to Gehenna."

"And then what?" he whispered at her neck, his breath warm and his hardened body pressed against her back.

She grinned at the panel, losing herself in proper affections she hadn't felt in years. She wasn't even sure how to act. "These buttons and levers each do something different... See, this one here is the pulse ram Emilia designed so we can get through the gate," she said with a hand wrapped around a hefty-looking lever. Then she moved her fingertip to a green square button near the top. "This button will release the scaffold to protect the tree. It's full of formulations that I made to help heal it. That's all of these buttons."

She closed her eyes at the tingle of his lips brushing against the back of her ear. "What are these ones here?" he asked, running his hand up her belly before briefly motioning to a row of buttons near the bottom.

"Those are for the aerosolizer at the back of the vehicle," she whispered when his mouth pressed against her neck.

"You've thought of everything," he said, letting his fingers walk along her nape, gathering her hair and twirling it to one side.

The bite of the cockpit's chill softened, and her heart beat a little faster. She fell silent, allowing herself to enjoy his touch, his kisses on her neck...

"Momma, is Daddy down there with you?" Cimma's voice cut through the air, and they both jumped and spun toward the hatch. Their daughter's little yellow eye peered through the crack.

"I told you to let them have some privacy, you little stinker!" Gale scolded her from the main level.

"Sorry, Papa! Sorry, Momma and Daddy!" Her giggles faded when she let the hatch drop.

Damaetra blew out a harried breath, chuckling as she turned toward Loren. He was so different, but so much the same. It felt like a dream. But dreams fade, and she felt the guilt of holding back her illness from him. That was a confession for another day. Today, she wanted to finish what he started.

Damaetra opened her eyes. How long had they slept?

She rose up on an elbow, trying to find shapes in the dark. It was cold again, her sweat dry and salted over. Rubbing a hip, she rotated it slightly, hoping she didn't overextend herself.

While she massaged her hip joint, Loren's hand slid over hers. "What time is it?" he mumbled.

"I don't know," she said. She leaned over him, not letting the darkness keep her from finding his mouth with hers. He reacted with a squeeze on her hip. It felt nice but dangerously close to painful.

Forget it, what was a few more minutes?

"Dilly! Dilly, we're here!" Emilia's singsong voice called from outside. The sound of doors squeezing shut followed, with the distinct crunch of footsteps dragging through the sand.

Dill turned back toward Ayala and Niklaus with the corner of his bottom lip between his teeth. "Guess it's *my* turn to lay some pipe," he said, wagging his eyebrows.

Ayala giggled as Niklaus wrinkled his entire face inward.

Dill leaped from his seat and bolted from the tent. "My darling queen! Come to Daddy!" His grand shouts caused Niklaus to curl a lip and roll his eyes.

Dry air blew into the tent as the clean and pressed Emilia ducked inside, giggling on Dill's arm.

Eva followed close behind with everything she owned in her fists, looking around. "Where's Nico?" she asked.

"Oh, he's in the bunker working on a few formulations," Ayala said, standing to give her a hug. "He's going to be so happy to see you! And you'll never guess who else showed up..."

Eva pulled back, gazing at her young friend and catching a glimpse of Niklaus grimacing and repeatedly poking a finger through his other fist. Ayala stuttered a change in subject.

"A-ah, but first, go see Nico. He seems like he's down in the dumps."

Eva hummed. "Really? That's unusual for him."

"Maybe I'm wrong, but he's been so focused on trying to fix things around here, make better formulas... I don't know."

Eva glanced at Niklaus, who shrugged.

"Alright, I'll go find him," she said, dropping her bags to the floor. "But this new person you won't tell me about had better be someone special!" She chuckled before descending the ladder to the network of bunkers.

Since she had entered Niklaus's tent, Nico's bunker would be just a passage away. It was the tattered, ivory-colored strip of cloth that separated the brothers, and it made no sound as she slid it to the side.

Nico sat hunched over his small table with his back to her, piddling with a handful of phials and shaking a leg. It squeaked with every jitter, but he didn't seem to care.

She slid silently toward him, running a hand up his back. It made him jump, nearly spilling the crucible of heated solution inside.

"Oh shit, Eva! You scared the crap out of me," he said, standing to fold his arms around her. "You're here for good now, right?"

"That's right," she said into his chest.

He kissed the top of her head and broke away, sitting back at the table to fuss with his experiment. She'd be lying to herself if that didn't feel somewhat dismissive.

"Babe, I have to tell you something," she said, taking the seat across from him. He glanced up at her, one corner of his mouth tucked in and showing off a dimple.

"As I was closing up the house, a man broke in."

The news arrested his attention. "Broke in? Who?"

"It was that guy... the one who killed Dag."

"Oh Maker, that's right... He's not being controlled anymore."

"No. And he had someone with him."

The crucible bubbled, and Nico paused to stir. "Who was with him?" The stirring rod clinked against the sides of the vessel.

"I don't know, but he really creeped me out."

Nico cursed under his breath, and the stirring became vigorous. "Our plans just got way more complicated," he said through his teeth.

Eva nodded, eyeing the crucible as the bubbles intensified under his whisking.

"As if I wasn't already pressed for time... my legs are rusting, the machine's not ready, and I can't get this stupid formulation right!" Just as he said it, the formulation burst from the crucible.

Eva threw herself backwards, falling to the floor in her chair. When she picked herself up, Nico sat there, stirring hand frozen over the vessel and face coated in light blue slime. He sighed, sliding his other hand over an eye to free it from the goop.

"I'm sorry, babe," he said, "I'm a little stressed out."

"I see that," she said, giving him a demure grin.

He set the stirring rod down and cleared his eyes and mouth. The failed formula slapped onto the sandy floor when he shook out his hands. "We're just going to have to work faster, I guess," he said with a sigh.

"Don't worry, if he finds us, we'll just get rid of him," she said, moving behind him to wrap her arms around his shoulders. The sentiment was easy enough, but she knew it was not so easy to get rid of a strongman. She pressed her nose and mouth into Nico's hair, letting the curls tickle her lip.

He turned suddenly to face her, and she broke free. "I bet no one told you," he said, widening his smile.

She raised her brow. "Told me what?"

"Lor came back!"

Eva bit back a frown. "That's not funny, Nico."

"No joke, he just showed up yesterday. I mean, he's been with Dame all day, but he'll come out soon, I'm sure."

Without another word, she fumbled through Niklaus's bunker, then through the green fabric flap between his and Verena's spaces. The room was empty, but she heard chatter upstairs.

Once she made it to the top, he was there, having an animated conversation with Dill and Emilia. He had his back turned and didn't notice her. That was, until she ran to him, putting him in a headlock and grinding her knuckle into his head.

"Ow, hey! Stop doing the thing!" he said, turning red.

Then she squeezed him, kissing his head where she knuckled it over and over and over. "I can't believe you're alive," she cried out, squeezing him harder.

"I still can't believe I'm here," Lor said, clinging to her. "I keep expecting to wake up and find myself back in the bog. I'm awake, aren't I?"

Eva took in a breath and laughed. On the inside, he was the same brother she remembered growing up with. He smelled like the beaches of West Cordan and nostalgic memories of family vacations during simpler times.

She sighed. "I sold all your stuff."

Lor chuckled. "Even my blanket?"

"Everything but your blanket."

Everyone turned when Nico clopped up from the lower levels. His pupils were wide, and remnants of the glossy blue formulation were smeared into his hairline. "Hey," he muttered, "I don't feel so great."

He tottered on his feet before falling to his knees, then flopped face first into the sand.

Eva cried out and ran to him.

Chapter 29

Mister Shadow

Loren

Everyone shuttled Nico to the sofa as Eva brought the formula mishap upstairs to Jack. "Interesting to meet you like this," she muttered, placing the crucible in his hand. Jack tittered and studied the remnants of the blue gel inside.

Every sound coming from Nico as he lay there, completely knocked out, was either a whimper or half scream.

"I thought you all were supposed to be immune to poisons and stuff," Eva said as she sat, cradling his head in her lap.

"Only when we take them by mouth," Jack said, pointing at the residue on Nico's face. He jabbed his little finger into the blobby formulation. He touched it to his tongue and smirked. "He'll be fine. He's just being a sissy. It's only a mild muscle relaxant."

"So... why is he screaming then?" Dill asked.

Jack shrugged. "Beats me. Maybe he has some unresolved stress or something." He eyed what was left inside the vessel. "I'm going to take this."

Before Eva could protest, Jack disappeared with the crucible back underground.

"I'll stay with him until he wakes up," Eva said as her hands moved through his hair.

"I'll monitor him," Gale offered.

"Yeah, alright," Dill said as he glanced at Lor. "Well, it's technically our turn for watch duty. Wanna come?"

Lor shrugged. "Sure, why not."

The day was clear, a rare one according to Damaetra. Lor wandered to the first wall of dunes separating them from the wilderness of the Span, hiding his face under spare goggles, dust collar, and hood. The sweat already bubbled and dried at the goggle seams, rubbing raw against his skin. The old utility belt he got as a gift from Krik'tha back when he was at Guild Central squeezed his waist, and it was stocked with a few non-lethal phials. Even the shooter he remembered hung there, loaded with fresh needles full of Ivory Saltpeter. He hoped Krik'tha was well.

"Use them sparingly," Dill warned. "We don't have the same access to the good stuff that we used to."

"I still can't believe you held on to these," Lor said as he adjusted the tight strap.

Dill chortled. "Waste not, I say. You stay here." He pointed to the ground and motioned toward one of the tent residents, Quint, and then to Niklaus. "Let's roll."

They separated down the line of dunes for a wider approach, and he watched them go. This was what life was like for his family in the desert, and it was their section of the row's turn for surveillance duty. Dangerous creeps from what they called the "death camps" could wander their way, putting the entirety of the Kanckette tents at risk. At least, that was what his wife told him. She protested against him volunteering, but he insisted, considering Nico's condition.

Once their shapes became nothing but silhouettes dotted along the dunes, Lor turned forward to face a man standing just in front of him.

"Oh hell—" he sputtered, jerking his hand over the shooter strapped to his side. The ancient stood there, not a day older than the day of Lor's wedding. Yet, his tattered clothes billowed over bony arms and legs.

"I've been hearing this word often. What is it?" Maron asked. Black hair flapped around his pale face, and his yellow eyes peered through it. Apparently Par wasn't much help in keeping his hair trimmed.

"Never mind that, what are you doing here?"

Maron narrowed his eyes. "I came to find you, of course. I felt your presence return."

Stone-faced and as intimidating as ever, his voice came out in a core-shaking pitch.

"You felt my presence? What, you couldn't feel it when I was banished?"

"No. You were under the effects of a Yeunish drug for a long time. I wanted to come sooner, but I thought it wise to wait until you completed your reunions."

Lor cracked a smile. "Your Northern Common has gotten better."

"It is so."

The stoic ancient stood in silence, staring at Lor, as if waiting for him to instigate further conversation. The truth was, Lor didn't know where to start. So, he eyed Maron incredulously, lingering longer than he intended. "How did you get here anyway? Last I knew, you didn't have a jumper, cruiser, or skip. No way did you walk..."

He grinned, and it was weird. "What makes you think I am *here*?"

Lor squinted. It *was* unusual to see him here. As an ancient, he probably had some stupid powerful way to use their connection, and he was just a projection in his mind. Lor reached out and pushed a finger into Maron's shoulder. While his body was tangibly solid, he barely moved.

Maron tittered at the gesture, shaking his head. "Anyway," he said with a sigh, "now that you are no longer under the drug's spell, it is easier to sense you, so here I am."

"Alright, so what do you need?"

"I need you to help us rid ourselves of the zlae'duch Cirv'e."

"Us?"

Maron squinted. "My wife and myself."

"Great." Lor sighed. That was a wound he wasn't ready to open. "Tell me something, then. How did my daughter reach me in the South and you couldn't?"

Cimma's screaming laughter bellowed near the tent line, and they both focused on her and her brother chasing each other.

"She is bonded to you by blood," Maron said through more distant squeals. "We are only connected by eneris, and so her connection to you is stronger."

"How would she have even known to do that in the first place?"

Maron glanced beyond Lor's shoulder again to watch them at play. "When she came of age, I presented myself to her and taught her. Once she left, I began to teach your son, but he is still very new."

"You've been talking to my children?" Lor glanced over his shoulder toward the tent line again. Cimma and Nate were joined in games by their older friends, Ayala and the ones known as Betta and Treece.

"Yes. Your little ones like to call me *Mister Shadow*."

Lor eyed Maron again, his pallid features framed in that choppy black hair, and he tittered. "That sounds about right. Can they see you now?"

"If I want them to."

Lor hummed. "Can't say I approve of that."

"It is not about approval, it is about fulfilling the mission."

"Yeah, about that," Lor said and crossed his arms. The goggle seal chafed his face even more as the heat bored into his skin. "I need an explanation of what your purpose was down *there*." He nodded to the black hump in the distance.

Maron grunted and narrowed his eyes. "That story is long."

"I have time."

"We do not."

"You owe me."

"I do not."

Impossible, stone-headed Igni. Lor blew out an exaggerated breath. "Fine. Show me how I can move through this little mind-space thingy like you do. Like you are now."

"Thingy?"

"Never mind, just show me."

"Very well. Close your eyes."

Before obeying, Lor glanced down the dunes at the shapes of his friends, then forward for any sign of death camp members.

"I assure you, they are occupied," Maron said.

If he traveled through the scope of the area to get here, there was probably truth in that. With a nod, Lor closed his eyes. Rather than a greeting from the blackness he knew before, nothing changed... Maron stood in front of him in the desert. It reminded him of the moment he met his son, yet Maron radiated golden light as he stood in front of his own door. It was dressed in all the swirling colors of a chromatic phial.

"Are we in the other mind layer already?" Lor asked. As far as he knew, there was no real name for what they did. Maron only nodded, not confirming a name.

"Where is your physical body right now?" Lor asked.

"Where it has been since my mission began."

Lor sighed. "You could have said at Gehenna."

"No."

That made Lor chuckle. It was absurd of him to think of any other kind of personality coming from Maron—a man strapped to a hole leading to an evil dimension for 1,500 years.

Watching the golden color swirling from Maron's sides, it made him think. No one had ever been able to enter this space with him, and he always wondered, so he asked. "What color am I?"

Maron made that same bizarre smile. "Gold of course, like myself."

Lor threw up his arms. "Yes, of course! Of course... I should have known," he said sarcastically.

"You see now, your door is open." Maron nodded beyond Lor's shoulder. When he turned, he saw the black gate, wide open and playing various scenes from his childhood, like the most boring holofilm.

"Hey, that's private," Lor protested as his awkward tongue-touch with Luci played out in front of them.

"Then close it."

"You know, I didn't take you for a funny guy. Har-har. How do I do it?"

Maron pursed his lips and narrowed his eyes at the replay of Par pressing herself against Lor.

"Hey, that was *not* me, I swear!" Fear worked its way up his legs, and the door opened wider.

"I know this," Maron grumbled. "Focus on protecting yourself."

"How?"

"You once participated in a wicked ritual. You remember this, do you not?"

Lor wasn't in a habit of performing rituals but knew of only one he was forced to do. "The ritual of self, you mean? When I took out my gold?"

"That is the one," Maron grumbled, a marked change morphing into his brow. Disappointment perhaps. "It has left your deeper self open and vulnerable. Vulnerable to the zlae'duch Cirv'e."

"That's weird, because I feel like I've been locked out for years."

"Drugs."

"Pardon?" Lor smirked.

"You swing from one extreme to the next. The effect of the formulation locked you up. Now you rush into openness without it."

"Wonderful."

"Hold on to the Maker's truths. Understand who you are, who your family is, and reject the evil of this world."

Lor laughed. How could he not? "If it were that easy, don't you think I would have—"

"Who said it was easy? You must practice before we approach the worm."

"So you have a plan then?"

The first fight Lor had in the South was now playing through the door behind him with a smirk from Maron.

"I have a plan, yes. You must confront Roseaarde's ruler. He is tainted by Cirv'e's corruption, and you are the one for the task of extracting it from inside his mind."

"The princeps? How do you expect me to do that?"

Maron tilted his head, pursing his lips as if Lor should already have the answer. "We are connected and must work together."

Lor hummed. The replay of his fight with Hahn was the next holofilm to embarrass him through the door. He shuddered at the sight of that man straddling him like that with his fists clenching his throat. It reminded him of the day they confronted the boatman and Hahn died. That was the day he found his daughter and connected with the Nazagora. It was a good day. The door creaked shut.

"Very good," Maron remarked.

Lor guffawed at his victory, pumping his metaphysical fist. Closing his door was like performing his heals—just remember the good things.

Remember the truths.

"Now," Maron said, breaking Lor's reverie, "before you travel to the leader, I have a task for you, and it is good practice for what you must do. Find my wife."

Lor chortled. "Eh, don't you think that's a bad idea? Besides, don't *you* know where she is?"

"I do, yes. Find a good spot where you will be left alone—"

"You didn't hear the part about it not being a good idea."

"Focus in on your chosen spot and find her. Make amends. We must work together. You from the inside, us from the outside."

Maron would not take no for an answer, but his idea was valid. It was going to be a pincer attack: the mental versus the physical. Thanks to the ritual of self, the three of them had a connection, and they could use that. He sighed. "Fine. I'll find her."

"She has been joyless for a very long time, I warn you of this."

"Yes, it's rather obvious, thanks."

"What Par had you do was an offense to the Maker. But all offenses can be used for good. Our connection is getting stronger again and may serve the Maker's purpose."

Lor only nodded. The pain in the plan would take him from his family again.

"Travel through the desert of minds to reach her. Do not engage with any of them."

"What's that supposed to mean?"

Maron clicked his tongue and shook his head. "This world is so different. And sad. There are evil men in the desert, and you must travel around their minds. Do not engage."

"Come on, be more specific... What am I expecting to see?"

"Doors. Lots of doors."

"Do I really need to do this on my own?"

"Yes. It is good practice." Maron glanced to the side, and Lor followed his gaze, watching Dill's short silhouette jog toward them.

"Yo, Lor... only been back a day and you're already delirious from the heat! Who are you talking to?" Dill slowed his jog, taking several deep breaths.

When Lor turned back to Maron, he was gone.

"Dammit," he uttered. "No one, just thinking out loud."

Dill laughed and patted him on the arm. "Sure thing, bud."

"I think we're getting close to a sort of plan... ish," Lor said as he came back through the tent with Dill and Niklaus. "First, I need to contact Karl or Zary. Dad? Do you still have your e-disk?"

"So, what's the plan then?" Dill said as he plopped into the chair at the table, finding a small spanner to fidget with. His single working eye rolled around in his eye socket, and he used a finger to stop it.

"I don't think I'll ever get used to that."

"Get used to what?"

"Never mind. It's going to take a two-sided attack. The machine, and... well... me."

Gale was about to hand Lor the e-disk but then withdrew and gave him a look. "What does that mean?"

"It's not what you think, but it's not good either. Let me talk to Karl, and we'll gather everyone to talk about it, because it's going to take all of us. Is Nico awake now?"

"Yes, he's improved and downstairs with Eva. Better to leave them be for now," Gale said, hesitant to hand over the e-disk.

When he finally did, he made sure to let Lor know that it was not traceable and could find anyone. The best person Lor knew that could get him in touch with Karl was Url.

When searching for Tur'laethe, he was listed as the servant to Baela Loestra. The bigger surprise was that he was also listed as "unmanned." As Lor took a second to think about that, he wondered if that was Baela's way of hiding their relationship from the cities. And hiding their daughter.

He swiped in their code and watched the holo static hovering above his palm until the call went through.

Url's face popped in and grinned the moment he saw Lor. "Hey, I'm glad you called," he said. "These creature things are eating a lot of the fish."

Lor sucked on his teeth. He didn't consider the food toll of having Nazagora on the shores of a small fishing town. "Oh, I'm sorry about that. I'll talk to Karl about it. Speaking of which, is he nearby?"

"Certainly." He turned his head and shouted for Karl. As he did, the holo shifted and showed Karl sitting right there with an annoyed look on his face.

"I'm right here, Url," he said as he stood to take the e-disk. A flash of the sun hit the holo, glitching it for a moment before Lor caught the underside of Karl's nose.

"Hey, how are things in the desert?" he asked.

All focus went into the remarkably manicured inside of Karl's nose. "Good, good. Hey, tilt your head down a bit, would you?"

After a few interesting adjustments, Karl showed up like he was meant to. "Sorry, haven't used one of these in quite a while. Anyway, anything new?"

"Yes, actually, I'm going to need you to start getting everyone prepared for my return. We're going to need the Nazagora in our plan."

"Url says the Nazagora are eating his fish."

Lor hummed. "Yeah, I heard. Um, well, can you ask one of the Beast Tamers to do something about that?"

"I can try. Maybe the people of Corl can get a taste of the Nazagora, eh?"

Lor paused, then shook his head. "Probably not a good idea if we want them to stay on our side."

"Right. Well, I'll have the tamers take them farther out."

"Hey, try feeding them some of that saxeroot we brought with us. It seems to grow well."

Karl shrugged. "Perhaps."

"I'll give you another call in about a standard week. It should be enough time for me to practice and get my family ready, then return to Corl."

"And the Nazagora?"

"They're going to take us where we need to go."

Chapter 30

Practice and Focus

Loren

Rehashing the plan to Lor's family wasn't easy. There were many protests, especially from Damaetra and Gale. He ran it over again in his mind, hoping he correctly interpreted what Maron said. And with the way that guy spoke, his confidence wavered a little. They were to take the machine to the tree, and he was to take the Nazagora to the capital. Their reactions to the plan were sound—the idea was crazy.

To give them a fighting chance, he had to do what Maron said and practice. The thought of seeing Par again set his stomach fluttering. He wasn't ready to ever see her again.

Too many people bustled in the bunkers, with a handful of people going over the schematics in the tent. Lor needed a quiet place, and despite the planning going on in the tents, the bunkers were just too noisy. So, tent side it was, armed with a pair of earplugs from Gale that he squished between his fingers.

A solitary spot behind the couch would do… It was out of the way and hidden from the entrance in case he lost himself. He didn't plan on losing himself again inside the hollow space between sleeping and waking, but the fear was real.

He shivered once before he settled cross-legged onto the ground and stuffed the plugs in his ears with a grimace until all he could hear was his own heartbeat and liquid brain matter. After a quick prayer, he closed his eyes and concentrated.

When he stood in the other layer and turned around, the tent was full of color, smoking off his friends and swirling together in an indescribable canvas. Each friend had their unique door behind them, but he looked for the one *she* owned. The mother of Foscans. Maron warned him that he would need to travel through the death camps to get to her. For now, he made sure his friends were secure.

So far, everyone's passageways were closed. That was good... they were safer to guard themselves. Damaetra's door was the white gold that he remembered, while Gale's was blue and silver. Nico had a shade of green with golden accents, and Eva's was yellow with golden details. A vibrant purple door with ivory trim stood behind Dill, and a softer shade of purple with the same ivory as Dill's guarded Emilia's back. The orange one lined in white stood behind Cae, while Niklaus had a grayish blue door, also lined in white.

One neat detail Lor pieced together was how each couple had coordinated accent colors, as if they inherited them together.

After passing through the hallway of his friend's minds, the path to Par became long and dark. A mineral aroma hovered in the atmosphere, and he knew it was the test Maron told him about. He only hoped he headed in the right direction, not ending up back on the East Coast or somewhere in the northwest mountains.

After what seemed like a standard hour, he finally came across dark sets of doors, disheveled and chaotic. Some propped open slightly, begging for entry, others sealed and molded shut. It ran shivers through him in the eerie quiet, the state of them in degrees of disarray. One door squeaked on its hinges in the breeze. It occurred to him that these doors belonged to the desert brigands—each open frame offering a wicked encounter.

Lor had enough wicked encounters to last a lifetime. He shuffled along, praying not to rouse whatever lay within. There were hundreds of these doors.

The path he took was a straight line through the thick of them, as it took almost as long to make it beyond the cluster as it did to reach it.

A part of him wished he could help them. He could enter and lead them in the right direction—to a life of good. However, he was only one man—one man with only a whisper of skill to accomplish something like that. But he had come far. He was walking through the desert of minds, on the instruction of an ancient. How neat was that?

Now free from the chaos of blackened doors, Lor peered behind his shoulder to watch them fade as he moved forward. He was close, he knew, and the faint shimmer of color brightened in the distance. So he ran to it.

It reminded him of the time as a child when he heard Eva's screams down the beach, as she had twisted an ankle running along the shore. With all the urgency of a brother desperate to help his sister, he ran to her. But even then, he knew that once he got there, he wouldn't know what to do.

His journey toward the distant door was much the same. He was desperate to fix the problem, not knowing what lay inside, or what to do when he got there.

He slowed to a trot, coming up on the new door—a delicate swirling color of stone, devoid of its former vibrance. At one point, the door would have been beautiful and inviting, much like the one he saw behind Maron. Now, its dulled silver handle had crusted over with a dark patina, and the stone had chips and cracks.

This was her door.

As he moved closer, it opened on its own, inviting him inside. When he entered, a flash of light pulled him through it and into a bright room.

Earthy decor dripped from the walls in shades of green and blue. White flowers dotted the ivy tendrils that curled in carefree whorls along with the blue and green life, and the furniture had been arranged in a circle. No tech distractions held this home captive, as each chair wore intricate carvings and colors, with a unique design to its owner. Except the chairs were all empty. All but one.

She sat with her back to him, her dark hair cascading over her chair, and she held something in her arms. Light from a window carved out overhead glittered across her strands, illuminating them in shades of warm red and gold.

"I wondered when you would show up," she said to him, not bothering to look but continuing to gaze down at the bundle she held.

He said nothing, only moved toward her, bending his knees to sit in a chair next to her.

"Not that one," she said, "that was Maron's."

Lor stood up and went to her other side and sat.

"Although, he refuses to come back here." She looked over at him. Her turquoise eyes were glassy and bloodshot.

"Who are you, Paerli?" Lor asked.

She tittered with the faintest smile. "I think you know."

The bundle in her arms shifted, and she patted the underside of it, as if it were her child. As to his question, he was pretty sure he did know, but to hear it from her was more important. And if she offered him her story, maybe he could help set her twisted ankle right, as if he knew how.

"Everything was taken from me," she said, rocking the bundle, "every thing and every one."

Lor watched her as she continued to look down at the child in her arms. A glimmer of a memory resurfaced as he watched her there. Drinking her eneris gave him insight he wasn't prepared for back then. None of it made any sense, and everything he'd received in visions since then were only fragments. Just enough information to confuse him and nothing more. But the more she rocked the bundle in her arms, alone in this empty, sunlit home, he got his clue.

"You burned down the tree, didn't you?" he said.

She pressed her lips together, looking up at the ivy-covered wall. "That was so long ago."

"Why?"

"How could I even begin to explain an age-old culture to you? You'd hardly understand."

"Can you at least try? I want to know," he said. Leaning sideways in the stone chair to look at her directly, he realized in that moment how quiet the infant in her arms had been.

"The past is the past. No sense in resurrecting it. I can tell you that it came at great cost to me."

Once she finished talking, the room peeled back, trading layers of warm light for gray. Dust motes floated lazily through it. The vibrant blue and green ivy threads recoiled into black petrification while their white petals disintegrated into more dust. A breeze blew in from an open entry, pushing black and yellow sand at the threshold in small eddies.

"Welcome to my home," she said, pulling back a section of blanket, revealing the tiny skeleton she held.

He shivered. The poor thing.

"My mind can only hold the image of what it used to be for so long. I'm surprised even the stone chairs are still here," she said.

They were worn, seat-shaped blobs, the carvings stuttered and skipped, leaving mere remnants of what was once there. Lor leaned into the dissolved back and dragged his fingers up the armrest, feeling the pitted wear of the ages. It surprised him that his heart ached to see them nearly gone.

"My husband, you know, Maron. He was from the East." She stood and placed the little bundle of bones inside a petrified cradle, then sat back down. "It was where the Igni came from, in fact."

He let her talk, only stiffening in the amorphous stone seat at the mention of the East.

Par sighed. Dark circles hovered under her eyes, and she tilted her heavy head to the side. "When they came to our land, we mistook them for hostile, and the war started. I'm pretty sure the North struck first, so that blood is on us. But, I mean, this was before I was born, so I don't know the details. I only know that the Igni ceded to prevent further deaths. And the Igni survivors assimilated with us. By the time I was born, a generation had already passed.

"It was my generation that actually began to choose them as 'matches'... like I had told you before... you know... back then."

Lor furrowed his brow, taking in a deep breath and letting it out slow. He wished he'd met this person during the program. This person in front of him was different than the one that was capable of hurting him then. Past Par was nothing but lies; present Par was human, the type of woman he thought he made friends with in the program.

"We hid our relationship from society, you know. The North didn't like us mixing with the East... but I didn't care. See these chairs?" She waved a hand around at the circle of humped stone. "There's one for each child we had together."

There were eleven chairs besides hers and Maron's. Lor sighed, thinking of Cimma and Nate. There was no doubt she had to watch them all die.

"Outside of all that, it was also my generation that began suffering the effects of the breach. We had no idea it was even there. Random people would complain of strange sensations from this or that, while Maron and I both felt its power on us.

"We didn't know what to make of it. Some called it the Maker's blessing, but he and I knew it was something else. Something we weren't meant to have. Of course people abused it, as they tend to do.

"Maron and I..." She paused and bit her lip. "We were the first to identify as Reapers. Although, we didn't have a name for it back then. We only gave it a name after I lost my second youngest by it... My very own hands."

Par glanced down at her fingers twined together in her lap—limp and open as if holding on to something small and invisible.

She sighed, and her chin knotted as she held back her tears. "He was just a baby. My little Dal'miko."

Something stirred in him, seeing her there like that, vulnerable in front of him for the first time. He didn't think she was capable of crying. That lump in his chest he felt for his children, terrified to think of his own hands sending them to their graves. He glanced over at Par, still looking down at her open hands with a face dull and sagging.

What could he possibly say to her? "Why don't you go be with Maron?" he whispered.

She tittered with a face-chewing pout. "Maron is a little upset with me right now. But he's still an Igni. He usually comes around." She paused for a moment, running her hand over her mouth. "You have my pendant, don't you?"

His eyes went wide. He'd completely forgotten about her pendant.

She sighed at his non-answer. "If you find it, destroy it. It's taking time, but its effects on me have waned."

"What effects do you mean?"

She wrung her hands together, glancing down at the swirling black and yellow whorls of sand on the floor. "Cruelty. Anger. Lust... anything Cirv'e sought to exploit in me."

"How long?"

"As long as I've been immortal."

"Did Cirv'e make you immortal?"

Paerli shot a look at him, an animalistic light in the back of them. "I sold myself to stop feeling pain," she said, then faced away from him. "It came to me one night, during my darkest moment of melancholy. A being of beautiful light, an ancient protector sent by the Maker." She paused, the reflective light fading in her eyes. "You were stronger than me. I bought the lie and made a pact with it. I was weak."

A being of light... it made sense she was swayed by something like that.

"I'm sorry, I guess I never truly answered your question," she said, tossing her hair to the side and looking at him for the first time. Really looking at him.

"Who am I? I'm just a regular Danashi woman from the North that fell in love with an Igni man from the East. We had many children together, and when I gave birth to my first, she was a beautiful pale child with white eyes and the black hair of her father. We were stunned, never having seen anyone like her. So we gave her kind a new name. We called her Foscan, after the Igni word, *fosca*, for *inner light*. All of our children were Foscan, as were the children of the handful of other Danashi people that took Igni partners in secret.

"You know what's interesting?" she said, looking back to him with a joyless smile. "Well, I find it interesting at least. While I, as a Danashi took an Igni partner, my Mesamen peers also took Igni partners. Even though Maron and I created something beautiful, the Mesamen and their matches created equally beautiful yet opposite children to ours... pale as sun-bleached parchment, bright eyes the color of gemstones, and the whitest hair, with a touch of gold. You should know exactly of whom I speak."

Of course he did. His own wife was an Igni descendant, and he had no idea. "The Anglia," he mumbled.

Par nodded. "Which is why, you see, the cities don't like your kind. They think the Yeunish are the Igni reborn, Anglia and Foscan together... such blasphemy to them. The East coming back to finish them. What they don't understand is that you're more than that. You're a perfect union of the East *and* the North."

Lor scoffed. "You say that like you're in awe of it, but you *hate* me."

She clicked her tongue and shook her head. "No, I don't. The worm does."

"Was it the worm then, who convinced you to hate your own children?"

She pulled her lips inward, taking a deep breath and closing her eyes. An eternity passed before she acknowledged his question. "Yes, of course," she said, "and it's all my fault." She swiped a hand across her face.

"What do you mean?"

"It's the reason Maron is upset with me, and the reason I can't find it in me to forgive myself."

Lor continued to watch her, hoping she would keep talking, even if he had a good idea of what she would say.

She traced the shallow symbol carved into the arm of her chair. "I'm the reason the Foscans are in servitude. It was me that launched the campaign against them and rallied to enslave them. My own children... Maker have mercy." Her voice muffled when she pressed her face into her hands.

"Par, what did we unleash when we opened the breach?"

She dragged her palm down her face and frowned. "We unleashed Cirv'e... and whatever Guild abilities were too big to fit through Maron's seal."

"Now you lost me," Lor said, scratching his chin.

Par scoffed. "Where did you think Guild abilities came from? Why do you think the program is on Heart Island to 'take courses' for the Guild? It's a direct line for breach influence, that's why. And it's also the reason the cult lives on the island. They either won't, or can't, leave. Cirv'e is free to beguile more than just the North's leadership. It got to its citizens."

"Hold on," Lor said. "Why was Maron attached to the breach at all?"

"Maron did what he could for a time. Because of the worm, I knew he wouldn't last. I just needed that little extra edge from you to get him off."

"Alright, I don't want to relive that, thanks."

"Yes, I suppose not," she said.

A hot breeze wafted through the door, and he choked on the dust.

"Are you alright?" Par asked, genuine concern on her face for once.

He held up a finger, and as he did, a muffled clang rippled from deep in his mind.

Par waited for his answer, eyebrow raised as Lor rubbed his throat. "Hold on," he said, tilting his nose upward and taking pointed sniffs, "do you smell that?"

Par tittered. "I don't smell anything."

He took in a deeper breath. "It smells like..." Another deep inhale. "Electricity."

Chapter 31

Reflections

"Look at 'em, Bas. Runnin' around like a bunch a insects." Hammer spit a stream of brown into the sand.

"Yes," his companion replied.

The wind kicked a gust of motes in front of them, blurring out the figures of children running around in play with their caretakers.

"I got some real specific jerks in mind when we go in, hear me?"

The pallid man inclined his head, scanning the line of tents in the distance. A pair of blue goggles hugged his deep-set eyes sitting beneath the thick white brows of an Anglian. He licked his lower lip with a plump red tongue.

"But I won't complain if there's more casualties." Hammer cracked his knuckles. "Just make sure you pull 'em for me good."

They began their journey to the camp with leaded footsteps, dragging minor trenches into the sand. "When you pull 'em, I want to taste it, got it?"

Bas grumbled, keeping his gaze on the tent line.

Hammer held his hand out, stopping Bas for a moment. "I forgot to tell you, they got Guild abilities."

A guttural hum vibrated from the Reaper's throat. "What," he said.

"Engineer and Formulator, I think. They might have some needler type weapons, so we gotta be smart about how we get 'em. They almost got me years ago, so yeah."

"Alright," Bas said with a nod.

"I wanna sneak up on 'em, got it?"

Bas nodded, jerking his chin up at the back of the tent line.

"Yeah, we should go behind. Good idea."

Not a soul saw them, and they crept beyond the tent backs, behind the track supports. It was a nice little ditch, enough to hide the tops of their heads as they made their way to the end of the line.

Even after accidentally toeing empty water cans, the children's play screams drowned out their trek. Good. They wouldn't see them coming.

Chapter 32

Return

NICO

It was almost time to set all the plans into motion. Lor's mind walking had improved, and the machine parts were mostly installed. Nico paced behind the Engineers, who sat on the floor poring over the schematics. Everything was finally coming together.

Emilia pointed at her parts, confirming that she was done with installation. "The aerosolizer is done too, so we should be able to load Dame's draughts in the back," she said.

"Is the panel connected already?" Dill asked.

"I was just down there early this morning," Eva confirmed. She glanced up to Nico with that puckered smile she always gave him when feeling playful. It made him crazy, and he gave her the same smile in return, biting at his thumbnail as his own vice.

The tent flap flew open, letting loose a hot breeze to blow their paper notes throughout the space. "Well, look what we have here," a deep, scratchy voice muttered in the shadow. Everyone spun toward the entrance, as a large man unfolded into their home, malice screwed up on his face.

"Get downstairs," Nico whispered, voice cracking. When no one moved, he turned to them. "Go, go!"

The women scrambled to stand as the hulking man took his steps forward, but Verena ran to her side table, snatching the taser she had engineered special for occasions such as these.

An electric snap cut through the air, followed by the metallic aroma of Verena's bolt barb striking Hammer. It sunk into his chest and he shook, stumbling into tables and chairs as he stared stupidly at the buzzing object sticking from his flesh.

During the distraction, Nico and Dill ushered the women and children to the bunker, closing the hatch for the first time in years.

"Stupid woman," Hammer said with a string of drool dangling from his lip. He shivered, yanking the barb free and dropping it to the sandy floor.

The tent was too small for a brawling strongman.

Nico stepped in front of Dill and the couch where Lor was, sitting behind it and deep in his meditations. "Look, I know you have unsettled animosity toward us, but, please, if we could just go outside—"

"Gladly," Hammer said as he bent over and snatched Nico's leg from under him.

The move knocked Nico to his back, causing his head to crush the schematics, punching a small hole in the paper before Hammer dragged him from the tent. Nico waved his hands, searching for something to latch on to—he was useless, dragging through the tent and out the front flap. The hot sand burned against his neck. When he plunged his fingers into the scalding grit, the skin rubbed into raw ulcers on his knuckles. He was no match on his back.

"Get inside your tents! Everyone!" Nico shouted as Hammer continued dragging him in front of the tent line.

Residents scurried inside in a panic, and children screamed. A few neighbors hovered with gaping mouths and tension in their stance as if debating whether to stay or flee. Nico's body left a deep groove in the sand as his head bumped over a hidden rock. It knocked him dizzy, and he shook his head.

An orange blast cut through his vision, striking Hammer across the back, disappearing as fast as it came. He paused and turned, dropping Nico's leg to face his aggressor as Nico wasted no time scrambling away. Ayala stood with a smirk, hands engulfed in flame.

"Yer one a them, are you?" Hammer said. "Let's see if we can snuff out that fire, yeah?"

He leaned over, gripping a stone half buried in the sand. When he pulled it loose, it was almost half Ayala's size fully exposed. It soared toward her. She ducked in time for it to miss her head, but she screeched when it shattered her elbow.

DAMAETRA

Not again. She wouldn't let him take her husband again, or her babies, or her friends. Damaetra paced in search of anything that could be used as a weapon, opening drawers, throwing back pillows, and rifling through piles of notes.

Cae followed close behind. "What do you think you're going to do against that man?" she asked.

"Something. I have to do something." Damaetra ducked into Nico's bunker, this time adding Eva to her tail.

"We are no match for a strongman," Eva pleaded.

Damaetra's fingers walked over Nico's formulations, swishing the phials in their brackets. There it was... in the back, behind a few phials of green, hung the chromatic formula. "I am," she said, swiping the neck of the phial.

Cae grabbed her wrist, tugging her back. "No, Dame, please, I'm begging you not to go out there."

The block in her progress wore creases in Damaetra's brow. "I love you, but for the love of the Maker, let me go."

"I won't."

"I'm not going to stay down here and do nothing like last time!"

"You were giving *birth* last time!" Cae's shouts made Nate cry.

LOR

First it was the hot breeze, then it was the clang of the bunker hatch. There was no mistaking the acrid smell of electricity that pulled Lor from his talk with Par. Even deep in his mind walk and the plugs stuffed in his ears, he felt the change in the atmosphere. The pull began in his gut, yanking him from Par's home in the mountain back into his spot behind Jack and Verena's couch.

No time to react. The moment Lor peered beyond the furniture, it was just in time to see the top of Nico's curly head getting swallowed by the tent flap.

The light stung, and he waved his arms around, trying to help himself from his meditation spot. A spare set of black goggles sat on the conversation table. They were snug but serviceable. Dill stood at the entrance, peering from the crack, and Lor jogged to him.

"I'm *useless* here," Dill hissed, "all of my weapons are downstairs." He tossed a gaze to the closed hatch.

"Don't... Stay in here," Lor said. "Let me handle this. I can't die, and I won't stand to lose any of you."

From the shadow of the tent, Lor watched the scene outside, catching the moment a boulder clipped Ayala. The hulking man responsible for the throw, and clearly proud of himself, was one he was all too familiar with... and all too sick of. Lor's blood boiled. That man had to go.

Waiting for the right moment, he watched as Nico stood once again, with Ayala screaming in Jack's arms. He wanted to heal her, but the moment was wrong... and no one had weapons.

Gale and Niklaus peered out from the tent across the way, catching him watching them. Gale made a short motion with his hands, telling him to turn around. He wasn't going to do that, making sure to let Gale know. Even in the shadow, Gale managed to show his disappointment, spinning his hand around again, to be met with another defiant response. Their silent argument was cut short by movement nearby.

A figure moved in a strange cadence toward the fray, and Hammer happened to notice. The one they called Treece wove through the sand, slinking in a bizarre dance, hands out with menace in her eyes. Damaetra told him no one had ever seen her demonstrate her ability—it was too risky as a volatile. Lor sucked in a breath, half in fear and half in anticipation. He'd never seen one before. Even if he knew the danger of activating their gift, he couldn't deny his interest. So he watched.

Hammer sneered at her, yet she didn't seem to care about her own safety when he readied himself to tear her apart. Her eyes pooled into blackness, odd and alien-like, with the most magnificent twirls of sprouting vines bursting from every plane of her body. Arms, legs, head and neck: there was nothing she didn't latch on to, wrapping Hammer in a cocoon of ivy.

Ayala cried out for her friend.

The curve of the girl's body morphed into a knot of vines and squeezed, not leaving a speck of the strongman to peek through them. Hammer toppled over, wriggling under her tightening constriction and gasping for air. He bucked like a worm in the sun, coiled within the green cocoon.

This was Lor's moment to come to Ayala's aid—at least he thought as much before Hammer's weak cry came from between a space in the vines: *Bas! Bas!*

When a cloaked figure emerged from behind the tent line, Lor hunched back inside. The new arrival approached Hammer's prison in a similar eerie shuffle as the volatile. A set of stark white fingers stretched out, wrapping around one of the vines. At once, a stream of silver pulsed like an open artery, forcing Treece to loosen her grip just enough to allow her prisoner to gain leverage.

And he took advantage of that, flexing outward and bursting Treece to pieces. Ayala shrieked for her friend again, heaving muffled sobs into Jack's chest.

Scarlet streams twirled in a ribbon dance, sputtering from each broken piece and painting the sand in star bursts. The pieces *piff piff piffed* into the grains, with the last of Treece coursing red into the yellow dust.

Ayala sputtered and gasped under a torrent of tears as Jack held on to her. The young man they called Quint bolted from his tent toward Ayala, passing the severed remains of his childhood friend with a choke stifled in his throat.

Hammer bent over to suck in a tidal wave of air, while watching Quint run by. His skin had gone redder than a blood fish, with the whites of his eyes to match. His entire body was covered in little pin marks, oozing thin trails of scarlet, as if he'd just stood in a blood rain.

Still pitched forward, he wiped a smear from his forehead and gaped at it. Then he rubbed his throat with a short laugh. "So she... was a volatile... yeah? Almost got me... I'll admit." He took hard breaths where he could, bordering on wheezes. "Hmph, they're all so different... What a waste." At last he stood upright with some effort, watching everyone around him. Each pinprick in his flesh was raw and angry, but he dusted himself off with a snarl, showing off a single crooked tooth in his upper jaw, too crowded with brownish teeth to let it sit right.

Hammer focused on Nico, extending an arm to the hooded stranger, who stood among Treece's broken remains. "Let me introduce you to my friend here."

The stranger cupped his hand in front of him, holding on to the puddle of silver. It reminded Lor of his days working in the morgue—days he wasn't keen to remember.

"His name's Bas," Hammer continued, "and he's gonna pull all you little pricks dry."

Bas held his hand toward Hammer and murmured something inaudible.

"Hell, why not?" Hammer grabbed the man's pale wrist and held the cupped palm toward his lips. The sucking slurp that followed made Lor sick. Gale and Niklaus grimaced in their hiding spot, and Ayala wailed again.

Jack demanded she and Quint get inside the tent.

Hammer's plump tongue crept out from between his lips, catching a dribble of sliver. "Mmm, tastes like a warm vegemeal bar."

Niklaus snuck out from the safety of his tent, clutching a long ripper blade, not unlike what Lor had seen before. It was eerily similar to the blade that took the eyes and legs of both his friends.

"You're a sick *freak!*" he shouted.

At the sight of his old partner, Hammer grinned wider, showing more of those stained nubs in his mouth. "Well, look who it is... The *yellow* twin. I hear there's a bounty on you in Secas."

"Rot in hell," Niklaus spat.

"You first."

DAMAETRA

"Don't knock my arm, or we'll all die!" Damaetra shouted as the phial of Last Grudge jiggled in her grip.

Cae let her go, holding her hands up. She didn't mean to lie to her sister like that. But she was getting in the way.

Damaetra marched back into Verena's bunker toward the ladder. "Someone help me with the hatch."

NIKLAUS

Hammer tittered. "So you think *I'm* the freak, eh? Coming from little baby Hare... Injecting silver since you were still in your swaddlers." He nodded at the blade in Niklaus's fist. "And who are you to talk all high an' mighty, with you cuttin' off yer own twin's legs and such."

"Hey, screw you, buddy," Nico interrupted.

"Screw *you*," Hammer said with a smirk.

"Nice comeback, dumbass," Niklaus said just before sprinting forward with his blade.

One cut was all he needed. Just one cut. But his ill-planned move failed when Hammer dodged and stuck a leg out, sending him flying. The blade soared from his grip, clattering against the small boulder between his and the Freelys' tents.

Hammer nodded toward the creepy Reaper, Bas. "You know what to do," he said.

Niklaus scrabbled backward, ankle bent at a bad angle, as the man slinked toward him.

"Back off, man..." his voice cracked. He tried to stand, but panic seized him, and his bent ankle was clearly useless.

Bas reached down, that eerie white hand connecting with Niklaus's sun-kissed leg.

"Get it off me! Nico!" Niklaus panted, trying to kick and thrash Bas from his leg.

Silver erupted from the pores in his shin, and he threw his head back with a yowl.

Nico bolted to the pair, striking Bas across the face with a spare howie rod he nicked from the random pile of train debris. It was enough force to knock him loose from Niklaus, and to blow out an eyeball, which rocked by its cord over his swelling cheek.

Bas slowly pushed it back in the socket.

"Tech eyes," Nico muttered.

The Reaper stood in silence, glaring down at Niklaus with a frown as the lens in his engineered eye readjusted.

"Back off," Nico warned, standing in front of his brother with the rod pitched back and ready for another swing.

Bas tittered, then sauntered toward Hammer, holding out his hand full of Niklaus's silver. That bastard sucked it straight from the man's palm with a grin, like sipping hot tea with a pinky finger stretched out. A smear of the blue-black remnant had smudged over his lower lip.

"Ass...*hole*!" Niklaus cried, voice cracking while he held his withered leg and scooted backward.

"Mm, MM! Tastes like coward, little Hare," Hammer cooed. "No wonder Par preferred me."

"Get wrecked, you son of a bitch!"

"I wonder if your brother tastes any different." Hammer leered up at Nico, who still brandished the howie rod.

"If you try it, I swear, your death will be magnificent." Lor swiped the ripper blade from the ground as Jack stood by his side.

GALE

It had to be in Verena's bunker somewhere. Gale pondered the hatch in Niklaus's tent. He stuttered down the ladder and nearly fell when he hit bottom. Next door, he heard the women arguing.

"Hey, hey, what are you doing?" he asked when swiping the curtain aside and finding Verena and Eva pushing at the hatch.

"We think it's stuck," Emilia said with her arms draped over each of his grandchildren. They sat on the floor, looking up at Damaetra as she tapped her toe behind her.

"You're not going out there," Gale said.

"Only I am," Damaetra said. She held out the phial of Last Grudge.

Gale gasped. "Oh Maker, I thought we had those buried for safety!" he said, pushing his hands forward.

"Well, this one was in Nico's chest," Damaetra said. "Besides, it has to be thrown and shattered to work, right?"

He eyed her. "Be so careful with that thing."

"What are you doing down here anyway?" she asked.

"I'm looking for my antique shooter. I believe I left it in here last."

The slice of a drawer opening cut through the conversation, and Verena brought the weapon to Gale, placing it in his hand. It was a dull gray, with patterns carved into it. Such a thing... old and fragile, yet powerful and fatal. He didn't have many projectiles left for it since the cities stopped making them a few seasons ago. He kicked himself for not buying more when he had the chance. What he had left was about twenty-three chances to nail these guys. Should be more than enough.

"Thanks," he said, curling his fingers around it.

Damaetra tugged at his arm. "I need to get out there," she said. "Can you help us get the hatch open?"

Gale studied the framing. Going long periods without shutting the thing warped the edges, possibly wedging it closed. If it was stuck, he had to get it open anyway, but now was not the time. Damaetra shouldn't be out there... But he knew the pull of a protective nature, because he felt it too.

"I'll probably have to get it from the outside. But Niklaus's hatch is open."

"I'll follow you." She smiled at him.

LOR

Hammer hummed until he rumbled in laughter. "Oh, Cricket. My, my... Look at *you*. Did you gain a whole stone?" He flexed his muscles, bulging out the irritated little holes in his flesh. Some of them oozed clear liquid, diluting the red to a pinkish gore running down his arms. "And you," he said, pointing a thick finger toward Lor, "I'm gonna enjoy letting your whole family watch you die again."

Hammer tipped his torso forward, stomping toward them and picking up speed. He held back a fist. As the five-knuckled meat hunk sped toward his face, Jack sidestepped as Lor ducked, sliding the ripper under Hammer's armpit. He howled when the blade bit into his arm. Now enraged, he slapped Jack's body, sending him flying into Lor. They tumbled together until Lor settled on top of the blade, slicing right down his old crescent scar.

Lor cursed and stood—blood pulsing from the yawning wound in hot streams.

Hammer grinned and stumbled to the side while pressing his other hand against the fresh wound under his arm. "Don't you know if you don't know how to use your weapon, you get stung by it?"

Lor glared at him, flicking the blood into the sand and watching the smug look on Hammer's face die when his arm knit itself. It made Immortal Green taste the best it had in years.

Hammer rolled his eyes with a grunt. "Oh yeah. Forgot."

Jack stood and dusted himself off.

Any joy Lor felt at Hammer's premature celebration vaporized when Hammer reached over to a different debris pile and flung a gear cap at Nico, striking him square in the forehead and knocking him back.

"No!" Lor ran to his recumbent friend, forsaking his surroundings just long enough to get snatched by the neck.

"Not today, little Yonch," Hammer sneered, squeezing and lifting Lor from the ground.

He nodded toward Bas. "You can't pull this one, sadly," he said, jerking Lor's head, "but man, I'd love to taste gold someday."

Helpless, Lor dangled from the strongman's grip. Stupid! He should have known better. His fingers slipped around the thick fist tightened over his neck, unable to find purchase. The oozing pus from Treece's thorny hug smelled bad, with a bitter remnant of poisonous slag. Hammer swayed a bit as he held Lor's neck, and while his fingers scrabbled at the fat fingers wrapped around his neck, he wondered if Treece's jabs weakened the strongman a little.

Several pops and the flood of Immortal Green signaled the sick realization that his neck had broken in a few places. Numbness captured his arms, and they fell slack, dangling at his sides.

Hammer sighed. "Can't *kill* this one neither... but what I can do is make 'im suffer." Every waxy, cratered surface of Hammer's pock-marked face wrinkled with wicked intent as his rotten mouth turned up in a grin. "I think I *will* try the better-looking brother. Two fer one... I get silver, and I get to watch the Yonch squirm. Go get him for me."

A gurgle sputtered from Lor's protesting lips. The repeated snaps in his everlasting spine had him wishing for his row with Hahn in the bog. Hammer tossed him away, and he went wheeling into the Freelys' tent pole with a clang. More Immortal Green for the break to his back.

Bas shuffled to an unconscious Nico lying prone next to his ailing brother.

"Get up, Nico," Niklaus whimpered.

As the Reaper advanced, he threw back his cowl. Lor couldn't move—his arms and legs still numb from neck and back breaks. He'd never had injuries like these before, and his immortality took its time. Now, he would have to lie helpless and watch his best friend die.

The howie rod lay loose across Nico's fingers, and Niklaus clawed for it, cursing his frozen leg. Just as his fingertips made contact with the hot metal, Bas kicked it out of reach.

More cursing and thrashing, with the mantra, *No! No! No!* as Niklaus cried out for his brother. Hammer licked his bulbous lips along the steady beat of his own knuckle cracks as the Reaper's pale fingers brushed against Nico's copper skin. Lor closed his eyes, yet the scene remained, coated in a random array of colored panic fog from all around.

No, please, Maker, save us...

A blast rang from the tent. Then another. Everyone jolted at the pops, watching Bas jerk back. A fan of blood sprayed from his shoulder, then his side. He fell to his knees in the sand, pressing a hand to his waist as red seeped from between his fingers. Gale marched toward the Reaper, pointing the antique shooter forward with both hands, letting loose another shot. It struck Bas in the ear, blowing it off and knocking him back.

Once Gale stood over him, he gritted his teeth and aimed the shooter down. Bas waved his arms around in a lazy stupor, searching for a spot of bare skin to rest his reaping hand. Before he could connect, Gale pulled the trigger, opening a hole in the pale man's forehead. Bas fell like a stone, a crimson puddle filling the grains around him.

"Now!" Gale shouted.

Damaetra emerged from Niklaus's tent, a phial in hand, sprinting toward Hammer. Lor wanted to scream, but his crushed throat only allowed a feeble wheeze. The linen fabric of her dress undulated with the twirling white-gold strands of her hair as she ran. She was all light and fury.

Still seething from the death of Bas, Hammer spun toward the pearled flash advancing on him. "Comin' back for more, yeah?" Hammer clamped his teeth, pushing out the rage from between them, while pitching back a fist.

When she was close enough, Damaetra hurled a phial... *the* phial. There was no way for Lor to know whether his immortality would stitch him back together if torn to shreds by Last Grudge.

It soared, neck over base toward Hammer's chest, and Lor felt his legs again, scrabbling backwards as fast as he could muster. Damaetra turned heel as soon as the glass left her fingers, stumbling with a roll back toward Lor, and he held on to her.

Gale took aim as the phial closed the gap, then blasted the fat bottom of the glass open.

A confetti of multi-colored fog spread before the strongman, yet he wavered there, fixated on the crimson flower blooming beneath his rib cage. He gaped at it and staggered, pressing dirty fingers over the fresh hole in his side.

Gale dragged Nico away, and Jack with Niklaus.

The colored fog grew, swirling like a freshly jolted motor, and Hammer pushed his free hand through it like a man just off a drinking bender. As he did, the scissoring wind struck, slicing clean through his wrist and severing his hand. He screamed.

The curdling howl he made at his bleeding stump morphed into a gurgling squelch from the razor storm, ripping through his throat and penetrating his flesh in a crimson buffet.

Now that the target was had, the sawing raze of colors slowed, releasing what remained of Hammer into a red mist in the breeze. The sun caught the red edge and cast a prism along it, fanning away as the rest of him dissipated.

Gale sighed, relaxing his grip on the shooter and lowering his arms. "Is everyone alright?" he asked, chest heaving.

Damaetra rolled to her side, clutching her hip with a grimace as she leaned into Lor. Gale ran to them, turning Lor's chin back and forth to examine his neck. Each touch made him wince, and the overwhelming flavor of grass and dirt penetrated every one of his senses so wholly that he wasn't sure if he'd ever taste anything right again. But the wheeze that pulled through his vocal cords improved little by little until he was able to clear his throat.

He slid an arm under Damaetra's shoulder. "Are you hurt?" he rasped.

She groaned and moved with his help until she sat upright, glancing at the Freelys' tent. "I'll be fine."

"Go inside and get back to the bunker," he said, nodding at the tent. "I'll meet you there after I help clean up this mess."

She nodded, clutching her hip. He handed her to Mr. Freely, who ushered her toward their connecting bunker hatch. Gale mumbled something about prying open Jack and Verena's hatch just before taking off toward their tent.

Lor rubbed his throat, swallowing a dry lump. The breeze suffocated the sounds of the desert. All but the distant pleading coming from behind.

Nico had come to, rubbing his sore brow while standing over his complaining brother. "Niki, we have to cut it off," he said.

Lor caught up to them as Nico knelt down to hold Niklaus's bicep and forearm. Dill had slipped from the tent and latched on to his other arm.

"No! NO!" Niklaus cried, kicking the functioning leg. It vibrated in place, throwing plumes of sand and forcing everyone to dodge the fan of grains. The wasted limb wouldn't move, emptied of its essence. He spit toward Bas's corpse three times.

"That looks bad, Niklaus," Lor said. "It needs to go. I can heal it after."

"You can *heal*?" Nico asked, raising a brow.

Lor shrugged. Standard years of healing and he didn't think much of it, forgetting his friends didn't know he could. "It's a Yeunish thing, I guess."

"Huh. This'll be interesting to see."

Still wriggling, Niklaus's body heaved in panicked rushes when he looked up at Lor with eyes wide and wet. "You can heal it like this, though, can't you? Can't you?"

The leg swished in the sand as he protested with his upper half. The irony of Niklaus losing his leg wasn't lost on Lor, but he couldn't help but feel a little sorry for him. He clicked his tongue. "I'm sorry, Niklaus, I can't put eneris back in."

Niklaus shook, pulling his face inward in a weeping grimace. "Caella! Caella!" he belted for his wife.

"Don't bring her out for this. You know we have to cut it off. Lor can heal it after."

"Yeah, you don't want to see what it's like if we leave it on," Lor said. Hahn's grotesque hands came to mind.

Nico nodded at Jack, who advanced toward the group while holding the ripper blade. Sweat made a beaded mustache on Niki's upper lip. His eyes went wide while panting in harried whimpers.

"Hey, I'm here... we're all here with you," Nico said with a gentle hush.

"No, please!"

"I'll make you a new one," Dill said. "It'll be just as good or better."

"You don't have the material!" Niklaus kicked again, tossing more sand.

"Secure his good leg," Jack said.

Lor pulled the good leg away from the other until he was sure it wouldn't get nicked by Jack's swing.

"We're here," Nico said over his brother's sobs.

Lor glanced up at his friend, comforting his twin. As always, Nico's ability to show grace was profound.

Jack stood over Niklaus, a firm grip on the handle and locked in position. He grounded himself with a short rocking motion, then raised the blade just enough.

"Don't cut my dick off!" Niklaus shouted as the blade came down, slicing a hand's width above the knee, halfway through. If a scream could reach the Promised Land, there was no doubt his made it there.

"Quick, one more!" Lor shouted.

Jack pulled the blade back in an arc of blood. It spattered up on Niklaus's shirt and chin, and he sucked his lower lip in and out while drooling. The blade came down again, finishing the deed with another hearty roar from Niklaus.

Lor kicked the husk to the side, scrambling to wrap his hands around the slippery, spurting stump, and closed his eyes.

The runner's chest heaved, and he panted through his teeth. It didn't take long for the bleeding to stop as the flesh glossed over in a dark jelly on the stump. It was an intense heal, a burning sear that simmered from deep within to close the flesh. The scab emerged to crust over the spot in a ring of discolored reds and browns.

After a standard minute, the wound had fully closed, a dark purple stain at the end. Much of his blood had crept out beforehand, turning his flesh pale. But Niklaus had calmed, sucking in deep breaths through his nose as he furrowed his brow at what remained of his leg.

A wet heave bubbled from Niki's throat as he sputtered vomit down his shirt.

Lor grimaced, turning to Nico. "He's going to be cold for a little while." He paused to dip his bloodied hands into the sand. "A heal like that uses a lot of body heat, so it's best if he stays outside to warm back up."

Nico nodded, kneeling next to his puke-covered twin.

Then Gale screamed for Lor from Verena's tent.

Chapter 33

Shattered

Loren

Lor nearly tumbled down the bunker ladder, finding everyone surrounding his wife. Damaetra lay on the ground, unmoving and deathly pale.

"Damaetra, baby, what happened? What happened?" Lor asked around the circle.

Caella was already in tears, and his daughter sat at Damaetra's shoulder, wiping the white-gold strands of her hair back with lower lip trembling. "Mommy," she croaked.

"She was trying to help me get the hatch unstuck, but she fell from the ladder," Gale said, kneeling next to them.

Nate had his face buried into Eva, clutching at her sides and refusing to look.

A tear pooled at Damaetra's eye—growing but not falling, and the small light from above sparkled in it. Her mouth turned down, and she made a series of pained gulping motions.

"Loren," she croaked, raising a weak hand for him. He clutched it and pressed it to his face. "I-I think I broke something." Her voice was shallow.

"She said she broke something," Lor repeated to Gale.

With a trembling hand, Gale lifted the side of her linen dress, pulling the hem up to her waist. Purple-black bruising crawled down the side of her left leg. "Oh God," Gale whispered.

"Loren," she whispered, "remember when we first met? You were so adorably awkward."

"I'll heal it, it'll be alright, just let me heal you."

"I fell in love with all of you that first week. All of you... all of my friends."

He hushed her. "You'll be just fine, baby, let me just heal you..." His hand shook as it hovered around her waist, leading toward her hip.

"And you were my first love..." Her voice weakened.

No one told him. When he placed his palm on her broken hip and closed his eyes, no one said a damn thing to him. So he fed her his memories. Every special moment from his childhood until now, he fed into her.

From him and Eva jumping the waves at a cold beach in West Cordan, to the first time he tasted sarga fruit. He showed her the day he first met her and how she was like something from a dream. Their friendship with Nico and Dill, the motes of light that danced over her nose in the hot spring, and the day he first made love to her all fed into her mind. The birth of their children and the friends he made in exile, all of it.

But no one said anything to him.

When he opened his eyes, she smiled at him. "I love you so much," she whispered.

The bruise remained, raging down her leg in dark webs. "Why can't I heal her?" he hissed.

Gale only looked at him from under his hand rasping over the stubble around his mouth. There were tears tracking down his sunburned cheeks.

"*Dad*, why can't I heal her?"

Gale ran from the bunker, shouting for Jack.

"Where are you going? Somebody answer me!" Lor shouted.

"Loren," Damaetra called to him, and he took her hand again, pressing her pale fingers to his mouth.

Lor shook his head. "No... no... I heal now. I can heal. There's nothing I can't heal." His voice cracked and quivered, knowing too well his limits.

"I should have told you," she said. The dark stain continued its spread down her thigh.

"Told me what?" he whimpered as he kissed her fingers, soaking in every violet-scented molecule of her skin. He asked, but he knew. It was the genetic bane of the Anglia, the one that took Haedrian, his real father. Wasting disease was what Gale called it. "I'm sorry I wasn't here for you." Lor choked out the words. "You are everything to me."

Jack's voice rumbled in the main tent in anxious pants. "It's still experimental," he said.

"Doesn't matter," Gale said.

Both men hurried down the ladder, Gale with a strip of cloth in one hand and his worn medic bag in the other. Jack clamped his teeth over the syringe cap, spitting it to the floor. They scrambled toward Damaetra, and Lor held her closer.

Gale threaded the cloth strip from the top of her hip around her groin and back, cinching the knot right above the webbing bruise.

Rubbing his face again, Gale rummaged through his kit. "I don't know if that'll work, but it might help." He pulled out a disinfectant patch, gently patting her hip with it.

"It's a start," Jack said, sticking the darkest eye of the bruising with the needle, pushing in a dark orange fluid.

Damaetra whimpered with her eyes closed. The pool of tears that had collected finally fell. When Jack withdrew the needle, a thin stream of watery blood slithered around her hip, staining the edge of her underwear before dripping into the sand. The square of gauze in Gale's fingers collected it, and he directed Cimma to hold it in place over the needle stick. Brave girl, she did it, lower lip stuck out and whimpering "*Mommy*" again.

Jack knelt at Lor's side, putting a hand on his shoulder. "Now," he said, "try again."

Lor nodded, licking his dry lower lip. When he looked down at her, she was looking up at him. He leaned down to kiss her, the scent of her violets warm and humid around them. Then he rested his lips on her cheek, closing his eyes and taking her in.

For the first time in what felt like ages, Lor found the white-gold lens under his lids. It had dulled, the entire surface full of widening cracks reminiscent of her lingering pain after her rescue from Gehenna. But it was more... way more. The mirrored surfaces exposed his reflection, staring back at him under pocks of delaminated grime.

As he watched the lens, it quivered open with a rusted squeal. Inside, the space was a beautiful home, shrouded in darkness. He had to go there, he knew... and he willed himself inside, letting the aperture squeak shut behind him.

Nothing but silence greeted him, with phantom shapes in the dark. Her floral aroma permeated the place, and he took a deep breath.

"Damaetra?" he whispered. Only his echo responded.

He took his first steps in the room, and a low table bit into his shin. Sucking in a breath, he pondered how a metaphysical piece of furniture could have possibly hurt.

As he reached down to rub the sore spot, a piercing shot rang out. He ducked his head, hearing the tinny wail in his ear and the sound of a vase shattering. The reverberation faded, and the faintest whimper came from his right. Whoever created the shot rifled through some drawers before cursing and tossing things about.

The small whimper came from behind a sofa to his right. The stranger didn't notice him or her, cursing some more and slamming the door shut.

The end of the hallway began to pool with blood.

Lor called for Damaetra again, and she slowly rose from her hiding spot, looking at him with wide eyes, wet and nearly black from her wide pupils. "Come with me," he whispered, holding out his hand. She hesitated but took it, and he led her to the back of the house, away from her dead father in the front hall.

Rather than find the sun outside, they entered into a long, darkened hallway, familiar to one he used to walk during first levels. Yet, like the home, it was difficult to see much other than the shapes of other children lining the halls. Their eyes glinted in the dark, watching them.

Even as he held her hand, the young version of his wife had grown a few years, still grasping him and glancing at all the child-like shadows. She tightened her grip as the low murmur crescendoed from the walls.

One nasty child stepped in front of them, a brown smear of filth slathered across his upper lip. With a giggle, he pointed at them. "Hey, look, it's the drug baby!"

His declaration roused the other child shadows into a raucous laughter, each shouting their own taunts and curses at her.

Daddy was a druggie, daddy was a druggie...

Drug baby dummy!

Hey Dumb-eetra! Are you a dummy?

They sang the chant through the hall, and it echoed, becoming one with the air. She clutched him tighter, and they ran.

Daddy was a druggie, daddy was a druggie...

They burst through the front entrance and stepped into the outdoors, letting the song of her bullies fade behind them. He had no idea... She only ever had nice things to say about her childhood.

They were outside now, still under cover of shadows. As they moved forward, the soft crunch of nature under their feet was traded for squelching, and Damaetra cried out with adult lungs.

Something yanked her head back, then forward again. It was then he realized something had sliced off her hair in a single swipe. She squeezed his hand for just a moment before vanishing. He swiped at the air in a futile attempt to hold on to her, find her. Calling her name, he only heard his own voice.

Lor cursed to himself, whipping his head back and forth and squinting to find her again. A warm, humid aroma of new growth, mushrooms, and moss wafted by, with a string of ash and rot twirling inside of it.

It was all too familiar, and he panicked.

Helpless, he watched as she relived her imprisonment in Gehenna. She shivered in a dank corner in the thin lavender dress he loved. Par did this to her. Paerli did this.

As he felt the anger rising, a slithering wetness split the mud and brought the cold to him. That dissonant voice he could never forget rose with malevolent laughter. He steeled himself to face this thing—scared to try for the first time since stopping Lapis Evening. But he was in *her* mind, and there was too much to lose here. Man up. But there was help. Underneath that incessant laughter was the tiniest whisper, landing right at the edge of his ear canal like a little gee fly buzzing its wings.

You can forgive her. Forgive Paerli.

He wanted to, and he didn't want to. Par's dark form hovered over Damaetra. He couldn't hear anything, but his wife shrank down, looked down, tilted her ear to her shoulder. Seeing her there, abused by her friend and those cohorts...

Forgiveness is a blessing. Save your wife.

The whisper dissolved, but the message had been delivered. Resolute, he squared his shoulders and saw Damaetra seeing him. They locked eyes as the laughter shook the walls.

"Get out," Lor said. "Get *out*!" His shout aroused the attention of Par and her gang.

The worm's laughter died, and it was silent once again. Lor ran to her, picked her up, and fled. The walls shook, dropping eggs of broken stone smelling of mushrooms. No one followed them—this was only a twisted memory, invaded by the worm. Showers of dust and stone rained around them, and Damaetra cried his name into his neck.

The pitch of her scream intensified as he squeezed through the cavern gap with her in his arms. "We're going to make it, baby, we already have," he said, feeling the sweat stream down his temple. One last push, and they tumbled forward, through the ground, landing in his basement. She fell onto his red chair, now holding their children and bathed in more shadow.

Lor threw his head back and groaned, a new realization that these vast time jumps were by design. Grief consumed her so wholly that only the bad overwhelmed her memories. The goodness was erased with time, leaving massive gaps in her memory. He had to watch her life without him play out.

She spent most of her time in the first few standard months sitting in his chair, staring out at nothing. Her eyes swelled, and the children cried for her attention. There was a journal, and she hand-wrote into it, rather than use a v-note.

She and the children moved to the desert with Gale, Nico, and Dill, where no one went looking for anyone—Niklaus's suggestion. And she wrote. One entry, once every standard year. No matter how curious he was to read it, the darkness blotted out her words.

"Don't forget the good, baby. Don't forget it," he whispered, moving toward her as she sat inside the tent's shadows.

Death camp brigands occasionally tried raiding their community, with increased frequency as the years passed. They killed a few, working with the other residents to push them back in cycles. The brutality stung at first, but then she became numb to it.

Then Cimma disappeared. Lor bit his lip.

Then her sister died, and he cursed under his breath. How much... how much more could she possibly carry?

"Don't ever forget the goodness." He touched her shoulder, and she leaned her head toward him. Kneeling next to her, she looked through him, but with a meek smile on her face. It was the kind of smile she made when getting struck by the feeling of giving up.

He wanted to try something different. The thing he wanted to try wasn't anything he'd done before, but he felt compelled anyway. Something urged him to do it, deep in his heart.

Taking her hands in his, he pressed his forehead to hers and pulled. He pulled the black corruption in her veins, and it wormed from her pores, snaking down her body and bathing her in pitch. All the bad moments, from the ten years without him, her sister's death, her daughter's disappearance, her imprisonment, the teasing, and her father's death—it came from her and sought him. It was the melancholy that seeded the rot that ate at her bones... all of it absorbed into his own skin.

The indescribable pain squeezed every inch of his bowels, and he wanted to scream. All her sadness and deep physical aching in one fleeting moment, and he feared he might implode right there. But he didn't even open his mouth to protest, only loosing a full body shiver in silence. The earthen flavor coated his tongue as each wave of sadness penetrated into his skin.

With a final, violent jerk, the darkness filled him—and when the last tails of her contaminated mind wriggled into his pores, the environment curled back like a piece of parchment, bringing back the light. It struck his eyes in hundreds of needles.

He found himself lamenting on the floor at her feet as the bright tang of Immortal Green faded from his tongue. She ran her fingers through his hair, combing her fingernails over his scalp in soothing circles.

And that was how it would be—he carried it for her. He would carry it for her forever. As long as she could walk in light, he would carry that darkness for her.

"I love you," he said, pressing his lips to her knee.

She cupped her hand on the back of his head, whispering the same.

An invisible string tugged at his belly, but he wasn't ready to go. Yet, the job was complete. He was yanked through the lens, back into the outer space of minds, and it closed with a wink. The last view he caught of the lens was how it shimmered anew.

Strange, being back in the real world. A shock of warmth crawled through his limbs, snatching his core. Several pairs of eyes watched him with anticipation, waiting for answers, while Damaetra lay in his lap in a deep sleep.

He checked for her pulse. If he remembered anything from living under a medic's roof, it was to always check for a pulse. Her skin had chilled from the heal, more so than even Niklaus, but the large artery at her throat thumped against his trembling fingers.

"She's alive, thank the Maker..." He blew out a jet of relief. "Is she going to stay that way?"

Gale felt the same spot, then turned her head back and forth, listening for her breaths. "I hope so," he said.

The purple bruising had stopped its travels down her leg. The spot where Jack's needle went in was nearly faded, and her white skin radiated outward, digesting the bruise in a pale spiral.

Lor looked up at Jack. "What was that formula?"

Jack pressed his lips together. "It was experimental... a mediocre push to help you find her, then know what to do when you did."

Lor nodded and glanced at his wife in his lap. "It worked as intended."

Her skin was so fair. Her face a peaceful mask. Lor brushed his fingers against her cheek, feeling her soft mouth with the pad of his thumb. How many people had he fed his memories of her to?

Even unconscious, her lips carried a subtle, satisfied grin.

Chapter 34

Death's Wake

Loren

Lor needed a nap. The intense healing of first Niklaus, then Damaetra, and last Ayala, had him wanting for rest, and he wasn't in the mood to explain his healing capabilities to anyone at the moment. Not even to Gale, who begged to understand. Under that exhaustion, he felt nauseating waves of "what ifs." What if he wasn't there? They would have died from their wounds.

Another wave of anxiety.

But by the Maker, he was there. And now, Damaetra needed warmth. If Lor could have hoisted her up the ladder to the main level, he would have. But his silver filigree blanket was thick enough to do the job for now, and he had no idea how long she'd be out.

The entire last standard hour replayed in his head. Watching Damaetra stand up to Hammer... he grinned at her gumption. After everything she'd been through, she still had it in her, and he loved her more for it. She held so much pain, and in that dark mess of hers, he was left with a lingering sense of something he couldn't quite put his finger on. Something like shame.

Whatever it was, it didn't reveal itself in the moment, but it came to him in a final whisper as he absorbed the darkness. There was nothing for her to feel shame for.

He scanned the war zone. What a mess.

Niklaus sat where he left him, dazed in a puddle of blood and puke but regaining the color in his cheeks. Nico sat with him, hand on his head.

Tent residents had emerged, weeping and talking in agitated whispers. Dill had come out to help them cope, offering his humorous quips to diffuse their fears.

The one called Betta held a thick bag he recognized as one normally used for shopping and trudged among the ruins of her volatile friend. Even from a distance, her frown reached him, while she plucked Treece's severed ivy cords from the area. Quint and Ayala ran to her and held her as she wept with the blood-soaked bag.

Nearby, the corpse of the Reaper Bas lay stiff and cold in the desert heat. A few children craned their necks from behind their mother's skirts to catch a glimpse of the monster in their realm, while their fathers walked the perimeter in disgust at the invasion.

"Nick!" Cae screeched as she ran from the tent toward her husband. She stopped short of his missing leg and fell to her knees next to him with a short cry.

Eva followed shortly after, bolting for Nico. He had quite the lump from that gear cap, but he smiled that dimpled smile at her and shrugged as he touched his forehead.

Seeing Cae and Eva run from the tent made him nervous that his children would wander outside in this mess. He only hoped Gale would keep them down there for now. They could stay with their mom and avoid the explosion of gore.

The hump of Bas lying there in an amorphous circle of blood made Lor curious. He'd never worked with an Anglian Reaper before, and the man had already begun to bloat.

Lor marched to the body. The desert had taken its share of the dead—dried lips peeled back over large teeth, dark blood jelly scabbed over a putrefying hole in his forehead and ear, swollen belly full of new gases, and the loose tech eye bulged from his socket.

The way he fell positioned him into a coiled child, hands curled inward under his chin. A piece of his skull sat in the sand like a little cap, blown from the back of his head. The navy sleeve of his Audun cloak had pushed back, offering a peek of sallow skin draped over protruding wrist bones.

"Look at him," Lor murmured to himself. "A tool of the cities. Just another evil abuse of the Guild."

The prickle of anger sat at his neck, and he rotated his head to shrug it off. Cae had told him just yesterday that he needed to look for the stars. Rather than simmer in the rawness of the attack on his family, it was time to sort out the riddle that only Horace-Greg knew how to deliver. Knowing Horace, he wouldn't say something like that if it didn't mean something.

As Dill continued his pilgrimage through the tents with Emilia joining him at last, and Niklaus out of sorts in his own mess of worry, Nico stood with Eva in his arms, chin on her head and vacant stare. Despite a knock to the skull, Nico was smart—possibly smart enough to help him solve this riddle. So he made his way toward them.

"You want me to heal that?" Lor said, pointing at the egg on Nico's brow.

He nodded, a small upturn of his lip as he continued his hollow stare over Eva's head.

Lor fed him the memory of when they met in school. For a moment he was afraid it would make Nico nostalgic for better times, but the memory did the trick, banishing the knot from his head.

"Nice," Nico said, draping his arm around Lor's shoulder and drawing him into his embrace with Eva. She hummed and wrapped her arm around Lor too.

There was a kindred sort of silence in that embrace, and within that space between his sister and best friend, Lor didn't feel the need to say anything at all. At least, not for a while, as they remained together for a good standard fifteen minutes.

"Nico..." Lor said at last.

"Hm?"

"I wonder if you can help me."

"Anything. What do you need?"

"When you went downstairs yesterday, Cae came up and told me a riddle she heard from Horace."

Nico stood upright and tilted his head back to look at Lor. "Horace? Wow, that's an old name. What did he say?"

"He told her to tell me that I need to look for the stars. Do you have any idea what that might mean?"

His brow crinkled as he pulled his lower lip into his mouth for a good think. "Nothing is coming to mind right now... but give me a bit to think about it."

"Of course. Thank you."

Nico nodded with another smile.

"No, I mean *thank you*," Lor said, "for being a part of my family."

A tighter squeeze came from Eva and a focused grin from Nico. The lines in his face softened, and his eyes got a touch brighter, as if some weight had been slugged from his shoulders.

Their unspoken agreement was cut through by Dill's shouts of revelation. "I can't believe how stupid I am! Why did I never think of this before?" He stood off in the distance under the tracks, holding up two rusted howie rods and pumping them up and down with laughter. "Niki, a new leg for you!"

Niklaus groaned nearby as Nico snorted back his laughter. "I'm sure it'll still be pretty awesome," he uttered.

"I know it will." Lor kissed his sister on the head. "I'm going to check on Damaetra."

The upper tent was still, with the groanings of his children buzzing in the bunker.

"Pa-*paaa*! I want to go outside!" Cimma brayed along with Nate.

"Absolutely not," Gale said, "you both are staying in the tents until tomorrow."

More groans. Lor descended the ladder, kneeling next to Damaetra as she lay on her bedroll, still unconscious. "How is she?" he asked as Cimma came up behind him, wrapping her arms around his neck. He reached up and held on to her dangling hand.

"She's getting warmer, thank the Maker," Gale said. "I've been measuring her vitals, and she seems to be pretty stable."

"Good. That's good." Lor bit his lip. He examined the bunker for the first time since that morning, disheveled belongings scattered throughout.

Books were strewn on the floor, bedrolls in a state of partial inflation from being tilted over, and pillows crumpled and tossed. "What happened in here?" Lor asked.

Gale tittered. "Ask your wife. She was determined to get to you. Made a mess of things."

Something in the way he said that made Lor sad. If she hadn't worked with Gale to toss Last Grudge, he was sure he would have watched everyone die by Reaping—another "what-if" nightmare that sent a shiver through his sides.

"Hey, do you mind if I sit with her alone for a while?" he asked.

"Yes, absolutely." Gale stood up and held his arm out for the children. "Hey, let's go wait for Quint and Ayala at the Freelys' bunker, alright? We can play games later."

Cimma slithered from Lor's back and went with Gale as Nate followed. Before disappearing through the thin fabric partition, Nate took a moment to turn back toward Lor. "I love you, Daddy," he said.

"I love you so much, buddy."

Nate smiled with his lips tucked in, then followed after Cimma and Gale. Once everyone was gone, he tilted his gaze down at his wife.

She seemed more at peace lying there. The peach flush he adored had returned to her cheeks, and her lips were pink. Her hands lay on her chest, and they rose and fell steadily. The ancient tech ring he gave to her faced him, odd markings displaying their mysterious language. He reached down and ran his thumb over it. How he wished he could enter her mind again. Better to let her rest. He prayed she was left with only the good memories, as the demure smile on her face would suggest.

When he pushed her hair back from her clammy forehead, his finger brushed up against a hard corner of something stuffed inside her pillow. Careful not to jostle her, he crept his hand into the space between the cover and the fluff, pulling out a tan-colored notebook.

In his travels through her memory, he remembered her writing in a journal. Was this the one? He glanced around and listened. No one was around to see him peek into her private scrawlings. It could have been looked upon as rude for him to pry. But now that he carried her pain, he had to know what she wrote.

The first page was blank. As was the second and third. He swiped furiously through each page until finally on the sixteenth sheet, she had scribbled with a light hand, *Maker forgive me.*

Chapter 35

A Most Unfortunate Row

Loren

Laughter barked from the level above from Gale, Nico, and Dill, but Lor was in no mood for joy. The tan journal pinched in his fist, he was ready for a fight.

The same nauseating illness of rage pumped in his chest, except instead of being fed by Par as it had so long ago, it was all his own.

Two deep breaths. He closed his eyes to the scene covered in the smoky chortles of his friends and father.

Two more deep breaths. The anger must be managed. The worm must not be allowed a foothold.

Two bursts of brilliant blue puffed across his vision when Gale recalled his actions in the desert. *Bam! Bam!*

Screw it.

Lor stomped into the main tent from the bunker, wagging the tan notebook in crazed jolts over his head. "I ought to beat you straight into the ground!"

The three of them were sitting at the table, having a nice drink and chatting without a care in the world. Lor's abrupt interruption made Gale shudder and turn around.

"Hold on, son, what's this about?" Gale said, pitching back as Lor advanced on them.

"Don't *son* me, me you son of a bitch!"

Gale seethed. "Back up, Loren."

Nico and Dill gave looks to each other. Nico started to stand, but Lor wouldn't have it.

"No, you sit down and witness this. Both of you!"

Their twin expressions and Nico's slow recline into the chair impressed on Lor that he'd become rather intimidating. But this fight wasn't against them, and he wouldn't apologize for it.

He slapped the notebook on the table between them, open to page seventeen: a journal entry written in Damaetra's handwriting.

"I found this inside her pillowcase, *Gale*," Lor sneered. "Read it. Read it right there!" He stabbed at a passage in the book, center of the page.

Gale cleared his throat, sliding his glasses from forehead to nose, and began to move his mouth over the words.

"No, read it out *loud*," Lor pushed the words through his teeth. "Everyone needs to hear."

Gale glared at him from over the rim of his dark spectacles. The shared discomfort traveled between them and his friends. Again, Gale cleared his throat and straightened the book in his hand. His voice shook as he spoke.

> "The Maker played a cruel game with me. The more I grieved my losses, the more I wanted him. I needed to feel whole over and over again... And when we came together, I felt a nagging guilt that I was angering God."

Each word that came from his stepfather's mouth descended into trembling. And as he read it, Lor knew his own face had changed, because the hot anger he came upstairs with now poured freely from his eyes.

"How could you do it, Gale?" he said, letting the drops slide onto the floor. "How could you sleep with my wife?"

"Oh shit," Dill whispered. They all turned to Gale.

"Loren, wait," Gale said, making a move to stand when Lor struck him across the jaw, sending him to the floor on all fours and nearly toppling the table. His friends knocked back their chairs when they stood.

The usual flavor of Immortal Green washed over Lor's mouth. A rough cut on his knuckle drawn by one of Gale's remaining teeth sewed itself shut. He snatched the journal from the table, shaking it in front of them.

"I read this whole entry. The whole thing, Gale. Remarkable stuff, truly. And, as a special bonus to me, I got to read all about it in such vivid detail!"

Now kneeling, still on the floor, Gale held his jaw. Blood ran from the corner of his mouth, and a tear dripped from his eye.

Nico came to him, possibly to recreate their moment in the desert. He wished he could succumb to the comfort of his friend, but he couldn't. Lor flicked the journal at Gale, and it struck him on his knee. "Have a read. It's so detailed that I know you smelled like *rich island coffee* to her. As a fun extra, I also know the color of your pubes."

He spit out the last bit, finally turning to leave with Nico at his side. Dill knelt next to Gale, picking up the dark frames that flew from his nose when he took the hit.

"She wanted it too," Gale mumbled through his bloody hand.

Lor turned once again to face Gale, with Nico's palm pressing into Lor's chest. "I'm sorry, what the hell did you just say?"

"Don't, Loren," Nico pleaded with him, "this is what it wants. This is what Cirv'e wants."

"I said, *she wanted it too*!" Gale shouted back, face twisted into something unrecognizable, and sputtering droplets of red into the sand before him. Dill dropped his face into his hand, shaking his head.

Lor relaxed, drawing his shoulders down, and stared at his stepfather on the floor. "I wish you had died that day."

Nico grabbed his arm and led him back into the bunker, beyond a resting Damaetra through the thin fabric flap and into his own place in the hive of desert basements.

"*Ouch*, Lor," Nico said when directing him to sit.

Lor choked on the thickening curtain of mucus in his throat. "Was there any woman in my life that Gale wasn't willing to take for himself?"

Nico sighed, leaving a bloated pause between them. Ten years. Ten long years! No matter what his friend said, it would only make him angrier.

The longer Nico remained silent, the more Lor grated over the thought of his stepfather touching Damaetra in that cockpit: the very place they made love when he came back to her. He wanted to scream. Instead, his throat bobbed as he fought it, knowing if he did, it would carry through the bunker hive and frighten everyone inside, including his children a few rooms over. He heard their faint laughter.

"Loren," Nico said at last. He squeezed Lor's shoulder, sending a pinch of the good kind of pain that released pressure stored inside of it. "We love you. You know that, right?"

Lor's lip trembled as he stared into the dark corner.

"Gale loves you more than anything," he continued.

He sucked his trembling lip under his top teeth, biting down and feeling that tiny jolt of electric pain. No Immortal Green yet, but just enough pain to distract him from the urge to punch Gale again.

Nico squeezed his shoulder once more. "I won't make excuses for him. We had all given up hope that you were alive." A tiny crack in his voice revealed the tiny crack in his crumbling mask.

"Damaetra was lost without you." Nico made another one of those miserable long pauses, intending it for himself to continue speaking without showing his own cracking polish. "And then Cimma disappeared, and her sister died... then Cae ran off for a while... Everyone processes their grief differently, and well, Damaetra processed hers as written in that journal."

The squeeze at his shoulder was the only thing keeping the pressure in Lor's system from bursting. Every dire emotion waved through his veins as he listened to Nico and relived the past two days. The past ten years.

"Kill me," Lor uttered, "please kill me."

Nico sighed and rested his brow atop Lor's sweaty head, covered in greasy blond strands. "I didn't tell you this earlier, but I do think it's important now..."

Lor felt his friend take two prolonged inhales of his scalp. Surely it didn't smell great.

Then he blew out the breath, hot air crawling down Lor's skull. "Gale... well, with all the noise on the day you were taken, he... um, ah, I don't know how to say this delicately...."

Another pause. Another dreadful pause.

Nico clicked his tongue and spoke slowly. "I'm just going to say it. Gale tried to kill himself after you were taken away."

Lor sighed, and that's when the guilt finally reached him.

"I stopped him, but just barely," Nico continued, swiping casually at his cheek. "We can't let the worm win. We just can't."

Lor sat upright, letting Nico's grip dig deeper into his shoulder. "How do you know this is the worm? How do you know it's not just humans being shitty humans?"

Nico tittered. "Humans are shitty because of the worm."

Nico had him there. He glanced into the dark corner again, a feeling of unease reaching out and brushing its cold fingers down his face and torso. "What do you have over there?" Lor pointed at it, feeling as though his arm might be swallowed by the darkness.

Nico squinted into the corner. His think face was just as Lor remembered: crafted by skilled Artisans in the finest stone. "Oh... Oh!" he blurted before grabbing a random stained rag that was draped over his Formulator chest on the floor.

With rag in hand, he disappeared into that dark corner, emerging with something clutched in his fist, wrapped in the protective, dirty cloth. When he unfurled his fingers, Par's pendant lay inside, black stone glittering with red stars.

"Look for the stars," Nico declared.

It was then it clicked for Lor. "We have to destroy it."

Chapter 36

Ten Years

Shattering Par's pendant was easier than Lor thought. One pop with a robust spanner, and the thing just cracked into several pieces, wriggling their way out of their golden setting. Nico had remarked at that fact also, pointing out that it had survived in pristine condition so long without blemish, to be crushed in one hit. Either way, the stars disappeared, leaving nothing but unremarkable black stone.

Nico left with the thing, vowing to obliterate it into powder until he was satisfied. Lor was just fine with that. Well, he hoped that with its destruction, he would start to feel better. And largely, he had felt the weight of the atmosphere lift a bit right after the stone cracked. Yet a part of that anger remained.

In an attempt to view the situation outside his own perspective, he *had* been gone for ten standard. Of course Damaetra was lonely and sad. There was a point where he even wanted her to move on. But Gale? Why did it have to be Gale?

Lor stroked Damaetra's hair, listening to the distant giggles and shouts of his children several bunkers over. Second sun was almost in the sky, and everyone was inside once again, but allowing him his space with her for a time.

That solitude was interrupted by the metallic squeak of shoes over ladder rungs. When Lor turned, his father stood there. The corner of his mouth had swelled with dried blood cracking over it.

He stuck a gray-colored journal toward Lor, stiff-armed and unsmiling. "I was an asshole," he said, jostling the journal in his hand and beckoning Lor to take it.

Lor studied him, but Gale held his position, offering the journal.

Seeing him standing there with a busted mouth scratched at Lor's guilt… knowing now about Gale's brush with suicide, then telling him he wished he had died… The sympathy war raged inside his organs until he finally stood, snatching the journal from Gale's grip. Then his father left him.

The gray one was the journal he'd seen in her mind. This was the one he tried to find… How did Gale know? A smart man could deduce such a thing, he supposed.

One hand squeezed the bottom edge of the new journal, the other flat on the top. What lay inside made his heart pump faster than he'd like. This was his wife's world when he was gone, and he had to know.

My Loren,

It's been a standard week since you've been gone. There are no words in Northern Common that could express how much you mean to me. When I look at our babies, I see your face in both of them.

I can't seem to find a way to open my mouth and speak. Gale and your sister, along with our friends, have taken on a great responsibility for us, and I'm forever thankful for that. I must be honest, I was afraid my depression would be the end of all three of us. It might yet be the end for me, but at least our children will be loved and cared for.

You'll be happy to know that my implant is gone. Gale removed mine, Eva's, and Emilia's too. If the cities ever try to track us, they'll only find the three of us huddled together at the bottom of the sea.

I finally named our children. In the hopes that our prayers are heard, I named our daughter Cimone'a, which means "the Maker answers" in Foscan. Our son is Nathanael, which also means "the Maker answers," but with the Anglian spelling of the Foscan name. I figured it fitting for their heritage, and for their future because I hope and pray for the Maker's answers. Both of our children deserve their father…

…And their mother to be fair.

I must swear to you that I will become stronger for them. Please forgive me for being selfish in my melancholy. I knew there was a risk for our children, but I never once thought it would be you I would lose.

Love always, Damaetra

YEAR 1

Dearest husband,

It is the one-year anniversary since you've been gone. When I think of anniversaries, I think of celebrations. Of course, I do not celebrate this anniversary, and I hate that it is our children's birthday. I wish you could see them.

Shortly after you were taken, we moved to the desert to live with Jack's wife, Verena, and their daughter, Ayala. And by "we," I mean me, Gale, Dill, Nico, and Niklaus. Remember him? He's another story I'll have to tell you about. We left because that horrible man that took you still wants to see us all dead. And I told you I'd protect the children against this war.

Anyway, Verena's been such a blessing for us—and she's an Engineer! It makes a hard desert life a little easier with her gadgets. Speaking of Engineers, Eva lives in your house and continues to work in the cities to help us out financially. Emilia, my two sisters, and mom, and Aedras also help out with what they can. Trust that we are taken care of.

Eloria is taking courses at Peakwood so she can get her degree in Law. She's in the accelerated program so she can get an internship as a roundsman within a year. I know you wanted that so bad, but trust me, you don't. She's doing it to get close to Hammer in the hopes she can push our family from his mind. I feel so bad for her, because in between courses, she has to find more creative ways of getting him to back off until she can be next to him. I miss my sisters.

Oh, you should know that Emilia and Dill are engaged! I never thought that was a thing that could happen, but consider me surprised. They're supposed to get married after the maelstrom, but it will be here in the desert, in secret. You know how that goes. She seems to be oddly perfect for him.

Our son, I call him Nate now, well, he's already started showing interest in moving around the tents, holding on to whatever his little chubby hands can find, and scooting here and there. He's so precious, and he looks just like you. Now Cimone'a (I call her Cimma), she is content staying still, watching everyone around her. She's very observant, and I can only imagine what goes on in that little head of hers. It's so strange to see how much she looks like me with that black hair, and, well... you know...

Cimma said her first word not too long ago. I'm not too surprised that it was *Mama*, but recently she added *Dada*. She says it so resolutely, as if you're standing just in front of her. It broke my heart.

They both have their baby bottom teeth now. I had to wean them when Nate decided to bite his Momma. Yeesh, just thinking about it sets my teeth on edge. I really miss you.

Love, Damaetra, Nate, and Cimma

Year 2

My Loren, my husband,

Another standard year has come and gone. Emilia is now Mrs. Storgut, and Nico has asked Gale if he may marry Eva. In truth, I thought it would have been them before Dill, but I'm just missing the mark all over the place. Either way, she said yes! I'm glad she matched so well with one of our best friends... and who better than Nico? (Don't tell Dill I said that.) They're planning on waiting until around this time next year. Nico agreed that we needed another happy event around the twins' birthday to help us cope.

So how have we been getting along in the desert? Well, like I mentioned before, we get funding from what we now call the "Triple-E Bank." Cae doesn't like being excluded, but her contributions are also a blessing... and she's done such wonders to temper Niklaus. More on that later.

Back to desert life: Gale, Nico, and Niklaus run errands for us to Secas. We've been slowly gathering supplies to build the machine. What's the machine, you might ask? Well, it's the *under*-underground vehicle we started building last year. Gale thinks we should try to heal Mount Gehenna back into what it used to be. He reasons that it might help reset the North into some kind of utopia... maybe push out the *worm*. And if it doesn't fix the politics of Roseaarde, well, we could probably make a home there. Maybe... if Par is gone.

I've been perfecting my formulations to help with the healing of the mountain, while our skilled Engineers have been building the machine. They all volunteered me to drive it when it's done. Well, I'm nervous about that... this isn't going to be an ordinary jumper.

The twins are now two standard years, and they couldn't be more different. Yet, they cry when they're apart... well, Nate cries... I don't think Cimma knows how. But she will whine. Oh, the *whine*! When she's not whining, and Nate's not crying, they babble and giggle at each other all the time. It's so cute, like they have their own language. Cimma's our little talker, though—she knows more words and started talking first. Nate is our walker. He found his way around the tents early, while Cimma didn't find her strength until quite a bit later. Gale said you were a lot like that too. You could have a smart mouth with him but weren't fast enough to run away. I had to laugh, sorry, baby!

Love forever, Damaetra, Nate, and Cimma

YEAR 3

My lost love,

Well, it's official, your sister is now your best friend's wife. It's so weird. I love them both but can't help but feel a little envious of the budding relationships around me. Especially since you've left your mark in every single member of this tent. Well, except Verena and her daughter, but everyone else.

Can you believe our children are already three? I can't. Cimma has grown rather fond of Nico, calling him "Unca Nino." Nate just copies her, so he says it the same way. Then there's "Unca Dew" and "Unca Nini." I'll let you figure those out. I won't even try to spell how they say "Aunt Verena." And of course, I'm always hearing, "Papa, Papa, Papa!"

Gale adores them so much, and they him. We gave them a taste of your favorite fruit not too long ago... you know, the sarga? Well, Nate didn't care for it, but Cimma *devoured* it. Gale finds them in Secas when he can, bringing them to her, and her eyes just light up. Aside from the occasional fruit, it's ration blocks like always.

We sometimes get charitable "drops" from the tracks above, but we're lucky we have funding for those shopping trips to Secas. I think Niklaus steals sometimes... old habits and all. Am I a bad person if that doesn't bother me?

So, Niklaus...

He apparently came to our wedding. In his own words, he was stalking Nico. I had a feeling he wasn't completely devoid of love for his brother, or redemption for that matter. Remember we talked about that? During his stalking, he ran into Cae while she was living with Nico. They started dating in secret, before he reconciled with his brother, which I find so interesting. Wasn't I carrying the twins then? They've been together for a long time now.

I try to think of all the little moments we were having together while she was sneaking around with him. It's the nostalgia in me, I know. Despite our somewhat sordid history with him, he's turned out to be quite a resourceful boon to us. Perhaps he feels he must pay us back in a way he knows how. He's still mouthy, but in a fun way. I like how he and Cae balance each other out.

He won't say it, but I can tell he misses Jack... They reconnected after his escape back here, and—dare I say it—even became friends. He blames himself for not doing anything when they came to get him. I can't blame him for running... not really.

Love always, Damaetra, Nate, and Cimma

Year 4

My dearest Loren,

Maker help me, our stubborn daughter refuses to go potty in the bucket. She stays in her swaddlers, and it's getting very old cleaning it up. Water is precious here, and we have to recycle it a lot of times (thank the Maker for Verena's tech!), but filtered or not, no one wants poopy swaddler water for their baths or their mouths. Nate is a good boy and tries to talk her into it. I mean, she's old enough that it's going to get embarrassing for her.

I've been feeling weak lately, and I'm not sure why. It could be the desert heat, but you'd think I'd be used to that by now. Perhaps it's just running around after the children. Cimma gets very stir-crazy, and she just wants to explore. I wish she could, I really do. But we are constantly surrounded by death—death in the environment, death in her bounty, the looming threat of Hammer coming to claim us, and all the little camps in the depths of the desert that sometimes wander our way.

The guys had to kill a band of them that got too close a few months back. Verena and I didn't even know about it until everyone returned... Gale with a broken wrist and everyone spattered in blood like one of Cae's abstract art pieces. They do what they can to protect us, but if we don't know where they are or what they're doing, how can we possibly know if something happens to them? If I lost them, I would probably just perish. I would turn to dust.

I'm sorry, I know I must hide those thoughts from our children... it's important that I stay strong for them. Every day I pray to see your shadow on the horizon.

Love eternally, Damaetra, Nate, and Cimma

Year 5

My husband, my love,

It's been a long five years without you. We pray for your health and safety all the time. I'm selfish in that I pray for you to come home to me. While Nico, Dill, and Niklaus have to suffer their significant others living across the country, they can at least be assured annual, month-long visits.

...I'm sorry, it's so inconsiderate of me to wish their ~~minor~~ hurt was mine too. At this point, it feels like the only ones who might understand what I'm going through are Gale and Verena. Not to say no one is sympathetic, but it's hard to live in this skin, holding out a hope that you'll return to me, when deep down I fear... no... I *know* you are already dead.

I have nightmares about it sometimes, seeing your pale body floating in a sea of green water, vacant eyes hazed over in death. God, I'm tearing up just thinking about it.

Cimma sits in my lap right now, watching the pen move over the paper, so curious. She's getting close to understanding letters, so I have to be careful what I write here when she's watching. But her being here is a comfort to me. She seems to always know when I'm not feeling well, even if I don my best mask. I think Nate does too, but he's a boy with his own curiosities and distractions.

The machine is coming along fantastically. With everyone pitching in to help, even other residents of tent city who believe in the cause, it's come together faster than we imagined. We have to take care not to purchase parts or eneris in bulk as to prevent raising any suspicions on any of the runners, so it's a little here, a little there... That's the part that's taking time.

I've already mastered the formulations that will go into the manifold. I just need to make sure they stay stable until we need them. Sometimes that's not easy to do. The preservation system I put in them shouldn't harm the tree, at least, based on the taste tests Nico and I performed.

Love always, Damaetra, Nate, and Cimma

Year 6

My dearest husband,

Everyone in the tents has a role to play, and Nico had one of his taken from him. It's his legs... they're not working properly anymore. We think it has to do with bits of sand getting jammed into his joints over time. He went flying when his right leg locked up and about landed on Verena's electrical trap. We told him to retire his shopping trips and focus on his offensive formulations until Dill can figure out a fix for his legs.

But Nico's not only working on offensive phials, he's been trying to find a replacement for Verdigris Mend, since we don't have gold eneris. Bless him, he works hard, but I can tell he's getting stressed out.

You won't believe this next thing—Cae proposed to Niklaus! Isn't that funny? She's always been the more hot-tempered of my sisters, and she probably got tired of him not asking. But, of course he said yes to her! They're going to wait a little bit too. Since everyone is so distanced most of the year, they're going to make it official after the maelstrom when they're all visiting for the month.

Off topic, but Gale has been teaching the children basic first aid. I think they're old enough to start learning that, right? They're six now, and they pick up on things really fast! Gale even started teaching them Foscan just for fun. I totally forgot he knew how to speak it. Sorry, I shouldn't have brought that up.

Love forever, Damaetra, Nate, and Cimma

Year 7

My amazing Loren,

I wish you were here. Seven years, and my soul aches, my bones ache, I feel weak... is it heartbreak? Mae'guae haer. I learned a Foscan word of my own. According to Gale, it means I love you. I don't know if I'll ever be able to get over you.

Cimma told me not too long ago with utmost certainty in her belief that you are still alive. Please don't misunderstand that I've been putting notions such as these into her head, nor has anyone in the tents. Her dreams are vivid and somewhat untamed. I heard her talking to herself outside once, and I'm so afraid she's developed a mania of sorts. She has an imaginary friend she calls "Mister Shadow," and the name alone has me on edge.

An even worse possibility than a diagnosis of mania... has she been speaking to the worm? Maker, I pray that she is not.

We heard rumors of Yeunish executions from Eloria. I'm not sure if these are happening in the cities, in the outer towns, to the banished, or what, but oppression has gotten so much worse. In a way, I'm glad we came to the desert, away from prying political eyes. We've been tried and tested out here. Our children are tougher than most, more aware, with more skill...

Cae says work chatter is getting bad. She can't even suggest a positive feeling toward the Maker lest she get fired. Mom and Aedras are going through the same thing, while Eloria has been hard at work pushing that strongman. I forgot to mention years ago that she got the job. Sorry about that. So much time passes that I often forget the things I've experienced. Good things roll off my back like warm grease, yet the bad things lodge themselves into my mind like a malignant tumor.

I love you, I love you, I love you.

Damaetra, Nate, and Cimma

Year 8

Precious husband, distant lover,

I think I'm getting ill with something I can't cure with a phial. Maker forbid we risk having anyone ask the cities for help. Control is getting tighter, surveillance wider, and the violence... well, it's wilder.

Nico has been trying to create something new for me, but he curses himself for not having "Yeunish intuition." You'd think I'd be able to help, but I find myself oftentimes resting here and there. I do hope it passes. But at least if I die, I'll return to you.

On the off chance you are alive and you ever do come back, you'll be surprised to see Dill. Over the years, he's slowly collected parts to make himself a pair of tech eyes. Once he finished making those, he needed to have them installed. That means Gale had to install them. And if you can guess, that means Gale had to remove Dill's natural eyes. We had some good pain relief phials and a phial and a half left of Verdigris Mend, so he did well. Niklaus says he screamed like a girl (that made me laugh).

It's so strange seeing Dill's face almost like it was all those years ago. Now, we have just one phial of Verdigris Mend left and still no replacement formulation. Even worse still, Gale's body is starting to reject Verena's patch. He needs a drop of it every once in a while to calm down the redness, but it's only a matter of time before he won't be able to run anymore.

An update on our children: Well, Cimma is stubborn, just like her father. She still talks with this "Mister Shadow" and insists that you need someone to bring you home. It upsets Nate quite a bit, but I can't seem to get her to stop. So stubborn.

Love forever, Damaetra, Nate, and Cimma

YEAR 9

Dearest Loren,

Our goal is to get the machine up and running next year sometime after the maelstrom. We're almost there, with only a few tweaks left. In the meantime, I've been teaching Nate how to operate the machine. I know it's my assigned duty to drive it, but I'm afraid for my future.

I have the wasting disease, like your birth father. I don't know who I inherited it from, but one of Gale's medical tomes said it could spontaneously occur in the Anglian race when "confronted with a war of stress." Does sadness translate into stress? Medical tomes use such odd language... but in a weird way, I understand. Maybe that makes me a secret ancient. I don't know what I'm saying, don't mind me.

I believe that this is happening because deep down I know you're dead. I've lost my hope that you are coming back to us. Can you see us? While in the Promised Land, do you know who we are? When I follow you in death, will we be together again?

I can take solace that your pain is gone, but mine still works through me. I'm surrounded by loved ones, yet I feel alone. I struggle to write in this book, knowing what I know about your fate. I just wish I could feel something other than heartache.

Yours eternally, Damaetra

Year 10

My husband,

Melancholy is a bitter sundown on us all. Forgive me, my love.

Love, your wife

Lor closed the journal, sealing his tears inside.

Chapter 37

Lor's Resolve

Loren

Damaetra lay still, hair pooled around her head in a sweaty halo. Eyes closed, cheeks flushed, her chest rose and fell slowly. Lor pressed a wet hand rag over her forehead.

He couldn't be mad at her. On a much deeper level, he understood what she went through… her suffering lived in his veins. While he dealt with his grief differently, Damaetra was a much gentler person than he.

Gale on the other hand? Well, despite the squeezing waves of anger that persisted in his gut, Lor did regret wishing him dead… right to Gale's face no less. After all, he lost both of his wives, his son, and his career…

If only he'd read the gray journal alone. Whatever nagging voice in the pits of his mind that urged him to simmer in his hatred had to go. There was work to do, and he had a family to protect. There was a world that needed to change. He caught himself rubbing his face to pink in the bad habit of his father, but the rasp of his dry palm against nose and cheeks was the distraction he needed to curb the rage, guilt, and sadness fighting for his attention.

He stood and looked down at her lying there, weakened and vulnerable. There was no way he would leave her in tent city while he went after the worm. Even if she was conscious, she had much healing to do. Corl was safe. It was time to make a real, tangible plan, and there was no more time to waste.

The children quarreled nearby about who would sleep next to their momma, with Verena tempering their conversation. Jack blew out a loud sigh and flapped out his and Verena's bedroll. "It's late. I'll go get Gale," he said.

"No, let me," Lor said. He didn't wait for a response before ascending the ladder.

Once on the upper level, there was a type of magic in the way second sun's purple rays arced into the tent. As serene as it seemed, there was nothing calming about the air. Gale sat alone on the couch—head in his hands with elbows propped on his knees.

Lor dragged his feet to stand in front of him, rousing Gale's attention. When he looked at Lor, his brows knit together and he pulled his lips to the side. The puffiness under his eyes either came from the hit or his own grief.

"I can heal that for you," Lor said, pointing at Gale's jaw. The blood he didn't bother to clean persisted at the corner of his mouth.

Gale put his fingers to the hard, dry spot. "No. Don't," he rasped.

Lor nodded, putting his hand down. The silence between them cut deeper than the ripper blade, and it was the kind Lor's Immortal Green would never be able to fully cure, he knew that. The scar would remain inside of him as Gale would wear that same scar on his face.

"I'm sorry that I... hit you." Lor's voice pushed aside the curtain of dead air.

"Don't be. It was a hell of a hit." Gale moved like a dead fish, leaning back into the couch and placing his hands at his sides. Aside from his initial acknowledgment toward Lor, his gaze remained fixed in his lap.

A restlessness of sorts stirred in his father when he ground his palms over the top of his thighs—as if he'd swapped his face-rubbing habit to one of lighting his own legs on fire.

After a moment of the back-and-forth swishing of his palms, his face crumpled inward with the deep reflections of someone studying his medic manual. "I'm so sorry," he uttered.

"I know you are. I've made peace with it." Saying those words betrayed his own thoughts. But he had to move on. He had to.

"I'd like to think I'm a better man than that."

Lor closed his eyes, folding his lips inward. The scene remained under his lids—a pensive Gale digging his legs with his palms in a colorless silence. The difference was his door, slightly parted behind him. It wasn't open enough to see fully, but Lor caught small clues that it was the day his mother died—Dag, his real mother—and it hurt to watch. Rather than his blunder with Damaetra, the real issue on his mind was that day. Gale had really lost so much then: the catalyst to now, where he sat in front of him, burning holes in the top of his pants, probably regretting ever involving himself in Haedrian's affairs.

"Say something," Gale said. Blue swirls lifted from his shoulders, and Lor realized Gale was looking right at him.

Lor opened his eyes, and the door vanished. "You *are* a better man."

Gale scoffed and shook his head. "I deserve this, you know?" He pointed at the red crust on his swollen lip.

"No." Lor shook his head. "You don't."

The silence that seemed to permeate every facet of Lor's relationships in the last few hours had begun to wear on him. "Let me heal that," he said.

"No." Gale turned his nose in the air, off to the side.

It could have been the rush of everything happening at once during his return home, but it was the first time Lor noticed the nick of flesh removed from the top of Gale's ear. All he could think about was that suicide attempt.

Lor sat on the couch next to his father.

"You raised me," he said.

Gale tittered.

"You lost Surai."

Gale nodded with a sigh.

"You lost me and Dag."

Gale pressed his lower lip under his front teeth and resumed the bonfire on his legs.

"You kept my children safe and cared for my wife."

Gale closed his eyes, lower lip still stuck under his teeth. He took in a deep breath. Once he opened his eyes again, Lor turned toward him.

"You don't deserve that." He pointed at Gale's lip wound.

Gale didn't argue back, only shaking his head in mild disagreement.

As he sat there, Lor surprised him with a hug, gripping him tight, and Gale hugged him back. What he knew Gale wouldn't expect was Lor's hand on the back of his neck, feeding him the memory of the day they sat together after Surai's death.

Lor was only ten years old, the age of his children. The stone funeral bench didn't offer much comfort as his legs listed back and forth while he sat and watched everyone mill around, away from the gardens where they buried her. To him, Surai was his real mom, and then she was dead.

After sending Eva with Dag, Gale sat next to him on that bench.

He said nothing, just sat with him there. The musky cologne of coffee coated his clothes, radiating around them and reminding Lor of home. Then he draped his arm around Lor, letting him cry into his side. Everything was warm, and the protection of his father comforted him, telling him it was all right to mourn for their losses and still be strong. They both were hurting, and Gale let Lor grieve.

There was a quiet bond in that moment—a little spark of connection between phases of rebellion against his stepfather. Lor didn't know the significance of that moment until years after it had passed, but Gale had given him a gift that day. And now, they both were hurting, and Lor let Gale grieve.

His reasons for fishing down to that tiny morsel of memory in the middle of their somewhat stilted relationship during his youth weren't entirely clear at first, but it made sense. It worked. The swelling in Gale's lip had de-escalated, leaving nothing but the crust of blood cracking into flakes. Even the raw redness encircling his eyes had faded.

Gale touched his lip and clicked his tongue. "Stubborn as always… won't even let me wallow in my injury." He smiled a little, and Lor responded in kind.

"Yeah, well, I'm going to need you in top shape for what's next, because this is the moment where we are going to change things."

PART 3

Chapter 38

The Plan

Loren

It broke Lor's heart to see them cry.

"Do you have to go, Daddy?" Cimma whimpered. She wrung her hands with Nate behind her turning a toe into the floor.

He knelt next to his daughter and beckoned for his son. They hung their heads, leaning into him as he held them. "I know it's hard to hear, my babies." Squeezing them a little tighter, he didn't like leaving them either after he had only just arrived. "I need to do this for us. For both of you and for your mom."

Not having his family present would dull his colors, and he prayed he'd be strong enough to face the evil.

Cimma whimpered again. "Mister Shadow said I need to give this to you." She pulled out a tie-wrapped bag from her pocket, smaller than his palm.

When he took it, he pulled the tie, and inside the curled fabric lay a twined lock of Damaetra's white-gold hair woven with strands from their children.

"What's this for?" Lor asked, pinching the braid between his fingers.

"He said it was how we could be with you while we are apart and give you strength in the other layer."

The braid was mostly white, with Cimma's black hair twisting through it.

Holding it to his chest, he smiled at them. "I'm coming back to you. I promise."

"Dill and Emilia are coming with me to the cities," Lor said. He pointed at Nico. "You'll have Eva, Jack, Verena, Gale, Niklaus, and Cae, along with my children. Ayala and Quint are staying behind with the Freelys and Betta to protect the tents in case things get wild. Let's hope they don't get wild."

Dill chuckled, cracking his knuckles.

"Maron and Par have agreed to meet you inside the mountain. But once inside, I need them to help me at the breach while everyone else stands guard or works on the tree. Am I missing anything?"

"So you're taking Damaetra to that little town on the South Coast? What's it called again?" Nico tapped his lip.

"Corl. As long as she's only semi-conscious, I want her as far away from any trouble as possible. We have friends there, and I think that's where she'll be the safest."

They both nodded, a mirror of concentrated looks.

Closing his eyes, Lor checked the other layer around his friends one last time. Two doors, shrouded in mist, and locked tight. Good.

Lor cleared his throat. "Are you ready?"

"No," Dill said with a chuckle.

Nico said nothing, but his smile carried the weight of fear.

Lor pressed his damp forehead to his friend's, and Nico closed his eyes. "I'm trusting my children's lives with you and Eva," he said. Nico tittered with the same trepidation.

"You've been the best friends I could have ever asked for, and I truly love you both. I'm coming back, I promise." It was the second promise he made that morning, and he hoped he could keep it.

A wave of warmth blew in from the tent opening. "Now let's have a kiss," Niklaus said, puckering his lips at them.

Nico choked out a laugh, breaking away. "Shut up, Niki," he said.

"I'm just messing with you." The genuine smile Niklaus gave made Lor regret missing out on the years of reconciliation and relationship building. But he had time. There was so much time left for him. Niki plunked into the nearby chair, and the welded howie rods squeaked over his ball joint knee.

"Remember, all of you... even you, Niklaus... don't let the worm inside. Lock your doors, stay strong."

"Same to you," Nico said.

"Hey, Loren..." Cae said as she crawled up from the bunker. "I forgot I was supposed to tell my sister another thing from Horace. Since she's still resting, maybe you would know?"

Lor angled his gaze down to his sister-in-law with a shrug. "With the riddles that guy hands out, I'm thinking a hard *maybe*? What did he say?"

"I might get this wrong," she said and paused, tapping her finger on her lip. "But he basically said, 'the order has your back,' or something like that. What does that mean?"

The order... It felt familiar, but it was an idea that sat on the hazy edge of memory. Just enough to know it was there and understand its importance, but a smidge too far to reach out and grab.

"He called it, 'the order'?"

"I think so. Either way, he said they're in the cities and they support you."

He nodded. Even if he wasn't sure who "the order" was, if Horace said he had friends in the city, he trusted that. Hopefully he would do him a favor and let the order know he was on his way.

He said his goodbyes to his family and new friends, praying he'd return in one piece. Praying he'd return at all. Giving Gale an extra-long embrace, they parted with a fond, "I'm proud of you," from Gale, and the first ever, "I love you, son."

Damaetra was light in his arms. She had moments of coming to, but her interactions were woozy and brief. Progress was progress at least. She woke up long enough for him to explain where they were going, eat a protein block, then take a good swig of water before lying down again. Whether she understood where they were going, he wasn't sure, so he hoped she didn't wake up again while they were traveling.

Lor carried her outside while she rested, shrouded in a cloak with a set of goggles fixed over her eyes in case she did happen to open them on the ride.

Dill stood by the sand skip, pulling out Verena's charger, then helping Emilia into the side car. "You ready for this?"

"Not really," Lor said, laying Damaetra in Emilia's lap. He tucked them in with the filigree blanket even if Emilia protested the heat.

Lor straddled the seat and stared at the panel, trying to remember how Url started it up. Guided by his gut, he made the correct moves to get the thing started, and the little electric engine buzzed to life. As Dill settled into the seat behind him, he glanced up for a moment and told the air, "Tell Horace, I'm on my way, Greg."

"Who's Greg?" Dill asked. He lowered dust goggles over his tech eyes.

Lor sniggered and told him not to worry about it.

Chapter 39

On the Move

LOR

Another mild day in Corl. A beautiful beach was dotted with residents underhand tossing bits of food from the new saxeroot crops to the Nazagora that floated in the blue. Children squealed in delight when the Nazagora rolled in the water, gulping up the morsels. From what Url said, the residents knew little of what their plans were. How blessed ignorance was, and Lor wished he could join them.

He wrestled with the idea that he was spearheading a revolt. It was dangerous, and he had no idea what he'd find in the cities. He had no idea what they would find at the tree, and how strong the worm actually was.

As long as no intense, town-smashing storms passed through, or any city-led invasions, Damaetra would be safest here. With Url and Zary taking care of her, Lor was resolute in that. For her sake, he had to succeed in this.

Damaetra lay in Zary's room, resting on a handmade white and green patchwork quilt, under his silver filigree blanket. The bed frame was put together with glazed branches from the coastal trees and wrapped with petrified night vines, flowers long gone. She was on her side, hands curled in front of her face. Then her finger twitched. Then her shoulder... and she yawned.

"Where am I?" she grunted as her eyelids fluttered halfway open.

Lor sat behind her on the bed, rubbing her back. "You're in Corl. It's a beach town where our new friends live."

"F-friends?" Her voice scratched out of her throat when she turned her head to see the three of them behind her.

"This is Zary, and her dad, Url." He kept his hand rotating over her back as her eyelids wavered.

"Hi, Zary. Hi, Url," she uttered as she lay her head back down and slowly flexed her hands in and out of fists, fighting to stay awake.

"Zary is going to take care of you for a little bit while I run an errand. I'm coming back to you," he whispered to her. Pressing his lips to her cheek, her skin was still warm, not too hot.

She nodded. "Where are the babies?" Closing her eyes, she yawned again.

"Gale and Nico are taking care of them. Get some rest, alright?" Her head only nudged up and down in two sluggish nods before she fell asleep again.

Zary stood nearby, hands clutched together in front of her chest. Her eyes reflected a pain only she knew how to show; he must go, but she worried for him.

"Thank you so much for watching after her." Lor pulled in his friend for a hug. She was almost as tall as him.

The warmth of her breath swelled at his shoulder. "She's like a part of my family now too," she said before pulling away to look at him. "Please, please... be so very careful. Remember your practice."

Lor let her go, squeezing her shoulder. Then he shook Url's hand. "Thank you for taking care of us."

Url had an impish face, with exaggerated Foscan features. He grinned wide enough Lor thought the corners of his mouth might touch his ears. As he shook Lor's hand, his eyes became glassy.

"Thank you for bringing my daughter home," he said. At once, he drew Lor in for a hug, squeezing right at the waist tight enough to force all the air from his lungs. He had a fisherman's strength; there was no doubt.

"Good God, man!" Dill's exuberance outside was loud enough to hear from Url's cottage. "These things are crazy weird!"

After saying his goodbyes, Lor took the three steps out the front door and clapped Dill on the shoulder. "Yep. And you're going to ride one."

"What? No way!"

"It's the only way." Lor grinned.

The Nazagora bobbed several paces past the shore in the water, with Davy and Oren sitting cross-legged on top of one of them, deep in conversation. Feeding time must have been over. Lor couldn't tell for certain, but it looked like they were sitting on Teddy.

Dill stared out at the ocean, clicking his tongue. The utility belt was already cinched around his waist, and he held a hand at the side where his shooter had been affixed. Lor wouldn't use it where he was going.

After a while, Dill pushed a heavy breath from his lips, vibrating them to a buzz. "Hey, Lor," he said.

"Yeah?"

"Remember when we met?"

"Yeah...?"

"Did you ever think back then that we'd hitch a ride together to the cities by alien?"

Lor laughed. "No, I didn't."

"Emilia won't like it."

Lor laughed again, knowing how true that was. He pulled out his borrowed e-disk and swiped a quick message to Gale.

NATE

It's time.

Dad's text to Papa came through, and he ushered them all toward the bunker.

Everyone rushed to the cockpit. As they hurried to take their spots in and secure themselves, Nate pulled out his mom's ring from a pocket and turned it in his fingers for a moment. The curved chair with motley fabric swiveled and sighed when Nate plunked into it, and he took a breath before sliding the ring into the ignition slot. A hum radiated from the panel, lighting up the buttons.

These levers and knobs had a specific order, and Nate closed his eyes to remember Mom's directions. After all, this would be the first time the machine had ever been fully activated.

As the family waited for him, he stared at the panels, freezing.

"What's wrong?" Cimma asked, leaning forward against her restraint.

Nate continued to stare at the panel with his mouth open before uttering, "What if I get us all killed?"

"What do you mean? Of course you won't kill us," Cae chimed in from the back while wrestling with her restraint buckle.

He didn't answer, just kept staring at all the buttons and levers with a blank look as if all knowledge he ever had fled from his mind.

Cimma unbuckled herself to stand behind him. She wrapped her arms around his neck, pressing her cheek against his. "You're the smartest boy I know."

Nate took in a breath. As Cimma lingered there holding him, he closed his eyes, taking in his sister's scent, and it reminded him of Mom.

"I love you, bubbie," Cimma said, "and as my older brother, I know you're the best for this." She kissed his cheek in two swift smacks and squeezed him again.

He blushed, smiling at the panel and all its blinking lights.

LOR

Gliding through water, Teddy the Nazagora held his cargo. Tucked inside the creature's pouch were Lor, Karl, Davy, Dill, and Emilia. The other Nazagora was the big female they called Champ, loaded with Rik and Oren, along with a handful of some of the better Yeunish fighters, including Ivon. They were his backup plan in case he needed strength behind him. The hope was that they were only along for the ride, nothing more. In fact, it was best if no violence was necessary at all, but he knew that was a childish wish, considering their plan was to storm the capital by Naz-back.

Both Teddy and Champ were fitted with a sturdy saddle of sorts, large enough for two riders each, while everyone else remained in the pouch. Lor and Dill volunteered to be the riders of Teddy, and Rik with Ivon as the riders for Champ.

They took a wide water route, stretching south from Corl, making a great loop around the pickup spot where he was branded, then toward the west-most angle of the peninsula holding the seven cities. Teddy and Champ knew their destination, because Lor shared it with them.

According to Eva, the most space for them to make their way through with the least number of potential casualties was between Wild Crag, the Shepherd city, and Pandemonia, the Weggevens city. Lor prayed there would be minimal casualties, or none at all. These people were mostly innocents, having been lied to, just like they were.

Teddy and Champ moved on auto. As long as Lor was tucked in their pouch, they had a direct line to his thoughts. It was still so weird.

He clenched the braid from his family at his chest and closed his eyes. In a way, being held by the Nazagora was a peaceful change as of late, since the darkness of the pouch left nothing to see under his lids, unless someone made a noise. No one talked over the soothing rush of water and slow rocking.

Lor knew the Nazagora swam fast. He didn't know it was that fast. It wasn't long before the swish of lapping water was traded for silence. The Nazagora waited for their instructions, as they had hit land.

NATE

Without making any mistakes, Nate activated each lever and knob in the correct order. The engine roared to life, vibrating underneath him. Cimma giggled as she let the vibrations travel up through her vocal cords while she *ooh-aah*'ed again and again.

"This is weird!" she shouted with another shuddering laugh.

To his left, Verena and Jack were strapped into harnesses, moving along the great panel on the side of the machine. It took a lot of electricity to run, and her job was to make sure to keep it running, made easier with Jack's help. Nate swallowed, turning back to the controls.

"We're good to move forward, activate the digger," Verena said, pumping a lever five times.

Nate obeyed, spinning the two cranks in front of him in unison, watching the scoop mechanisms unfurl from the nose of the machine. As he turned each one, they moved back and forth, spading out the sand in front of them. But once the area was clear, they swished through the air, and he had to at last move the machine forward. This was the part that made him the most nervous.

A gentle push from the accelerator set at low throttle and the machine rolled forward ever so slightly, continuing its dig through the ground. Sweat tickled his brow, and he swiped at it, knowing everyone inside that machine relied on him... and relied on him not to kill them. The movement was jarring, having never felt its engine rumble or its belt crawl forward. He didn't have time to wonder about it, fixing his focus on the diggers for now. Each shovel poked into the wall of sand with minor resistance.

Papa sat next to him near the controls and pointed at the panel. "Do you remember how to move upward?" he asked.

Nate nodded, eyeing the angler dial and cranking it up a notch. Verena continued her movements along the great panel and telling Jack what to do while pushing power into each thing Nate did. As the angler rose a few degrees, he felt his belly flop. He never did well with the feeling of tilting backwards like that. At least he could rest his back against the motley chair as they ascended through their underground spot.

Schup-schup. Schup-schup. Schup-schup.

Each digger worked together as the machine tilted them farther and farther back. Everyone leaned back, looking nervous. Verena and Jack had locked their special shoes into the panel, keeping them level with it, even in their harnesses. Jack furiously pumped one of the levers at her direction, grinding power to the angler.

Schup-schup. Schup-schup. Schup-schup.

"I'm getting dizzy, bubbie," Cimma whined.

Nate checked the short-wave detector. "Almost there."

Schup-schup. Schup-schup. Schup-schup.

"Almost..." Nate bit his lip.

The rest of the cabin filled with groans as their ascent continued.

"Almost..."

Schup-schup. Schup-schup. Schup-schup.

Nate slammed his fist down on a green button, letting loose a pulse shot from the nose of the machine. A cone of sand blew forth, and the machine crawled out into the open at last.

LOR

The Nazagora waited for their instructions, but Lor wasn't familiar with this side of the peninsula. The short time he spent in the cities was more on the southeast side.

In the tight creature pocket, he slid out the e-disk Url gave him. The holo projection bent along the inner pouch flap, distorting the map. He moved it back and forth to try to make the image clear, but the best he could do was position it so that the whole map lit up on the underside of the Nazagora's pouch. Even if the route was somewhat visible, he would have to rely on his earlier effort at memorizing the map.

Karl lay next to him, face down and buried in his arms, mumbling something about regrets.

"Too late for that," Lor said as he examined the distorted directions.

The roads bent around imperfections in the fleshy pocket, but he found a route. Looking at the map was good, but there was nothing like seeing with his eyes. He slid from the pocket, telling his companions to wait while he examined their surroundings.

Their beach was empty and inhospitable. Rocky outcroppings surrounded the shore as white caps swished and crashed into them. The Nazagora lay on the only section of sandy bank not getting assaulted by waves of salt water. This was good. No one knew they were there just yet—no sense in creating chaos until closer to the spire. The spire... a gleaming white beacon in the distance. It poked its steeple over the clearing in the stones. Lor caught the very tip of it.

"There." He pointed toward the steeple, hoping Teddy understood him.

It was unknown to him whether the Nazagora could climb. They could swim well enough and stand tall, but the undersides of their tentacles were rough and scaly rather than sticky. There was no harm in trying. If it didn't work, they'd have to try another angle onto the shore.

He patted the outside of the pocket, beckoning Karl and company to come out. They obeyed, looking around. Lor pulled out the e-disk again, murmuring to Karl that the spire was just up ahead and was ready whenever he was.

"I have nothing to lose," he said.

"Do we get on now?" Dill asked, tightening the saddle strap under Teddy's front tentacle.

Lor glanced at the tip of the spire again, folding his lips inward. "Yes, let's get on now."

"Righto." He gave Emilia a quick kiss, and she handed off her pulse shot along with an extra one before climbing back inside with Davy and Karl.

Dill jogged over to Ivon, giving him the extra pulse shot and a quick lesson on how to use it. Lor watched him take the handle, rotate it around a few times on its fulcrum, and aim, letting loose a short wave disturbance that boofed against the rock wall. A few smaller pebbles rained from the side, with a small plume of dust. Ivon nodded, taking the shot and examining it before trying it himself.

The pulse shots were only precautionary and non-lethal—a means to push back anyone that got too close or threatening. Lor hoped they didn't have to use them, but they would most likely need them.

Rik and Ivon checked their saddle on Champ and mounted her back. She rocked back and forth slowly, dipping up and down with gentle nods. Lor and Dill mounted Teddy, and he mirrored Champ's movements.

From Teddy's back, Lor saw more of the spire, touching his back and communicating to him where he wanted to go. Once Davy got the message from within the beast, he directed Teddy forward. It was still so strange to have such a connection with a creature like the Nazagora.

Teddy responded and Champ followed, making their move up the rock wall. Each tentacle slapped against it, shaking them in their saddles, with the crunch and screech of hardened scales piercing rock.

It couldn't have been more than three times Teddy's height to reach the top. And when he did, the screaming began.

"Shit! Go, Teddy! Go to the spire!"

NATE

The dunes were quiet. Even with the sun coming through the front glass, it was eerie, as if anything could happen. Nate sat rigid in his chair, fists tight around the steering wheel. No one spoke, leaving only the low rumble of the tread to vibrate in the cabin.

Verena lounged in her harness with a yawn as Jack spun the power crank every once in a while when the engine sputtered.

"It can't be this easy, can it?" Uncle Niklaus said from the seats in the back.

"Surely not... but I wouldn't complain if it were." Papa squinted through the glass, scanning the dry horizon with his lips pushed forward. Then his mouth dropped open. "Nope, definitely not."

Papa was right—several shadowy clusters ran at them, whether out of curiosity or something else, Nate didn't know. Best to prepare for the worst. The blue button next to the green pulse button was the one he remembered Momma said was the shield.

His sweaty palm pressed into it, and a short buzz rippled through the cabin as Verena reassigned herself to the panel with Jack.

Nico groaned from his seat in the back. "These are deep desert brigands. There's no telling the depth of their madness."

That warning did nothing for Nate's confidence, but Uncle Nico knew what he was talking about. Firey hands like Ayala's ignited in random dots along the line, with white frost fists like Quint's.

"What do I do?" Nate cried.

"Just drive!" It was Aunt Eva's voice, firm but panicked.

Nate pushed the throttle forward, picking up speed as the crowd of brigands closed the gap between them.

Just outside the front glass, another swarm aimed a variety of engineered weapons at their machine, releasing their payloads into the shield. Each blow popped or exploded, followed by screams from his sister and shouts between the adults behind him.

A few Weggevens fire elementalists readied themselves, hurling fistful after fistful of fire and ice. They were getting pelted all over by elements and engineered weapons when the high-pitched bleeping started.

"How are they not dying?" Uncle Niklaus shouted. Nate craned his neck toward the ones they passed, watching them collapse and seize in the sand.

"They *are* dying," Papa confirmed.

"Let them kill themselves then!"

"It's not stopping the Engineers!" A few more pops hit the side.

"Our shield is getting weak!" Nate shouted through the alarm, flipping another switch. The adults shouted at each other, a mix of directions and plain yelling. The budding sweat around Nate's temples now crawled down his face.

"Ready!" Verena shouted from the panel.

"Activate the boost!" Aunt Eva's voice warbled as they rolled over rough and hilly land.

Nate obeyed, pushing a heavy black and yellow striped lever forward. The machine picked up speed, catching one of the closer Engineers under its belt. The squelch of wet bones carried through the cockpit, and Nate frowned.

"I just killed someone!" he cried out.

"He was a bad man!" Cimma shouted from her seat as she bounced.

LOR

Live instrument music blared and squealed as the musicians ran mid-song. They had just landed right in the middle of a celebration. A banner scrawled in bright blue and gold letters declared: TWENTY-FIVE STANDARDS! An anniversary of sorts, with several people dressed in fancy suits and dresses scattering away from the beasts bounding through their party.

The screaming faded into the distance as a row of roundsmen lined up in front of their path, aiming shooters at them and calling to them through an amplifier.

"Halt!" one male voice shouted.

They approached at a steady speed, and the roundsmen didn't move. Not very smart.

"Only make a path!" Lor shouted to Dill, who rotated his pulse shot and aimed at the center of the roundsmen. Ivon copied Dill and aimed in front of Champ's path.

A pop rang out, with the whiz of something screaming past Lor's ear. Dill blew his pulse shot, sending five roundsmen wheeling through the air and opening their path. A second pop, and something struck Teddy in the side.

He wailed, a gurgling cry from his alien head ridge, and tilted to the left in a series of struggling thumps.

Lor clamped his teeth and placed his hands on Teddy's head, feeding him the memory of the tome. Whatever had struck him became only a memory as the beast straightened up and sped forward once again.

Ivon pulsed a handful of roundsmen in front of Champ, looking over to them to check in. Lor nodded back at him when another pop rang out, striking Ivon right in the chest. A burst of raw crimson sprayed from his mouth before he flew off Champ's back.

"Ivon!" Lor screeched.

NATE

There was no time for tears. Nate had killed someone. Cimma said he was bad, so that was good, right?

The highest throttle had Verena and Jack in a frenzy against the great panel. There were no more brigands to worry about in their wake when Nate left their squashed and writhing silhouettes in the dust. No one else seemed to care.

"We can probably slow down a bit," Uncle Nico said to them.

"Oh, sorry!" Nate pulled back the throttle, and the machine hummed to its original vibrations, crawling toward the black mountain. He tried to hide his sniffles and focus on the mountain.

Nate didn't fear the mountain like the others at the tents. It was where Mister Shadow lived, so it couldn't have been all bad.

"There's the wall." Papa pointed forward. "Do you remember what to do?"

Nate nodded. They would need to knock a hole in it. Aunt Emilia made the thing in the front that would do it. She called it the gut punch, and it was the light purple colored lever. It was her favorite color.

Cracks webbed across their front window, with some still spreading.

Their shield was nothing but holes.

"We're going to have to speed up again," Cimma said. "Look." She pointed at the guard roundsmen at the gate, pacing wildly and swishing their hands in front of them, telling them to stop.

Everyone's heads jerked back when Cimma pushed the throttle forward with a grin. "Sis-sy!" Nate shouted, gripping the gut punch lever.

"Better now than never," Verena said, setting to work on the panel once again with Jack.

Nate whimpered. He didn't want to kill any more people. The tread hopped over rippling sand, and his hand got hot and sweaty over the purple handle.

"Move!" he shouted inside the cabin. Even though they couldn't hear him, they obeyed, several bodies diving to the side as he thrust the gut punch.

A great section of the wall crumbled, and they rolled the machine right through it.

"Don't forget the aerosolizer!" Aunt Eva said.

Right, gotta knock them out. Nate pressed a series of buttons. One released a puff of Lapis Evening, another made a cloud of Pink Poise, Mom's numbing formula. The roundsmen dropped to the ground.

LOR

Ivon hit the ground, rolling away. Champ began thumping hard toward the roundsmen row, who kept their weapons fixed on them.

"Rik, no!" Lor shouted. It was too late.

Champ demolished a team of roundsmen with her toughened scales, pressing them flat into the ground, splitting open their sides and crushing their heads. She was on a rampage, and Rik was furiously feeding her his rage. Dill twirled his pulse shot over and over and over, sending waves of knock-backs as the roundsmen aimed their weapons. Champ flicked away their cruisers as if they were gee flies.

Between obliterating several of them and knocking the rest out, Rik relaxed, slowly heaving with a scowl. The celebrants were gone, the roundsmen were dead or knocked out, and the spire was still too far away.

"Rik, we have to go. Rik!" Lor shouted at him.

Rik turned to him, clenching his jaw with a curt nod.

That could have been Lor in that row of Law men. It was Gale's friend Greg at one time. He sighed, setting his sights back on the spire.

Maker forgive us.

NATE

"They weren't even armed," Papa said, craning his neck back to see the roundsmen lying in the sand, sound asleep.

"City cuts," Aunt Cae murmured.

"I can hardly see anything," Nate cut in. If he tilted his head back and forth, maybe he could see through the blackish mist.

"You have to rely only on your short wave now, bud," Papa said. "It's not far."

Glancing down at the little beacon, he did see there was a large mass in front of them. He lowered the throttle, chugging through the smog. He grinned—possibly the only one besides his sister excited to see the inside of the tree. In fact, Aunt Cae seemed even more angry for some reason.

As they got closer to the big mass, the machine began beeping.

"Proximity," Verena said, slowing down on the levers and cranks. Jack followed her lead.

The machine sputtered to a stop, idling in place. Everyone began whipping off their fasteners, standing up and stretching. Nate wasn't looking forward to this part. Cimma hopped from her seat, giving him a quick peck on the cheek before moving to the back of the machine.

Nate double-checked everyone was leaning their backs against the back wall, strapped in place. Verena remained at the panel as Jack left her to stand in the back with everyone else.

"Ready?" Nate asked. Everyone nodded and murmured. He looked to Verena, and she spun a crank.

With that, Nate spun his own crank, activating the angler and slowly tilting the machine back. The nose scraped up against the tree, dragging upwards. He pressed the button activating the scaffold.

Legs sprouted from the belly of the machine, grasping the tree and latching on, scooting them toward it until they were completely vertical. Cimma giggled as the blood rushed to her head. Nate didn't find it terribly funny. It made him dizzy. The machine came to rest, belly against the tree.

"Press five first, then three and four," Uncle Nico said from the back.

Nate nodded, obeying the command. The five button was orange, and it fed one of Mom's healing draughts into the tree through the scaffold. Once he heard the pumping sound, he pressed the yellow three button. It began feeding Mom's nature draught into it. The four button was white, and so was the draught that went into the tree. Each formula was squirting into the tree.

"Let's hope they work," Papa said, unbuckling himself from the wall.

Everyone followed, and the sound of clicking belts releasing filled the cabin. Verena floated down with her harness, removing herself from it. Nate set everything to idle and unbuckled himself as well.

"Someone help," he whimpered. Everyone else stood upright on the back of the machine, while he sat backwards in the motley chair. Jack was the tallest, reaching up and lowering him down to the rest of them.

"You did so good, bubbie," Cimma said, throwing her arms around his neck. He blushed with a small grin.

"Well done, kiddo," Papa said as he ruffled his hair.

Uncle Niklaus cranked the new door open, the one that was in the belly of the machine. When it opened, the most awful smell came in. It was like dead things and dust.

"Ew, do you smell that?" Aunt Cae pinched her nose.

"It's the worm," Uncle Niklaus said as he darted his eyes around.

Nate wasn't scared of the worm. He didn't like the way it smelled, but he wasn't scared of it. Mister Shadow was able to hold it back forever. Why would he be afraid of it now?

The hole in the tree wasn't exactly lined up with the belly door, and they all had to squeeze through the gap to the inside. As soon as Nate's eyes adjusted to the dark, he saw the inside of the cavern... It was beautiful.

Chapter 40

Going In

Loren

The streets were empty. Lor looked around at how eerie it was. A crumpled napkin blew across the road. There were barriers placed across the main roads with signs warning of street closures and street signals flashing. Dill's dreadful humming of Salt Fire's "The Last Warning" petered out as he glanced around.

"I really... really hope this isn't a bad sign," Dill whispered.

Lor agreed, glancing over at Rik. His face was wrenched inward and he didn't speak. He and Ivon were close. They were all pretty close, really... Lor regretted not having the chance to save him.

The spire loomed before them, welcoming and terrifying. One thing he remembered about the spire were all the buzzing gadgets swarming in a spiral around it, always monitoring. It was strange to see only the gleaming white of towering stone, monitor-free. Renae didn't have his eyes on them, and there was a chance he didn't even know he was blind.

"Let's get this over with," Lor said, reminding himself of the first time they came to the spire. It was the day he, Dill, and Nico applied for jobs.

They pressed forward, allowing the automatic doors to swing inward, allowing them inside, Nazagora and all.

"What the hell?" Dill marveled at the guest entry. White, marbled walls stretched over several stories high, with matching floors and pearled veining crawling through it. Several clear glass monitors lined up along the arcing countertops where there should have been dozens of assistants. There were no assistants. The lobby was completely empty—no helpers, no roaming workers, nothing.

Climbing from his perch on Teddy, Lor landed on the hard marble, echoing through the lobby. He patted Teddy's side, and he rocked slowly a few times before Karl, Davy, and Emilia slid out to meet them. Karl held the ancient text tight against his chest, protected by a sealed bag Url gave him to keep it dry. His dark eyes widened as he craned his neck around for signs of city workers.

"It's empty," Lor told him. "Must be the order. I hope it's the order."

Champ also shook slowly when Rik gave her the signal and let her occupants out. Once everyone was released from their organic taxis, Url's e-disk buzzed in Lor's pocket. It was only a single message: *We cleared the path, now don't screw up. The Guide says hi.*

"It *was* the order." Lor smiled to himself. He was relieved but worried, afraid he'd squander their opportunity by doing something like screwing up.

An elevator near the back of the lobby opened, and all eyes locked in on it. "I guess we get on," Lor said.

Both Nazagora followed them to the lift that was built large enough for bulk deliveries. Lor guessed it was spacious enough to hold fifty people.

They stepped inside, the remaining nine of them with the two Nazagora and room to spare. The lift panel lit up. Twenty-four floors, with a metal key poking out from a slot next to the twenty-fifth. A small note dangled from the end of it, written in a tight hand: *penthouse*.

"That's where he's at," Karl said. "Based on what we've seen here, there's no telling whether or not he expects us."

"How could he not?" Lor asked, pinching the key and cocking it to the side. Even if the monitoring tech wasn't floating around the spire, he couldn't imagine Renae wouldn't know.

The doors slid shut and the pulleys activated, rumbling the floor and bringing them up. The Nazagora shivered in place, low to the ground like frightened cats. What a foreign place this was to them. There was no conversation inside the lift, only anticipation. Dill fiddled with the strap of his utility belt, and Emilia held the pulse shot at her side. Karl kept his tight grip on the ancient text. The other fighters stood stoic, watching their own reflections in the hazy metal doors. Even Davy was quiet for once, taking a moment to rest his hand on Teddy's head to calm his shaking.

The lift squealed as it settled on the twenty-fifth floor, landing with a soft thud and letting the doors roll open. Before them was a long white corridor, a single door at the end.

As they stepped from the lift, Lor turned to Rik. "You and Oren stay at the elevator here with Champ. Pick someone else to stay here with you."

Rik nodded, pointing toward extra fighter Al'anej "Lane" Keli'ro, then rested his hand on the beast.

After confirming their choice, the others made their way down the long hallway. The only sound was the slithering creep of Teddy's tentacles sliding over the tile and occasionally flicking the wall. Karl muttered to himself, continuing to embrace the ancient text.

The hall's brightness and stark whiteness swallowed any shadow they might cast, and Teddy's black flesh was a dark void behind them. They passed glass-lined walls and rooms of opulence: a fitness center, a break room, a theater for holofilms... Renae was only one man. It couldn't have been just for him. If it was... what a waste.

Once they made it to the end of the hall, they stood before the pristine white door, no looking glass at all.

"Stay here, watch and wait. I don't know how violent this is going to get." Lor rubbed his hands together. "Just stay right outside the door."

"Dude, why not just let Emilia knock him out with her pulse shot?" Dill said, raising his brow and pointing at her. She raised the hand-held device up, aimed at the ceiling while holding on to it only by its handle.

"I need to see if I can reason with him first. If he sees everyone swarming in, he may attack. Who knows what kind of security he has in there."

Karl put a hand on his shoulder. In the over-bright tech light, the lines in his face were more pronounced. "I will find the right passage while you talk to him. It may draw out the worm inside of him."

Lor nodded, looking to everyone around him, the weight of responsibility for their lives hanging like a noose around his neck. Teddy hovered behind them all, his little black eyes watching as Davy patted his side.

"If it gets bad, I'm shooting," Emilia said as she re-holstered the pulse shot.

"Deal," Lor said. "I'm going in."

Reaching for the door handle, his hand seemed so filthy against the pristine entry. It wasn't locked, sliding open to the grand white penthouse with a long black table in the center. At the head of it, there was an ornate black chair, padded in gold threads, with the man himself seated in wait. Renae grinned.

"I knew something was up," he said, folding his hands in front of him. A black jewel set in gold was wrapped around his finger.

Lor turned briefly to the others waiting at the open door, peering inside, dutifully remaining in the hall.

"I see you brought your pets." Renae opened a small case next to him, withdrawing a smoking cane to clamp between his teeth. "And my dear nephew," he continued as he lit it. Red smoke drifted from his nostrils.

"We need to talk," Lor said while squaring his shoulders.

"Do we now?" Renae stood, strolling toward him wearing a neatly pressed black suit and red tie, with cuff links to match. His whole presence screamed with the colors of that cursed ring.

"Yes, I think we do." Lor watched the man advance, anchoring himself in place and bracing for the next move. The red smoke finally caught up to him, filling his nostrils with an acrid stench. Iron and blood.

The closer Renae got, the more frantic Dill's whispers in the hall became, stifled by Karl and Emilia.

Shoot him! Shoot him!

Shh! Not yet!

Stop, or we'll all get it!

Renae smirked with that cane between his teeth, scarlet swirls puffing from under his tightly manicured gray mustache. Lor wondered at what point in Renae's life he had become enticed by the worm.

Renae stopped a single pace in front of him, close enough for Lor to see the pores in his cheeks. The princeps studied Lor's face and released more pungent smoke. "So you're a Reaper too, are you?" he said with a smirk. "I sense your pathetic vibrations. Yeunish garbage."

Lor raised an eyebrow. "Do you hate the Yeunish, or do you envy that we're not bound by your Guild rules?"

Renae barked out a laugh as more red smoke puffed from his mouth. "Envy? I don't feel envy for your kind."

"I wasn't talking to you. I was talking to the worm."

Renae paused, eyeing him as he began to pace. "You know, your little friend here hasn't been honest with you," he said, nodding at Karl, who strolled inside next to Lor with the ancient text open in front of him.

When Lor looked over at Karl, his red-brown eyes glared at Renae over the edge of the tome.

"We all have our secrets," Lor said.

"Quiet." Renae jabbed his hand to the side. "He was the first, you know. My dutiful nephew."

Lor sighed. They didn't have time for this. "The first *what*, Karl?" he asked.

As Renae pondered his nephew with a smirk, Karl tilted his head toward Lor. "I was the first one to persecute the Yeunish. And now I don't. But I've already done my penance for that, haven't I?"

Karl shifted, continuing to glare at Renae.

"H-how is that even possible? The Yeunish have been persecuted for, what, over a thousand years?"

"Now you're getting it," Renae said, taking the smoking cane from his lips and stubbing it out on his palm. The open burn sealed shut as he flicked the butt end to the side. "But my nephew's heart went all soft when he met old what's-her-face. The one with the lazy eye." He continued his pacing prowl in front of them.

"Her name was In'gaera, and she did not have a lazy eye. Last I recall, you plucked it out of her head!"

Renae laughed. "What can I say? She was a distraction. And she saw too much."

Karl scowled at him.

"Don't let him get into your head—" Lor warned.

"The esteemed one-eyed Inga!" Renae interrupted, raising his arms in the air. "The Yeunish Reaper! Healer! Abomination! Like you."

He turned his attention to Lor, eyes blackened over with malice. Lor furrowed his brow, opening his mouth to speak as Renae put a finger to his own lips to shush him.

"Heal this," he said, whipping out a pocket switch and jabbing Lor in the neck.

The steel stung when it pierced his throat, cold on the back of his tongue and hot when it was yanked out. Dill's whispers grew to curses and shouts. Lor shot a hand up to the wound as the dark blood plipped on his boot and stained the white floor. A direct hit to the jugular, and it made him woozy. Immortal Green mingled with the tang of his blood, but he held his neck, watching Karl watching him.

Renae got close. He tilted his head and gazed into Lor's eyes with his black ones. "What was it you were saying again?"

Lor baffed Renae in the forehead with his own, forcing the princeps to snap his head back.

"I didn't survive ten standard years in *hell*, away from my family..." He ripped a quick punch to Renae's eye socket with a sick thump and he stumbled backwards. "...participating in ritual fighting..." Lifting a bloody boot, he stomped Renae's insole, breaking his ankle and sending him to the floor with a cry. "...to be taken down by a pathetic puppet!"

When Lor pinned Renae to the ground, he began to screech in a series of inhuman wails.

Everyone in the hall howled and covered their ears. Even Champ and Teddy called out in pitiful alien ululations. Only Karl remained calm, holding the ancient text open.

Lor thought his ears might bleed from the throaty screeching. Between pressing his ear to his shoulder and grabbing at Renae, Lor wrestled with him, attempting to cover his mouth. Fire ran through his muscles as the possessed man thrashed against him.

Lor's hand covered more than half the princeps's face, and he mashed his palm into his open mouth. Renae bucked hard, clamping down to draw blood. Lor hissed at the sting. His own red stains smeared across Renae's cheeks as he writhed beneath Lor.

This had to stop—there was no time! There was no way he could relax enough to go mind-diving while the man chewed at his palm. Renae began slamming his head against the tile, gnashing his teeth and shredding his fleshy gag. It really, really hurt.

"Karl, do something!" Lor said in a panic. Enough of his palm had been punctured to feed Renae a modest meal as Immortal Green flooded his sinuses.

Karl cleared his throat and finally spoke. When he did, his voice came through in the musical sounds of Eastern Common. Renae pulled his growl inward when he heard it, spewing muffled curses at his nephew and writhing. The passage, whatever it meant, was enough to cut off the screams that brought everyone to their knees, allowing Emilia to march inside and bounce off a pulse shot. Right in the face. Lor had barely moved his hand in time, catching a numbing reverberation from the shot.

The blast threw Renae's head back hard enough to crack the tile before he went silent.

"I don't know how long he'll be out," she said.

"I'll try to be quick," Lor responded, wiping his hand down his pants.

"We will do our best to keep him out while you do your work," Karl said, flipping the text to another section, "but I have a bad feeling his ridiculous screaming could have summoned help."

Lor nodded. "I'll be quick," he repeated, sitting on the ground next to Renae.

He reached into his pocket and felt the braid there, pinching it between his fingers before closing his eyes. The feel of the little strands rubbing against each other almost brought the smell of violets to his nose.

The scene before him was a version of the room, covered in corruption. The white walls stained in black, roiling from the floor; it floated in the air like the dead embers of a fire, yet dripped around the room in oily dregs. It surrounded Renae, prone on the floor.

Just behind the fancy chair was the portal he remembered from his nightmare—dark and pulsing with mal energy.

Chapter 41

The True Realm

NATE

Even if it stank in there, the inside of the tree was amazing. There were trees *inside* the tree, some stuck to the walls, with their branches stretching to the middle with lots of leaves and glowy flowers. There were things in that cavern that Nate had only seen in books, and some things he didn't know existed. Brown mushrooms the size of his dad sprang out of the ground, with twisting ivy wrapped around their stalks in blue-colored night lights. He had no name for such things.

"It's changed," Uncle Niklaus said. He looked around but didn't appear happy to be there.

Nate was beyond thrilled. Cimma was silent as always, but the look on her face told him everything; she was in awe too.

"So where are they?" This time Uncle Nico looked around, a frown on his face.

The rhythmic pumping from the machine echoed inside, bouncing off swaying leaves and making hollow thuds against the huge mushrooms all over the place.

Papa put his arm around Nate and Cimma, drawing them close. There was a dark trail leading off into the shadows. It was the only thing about that place that made Nate nervous. As he stared into it, something moved.

Whatever was in the shadow spoke. "It's been a while." It was a woman's voice.

Papa squeezed Nate's shoulder, almost painfully, and Cimma whined from it.

"Papa, that hurts," she said.

The woman in the shadow stepped into the light of the glowing flowers.

Once Nate was able to see her, he'd never seen anyone so pretty. Her hair was long and dark, eyes the color of sea illustrations in his first levels book. She smelled like fruit, and it was better than the smell in the cavern.

Uncle Nico tucked Aunt Eva behind his back and stared hard at the woman. His face didn't look like he was happy to see her.

"Par," Jack cut in, guarding Verena in the same way.

"Long time no see, Cricket," she crooned.

"It's Jack."

The woman smiled, sadness reaching her eyes. Then she found Uncle Niklaus. "Hare, you've cleaned up."

"Don't you dare talk to him." Aunt Cae was furious. She stood in front of Uncle Niklaus and got red in the cheeks. "And his name is *not* Hare."

Nate didn't understand... Why was everyone so angry with this woman? Wasn't she supposed to help?

"I see," Par said, glancing over her shoulder into the dark. When she did, Mister Shadow came forward.

Nate grinned as his sister gleefully called out to him.

"Wait, Maron was your Mister Shadow?" Uncle Nico put a hand on Nate's arm.

"I told them not to call me that," Maron interjected, "but it is so."

"Ah, so you speak Northern Common now."

"It is not hard to learn."

"Good, because we need to get started as soon as possible. Lor is probably at the spire by now."

"Very well. Follow us to the breach."

"Mister Shadow," Cimma called to him. She wrapped her small arms around his waist and squeezed. "Be safe inside."

"I will try, young one." He held her too.

Nate stood nearby, but he wouldn't go, still thinking about the sound of that squashed man from outside. He waved with his hand hip high. Maron understood and nodded with the same grin he received in return.

NICO

Gale agreed to manage activities top side, while Nico, Eva, and Jack followed Maron and Par through the umbilicus.

The walls were strange, covered in the same luminescent plant life as the cavern, but waterlogged and swollen with discolored juices. They oozed thick and pus-like through crevasses and almost appeared to be breathing. Nico shook his head and studied the glossy walls again, but they remained still.

"This is giving me the creeps," he uttered, flashing a tech light pen up and over the arched tunnel. Eva walked close enough to him that he felt her heat.

"It has festered since I've been removed," Maron said.

"Interesting... You'd never know by seeing how much it's grown up top."

"Indeed. Life finds a way."

Paerli strolled close to Maron without a word. Her face was contorted into a sort of deep think, a reflection of her past transgressions. At least, that's what Nico hoped. They didn't talk much. Nico was focused on memorizing their trail for the way back.

Their path widened and opened up to a room of sorts, covered with the same soft, fleshy infection, with smaller black roots twining along the perimeter to meet at the hole in the center.

There it was. The nightmare of legend.

The breach was odd, like a malleable wound, similar to the thickness of fat under flesh. The secondary roots decorated the edges before the mouth swallowed them. There was enough light to see a few paces inside, and a tarnished golden film clung to the sides. Maron frowned at it.

"Maker have mercy..." Nico whispered. Taking care to cover his nose and mouth with the collar of his shirt, he shuffled toward it, cocking his head at an angle to see inside. There was no sign of the worm yet.

Reaching out a hand, he pinched one of the roots being sucked inside and grimaced. The same discolored liquid from the umbilicus passage squeezed out from his touch. Jack's disgusted grunt came from behind him as Eva told Nico to step aside. Before he did, he caught a glimpse of the mushy floor inside, remembering his living nightmare.

Eva stepped up next to him with a set of homemade brackets and went to work, connecting them to the soft wall. Each hammer blow was a dull thud, thick and wet. A stinking funk wafted from its center. She didn't once try to look inside it, keeping her focus on her task. Smart.

"Let's get this done," Jack said, taking off his pack-sack and placing it delicately on the loose dirt floor.

Nico moved to Jack's bag and withdrew a length of twine. "Take this rope," he said. It was tied at both ends with loops, and he handed one end to Maron. "Wear it around your waist. This is how we'll communicate. It's not much, but I want you to tug once when you are on your way back. Tug twice if you're not coming back."

"I understand," Maron said, taking one end.

Nico nodded, then raised an eyebrow to Paerli. "Par?"

She jerked her gaze toward them and fanned her hand. "Yes, I get it. Once to come back, twice to die."

Nico sighed. "That's not what I said—"

"Yes, I know. I know what to do, Nico."

"Alright, then. When I get your signal, we're going to crank these brackets closed to seal the hole... It's a lot like a bolt lock. Do you understand?"

"I understand," Maron said, looking over at his wife.

"Yes, yes," she huffed, peering into the breach as Eva attached a telescoping pole crank between two of the brackets.

"Once they're bolted closed, Jack and I have created formulations that are meant to make the seal permanent. So it's very important that you give me the correct signal. I won't accept weak tugs; they must be firm. Do you understand?"

"I understand." Maron gave it a good yank, and it pulled Nico forward a step. "Like this?"

"Yes, that's perfect. Do it like that."

"How do you know your formulations will create a permanent seal?"

Nico shrugged and draped the other looped end around his own waist. "I don't. But we can hope. And if it works, even temporarily, we'll pass the knowledge through generations. If you succeed in destroying the worm, we don't have to worry as much about it. Right?"

"In theory, that is the case." Maron glanced at Par as she dropped the loop around her waist and pulled it taut.

When Par checked the loop knot around Maron's bony waist, she glanced at Nico. "I hope you brought some phials we can use against it."

Jack handed Nico the pack-sack, and he nodded while rooting through it. "I did one better and also brought these pre-loaded shooters with something to help weaken it."

Paerli watched Nico pull out the classic manual shooter, and her fingers brushed against the dip in her neck. "Ah, yes. Lor shot me with one of those once... I see you grinning, you know."

Nico let out a breathy chuckle. "Sorry, but to be fair, you were attacking us."

Par sighed and pushed her lips to the side.

"You're going to need these too." Nico withdrew two utility belts: the one he wore during their original fight and the one Lor wore. It didn't matter which one Maron would wear; both of them would be too loose on him.

Nico gave them a quick lesson on how to discharge the shooter, and Maron took to it as easily as if he'd made the thing himself. Par less so, but competent enough. They were stocked with small phials of Red Mash, as well as a few of Nico's own cocktails, including Obsidian Blast Core, which dangled from their belts. The needles were filled with Ivory Saltpeter, which he told them was meant to make it weaker.

"Hey, I know I said tug hard to communicate"—Nico yanked at his end of the rope—"but if you could do us a favor and once you're where you're supposed to be, could you give us three soft tugs... like this..." Nico pulled the rope three times.

Maron and Par both repeated the gesture, and Nico drew his lips inward with a serious nod. "Yes, that's good."

Their bodies disappeared into the shadow of the breach, and Nico clenched Maron's knot at his waist. He looked to Jack, who wrung his hands around Par's knot resting on his belly.

"Maker help us," Eva whispered.

PAERLI

The small pen light didn't do a whole lot for visibility. Once they were far enough inside, Par's eyes adjusted to the dark, and a hint of blue algae glowed faint against the bowels of the breach. She clicked off the pen light, letting that dim glow become a bit brighter. She ran her hand down Maron's arm, twining her fingers in his, and he squeezed them.

"Don't leave me," she whispered. "Protect me from it."

The fact that she'd succumbed to it before made her worried it would happen again. What promises it would offer this time, she couldn't possibly know. Maron squeezed her hand again, tugging her a little closer to his side.

"It is a liar. Do not listen to it," Maron warned. She knew that of course.

The smell of the breach churned so foul in her nose. This was Maron's world for too long. She glanced up at him, his eyes fixed in front of them, dark hair getting long again. Last she'd cut it was several standard months ago. It was the first and last time he revisited their home.

"I failed you," she whispered.

"Hm?" Maron glanced down at her, those yellow eyes visible in the dark.

She repeated herself, taking a deep breath of the cavernous funk. Rather than gag on it, she embraced it. She deserved it.

Maron stopped and tugged her hand to face him. "You must not go inside with thoughts like these."

"I'm sorry, I know, I just—"

"Do you want forgiveness?" His tone was kind, and he held both her hands in his.

Even in the dark, his eyes searched her. She fought back tears; it had been so long since she felt them at her eyes. A croak came from her throat.

"Do you want forgiveness?" he repeated, clasping her hands together in his. They were large, mostly covering hers.

She sputtered, no longer able to hold it back. Years of suppressing emotions outside of rage, greed, and lust, her grief caught up to her in that dank lair. "Yes... yes, I want forgiveness. Please forgive me, Maron, my husband. Please forgive me for harming our children. Forgive me for hurting you. For hurting myself."

By the time she was done confessing, her voice was small, a cracking stutter through ages of repressed sadness. He drew her in and held on to her as she cried into his dirty shirt. Ten standard years she spent ruminating on her failures, recalling every stupid, harmful decision she made that created chaos in her path and death in her wake. She had to let go, and she prayed, for the first time in a very long time, that Maron would let her let it go.

He remained silent for a moment, and she heard his heart thumping slow in his chest, punching her ear with a strength she only wished she had.

"I forgive you," he told her in Eastern Common. Ages had passed since the last time she heard the musical language spoken, but it reached into her, grabbing the piece of herself she remembered from all that time ago, and she regretted waiting until now to capture that feeling.

"Hold on to that feeling. Hold on to the goodness it brings you," Maron said. "You will need it inside, and you will need it for Loren."

She nodded, pulling back and threading her fingers through his. "Let's get this over with," she said.

They wandered farther inside, crossing over a hidden threshold that rippled the borders of the space between; and it was here that they finally entered the true realm of the worm.

It was bright. Blinding. Par saluted and squinted, finding it did nothing to help ease her eyes, already burning from crying. The walls were pure white. Each filth-crusted wrinkle in Maron's face seemed even blacker than before.

She had the faintest memory of this room. The same room she met the worm, fresh after her husband volunteered to seal the breach—when she was alone, self-loathing and vulnerable to its suggestions.

She glanced behind her at the trail of rope. The end of it disappeared into the invisible barrier, appearing as a blunted rope end stuck to a white wall. She gave her rope three soft tugs, receiving three in return.

"Remember to tell Nico you're here," she said, nodding at Maron's rope. He used his free hand to give the required three gentle tugs.

The rope responded. At least they knew they could still connect to the outside.

"Maron..." Par whispered, squeezing his hand, "...do you see it?"

They stood several paces far from it, a spectacle she cared not to remember. It was pure light, pulsing with brilliant tendrils all around, swaying on its perimeter in multiple bright colors. She tilted her head down, trying not to look. It was like a copy of the breach hole, complete with the blackened vines being sucked into its center, yet alive and moving with what seemed like contentment, or concentration. Not a black void worshiped by the cult on the island, but a disk of light, too bright to stare into without going blind.

It didn't sense them as it hovered in place and breathed: in, out, in, out...

Par poked Maron's hand, tilting her head at the shooter on his hip. Maron nodded and drew out the weapon, raising one hand to aim, with his other hand still twined with hers. The shooter *thwanged* as Maron fired three rapid shots into the center of the light void.

It screeched and spun around to face them with a darkened, segmented visage of twisted hatred.

Chapter 42

Nothing Is Real

DILL

"I've got a bad feeling," Dill murmured.

Just as the thought crossed his mind, Rik and Lane backed up from their position at the elevator, with Champ sliding over to hug the wall.

"Something's coming," Rik shouted through the hall.

Dill cursed, looking over at Emilia. She swiveled her pulse shot and held it at her side, charge at the ready.

Karl continued speaking in the strange language, stopping long enough to shout something about the princeps calling for backup.

This time Emilia cursed, calling for Rik to back up to the center of the hall with Champ. Davy stroked Teddy nearby, and he gurgled, sensing Davy's fear.

"Here they come..." Dill readied himself, gripping his needler in one hand and a short, dagger version of the ripper blade in the other. He glanced at his wife, standing next to him. Never one to tarnish perception of her class, she still wore those lovely pearls around her dark neck.

Emilia looked back at him, her face crowded with concern, pulse shot tight in her hand.

The elevator pounded with restlessness inside of it, as Champ and her allies backed away slowly. Each floor ticked closer... 21, 22, 23... The banging intensified.

LOR

The inside was like he remembered: dark and muddy, full of despair and excrement.

Maker help me...

"Ssso you think you can ssstop me, do you?" The disembodied voice echoed from within one of many endless chambers.

Don't engage.

Lor looked around. The surroundings weren't well lit, only dark shadows cast by the familiar pinhole of light in the distance. He had to feel around with his feet. The slithering *schlup* crept across the walls, echoing as if the thing was all around him.

"Who do you think you are, Yeunish ssscum?"

Don't engage.

Inside this hell, he had no way to know if Maron and Par made it. For now, he had to assume he was alone. The only salvation for not only his people, but for the man whose mind was enrapt by this evil.

What was he looking for? In his memory of being in this place before, he never saw the worm. If he saw it, what would he do? A steady series of drips resonated in skewed syncopation.

"Allow me to help you, ssson of the Maker," it cooed at him.

Don't engage.

No matter how much Lor told himself not to engage, he couldn't help but feel its presence—the slick chill of its voice reaching down into his bowels.

In a way it knew this, and before he could push it out of his mind, a nicer kind of light swelled in front of him, and with it, a figure. It was his mother, Dag the Small. Gale called her Els'daegal.

"Mom," he uttered, bewildered.

"Mae'guar haer, my son," she said, reaching out for his hand.

Her cold fingers brushed against his. Her face, lovely. The long black hair she normally wore in a tail had loosened around her head, creating a dark and shiny veil, while her eyes—those piercing white eyes—peered through it, straight into him.

Another figure strolled up to her, tall and slender, just like him. Yet, the stranger was whiter than a specter, wrapping his arm around Dag and smiling at Lor. Though he never knew his birth father, he knew this was him. Haedrian, the gentle and wickedly smart surgeon, who died. Was this the afterlife? Was this really what the Promised Land was like? The dis-rhythmic dripping continued, and the bleakness in their surroundings crawled into his belly, squeezing it. This was not what he expected of the Promised Land.

"Hello, son," the Haedrian specter said to him, "I've been wanting to meet you for so long."

The man's face was much like Lor's own, yet more refined, with the skin of an Anglia and carrying a set of jewel-green eyes.

"Dad...?" Lor didn't mean to say anything at all.

"That's right, son. We've missed you... Come with us to the home we've made for you."

Haedrian moved to Lor's side, wrapping his arm around his shoulder, guiding him toward the darker knot in the depths. Lor took one heavy step, then two, trudging through the silty loam. It was like beach sand, and he could almost smell the salty tide, cold and humid air carrying the scent of beached fish and the predator birds that circled them. It reminded him of vacations at West Cordan with Eva and Gale.

Wait. Gale.

As he took more steps toward the darkness, his mother's pleading eyes on him and his father's guiding arm around him, he dug his heels into what he knew wasn't really the sand of West Cordan. "No," he said.

"What's the matter, son?" Haedrian said, still attempting to pull at his shoulder.

Lor sighed. "You're my father, yes, and I wish I could have known you. But Gale is my dad. I'm sorry."

Haedrian's smile faded into a deep frown, continuing downward until the corners of his lips dripped into sludge. The bags under his eyes breathed in and out before melting toward his chin, then the rest of him collapsed into the mire at his feet.

"What have you done?" Dag cried. "My son, what did you do?"

Her cries pierced the dripping dark, and she wailed for Haedrian, cursing Lor for his recklessness. This was not the Dag he knew, the one who loved Gale.

"You're not my mother," he said to her. She wailed once more before joining Haedrian in a gelatinous pile at his feet.

More slithering passed over and around the tunnel walls—frenetic and louder.

"I sssee what you do with my giftsss to you," the voice whispered from the darkness.

Don't engage.

"How about thisss?" It giggled and left.

Lor prepared himself for what he was about to see. A vision of Gale now? Destroyed by his own hand? A vision of Eva, or Nico, or Dill?

In the same way, a gentle light swelled before him, as a figure walked up to him through it.

"You left me, Loren," she said. Her long white-gold hair draped over pale shoulders, her violet eyes damp as the remains of tears clung to her eyelashes.

The feel of her soft hands drifted into his, and she held on in the space between them. If he had proper reasoning, it would have told him she wasn't real, just another trick of the worm... but what if she *was* real? What if she died when he came here, and she was here now, in front of him?

"Damaetra," he whispered to her.

"I've missed you for so long. Melancholy is a bitter sundown on us all," she said. The words were familiar to him, but he didn't know why.

"I've missed you more than anything." He couldn't help himself. She had to be real, standing there, holding him in that space. Even the edge of her ancient tech wedding band rubbed at his finger.

"Remember when you asked me to marry you?" She smiled, tilting her head.

"Yes, I remember," he whispered.

"It was one of the happiest days of my life. You helped me remember it when you took away my pain."

A slight twinge of the black grief that raced into his pores itched his skin at the thought of healing her. But it was for nothing, because she was here, gone already. And he'd left her to die in Corl.

"I'm so sorry, baby, I'm so sorry. I tried." Then he wept, and her hand moved to his cheek.

"I know you did." She guided his head to her breast, patting his hair as she held him. Small kisses pressed into his scalp as she lamented his sorrow.

A sharp snap cut through the air, and Damaetra's ghost screeched before it vaporized. Lor nearly toppled forward but caught himself, dazed at her sudden disappearance.

"You'll sssuffer for thisss, you Igni bassstard!" The voice crawled through the cavern, spiraling down the dark tunnel.

Lor cursed at himself for falling for it. Maron and Par had made it to the worm. And now, he knew what he had to do.

Chapter 43

Death Cycles

The Physical Realm

The light pulsed and raged, a deeply wrinkled face of madness in the center of it. The shimmering tendrils stood on end, and it looked like the sun. Its screams vibrated through the white space, and Par shuddered in Maron's grip.

Maron aimed the shooter at it once again. "Your time is done, zlae'duch Cirv'e," he said.

"It is *your* time that is done, last of the Igni." Its voice came from everywhere.

Par panicked and tossed a red-colored phial at its center. It absorbed the glass, turning its mealy face toward her. Maron stepped between them.

"We must lead it back through the barrier before we can harm it," he said.

They began to back up when a tendril whipped out and lashed around Maron's waist, yanking him forward. The friction of his hand burned against his wife when he was ripped from her grip.

Her feeble shouts for it to come for her instead were ineffective. The tendril squeezed and burned, and he had no way of loosing himself from it.

Maron's rope tugged and rippled, and Par wished they had come up with better instructions for how to interpret jerking yanks rather than solid pulls. As she watched Maron struggle under Cirv` e's grip, she hoped Nico was smart enough to know not to start sealing the breach as she tried to come up with an idea—any idea.

NICO

The stench was unrelenting. No matter how long they stood near the breach, Nico couldn't get used to it. He glanced at Jack, who continued to wring his hands over the knot at his waist. As much as Nico still hated Par, he worried for them both. This was the moment they'd been waiting for, and he stood sentinel, bored, and full of the cavern's stink.

Eva tightened and re-tightened the brackets around the soft breach border. She was always good with mechanical type things.

"Ugh, this wall is so soft, I'm afraid the brackets will tear free." Eva readjusted the telescoping rod.

Nico tittered. "If anything, they'll have to—" He blew out a hard grunt as his rope yanked him forward.

Eva's scream sounded like a whisper when his forehead slammed against the telescoping pole, and he tumbled inside the breach.

The rope dragged him through the mire, and the echoes of Jack and Eva shouting his name from outside. He rolled and gripped the rope, hoping to right himself and dig his heels in. After rolling a few times, he locked his new knees, catapulting him upright, almost stumbling forward and falling again. But he dug in, grinding his metal heels into the soft grime.

He was deep inside the breach, almost beyond the dimly glowing life plastered on the walls. Eva's voice was a distant call, shouting his name, asking if he was all right.

"I'm fine!" he shouted behind his shoulder. *I'm fine...* He blew out a breath and rubbed his forehead.

The rope no longer tugged but remained taut, hovering before him in midair.

The Mental Realm

In Lor's last conversation with the worm, he didn't dare wander into the shadow. Now, he chased after it. Maron for sure was on the other side.

The floor sucked at his feet as he ran toward the pinpoint of light in the distance. Each footfall was heavy, cumbersome... he had to remind himself that this was only in his mind. It was only Renae's mind.

The dim light burned his eyes, forcing Lor to squint. The more it burned, the closer he felt. The slithering echoes slurped up into a cone of silence, possibly into the light that he ran to.

He made a quick bid to the Maker and got an immediate response. Karl's recitation of the ancient text called to him as if he was standing mere paces away. In a way, he really was only paces away, but Lor was so deep inside Renae's mind, he could have been continents away.

The passage Karl chose couldn't have been read at a better time. Any other time, Lor would question the musical notes of Eastern Common, but this time, he understood the passage fluently. It made him lightheaded and giddy all of a sudden. There was information in that specific verse that he could use, and he repeated it to himself as he ran to the light. Two could play the illusion game.

DILL

"Hold them back!" Dill shouted when the elevator doors opened.

A wave of roundsmen poured through, storming the hall. Their eyes were voids, controlled by something, possibly the worm. The droves of innocent men and women of Law weren't in control of themselves and weren't aware of what they were doing, which is why Dill felt bad when he had to stab one in the neck.

Champ beat a few of them into the wall as Lane tackled another to the ground. Pulse shots blared left and right, redirecting one of Dill's needles into the cheek of another, who collapsed under the effects of Lapis Evening.

Oren punched one of them in the balls, and Dill grimaced when the man fell, clutching them.

Karl recited the Eastern Common verse, and it had a nice beat to it. Dill hummed along, firing two more needles into a lady roundsman.

"Sorry!" he said between hums.

Emilia pulsed one coming right for them, knocking him back into Lane and Rik, who shook him off and continued throwing punches.

The Law lost all intelligent thought, pursuing them in disorganized fury down the once pristine hall, now marred in scuffs, holes, blood, and hair. Teddy stood high on four tentacles before leaning down and chomping two of them in half.

Emilia screamed.

The Physical Realm

"I've been waiting for the day I could finally kill you," Cirv'e hissed, holding Maron up. He continued to wriggle within the rope of light. "You set me back for too long!"

Par grabbed Maron's rope, hoping to yank him free and lead the worm through the portal. When she tried pulling, the worm smacked her back, and she flew far enough to nearly pass through the barrier herself.

"Don't get me started on you," it said to her. The face in the center morphed, appearing like a looming god. It was the same face she remembered—loving, full of promises, even if she wasn't aware of the ill intent behind them.

But she knew this time, and she knew how it twisted her mind. She stood up and faced it, staring directly into its eyes, even if it burned.

"You turned me against my children," she said, gripping Maron's rope again.

It laughed at her.

"You turned me into a prostitute." Her fingers flexed around the rope.

It squeezed Maron and he grunted.

"You made me do unspeakable things..."

It roared with laughter, shaking the room with a series of thunderclaps. Once it was done mocking her, it was silent for a moment, the only sound being Maron in his struggle against the light prison.

"And yet," it cooed at her, "you were so easy."

Cirv'e squeezed Maron again and he screamed, arching backwards and wrenching his fingers around the tendril at his waist. Par gave Maron's rope three hard tugs from the other end, until Nico tumbled through the barrier, his mouth open.

"WHAT IS THIS?" Cirv'e shouted as darkness dribbled down the sides of the white walls.

"You are not welcome in my presence!" It zeroed in on Nico and dropped Maron, while the black ooze made its way down around them.

When Maron landed, he ran to Par. She held on to him as Nico scrambled to right himself. They huddled together, watching as the dark liquid dripped down the walls, ice crusting the edges of the new stain and coating the whole perimeter of the room.

Cirv'e's disk of light dulled, its multicolored tendrils curling in on itself as it floated to the ground. When it touched down, it collapsed into a squirming pupa. It flapped on the floor, eyeless with no mouth.

"This is what you are." Lor's voice came from everywhere.

The three of them, while huddled near the barrier, glanced around the room.

What followed was a worm's nightmare, played out for them in a 360 display all around: a frenzied holofilm of creation, abandonment, feathers, and disease. Scars, and rebirth, taking flight as a butterfly, and getting gobbled by a chitter bird. Then the cycle began again in increasingly horrific ways.

Maron concentrated on the scene as the sightless, speechless Cirv'e flopped uncomfortably.

Par bit her lip and glared at the thing's tortuous life cycles playing out before them.

Nico raised his brow, looking back and forth to the barrier behind them.

But as the holofilm continued, the truth began to spill out. It wasn't a worm, not really. It was made to become a worm by its past wicked plottings, banished to the icy blue crater of its own hell, dotted with black stones, filled with red stars. The tortured were here, wailing for mercy, and it burned with them. It was here where the end began.

"This is how you will die," Lor proclaimed as distant fire rained toward it from the holofilm.

Each meteoric hit thumped closer and closer as the worm writhed.

"No!" it shouted through the rattling walls.

"No!" Fiery stones thumped closer.

"I won't!" The floor shook.

"I WON'T!" The worm pounded toward Maron, Par, and Nico, slamming its head and growing larger and angrier.

They stood their ground, Maron telling them to wait. The worm humped closer, slowly morphing back into its disk of light.

"Wait..." Maron repeats, gripping Par's hand.

It lifted from the ground, mere paces from where they stood.

"Now!" Maron shoved Par and Nico through the barrier, diving after them.

Cirv'e gave chase at enough speed that its disk slapped into the border, vomiting a large, segmented worm into the space before them and into the dark slop of the breach. Its face wrinkled inward, enraged and hissing with pointed teeth. It had the face of a man, probably beautiful once, corrupted by its own deeds.

Now vulnerable, it opened its mouth to speak, taking three needles of Ivory Saltpeter into its soft palate. Maron lowered his shooter, backing away while the worm seized in great wallops. Par delivered three more shots to its face, neck, and tail before it slowed, rippling in weak protest on the dark floor.

The tail swished back and forth sluggishly, and it reminded Par of a long time ago, when she was still a child. There was a small lizard on the stones in front of her parents' home. Curious, she poked at its brilliant blue tail. When it popped off so the lizard could escape, the leftover tail swished back and forth. Back and forth. She watched it for a while when her dad, someone she hadn't thought about in hundreds of years, found her there, staring at it. When she asked him why the creature ran from her, he declared that she scared it away.

As she watched Cirv'e swish back and forth, her father's voice repeated in her mind. They had weakened it—scared it—there was nothing it could offer them anymore. They were done. She took Maron's hand and squeezed, and he squeezed back.

It looked at them with its weird, human-like face and took labored breaths. "Without me," it wheezed, "you will both die."

Par sighed and closed her eyes, revisiting the long, painful path of life, her endless bouts of injury and regrowth, and her years spent buried at the bottom of the sea. "Thank the Maker," she said. Maron chuckled.

It glared at them, its soft middle swelling and deflating slowly. "Without me, there are no Guilds..."

Nico put up a finger. "Ah, yes," he said, "thank the Maker."

Par laughed, withdrawing a phial of Obsidian Blast Core.

Cirv'e slowed its undulations, a yellow foam bubbling at its pointed mouth. It wheezed again. "Without me, there is no tree..."

The three of them looked at each other and shrugged. "We'll leave that up to the Maker," Maron said.

The worm widened its mouth and wailed. Par chucked the phial of Obsidian Blast Core right into its maw, straight down its throat. It gulped, eyes wide.

"No, I didn't mean to," Cirv'e groveled to no one before a chunk of meat exploded from its segmented middle.

It rolled its eyes back and flopped to the ground.

The three of them watched its flesh dry and flake, wafting down into just another layer of ash on the dark floor.

"Is it done?" Nico asked.

"God, I hope so," Par said.

"What was it? What was the worm?"

Maron furrowed his brow, staring into the mound of ash. "An old servant," he said, "of a time beyond our understanding."

Nico tittered and shook his head. "That... doesn't help."

"Nico!" Eva called over and over. They were far from the opening.

Par smiled, the first genuine smile in years, as she gave her rope one rough tug before they headed toward the exit.

Chapter 44

It Is Done

Loren

The roundsman with his forehead against Emilia's pulse barrel woke up. Hypnotized irises blinked into a bright shade of hazel before he backed away, arms up.

His team followed suit, with one screaming at the sight of Teddy looming over him. Dill lowered his shooter in one hand and tucked away the ripper he held in the other. Blood leaked from his split lip, and Emilia's pearls rolled all over the floor, the broken string still dangling from her neck with two pearls clinging to it.

Rik's torn sleeve was in the hand of another roundsman, who shook his head and dropped it as if it were diseased. Lane stood over a different roundsman, shirt in his fist and rearing back for a punch. But he let the man go, and they all turned their attention to the door at the end of the hall.

Renae stood half-tilt, leaning on Karl and adjusting the cuff of his sleeve. His hair was mussed out of place and mustache frizzed over his lip, stained red.

"Take the rest of the day off, men," Renae declared, waving the roundsmen off.

They blinked at each other, dazed and searching the hall. When Renae shooed them away again, they began to stash their standard issue hollow rods, moving toward the elevator and taking second glances over their shoulders at their disheveled leader next to the two giant black creatures watching them.

Once they loaded into the elevator and began their descent, Renae fell to his knees and wept.

Lor squeezed out from the penthouse and ran to Dill, wrapping his arms around his friend while Karl laid a hand on his uncle's shoulder.

"I...I..." Renae stuttered with his head in his hands. He stood abruptly and walked right past Teddy to the private bathroom and shut the door. In the hall's silence, the squeak of a sink and rush of water came from behind the door.

Lor made his rounds to everyone in the hall. A few dings and bruises here and there, but nothing life threatening. He had asked the Maker for that, knowing when he heard the truth in Karl's verse and made the choice to vanquish the worm, he'd lose his ability. No Immortal Green would touch his tongue ever again, and no one would receive his memories to knit their flesh back together.

When he laid a hand over Dill's cheek, he tried briefly to correct the split in his lip. After nothing happened, he shook his head and Dill nodded, pressing his lips together.

Emilia examined her pulse shot, confused. "Why can't I sense the tech anymore?"

"The worm, Cirv'e, is dead." Renae stepped from his private bathroom and closed the door. Everyone spun to look at him in silence, watching him adjust his cuffs. "I wouldn't blame any of you if you'd like to see me dead too. I have a lot to answer for."

Renae continued to preen his suit, hair, and face. His gaze went anywhere except to the carnage of his hall. The two Nazagora beasts hardly made him flinch.

The e-disk buzzed in Lor's pocket, and a message hovered there from an unknown number.

Is it done? was all it said.

Private number or not, his response went through.

It's done.

He glanced up at Renae, who still refused to look at anyone, for his own reasons.

Meet us in the atrium. The words hovered under his last message.

Lor leaned over to relay the message to Karl, who nodded and beckoned that everyone follow.

"I will meet you shortly," Renae said. "I have a few moments of reflection to do."

"Very well. Welcome back, Uncle," Karl said, squeezing Renae's arm. Renae slow-blinked with a nod and a tight grin, spinning the ring on his finger and twisting it off. The black stone had faded, no glimmer of red stars, no vibrations of maleficence. He curled it in his fist and nodded again before Lor ushered his friends to the elevator.

As the doors closed on the gore-smeared white hall, Renae stood in the middle of it, hand on his face and peering through his pinky and ring fingers while shaking his head. It was a mess.

At the ground floor, the elevator doors opened, and they were greeted by the elusive Order: a group of well-dressed, color morphing contact wearing Yeunish men and women.

"What in Gehenna...?" Dill whispered, scanning the group. Emilia clung to his arm, and the Nazagora hid in the corners of the elevator, still apparently frightened by it.

Lor was able to coax Teddy and Champ from their hiding spot, and they obeyed with loyal conviction rather than Guild taming. Even as beast taming became a thing of the past, they still nuzzled next to Davy and Oren while cowering low to the floor.

The tallest man in the front with the gray contacts stepped forward, eyeballing the Nazagora. His black hair had been cropped close to the sides of his head, with the top swept back in a stylish coif and silver streaks running through it. Not a wrinkle creased his crisp stone-colored button-up. He reached out a hand to Lor.

"In the cities they call me Perci," he said, gripping Lor's hand with a solid shake and gaze still shifting toward the black creatures undulating nearby. "My name is Haes'perskel Lina'scera. Horace sends his regards."

Lor grinned. "Great to meet you, Perci."

Perci explained to them that the order worked under Audun's nose, as ordinary servants within each city's boundary. Cooks, janitors, accountants, administrators, medics, bankers (Perci's role) ... they infiltrated all but Law. Lor breathed out a sigh to hear that he hadn't actually been a part of any Yeunish massacre when Champ took out that line of roundsmen. The look on Rik's face agreed, and he gave Champ a pat on the head.

The order had plenty of setbacks from the past several years, as they had set these plans in motion even before Lor entered the program. Once the breach was opened, they desperately needed to make their efforts a priority, yet the dark creep of breach influence on the cities prevented them on enough occasions they feared they'd already lost.

As Perci told that part of the story, his voice choked off at Renae's entrance into the atrium. The man's presence alone was enough to silence the entire room as his shoes clacked over the tile toward them.

He settled in line with Lor's group, feet shoulder width apart, legs straight, and arms dangling forward with one hand cupping the other wrist while glancing at Perci. "Go on," he said.

Perci cleared his throat and continued, sharing that Horace relayed to them a new plan that could work, made possible by Lor's family. All they had to do was wait for the signal to execute their backup to the backup plan, which was simply to clear the way.

Renae sighed, nodding his head and closing his eyes. "I owe everyone... a great debt," he said. "I have been merciless. I have been deceitful and cruel. I will pay a toll for this, I swear it."

He turned to Lor and his group with his shoulders back and light-colored eyes burning into them. "I owe the lot of you not only the sanctity of the cities, but also my life. Ask, and you will have it."

Dill rubbed his hands together, and Emilia nudged him. Lor glanced around at everyone in their silent expressions, wheels turning in their minds, unsure of what to ask for. Truth was, their lives were molded by exile, not just him and his Yeunish friends, but Dill in the desert and Emilia in hiding. He only knew he wanted to spend his days with his family, rebuilding their lives and the tree, unbothered...

And fully funded.

Karl remained in the spire, offering to help his uncle with reshaping the city. There were some good rules worth keeping, with many needing removal, and Renae would need help sorting through all of it, including creating new rights for not only the Yeunish but also the Foscans. Now that there was a timer on the rest of their lives, he needed all the help he could get.

Karl also requested reprints and translations of the ancient text, with new coursework in Eastern Common at Peakwood Academy.

The Yeunish order were lifted to high positions in the spire, no longer requiring their disguises or remaining hidden underground. Perci landed the role of managing the treasury, so each pay period Lor and his family would receive was signed off by him. A few others were assigned to help Renae and Karl with their work. As far as Lor knew, they were happy not to have to hide themselves any longer.

When they left the spire, they took a ride to shore by Naz-back until it was time to say goodbye. Davy cried into Teddy's head ridge as the beast nudged him back with affection. Rik and Oren stroked Teddy's and Champ's heads, with Oren even planting a small kiss on Champ. The two of them slid into the water, twin black bodies swerving toward the horizon until their little bubbles dove under the surface.

Davy sobbed the entire jumper ride back to Corl.

When they arrived in the small fishing town, the children murmured and the Yeunish refugees shrugged at the horizon. After the worm had been defeated, the unattached Nazagora just *left*, swimming back to the South. Fresh tears sprang from Davy at the news, and Zary pitied him, offering him comfort... which he very much appreciated.

Url gaped at the array of gifts from Renae—new rods and lures along with packets of heirloom seeds from plants long extinct from the North. Zary received Karl's promise of a first print run copy of both the original and the translated ancient text, with distance learning lessons in Eastern Common.

Rik, Davy, Oren, and the others that accompanied them in the fight for the spire were first offered immunity for the deaths of the roundsmen, then also the choice of wherever they wanted to go, on him. Of course, Davy chose to stay near Zary, with Rik and Oren choosing Corl as well.

The remaining Yeunish refugees took their week of mourning for Ivon, then some chose to stay in Corl. Others asked for rides to the cities, Secas, or the mountains.

On their first day back in Corl, Lor went immediately to Url's home, searching the rooms and finding no sign of Damaetra. He passed the bawling Davy in Zary's arms, plunking into the sand in a frantic search for his wife. Url tapped his shoulder and pointed toward the shore with a smile.

She stood there with her back to him, looking out at the wide blue sea. Her hair tossed and coiled in the breeze, shimmering under daylight. It reminded him of the first time he saw her—pensive prayer toward the great expanse. He ran to her while calling her name, and she turned, limping toward him and using all her might to leap into his arms, wrapping her legs around his waist.

"I came back for you," he repeated to her, planting kisses on her mouth, her cheek, her neck, "I came back for you."

She wept in his arms, settling her face in the crook of his shoulder. "I knew you'd come back for me," she said.

Chapter 45

Ten Years

Loren

Chitter birds squawking signaled morning. It used to be a tinny alarm from an e-disk, the slit of faint light coming from a meager window, or the rise in heat and humidity from wild, barren lands. Life in the mountain zone of the tree was different.

Lor sat up at the birdsong and yawned, glancing over to Damaetra curled up next to him. Every year, she gained more feeling back in her hip to where she walked almost normally again. He rubbed her leg, and she rolled over, yawned, and shuddered.

"Will you take Eoin to the gardens with you this morning?" she asked. The back of her hand was on her forehead, and she squinted at him.

Their son gurgled in his cradle as if he sensed they were talking about him. Lor laughed and stood. "Sounds like he's thrilled to go." He bent down to give her a kiss. "When you and Eva get back from Montaegar later, we're having our send-off dinner for Quint and Ayala."

"Oh, that's right." She yawned again and sat up.

Lor strolled to the cradle, picking up their chunky six-month-old son. His little white hand playfully slapped Lor's cheek.

"I think they'll like living in the cities. Life is too slow for them out here," she said.

"Yeah, you're right. Renae said he had a nice setup for them when they get there, so that's even better."

Damaetra hummed and smiled at him with one eye still squinted shut. "Hey, I'm going to wake the other children, so if you could feed him real quick, I'll love you forever."

"Deal," he said, giving her another quick kiss before she tickled Eoin and left. He giggled and leaned into Lor.

Eoin was certainly hungry, eating fast enough that Lor was *almost* first to show up at the gardens. He looked around at their small community, built and paid for by the cities. Nico was at a nearby plot, crouched down and showing his daughter, Lulu, the giltberry vines while she was knuckle deep in her nose. Brushing her hand away from it, he noticed Lor and waved.

As Lor walked over to them, Lulu called after Eoin while holding her hands out for him.

"Ah-ah, I know where that finger's been," Lor tutted, patting her bright red curls.

She blushed with her lips pressing inward in a wide grin before bending down to examine the giltberries and her nostril again. Nico took Eoin and received the same face-slap treatment and giggling mirth.

"Have you talked to Maron or Par this morning?" Lor asked, planking his hand over his eyes and casting his attention to the East Coast. The tree still had some growth to do, but it had already sprouted a nice thick green stalk out of the black, large enough to begin housing many new creatures in its canopy.

"Not yet," Nico said, pulling out a new model e-disk. He fumbled with the right movement to activate it. Eoin jiggled in his arm, making it difficult, but he finally got it. "There's a message from Maron, though."

Lor leaned over to read it. "Nice. Nate's second year apprenticeship is going well... Hopefully he'll let him take some time off to spend with his girlfriend."

"Eva and Dame are bringing her back with them later, right?"

"That's the plan."

Nico sighed and bounced Eoin. "Well, I'm glad Nate found passion in something. I know he was really bummed when the Guilds fizzled out. Especially since he had a real aptitude for Engineering."

Lor tilted his head and shrugged. "I mean, he could have gone to Heart Academy to learn."

Nico tittered. "Too much math."

Lor laughed and glanced at the tree again. "Can't blame him. But he's actually pretty great with the tree."

Children poured from Lor's home, chatting among themselves and spilling into the gardens. Damaetra came out after, wearing her pastel blue sundress with hair tied up in the two buns atop her head. Cimma followed behind, spotting Lor and Nico. She bent down to rest her cheek on Damaetra's head for a short hug, then trotted over to them, taking over baby duties.

"So you just walk on past your other brothers and sisters?" Lor tsk'ed. "I know who your favorite is."

Cimma giggled. "Hey, we had breakfast together. We're already tired of each other."

"Fair enough."

Nico examined her with a squint and half smile. "Hey... have you grown again?"

One thing about Cimma was that she loved when Nico pointed out how tall she was next to Lor.

"Hm, I don't know... We'd better check," she said, moving behind Lor to press her back against his.

Lor sighed and rolled his eyes with a smile while Nico put on his very serious think-face. "Ah-haaa... I think you're just about even now."

"Well, just so you know, you stop growing when you hit twenty," Lor teased.

"Says who?" She put a hand on her hip.

"Actually, there are medical papers that suggest your dad is correct," Gale said as he strolled up to them.

"Pa-*paaa*!" Cimma whined. Nico and Lor laughed.

"Although, the evidence may not apply to the Yeunish." He smiled and winked at her.

"Yeah, *yeah*." She put her arm around Gale in a half hug, passing her baby brother to him.

A warm set of arms wrapped around Lor's leg as the round face of his other twin daughter smiled up at him.

"You'd better watch out, Cim," Lor said, "because Belle just might catch up to you someday." He stroked the black hair of his young Yeuni daughter holding him.

Cimma shrugged. "I'd still be taller than you."

Lor let out a mocking cry. "You are such a sass!"

Belle giggled at his comment and ran off to her identical sister playing in the dirt with their other brothers.

Damaetra sauntered to their group, giving Eoin a kiss, then wrapping her arm around Lor's waist. "We're set to leave whenever Eva is done helping Dill with Emilia. She can hardly move anymore and is due any day now."

Gale pinched Cimma's arm. "You think you're ready to take the lead on this delivery?"

Cimma threw her shoulders back and stuck her chin in the air. "I'm more than ready."

"Excellent. I think you'll ace Academy next year."

She chuckled. "It's almost like I'm cheating having you here to pre-teach me medicine."

"Someone needs to take up the duties after me. I'm getting too old these days." Gale rubbed the top of his head pink.

The door for Dill and Emilia's home swung open, and Eva emerged with her and Nico's twin daughters following. Just like the beauty queens they wanted to be, they fussed over each other's matching yellow dresses, talking in an exaggerated slant about popular styles and how to wear their thick red hair.

Eva waved to the group, beckoning for Damaetra.

"I'll see you when we get back," Damaetra said to Lor. She held on to his waist, looking up at him with the light filtering through her bright blue-violet eyes.

"I'll be counting the minutes," he said, pressing his forehead to hers and closing his eyes.

Sometimes, he swore he would catch a glimmer of the colors he used to see under his eyelids, but he knew they were long gone. It was bittersweet—their complication a stumbling block in his past, yet a boon in times of need. With his skin touching hers in that moment, he could only summon the faint memory of what her color once was.

She left with Eva, and he watched her go, with their son's babbling in Gale's arms as the soundtrack to her departure.

"Well, it's about *time* you all woke up." Niklaus jogged down the few steps from his front door with his eldest daughter on his back. A mixture of groans and giggles came from the group.

Lor nodded with a grin to the white-haired girl hanging on her dad. "I hope you're not training Eloria to have the same smart mouth."

Niklaus chuckled. "What do you mean by that? She inherited her smart mouth from Cae, not me."

"Yeah, see Uncle Lor? The key word there is *smart*," Eloria chimed in. The group laughed as Niklaus blushed with an eye roll.

Cae strolled up shortly after, holding their year-old twin sons on each hip. The boys had wild curls the color of bone and deep dimples, just like their dad. Cae implored Niklaus to take one, and he let Eloria slide from his back to grab Deaclan. She leaned over to whisper something in his ear, nibbling his lobe a little, and he grinned.

"Secrets are no fun," Eloria said while holding out her arms for her other brother, Finn.

Niklaus laughed. "You're too young for this secret."

"Hey," Cae said, handing Eloria her brother, "do you guys ever miss your Guild? I know it's been a while, but I was just thinking about it."

Lor pressed his lips together. He really missed his Guild. Especially when he stubbed his toe, breaking it on the doorframe three standard years ago. It was his big toe, and he hobbled for weeks afterward without the crutch of Immortal Green.

Niklaus glanced down at his prosthetic leg, while Gale scratched the spot on his arm where the patch used to be, and Nico licked his lips.

"Maybe a *little*," Nico said. "I realized I'm no good at actual formulation chemistry... without eneris."

Gale clicked his tongue and shrugged. "I really didn't run much except in the desert, so I'd say no."

"I *really* miss it," Niklaus said. "Except for swallowing bugs and sand in my goggle seals... and wearing out my shoes and burning my feet... chapped skin and..." He stopped and looked up at the sky. "I mean, it was fun while it lasted."

Lor reached out for Eoin again, taking the pudgy boy and looking into the violet eyes he got from his mother. Eoin grinned, a solitary tooth poking from the bottom gum, and he made a low cooing noise at Lor. Life for their children would be harder work, but they could do it. They'd been doing it.

"We're better off without them, I think," Lor said.

Cimma was quiet. She had already expressed her lament that she lost her colors. They reminded her of Lor, and now they were gone. He never really understood what the colors meant, other than it was a temporary gift from the Maker to do what they needed to do in times of need. Personally, he was glad to be rid of the mind walking. It was a lot of responsibility.

He reached out and squeezed Cimma's arm, and she gave him a half smile in return.

"What about your immortality?" Nico asked.

Lor tittered, pursing his lips and thinking about that never-ending flow of Immortal Green. It was a miracle he survived that long after losing it, and the thought was a regular visitor in his mind.

"I couldn't imagine living lifetimes without all of you," he said.

Nico grinned, patting his shoulder, and Gale bobbed his head with a smile. Cimma wrapped her arm around his waist, leaning her head on his other shoulder.

Niklaus chuckled. "Aw, I'd give you a big wet kiss if Cae wasn't watching."

"Da-*add*!" Eloria groaned, and Cae laughed.

"Well, on that note," Nico said with his lips pursed at Niklaus, "I'm going to get back to work on the gardens."

"I'm helping today," Cimma chimed in.

"Me too!" Eloria said while handing Finn back to Cae.

Lor nodded. "I'll come help in a little bit, as long as Dad's willing to watch Eoin."

"Of course I am," Gale said, holding his arms out for the boy.

Once Eoin was secure, Gale wandered back to his home between the others along the mountains.

Lor watched them go, lingering on the bobbing head of his son. His other children laughed and played nearby, with no danger of brigands or worries of anything more than skinned knees.

Miracles. All of them.

For some reason, and Lor thought he might have known the reason, the Maker saw fit to bless the group. The women bore children beyond an age when they could, and many at that. It seemed every annual trip to visit Jack and Verena in Corl, they had news of another on the way. That was despite her closed womb after Ayala's difficult birth.

Their lives had been put on pause to fulfill a mission, and the new life was a gift that they'd live the rest of their days for.

Lor stood on that small hill, watching all the children moving around the gardens and seeing his friends, old and new. Roseaarde had changed, and he with it.

And to think, had Gale never forced him to try something new, leave his comfort zone, and to enter the program, this reality never would have happened—and he lowered his head to thank the Maker for it, trials and all.

Epilogue

Dust motes shimmer in the yellow light cutting through the shattered window. Layers of age decorate each surface. Turum uses a gloved hand to run fingers through the detritus, hearing the jagged pieces of grit scrape across the dull marble counter even through the insulation of his suit.

"You can take your helmet off. Air's good," Maerya strolls inside, the hiss of her helmet liberating from her collar. She takes a good breath through her nose, exhaling through her mouth. The flexihood that protects her hair barely contains the black curls that frame her pallid face.

Turum grunts, releasing the hermetic seal on his helmet, taking in the brighter colors that his gray-tinted shield had been hiding. All that remains of this ruin are partially collapsed walls and what appears to be a very old food prep area.

"This is amazing," Maerya says, methodically opening and closing storage boxes mounted to the crumbling walls. Some boxes hang limply to the side, missing doors and raining dust every time she jostles them.

"Careful, these structures are incredibly old," Turum says, rubbing his chin and glancing over at a carved decoration on one of the more intact, inner walls.

The shuffling ends, only for Maerya to move to another section of the ruins, marveling at some new find. "Wow, look at these..." She pulls one of the empty frames from the wall, turning it around and tapping the back as if doing so would make it spring back to life. "If I were to guess, this is a second generation holoframe. I'm always shocked at how advanced they actually were back then."

Turum strolls toward her, running his now bare hand along the wall, letting bits of chalky plaster drop from weaker cracks. The feel of it is strange. "Rumor has it they had help," he says.

"Ooh, it goes down some more!" Maerya hardly pays attention, lost in the wonder of their find, already halfway down to the platform below.

The stairs she found are rickety and chewed, and no matter what kind of warning Turum would give to her, she wouldn't be turning back. A skeleton of old building material encages him, shuddering with each footfall. Yet, the distance is short enough that he's confident he'd be fine even if a foot went through one of the landings.

On the ground and exploring more of the ancient relics found in this lower chamber, Maerya nearly falls over after letting out an excited cry.

Turum lands on the gritty floor and turns to her. "Steady now. What is it?"

"It's a book! I can't believe it, it's a book!" Maerya bends over, sliding a heavily yellowed tome from under a pile of shredded, shattered, and moldy debris of different kinds. "How did it survive? Do you know how much this thing is worth?"

Turum clears his throat, bending down to take a look. "Priceless. It probably survived by being under cover of this structure so high up here. High enough even raiders couldn't get their hands on it. Let's take a look."

The thing is incredibly delicate and weathered. The title has been worn away and the cover hangs from the binding. In institution with Maerya, Turum has learned about books. They were the old way of passing information from one generation to the next, whether it was history or cooking recipes. His fingers dance over the cover for a few seconds before he runs them from top to bottom, feeling the rough grain created by missing layers of protection. Maerya hovers, breathless behind him, watching him press his index finger against the cover's edge and open it.

A bit of powder shimmies from the bottom, and Maerya sucks in some air. "Did we bring any pocket seals?" Turum says when he turns to her.

"I think I have one on me." She stands and pats her leg pouch, pulling out a medium sized, transparent square.

"I'd like to preserve this as much as possible." Turum tries to turn the first page, only for it to succumb to a susurrus of flaking paper. They both gasp at the loss. "Every single page is going to need a meticulous paint-over of rosin bonder. If we can get this back to the tree in tact, I can ask Emi to do it."

Maerya clicks her tongue while opening the plastic square to prepare it for preserving what remains.

A bit of ink is still visible on that first page, just above the piece that broke off. He can barely make out what it says, but he recognizes it as the old formal version of their own language. "This book predates even the old Yeunish war. You can tell by the way it still refers to the language as Eastern Common. See there? Huh." Turum is afraid to move his hand, worried for another collapse of precious pages.

The ancient paper has indentations where someone once wrote on the page, difficult to read up close as all the ink is missing. Maerya holds open the pocket seal. Being the perfect distance to make out some of the letters, she stops for a moment to tilt her head at the indentations. "Does that say... Tarlinsas?"

Turum turns his head to one side, then the other, squinting at it to make sense of the word. There's no way it says that. There's no way it says what he thinks it says. "No..." He pauses, angling his gaze once again. "No..." he repeats.

"What is it then?"

Turum turns his head toward Maerya, who is now standing to his left. She's holding out the pocket seal for him to drop the payload into it, but he doesn't. Not right away. Instead, he taps his breast pocket, the one with his name etched under resin in a gentle blue glow: T. Turtingas.

He titters at her confusion. "It says Turtingas... E. Turtingas."

About R.E. Holding

R.E. Holding was born in Iowa in 1979 and now lives in the hills of Missouri with her husband. When not writing, she is a full-time scientific project manager and soap artist who likes to cook, paint, draw, read, and learn.

Her interest in horror, science fiction, and fantasy goes way back to when she "accidentally" watched Poltergeist at age 5. While fascinated by the spooky cinematography, her irrational fear of clowns persists to this day.

She grew up in the Midwest in the 80s and 90s, often finding herself on the dirty low-pile carpets of Waldenbooks reading the newest Christopher Pike YA horror. She's an avid lover of stories of all kinds, whether it be through books, movies, tabletop games, etc., with a particular penchant for the things that go bump in the night. A scientist by day, she writes horror, sci-fi, and fantasy at hours unacceptable to the human condition. She manages Cliff Cave Books, LLC as well as a soap making site, L.H. Soaps & Sundries.

Thanks for reading!

If you loved this saga, would you consider writing a review? Reviews really help indie authors continue to do what they love and bring wonderful stories to you!

www.ingramcontent.com/pod-product-compliance
Lightning Source LLC
Chambersburg PA
CBHW020510140726
48132CB00028B/247
* 9 7 8 1 9 6 3 1 2 5 3 5 1 *